AMONG THE KING'S SOLDIERS

★ ★ ★

THE HOUSE OF WINSLOW SERIES

1. *The Honorable Imposter*
2. *The Captive Bride*
3. *The Indentured Heart*
4. *The Gentle Rebel*
5. *The Saintly Buccaneer*
6. *The Holy Warrior*
7. *The Reluctant Bridegroom*
8. *The Last Confederate*
9. *The Dixie Widow*
10. *The Wounded Yankee*
11. *The Union Belle*
12. *The Final Adversary*
13. *The Crossed Sabres*
14. *The Valiant Gunman*
15. *The Gallant Outlaw*
16. *The Jeweled Spur*
17. *The Yukon Queen*
18. *The Rough Rider*
19. *The Iron Lady*
20. *The Silver Star*
21. *The Shadow Portrait*
22. *The White Hunter*

THE LIBERTY BELL

1. *Sound the Trumpet*
2. *Song in a Strange Land*
3. *Tread Upon the Lion*
4. *Arrow of the Almighty*
5. *Wind From the Wilderness*

CHENEY DUVALL, M.D.
(with Lynn Morris)

1. *The Stars for a Light*
2. *Shadow of the Mountains*
3. *A City Not Forsaken*
4. *Toward the Sunrising*
5. *Secret Place of Thunder*
6. *In the Twilight, in the Evening*
7. *Island of the Innocent*

THE SPIRIT OF APPALACHIA
(with Aaron McCarver)

1. *Over the Misty Mountains*
2. *Beyond the Quiet Hills*
3. *Among the King's Soldiers*

TIME NAVIGATORS
(for Young Teens)

1. *Dangerous Voyage*
2. *Vanishing Clues*
3. *Race Against Time*

99A

AMONG THE KING'S SOLDIERS

★ ★ ★

GILBERT MORRIS & AARON McCARVER

BETHANY HOUSE PUBLISHERS
MINNEAPOLIS, MINNESOTA 55438

Among the King's Soldiers
Copyright © 1998
Gilbert Morris and Aaron McCarver

Cover by Dan Thornberg,
Bethany House Publishers staff artist.

Published by Bethany House Publishers
A Ministry of Bethany Fellowship International
11400 Hampshire Avenue South
Minneapolis, Minnesota 55438
www.bethanyhouse.com

Printed in the United States of America by
Bethany Press International, Minneapolis, Minnesota 55438

Library of Congress Cataloging-in-Publication Data

CIP data applied for

ISBN 1–55661–887–5   CIP

Dedication

This book is dedicated with a very special love
to the four most precious gifts God has given me,
my nieces and nephews:

To Heather Bradford

You are the first and the one most like me I think. (Don't hate me
for saying that!) It has been a joy watching you grow up into such
a special young lady. God will use your quiet spirit and intelligence
to do wonderful things for Him.

To Matthew Bradford

You are a wonderful mixture of strong body and tender heart. This
is shown through your athletic talents and your early response to
God's voice. Always listen to Him, and like Samuel, God will use
you in mighty ways.

To Kaitlin Slatton

From the first, you have always been the young lady. You already
possess deep insight and understanding far beyond your years. I
can't wait to see how God will use these gifts to minister to others!

To Daniel Slatton

You have a gift of making others laugh. I love your "embrace life"
attitude and hope to cultivate it into my life. I know God has many
wonderful adventures just around every corner of your life.

I love you all so much!!! You have brought so much joy and happiness into my life. Always know that you have an uncle who will love you no matter what and who thinks you are all the greatest! I will always be there anytime you need me. My prayer for each of you is that you surrender your life totally to God and follow His path for your life, as this is the only Way to true happiness. Thanks just for being the wonderful gifts you are!

GILBERT MORRIS spent ten years as a pastor before becoming Professor of English at Ouachita Baptist University of Arkansas. During the summers of 1984 and 1985 he did postgraduate work at the University of London. A prolific writer, he has had over twenty-five scholarly articles and two hundred poems published in various periodicals, and he and his wife live in the Rocky Mountains of Colorado.

AARON McCARVER is the Dean of Students at Wesley College in Florence, Mississippi, where he also teaches drama and Christian literature. His deep interest in Christian fiction and broad knowledge of the CBA market have given him the background for editorial consultation with all the "writing Morrises" as well as other novelists. It was through his editorial relationship with Gilbert that this book series came to life.

Contents

PART IV:
MOUNT UP WITH WINGS AS EAGLES

Character List

The lands over the Misty Mountains are being turned into frontier homes as the settlers struggle to bring freedom and the light of God into this rugged land. As they work to establish new churches, they answer the call to serve their new nation and fight for what they have built. Hawk and Elizabeth Spencer join in this struggle but find they must rely on God to help their children through their own battles of the heart.

Jacob Spencer—Finally reconciled with his father, his newfound faith in God will be put to the test as he must face the past he thought he had left behind and choose the future love of his heart.

Sarah MacNeal—The loss of her father and a burgeoning love led her to close her heart. When a possibility for new love comes, she must decide if she can open her heart again as she faces the risk of another loss.

Amanda Taylor—She has already given her heart to Jacob Spencer and dreams of the day when they will marry. But a girl from his past threatens to destroy her dreams.

Seth Donavan—A Scottish Highlander, he fights for the British Crown against the colonists. When he agrees to a mission of subterfuge, he loses his heart to a beautiful girl and must choose where his true loyalties lie.

Joseph Foster—A young man of the frontier who pursues the heart of Sarah MacNeal. When another man shows interest in Sarah, he will try anything to win the desire of his heart.

Anabelle Denton—A true Southern belle, she is accustomed to getting anything she wants . . . and she wants Jacob Spencer, no matter what the cost.

Among the
King's Soldiers

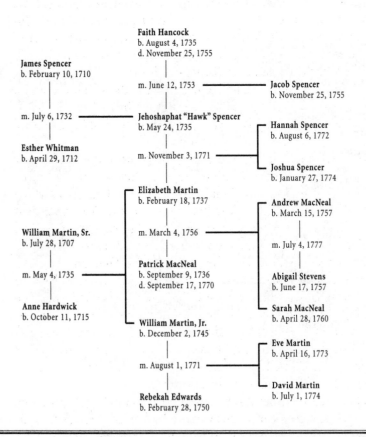

Faith Hancock
b. August 4, 1735
d. November 25, 1755

James Spencer
b. February 10, 1710

m. June 12, 1753 —————— Jacob Spencer
b. November 25, 1755

m. July 6, 1732 —————— Jehoshaphat "Hawk" Spencer
b. May 24, 1735

Esther Whitman
b. April 29, 1712

Hannah Spencer
b. August 6, 1772

m. November 3, 1771 ——

Joshua Spencer
b. January 27, 1774

Elizabeth Martin
b. February 18, 1737

Andrew MacNeal
b. March 15, 1757

William Martin, Sr.
b. July 28, 1707

m. March 4, 1756

m. July 4, 1777

m. May 4, 1735 ——

Patrick MacNeal
b. September 9, 1736
d. September 17, 1770

Abigail Stevens
b. June 17, 1757

Anne Hardwick
b. October 11, 1715

Sarah MacNeal
b. April 28, 1760

William Martin, Jr.
b. December 2, 1745

Eve Martin
b. April 16, 1773

m. August 1, 1771 ——

David Martin
b. July 1, 1774

Rebekah Edwards
b. February 28, 1750

Prologue

*M*y, don't you look elegant!"

Seth Donovan almost broke stride as he twisted his head to steal a glance at Isaac. His younger brother's face was aglow with excitement, and for one moment Seth was totally filled with apprehension. *He doesn't know some of us are going to get killed,* he thought. This younger brother of his had always been a hasty, impetuous sort of fellow. Now at the age of eighteen, Isaac approached war as he had always approached a game of skittles or kit-cat.

A cheer went up from a line of marching soldiers, and the sound of bagpipes in the air caught Seth's attention away from Isaac. At that moment they were passing a group of officers, but his eyes were on the woman on the snow-white horse.

Flora McDonald, in her mid-fifties, still retained traces of beauty and a dynamic excitement. All his life Seth Donovan had admired this woman, who was a national heroine in Scotland. Now as he passed by, he studied the clear blue eyes and the rich, abundant wealth of hair now slightly marked with gray. She caught his eye and smiled and raised her riding crop to her forehead. Flora McDonald was elaborately costumed for the parade of the Highland soldiers. She wore a double-breasted jacket with the skirt curving back to form short tails. The color was a sky blue and matched her eyes. The front skirts of her jacket were rounded at the seam and flared out at the waist, fitting her figure admirably. The sleeves were long and tight-fitting in the enclosed cuffs, and she wore a cravat around her neck. She wore a small hat of crimson with a large ostrich plume. All in all, she was a woman to be admired.

As Seth returned her salute, smiling back at her and lifting his musket, he thought of how this woman had saved a king's life—at least a king in the eyes of some. When the Stuart King James II, who had ruled England from 1685 to 1688, fled the country, his son James had become true king of England in the eyes of those who favored the Stuarts. Despite the fact that there was little encouragement for Prince Charles Edward from England itself, the exiled Stuarts traveled the Scottish Highlands to enlist the support of the Highland clans. They raised an army of Jacobites, and on April 16, 1746, at the Battle of Culloden, their forces were crushed by George II's son William, the duke of Cumberland.

After the battle, Charles Edward, known as Bonnie Prince Charlie, fled for his life. A bounty of thirty thousand pounds was offered for his capture, and he seemed doomed to that fate.

It was Flora McDonald who saved Bonnie Prince Charlie. Disguised as an ailing Irish maid, she put him in a boat, bundling him up in a bonnet and cloak and shawl. At the risk of capture, she avoided the British patrol vessels. In spite of high winds and stormy seas, they reached Skye and made their way to Portree, where the prince exchanged his disguise for kilt and plaid and then sailed for France.

As the bagpipes squealed and Flora passed from his sight, Seth Donovan was filled with a thousand memories, for Flora McDonald had practically raised him and his brother, Isaac. Their own parents had died at a youthful age, and they had looked to Flora and her husband, Allen, for what advantages they had.

He remembered how upon hearing that the McDonalds were immigrating to the American colonies, he had said to Isaac, "We are going with them, my boy. It's America for us."

As the troops marched on, Seth could not help but be proud of what was happening. It had not been destined for Flora and her husband, Allen, to enjoy peace. When the Revolution had come to America, they were drawn into it by Josiah Martin, the Royal Governor of North Carolina. He had persuaded the McDonalds to join the British cause and had made Allen a colonel in the young army.

The air was cold from the snows that lurked in the February skies of North Carolina, but at that moment those Highlanders who marched proudly along with their muskets, most of them garbed in the attire of Old Scotland, were excited. Seth himself was proud of his uniform. He wore a short red coat jacket with dark blue facings and brass buttons, and his tartan kilt was green with alternating black and dark blue stripes. His sporran—what non-Scottish people called a purse—hung from the front of his waist below his cartridge pouch. It was made of brown goatskin with the hair left on. Around his waist hung a belt cartridge of black leather, and at his side the sword tapped against his legs. He wore a cap of black bearskin, and the garters of his stockings were red. He made a colorful figure, and pride swelled through him. As they were called to a halt by Colonel Donald McLeod, the senior officer, the troops broke rank and milled around restlessly.

"What are we waiting for, Seth?" Isaac demanded. His cheeks were rosy red, and he thumbed the hammer on his musket nervously.

"I suppose they're going to have an officers' meeting. I don't think we're invited." Seth Donovan was a very tall man of twenty, two inches over six feet. He was almost a full four inches taller than his brother and towered over most of the Highlanders. He was broad shouldered with a deep chest and a muscular, lithe frame. There was a strength in him that lay beneath the surface, and despite his physical strength he was a man of intensely quick reactions. His blue-green eyes were constantly in motion, and he grinned suddenly and slapped Isaac on the shoulder. "Don't worry. We'll get action soon enough."

Almost at once Colonel McLeod called them to advance, and soon the marching column of two thousand men made a dramatic sight, the drums beating, pipes playing, and flags flying.

The Highlanders headed east to the coast. They marched mostly at night and crisscrossed creeks along the way, successfully eluding Colonel James Moore, who commanded 650 North Carolina Continentals. Moore's group had been sent to head the men off on the Black River. Realizing that he had been outmaneuvered, Moore sent Colonel Richard Caswell with eight hundred Rangers to cut off the Scots at a spot called Moore's Creek Bridge. They made quick time, and as soon as they reached the bridge, they met with other troops commanded by Colonel Alexander Lillington. Quickly the two officers set the men to constructing earthworks on the west side of the small, sluggish creek. Soon, however, it was decided to abandon these works and to cross over to make their stand on the east side of the creek.

"Take up the boards from the bridge!" Colonel Lillington commanded. And with a will the Rangers went to it, leaving the structure but removing the boards as they went. As if this were not enough, Colonel Caswell said, "Grease those timbers with whatever you can find!" This order was carried out, and soon the American Rangers were in place, awaiting the arrival of the Highland troops.

———————

"I wonder how many stars are up there, Seth?"

Seth Donovan looked over at his younger brother, who sat across from the small fire roasting his bit of beef on a stick. He turned his own, examined it carefully, and then deciding it was done, he pulled it out of the small blaze. He tentatively pulled off a bit, burned his fingers, then finally put it in his mouth. "Good beef," he said. He grinned, his white teeth flashing in the firelight as he added wryly, "I don't suppose the rebel who donated this cow to His Majesty's armies will miss it much."

Isaac returned his brother's smile. The two were very close. Having been raised alone without another brother and no sisters, and with their parents dead at an early age, it had seemed a father-son relationship as much as brother to brother. Isaac was an impulsive young man, and it had been Seth Donovan, the steady one, who had kept the two out of trouble. Now he looked up at the stars, glittering and twinkling like tiny pinpoints of light, and belatedly answered his brother's question. "More than a man could count," he murmured.

"And the good God made them all," Isaac said, "and He has names for them, I'll warrant." He looked across the fire and then grew more serious. Though younger, it was he who worried about his older brother more than the other way around. "Are you afraid of getting killed in the battle, Seth?"

"Don't think about it. What will come will come."

"But if you don't know the Lord Jesus, you'll spend eternity in the torments of hell if you get killed."

Seth shifted uneasily. His younger brother, for all his impetuous ways, had become a Christian two years earlier, and a good one at that. He had given up his sinful ways and had done all he could to persuade Seth to become a Christian. Now Seth shook his head and said, "Don't preach at me, Isaac. You can't push a man into the kingdom of God."

"Not pushing you," Isaac said quietly. "I am trying to plead with you to trust in the Lord God. Neither of us knows if he'll live."

Shoving the thought of death away, Seth laughed. "Don't worry about it. We'll be all right. At the sound of the first shot these rebels will run. That'll be all there is to it." He leaned forward and, anxious to change the subject, spoke of the political situation. "You see, the way it is, Lord Cornwallis is going to bring a strong fleet, eleven warships, so I hear, under Sir Peter Parker. They'll land off the Cape Fear River."

"Why not in South Carolina? That's where the good harbor is."

"Because Governor Martin wants it to be here in North Carolina. He convinced Cornwallis that if North Carolina were in the hands of the king's soldiers, it would be simple enough to take South Carolina, and then we'd have the best fleet on the coast. Big enough to accommodate all the ships of the world, I suppose. It'd furnish a base of operations that would go all the way to the James River in Virginia and all the way down to Florida."

Such had been the plan, but nothing was certain. The Tories of North Carolina had not risen up as Governor Martin had promised the British. This relatively small group of Highlanders was practically the only force available to fight the king's battles in the South

"We'd better get to sleep. It'll be a long march tomorrow, but we'll rout those rebels, Isaac. You wait and see."

"All right, but I'm praying that you'll find Jesus Christ as your Savior. I worry about you, Seth. Indeed I do." Isaac came over and, with an unusual gesture, put his arm around his brother. He hugged him closely, then said, "You're all I got in this world, and I wouldn't want to do without you in the other world."

Surprised by the expression of affection, Seth grew rigid; then he slapped Isaac on the chest, saying, "To bed with you! Nothing's going to happen."

Later, however, as Seth lay on his back staring up at the stars, he thought long about what Isaac had said. In all truth, he had been drawn to God by his younger brother's life. Christianity had suddenly become real, for he had seen it demonstrated in his own brother. The change was so evident, so dramatic, that he knew it had to be of God, not of the will of Isaac Donovan.

The boy's got some truth in what he says, Seth thought as he lay there. The inverted bowl of heaven overhead was dark blue, almost purple, and the skies were adorned and decorated with millions of small dots. Donovan had scarcely ever seen such a demonstration of lights in the heavens, and he thought, *Surely there has to be a God. These things couldn't make themselves. I know Isaac's right, and as soon as I can, I'll turn my thoughts to religion. But first we've got to fight this battle and drive these rebels out of this country.* Seth Donovan had a deep loyalty to the Crown. He well knew that the king of England was not a perfect man. He had many faults, but for him the kingdom of England, Scotland, and Ireland was one. For a Highlander Seth had an unusual loyalty to the Crown of England. He had never questioned this, and now as he lay there silently, he thought of Isaac's words and seemed to feel again the warm pressure of his brother's embrace.

"When this battle's over I'll talk to the minister," he murmured to the stars overhead and then closed his eyes and finally dropped off to sleep.

"Something's wrong with that bridge."

Isaac turned to stare at his brother with consternation. The two had marched for hours, and day was now beginning to break. They had been called to a halt by Colonel McLeod and were now tersely waiting the next command. "What do you mean something's wrong with the bridge?" Isaac asked.

"It doesn't look right." Seth searched the ground in front of them and pointed suddenly. "Look, Isaac. See those earthworks?"

"Sure I see them, but they're empty. Nobody's in them."

"That's right. They changed their minds. They were going to make a stand there, but now look. They're over on the other side. They're hiding behind logs and trees, and they've thrown up some earthworks there. They're just waiting for us to cross that bridge, and there's something wrong with the bridge."

The bridge itself was out of his view, and finally, unable to keep his curiosity any longer, Seth Donovan stood up. He took one straight look, then crouched down again, when a sergeant barked an order. "They've taken the boards off the bridge," he said.

"What are you talking about, Seth?"

"Just what I say. The framework is there, but they've stripped the boards off."

"Then how are we going to cross?"

"I hope we won't," Seth said. Something about it seemed all wrong, and he shook his head. "I'm no soldier, but I see what the rebels want us to do. They want us to come across that bridge clinging to the timbers. They can pick us off one at a time that way. If I were Colonel McLeod, I'd be wary of doing what the enemy *wanted* me to do."

But Colonel McLeod was a headstrong, impulsive man. He had come to fight and now was determined to win. He had red hair and it glowed in the sunlight as he stood up waving his sword. "Ready, men? We're going to wipe the rebels off the face of the earth!" his voice rang out.

"Get ready," Seth said, grimly shaking his head. "It's a mistake. They'll cut us to pieces."

"But we've got to go. It's orders," Isaac said. His lips were drawn tightly together and he was pale. He checked the load in his musket, as did other men up and down the line.

"Charge, men! King George and broadswords!" Colonel McLeod screamed.

Seth leaped to his feet and pushed everything out of his mind except the bridge. Encouraged by the squealing bagpipes, sounding almost like animals in pain, the Highlanders charged down out of cover to the bridge. Seth was not the first to get there. He saw others scrambling onto the timbers. One of them leaped from one cross board to the next, then suddenly his foot slipped and he fell into the waters below, his musket spinning in the air and splashing after him.

"The boards are greased! Watch out! We can't do it!" Seth yelled.

At that moment a fusillade struck the Highlanders' front line. They were cut down as with a scythe. Colonel McLeod was killed instantly as nine bullets slammed into his body.

All around Seth men were falling and screaming, and there was no leadership. He looked up and said, "Look, it's a countercharge! Get off this bridge!" He turned to see Isaac raise his musket and fire a shot, and he yelled, "Come on, Isaac!"

"All right, I'm coming!" Isaac yelled. He turned to step, and then a bullet struck him. His musket fell between the timbers and he collapsed, gripping one of the uprights.

"Isaac!" Seth screamed. He dropped his own musket, leaped forward, and grabbed his brother around the waist. He went sick as he saw the blossoming crimson on his brother's chest. Picking him up,

Seth threw him over his shoulder and scrambled back to shore. All around them he heard the screams of the dying and the curses of those who remained to fight. As he made for the woods, he glanced over his shoulder and saw that the Americans had found fords and were flanking the Highlanders. Seeing their plight was hopeless, and most of their officers were dead, the Highlanders broke rank and ran.

Seth Donovan ran until he could not breathe, his breath coming out in huge, panting gasps. The sounds of the battle grew quieter as he went deep into the woods. He fell to the ground, cushioning Isaac's fall, then rolled his brother over. "Isaac!" he gasped. "Isaac, speak to me!"

At first he thought Isaac was dead, but then the eyes opened, and Isaac lifted one hand feebly.

"Seth—"

"Isaac, you'll be all right. I'll get you to a doctor."

But Isaac Donovan was too far gone. He looked down at the blood that stained his chest and shook his head. "I won't make it, brother," he said. Isaac held his hand up and Seth grasped it.

"You can't die!" Seth whispered. "You just can't!"

Isaac was slipping away quick. His eyes fluttered and he whispered something. Seth leaned down quickly and placed his ear to the faintly moving lips. What he heard was "Going . . . to be with . . . Lord Jesus. I'll wait for you . . . Seth . . . I'll wait for you."

And then Isaac's body slumped.

Tears flooded Seth Donovan's eyes as he sat there holding the body of his dead brother. A hardness came into him then, and a fury burned at those who had killed Isaac. He looked blindly back toward where the battle was still going on, hearing the faint popping sounds of muskets, and he whispered, "I'll never forgive you for that, for killing my brother! Never!"

Overhead, soft white clouds drifted across the slate blue skies of February. It was peaceful enough, but beneath the clouds, Seth Donovan, holding the body of the only person he loved on this earth, was filled with anger. The tears that ran down his face stopped, and a coldness settled on him as he looked at the face of Isaac and whispered, "I'll be revenged for you, brother. Your death will not be forgotten!"

PART I

An Eagle Stirs Her Nest

July 1777

"As an eagle stirreth up her nest,
fluttereth over her young, spreadeth abroad her wings,
taketh them, beareth them on her wings:
So the Lord alone did lead him,
and there was no strange god with him."

Deuteronomy 32:11–12

Sarah

One

$\mathscr{S}$arah MacNeal looked up at the blue of the sky and thought abruptly, *Why, the sky is the same color as alder when it burns in the fireplace!* She had always been delighted with the brief spurts of blue fire that sometimes emerged from the thick chunks of alder wood that burned in the fireplace. She always looked for it among the reds and yellows of the flames, and then when the wood had exploded and popped and produced a brilliant, clear blue flame, she would clap her hands with delight.

The thought delighted her, for she had a clever and imaginative mind. The idea of a whole enormous sky with the same delicate tint of blue as the tiny sample from the alder pleased her. She stopped where she was and looked up, noticing the white smudges of clouds over to the south. They were the only ones in sight in the blue canopy above. Taking a deep breath, she said aloud, "I love it when the sky is so blue it hurts your eyes, and the grass is so green it doesn't even look real!"

For a moment she stood there savoring the day. At the age of seventeen, Sarah was a young woman coming out of girlhood who possessed a figure somewhat slender but which would mature as she grew older. Her eyes were pale green, the same as her mother's, under beautifully arched brows, and her hair, fiery red, hung down her back in long ringlets. This was a gift from her father, Patrick MacNeal, a Scotsman who had died on the journey to the wilderness across the Appalachians. Her face was oval, and her eyelashes were long and thick and darker than one would have imagined for one with such red hair.

Laughing at herself for no reason as she often did, Sarah began to move through the grass that sometimes was almost waist-high. She was wearing a simple light blue dress with fitted sleeves. Over it she wore a pinafore with a large pocket stuffed with a mixture of herbs and wild flowers.

On her head she wore a white mobcap with pleats around the top to frame her face. Despite the heat, she wore a stole over her shoulders made from scraps of material. It was a colorful piece of work, gleaming with yellow, violet, pale green, blue, and dark purple blocks of material.

She made an attractive sight, although no one was there to see her, and as she moved among the tall grass into a meadow, shaded and flanked by towering first-growth oaks, she stopped from time to time to pluck the wild flowers that bloomed abundantly in the spring. Sarah made a game out of picking the flowers, trying to find as many colors as she could. She had already found a bed of pepperwort, small flowers with a pleasant, pungent taste, white as cotton. She had hunted then until she found a group of small lady's slippers and delighted in the pale yellow lip of the flower. For some time she sought for red ones and finally found them in a carpet of Indian paintbrush, her favorite of all the wild flowers. They were a hairy plant, six inches to a foot high, and their blossoms reddened the meadow to a brilliant scarlet. She stuffed these inside the pocket of the pinafore and moved along until finally she came upon a flower that her mother had taught her to call Quaker lady. It was no more than three to five inches high, very small, with a delicate blue blossom almost lilac in color. Carefully she picked a nosegay of these, winding a string she had brought with her around the stems, and then moved on across the meadow.

As she circled a group of hickory trees, the sound of squirrels chattering caught her ears and she looked up to see two large gray squirrels perched on a branch watching her with their bright, beady eyes. Picking up a stick, she tossed it toward them, and they chattered angrily, then scampered away.

When she came out into a flat pasture, Sarah glanced up with surprise to see a man at the end of the field. She stopped dead still, her eyes staring and her face paling with the shock.

"Philip . . ." she whispered and dropped the small group of flowers to the ground. Her heart was beating as rapidly and as loudly as a drum, and she seemed somehow to be paralyzed, unable to move.

"Philip . . ." she whispered again. As the young man started toward her, the thought echoed in her mind and spirit, *But, Philip, I thought you were dead!*

Philip Baxter, however, was very much alive, and he ran toward her, holding out his arms to her.

Quickly Sarah started to run, but she was too shocked to say a word. As she hurried toward him, a shot rang out, and a slight puff of smoke issued from a group of scrub oak covered with vines.

Philip Baxter suddenly was driven to one side. He fell to the ground and writhed feebly and then lay still.

Sarah cried out, "Philip!" and ran to where he lay. When she reached his side, she rolled him over, but it was not Philip Baxter who lay there but Patrick MacNeal, her father, who had lain in a wilderness grave for years!

Horror and shock as she had never known swept through Sarah MacNeal. She stared at the face of her dead father without comprehension and then closed her eyes. As the blackness closed in around her, she began to scream. She cried out, "Papa—Papa!" in a high-pitched voice that seemed to echo in her head and then . . .

Suddenly Sarah realized she was not in a meadow with her pinafore pocket full of wild flowers. There was no Philip Baxter, and there was no Patrick MacNeal.

Opening her eyes suddenly, she glanced wildly around as the features of her small room came into focus. She saw the cattails she had placed in a woven basket. They seemed to move slightly in the breeze that came in through the single window of her room.

And then the door burst open and suddenly her mother was there sitting on her bed putting her arms around her.

"Sarah, what is it?"

Elizabeth Spencer held the young woman as sobs began shaking her like a reed in the wind. She held her even more tightly, whispering, "Was it a nightmare, Sarah?"

Sarah clung to her mother as a drowning person might cling to the arm of a rescuer. "Mother, I . . . I dreamed I was in a meadow picking flowers, and then . . . I looked up and saw Philip!"

"You saw Philip?"

"Yes, he ran to me and was holding out his arms to me," Sarah said, her voice barely audible among the sobs, "and then I heard a shot and he fell down. But when I ran to him and turned him over, Ma, it wasn't Philip. It was Papa!"

Elizabeth Spencer held her daughter tightly, stroking her hair and whispering, "It's all right, Sarah. It was only a bad dream."

"But it was so real, Ma!"

"I know. Dreams often are, but you've been so upset since losing Philip."

"But I've never had a dream like this."

"And I pray you will never have another one like this," Elizabeth said. "When you get through this time, you'll look back on Philip as a wonderful memory. As long as he lives in your memory," she said quietly, "he's not gone."

Elizabeth had sensed the deep affection her daughter had had for young Philip Baxter. It might not ever have come to be fully developed love or a marriage, but the seeds of it were there. Young Baxter had been cut down by a bullet, his youth blotted out instantly, and Sarah had not yet recovered from the shock.

Elizabeth thought quickly, *I've got to get her mind off of this.* Instantly she began to speak, "It's all right, Sarah. It was just a dream. Look, it's almost dawn. Why don't you get up and we'll fix breakfast. After all, it's going to be a cabin raising for Andrew and Abigail."

Sarah pulled back slightly from her mother. She brushed her hair back and then brushed the tears from her eyes with both of her hands. "I'm sorry. I didn't mean to bother you, but it was so frightening."

"Well, it's over now," Elizabeth said as cheerfully as she could. "Now, get out of bed. It's going to be a big day. You've got to go see Andrew and Abigail. Your brother's a married man now."

"All right, Ma." Obediently, Sarah swung her feet out and stood there in her shift. She thought of her brother, Andrew, who had been married only a week. It seemed strange for her brother to be married.

"Well, he's grown up and now you'll have a sister."

The fright was fading now from Sarah. She was a strong young woman who had suffered intensely over the loss of Philip Baxter. Everything she did, as a matter of fact, was intense, and now she firmly put the thought of Philip and the dream out of her head and turned it toward the things at hand. "I'll get dressed and make breakfast for you and Pa."

"All right, if you feel like it. Are you all right now?"

"Yes, Ma, I'm all right now."

"Good!" Elizabeth kissed her daughter, then turned and left the room.

As soon as she was gone, Sarah walked over to the window and stared intently into the sunrise that was beginning to turn the dark sky a pale gray. She loved the early hours of the morning, and now she busied herself dressing, blocking out her sorrow and grief and agony over the death of young Philip Baxter.

When Elizabeth returned to her room, she found her husband already out of bed and waiting for her.

"What was it?" he asked.

"A bad dream. I think it was about Philip and about Patrick."

Hawk Spencer nodded. "She's had those before, I think." Spencer was a solidly built man of six feet. At the age of forty-two his hair was still thick and black as coal, slightly wavy, and worn short. He was wearing only a pair of drawers made of natural linen, and his upper body swelled strongly. His deep chest swept up over a lean waist, and his skin was dark from the years of being outdoors. He came over now and put his hands on Elizabeth's shoulders. "You're worried about Sarah, aren't you?"

"Yes, I am." Elizabeth looked up and then put her arms around him and locked them. She was, at the age of forty, still slender despite bearing four children. She had a heart-shaped face with a pert nose and a smooth complexion. Now she thought suddenly of her first husband, Patrick. It was something that happened only rarely now, for after her marriage to Hawk Spencer, God had given her rest and peace from her grief. Now, holding on to Hawk, she whispered, "She doesn't show it, but Sarah's terribly shocked over Philip's death."

"I know. She's like you. She feels more than she shows."

Leaning back, Elizabeth looked up. "Do I do that?"

"You always did, but I've learned to know something of what goes on inside you. That's what happens to a man and a woman when they live together. But a young girl like Sarah keeps things bottled up, and I don't think that's good."

Elizabeth put her hand on his chest and stood there silently for a moment, looking up at him. Suddenly she said, "I've been wondering about something."

"About what?"

"I wonder if it's right for Jacob to take her to Williamsburg for this visit."

Hawk said with surprise, "I thought it was all settled! You said it would be good for her to go."

Elizabeth turned away. She moved over toward the washstand and looked down at the basin and the pewter pitcher for a moment, then poured some water into the basin. "Why don't you go ahead and shave," she said.

"All right." Hawk moved over and began lathering his face; then taking out a razor from the top drawer, he stropped it and began pulling it down his face. He winced as the razor cut through the whiskers, and his eyes watered with the pain of it. He was aware that Elizabeth was watching him, and he asked as he carefully moved the razor over his throat, "Don't you want her to go?"

"Yes, but she won't know anybody there. I've been thinking.. What if I ask Amanda to go with her?" Amanda Taylor was one year older than Sarah. She had led a difficult life, for she had been beaten by her father, Zeke, as had her mother, Iris. Amanda had blossomed, however, since the death of her father.

"That might not be too wise, Elizabeth." Hawk reached out and pulled off a towel from the bronze rack and dried his face. "I'm not very smart about these things, but I think she's in danger of falling in love with Jacob."

Jacob was Hawk's son by a previous marriage, and now he thought of the young man who looked so much like him. "I'm not sure it'd be good to put her in his company for a long visit like that."

"Would you object to her as a daughter-in-law?"

"Not at all," Hawk shrugged. He moved over and began to dress. Pulling on a pair of white socks, he then put on a pair of dark brown knee britches. Glancing up at her he said, "I'm afraid she might get hurt."

Elizabeth was surprised and said so. "I didn't think you noticed things like that. Most men don't."

"We're smarter than you think we are." Hawk pulled a white linen shirt over his head, then came to put his arms around her. "One of these days you're going to learn what a brilliant fellow you're married to."

"Oh, you!" Elizabeth always enjoyed the mild teasing she got from her husband. Now she put her hand up and rubbed his smoothly shaven cheek. "That's nice," she whispered. She pulled his head down and rubbed her own silky skin against it, then she stepped back and said, "I think it will be all right, Hawk. If you agree, I'll ask Iris if she'll let Amanda go."

"It's up to you. Whatever you think."

"Well, all right."

Hawk stepped into a pair of moccasins, which he found more comfortable than any shoes made by a shoemaker, and then turned back to her. He put his arms around her and whispered, "I thank God for bringing you into my life, Elizabeth. He has certainly been good to me."

Elizabeth savored the strength of his arms around her. She held him tightly and did not answer, but her heart was saying, *He has been good to me, too. In fact, He has blessed us all!*

The New Minister

Two

$\mathcal{A}$ndrew MacNeal reached out and took the hand of his bride. They had been married only a week, but somehow Andrew could not yet get it into his mind that he was actually a married man. He was not above average height, and his short blond hair with brown highlights glowed in the early morning sun as they approached the Spencer cabin. He had sparkling light blue eyes and bronzed skin from being outdoors all the time. He had a strong, stocky build and a deeply arching chest. At the age of twenty he was at the prime of his physical prowess. A happiness he had never dreamed possible swelled up inside him, and he reached out to take Abigail around the waist and pulled her closer.

"Good morning, wife."

Abigail, surprised, looked up at Andrew's eyes. "You've already said good morning. Did you forget?" She smiled, and a gleam of coquetry sparkled in her eyes. She was not a tall woman, but shapely and very attractive. She had a heart-shaped face, a flawless complexion, and a pair of gray-green eyes. She laughed at his expression, saying, "I declare, Andrew, you do act funny!"

"Funny? What are you talking about?"

"Oh, I don't know! You're just funny, that's all."

Andrew grinned at her and suddenly stopped, pulled her around, and putting his arms around her, he kissed her firmly on the lips. She returned his embrace and caress, but then pulled away. "Now, you stop that! Behave yourself!"

"All right, I will—for now." He turned again and said, "I smell bacon. I hope they made enough for us."

"Why, you already had breakfast once."

"I always say a man can't get enough of a good breakfast." They approached the cabin, which was set back from a large creek with a background of tall sycamore trees. "Hello the house!" he shouted.

Almost at once the door opened and Hawk came outside. "Morning, son." He turned to the young woman and a twinkle came into his eyes. "Good morning, Mrs. MacNeal. I hope you're enjoying married life."

Something about her father-in-law's expression embarrassed Abigail. She flushed suddenly, a rich color touching her neck, and she murmured, "Good morning, sir."

"You're just about in time for breakfast. I thought I'd have to eat it all by myself. Come on in."

The two entered the house, which was made of logs, as were all the houses in the settlement. There were no sawmills to make boards, and what few boards were available had to be laboriously hand sawn. The main room of the cabin was familiar enough to Andrew, who had lived there for much of his life. It was a large room, some fourteen feet wide and twenty-two feet long, much larger than most cabins. The logs were chinked with clay, and a huge fireplace dominated one end. A fire crackled merrily under the blackened pot that hung by hooks, and Elizabeth, who had been bending over a skillet placed on the coals, turned and said, "Well, I wondered if you would make it this morning."

Sarah, who was setting a table with hand-carved wooden plates and mugs, came over and gave Abigail a hug. "Hello, Abigail," she said. "Are you ready for the cabin raising?"

"Yes. I can't wait to get in my own home. It's nice," she said, "that Iris let us use her place, but I want my own."

Sarah smiled warmly. She and Abigail had been close friends in a way that only young girls cut off from civilization in a frontier settlement can be. There was little enough to entertain young people, and the two girls had grown very close. Sarah had been deliriously happy when Abigail had finally agreed to marry Andrew after a rather rocky courtship, and now she said, "You go sit down. Breakfast is ready."

At that moment Jacob Spencer joined them.

"Good morning," he said. He was wearing a fringed hunting shirt of linen over a homespun checkered shirt. He also was wearing leggings and moccasins in Indian style, and his britches were of deerskin.

He came over at once and shook hands with Andrew. "Hello, Andrew," he said. "How are you enjoying married life?"

It was Andrew's turn to blush, for Sarah giggled at the question. "Fine," he said quickly. He managed a smile and said, "I hope you're ready to go to work and build this woman a house." He was glad the two of them had finally worked through the rocky beginning of their acquaintance.

Jacob was the son of Hawk Spencer by his first wife, Faith. It had been a traumatic thing for Hawk when his first wife had died in childbirth. Unable to stand his grief, he had fled to the wilderness, leaving his parents to raise Jacob. It had only been recently that he had gone back and brought Jacob to the frontier.

Andrew and Sarah had welcomed Jacob as their stepbrother, for their mother had married Hawk.

Everyone in the cabin was well aware that there had been a rivalry for Abigail between the two stepbrothers. Hawk leaned his back against the cabin wall and studied the face of his two sons carefully, one of blood and one by adoption. *I reckon they're all right*, he thought with relief. He was pleased to see that there was no remnant of ill feeling in Jacob for having given up Abigail to Andrew. *He's going to be all right. Both of them are,* Hawk thought. Aloud he said, "Let's sit down and get with it! If we're going to work today, I've got to have a good breakfast!"

And it was a good breakfast. It consisted of johnnycakes fried golden brown and served with freshly made apple butter, crisp bacon, dressed eggs, biscuits, fried potatoes, and hot black coffee. Talk went around the table, and there was a great deal of laughing and jesting. The two youngest Spencers, Hannah, almost five, and Joshua, age three, were seated by their father. Hannah was a quiet child, very well behaved, while Joshua was loud, vociferous, and demanded attention every moment.

Finally Hawk pulled him up into his lap and said, "Son, you have got to learn some manners from your sister."

"No, Papa!" Joshua protested. "I best!"

Elizabeth laughed ruefully. "That's speaking right out! You remind me of your father."

Hawk grinned and held the boy closer. He swept his eyes over the handsome face of the boy, admiring his brown eyes and brown hair. Already the face was speckled with a few freckles and large dimples. "We Spencer men are always special. I've been hoping you'd notice that, wife."

Elizabeth scoffed. "Special! I should like to see what you've done that's so special!" She swept up Hannah and held her closely, smiling and squeezing her. "Don't pay any attention to your father. He's just teasing you."

"All right," Hannah said and smiled sweetly.

"You take these children out so we can clean up," Elizabeth said. "Make yourself useful."

"Sure," Hawk agreed and picked up the two children, one under each arm. He left the room, followed by Jacob and Andrew, and the women began cleaning up after the breakfast.

Abigail moved over to stand beside Sarah. She had been concerned about Sarah for some time, ever since the death of their friend Philip Baxter, and now she said cautiously, "Are you all right, Sarah?"

Replacing the mugs on a shelf fastened by pegs to the cabin wall, Sarah turned and said with some surprise, "All right? Why . . . yes. Why shouldn't I be?"

"Oh, I don't know. I just thought you've been looking sort of pale lately. Maybe you haven't been feeling well."

"No, I feel fine."

"Are you excited about your trip to Williamsburg?"

"I think so," Sarah said cautiously. "I don't know what it will be like."

"It'll be fun for you, a change. I want you to keep a diary while you are gone, and when you get back you can read it to me." Abigail smiled, then said, "You'll have all sorts of young men calling on you there. Write about all the parties and the dresses and the dances."

"Oh, I don't know about that," Sarah said. She seemed more subdued than usual, and Abigail would have said more, but at that moment two women entered.

"Well, hello, Iris. Hello, Amanda."

The two women, obviously mother and daughter, greeted the others at once. Iris Taylor was a slight woman of forty-two. She was only a couple of inches above five feet, but despite a rather worn expression on her face, she now was more cheerful than anyone had ever seen her. Her husband, Zeke, had died only a few months earlier, the victim of the same Indian attack that had cost Philip Baxter his life, an attack that Zeke had helped to plan and orchestrate. Her marriage had not been happy, for Zeke Taylor had been an abusive man toward his family as well as to everyone else. It had been a hard life for Iris Taylor, but she had maintained her faith in God, and now the only good memory she had of her marriage was that her husband had been converted to Christ on his deathbed.

Amanda Taylor was slightly taller than her mother. She was slim but showed the promise of a mature figure at the age of eighteen. There was a wonderful prettiness about her, for she had long straight hair so dark brown that it appeared almost black at times. Her best feature was her large brown eyes, which were liquid and expressive. She was possessed of an innate shyness, a result of abusive treatment from her father, but now she smiled sweetly and said, "Good morning, Abigail. Sarah, how are you?"

The women stood speaking together, and Elizabeth came over to greet the two women with a quick hug and a smile. "I'm so glad you could come."

"Why, I wouldn't have missed it for anything," Iris smiled.

"Iris, I'm grateful to you for letting Andrew and me use your house." Abigail laughed shyly, saying, "I guess we would have been out under the trees if you hadn't been so kind."

Iris said at once, "I was so glad to be able to do it."

Soon Abigail, Amanda, and Sarah turned and went outside. Iris commented, "I suppose it's time for me to go back to my home." By home she meant the house where she had lived with her husband, Zeke. He had beaten her badly, and Hawk and Elizabeth had brought her to stay with them—at least on their homestead. She had stayed in a house inhabited formerly by Sequatchie, a Cherokee friend. "It was good of Sequatchie to let me have his place, but I'm sure he'd be glad to get it back."

"I don't think so. Why don't you stay for a while?"

"Oh, I don't believe I should," Iris said.

Elizabeth changed the subject then, saying, "Iris, I have a favor to ask of you."

"A favor? Of me? Well, whatever is it, Elizabeth?"

Elizabeth came over to stand in front of the smaller woman. She said persuasively, "I've been thinking it would be good if Sarah didn't have to go to Williamsburg alone. What would you think if Amanda went along with her for company?"

Surprise washed across Iris Taylor's face. "Why, I never thought of it," she said. "It's so far."

"I know it is, but it would be good for Amanda to travel a little bit, don't you think? And it would be so good for Sarah. They're such good friends, and young girls need to do things together."

"Why, I suppose you're right, Elizabeth, but I don't even know that Amanda would want to go. She's so shy."

"Oh, I think she might, especially since Jacob is going."

Quickly Iris scanned Elizabeth Spencer's face. A smile turned the corners of her lips slightly upward. "She does admire Jacob. I suppose everyone's noticed. She thinks she's being very sly about it, but I know her."

"Well, she's such a fine girl, and she and Sarah and Jacob are close to the same age. They could have a very fine time together. And I think it would be good for the girls to learn a little bit more about how people live in other places."

Iris frowned and appeared to be thoughtful. "I suppose you're right. All Amanda has ever known is a rough life. But she doesn't have anything to wear."

"We can do something about that." Elizabeth smiled persuasively. "Just say she can go." She hesitated for a moment, then said innocently, "And you could continue to stay near us in Sequatchie's cabin."

"I suppose I could do that."

"I think you ought to. Sequatchie would miss you if you went away."

A faint color stirred in Iris Taylor's cheeks. She had become, in truth, very fond of the stately Cherokee chief, and it had occurred more than once to Elizabeth that, perhaps, something might come of this now that Iris was a widow.

"Well, I'd miss him, too," Iris said. She hesitated only for a moment, then added, "Well, if Amanda wants to go, she has my blessing."

"Good," Elizabeth said. "It's all settled then. Why don't you go talk to her about it now, or would you rather wait until you get home alone?"

"That might be best." She turned quickly, saying, "There's someone coming."

At that moment George and Deborah Stevens arrived. They were Abigail's parents, and as soon as George had greeted Elizabeth, he turned and went out in search of the men. He called back, "Here comes the preacher and his family!"

Going to the window, Elizabeth looked out and said, "Look, who's that stranger with Paul and Rhoda?"

Iris came over and looked out. "I'm sure I don't know. I've never seen him before."

"Well, he's welcome, whoever he is. Come along. Let's find out."

They stepped outside on the porch and Hawk turned to them. "Well, Elizabeth, you ought to be happy. We've got a newcomer. May I introduce Reverend Samuel Doak."

"I'm pleased to know you, Reverend Doak," Elizabeth smiled. She curtsied and said, "It's always good to have another minister in the neighborhood."

Samuel Doak was a serious-looking man with large, expressive dark eyes and a firm mouth, which was now smiling. "Thank you, Mrs. Spencer. I've heard such good things about you from my fellow minister."

"I didn't tell him any of the bad things about you, Elizabeth," Paul Anderson said. Paul Anderson turned his light green eyes on Elizabeth in a smile, for she was a favorite of his. He was only forty-one and had been a good friend to Hawk Spencer in Williamsburg, where the two had grown up together. He had traveled on the wagon train west with Hawk, where he had fallen in love with Rhoda Harper and married her.

Now Rhoda came to stand close to her husband. "He's a fine preacher, even if I do say so to his face," Rhoda smiled, looking at her husband in admiration. Her background had been very rough in Williamsburg, and she still felt at times unworthy to be the wife of a minister.

Reverend Doak was quick to respond, Elizabeth saw, for his eyes went to Rhoda at once. "Mrs. Anderson is too kind," he said.

"Not at all, Samuel," Paul said. He was carrying their three-year-old Rachel in his arms, a beautiful little girl with sandy blond hair and light green eyes. Even now she was pulling at his ear to get his attention. "He is the finest preacher I ever heard."

"Then you can't have heard many preachers," Doak said.

The group stood there speaking for a while, and when they had all gathered, Paul made a general introduction of the new minister. "Reverend Doak has blessed us already in this area. I think he's the first Presbyterian preacher after Charles Cummings in Tennessee. He's been a student at Princeton and has a baccalaureate degree, so he's a fine scholar, but he's an even better preacher."

As those who gathered around, and others who were not there, were soon to learn, Samuel Doak was indeed a man for all seasons. A scholar and an educator, his impact on the Watauga area was to be tremendous.

"I've been commissioned," Doak spoke in a clear, caring voice, "by the Presbyterian church to serve in this area, and I'm glad to be among you."

"Praise the Lord!" Hawk said with exuberance. He had been away from God for years, but when he had come back, it was with his whole heart. He had spent his early years over the Appalachian Mountains under Sequatchie, learning the ways of wilderness living, but since his marriage, he had left that life and now wanted to see the settlement prosper, and he expressed his feelings to Reverend Doak. "Anything I can do, sir, I will be happy to do it. We're so glad to have a permanent minister."

"You'll be pleased to hear that Reverend Doak is also an educator," Paul Anderson said. He looked at Elizabeth, adding, "I know you've been worried about the children."

"Oh, how wonderful!" Elizabeth exclaimed, her eyes bright with joy. "Will you be establishing a school in the area soon?"

"As the Lord leads, so we will do," Reverend Doak smiled.

Hawk stepped back and stood beside Elizabeth as the settlers gathered around the new minister to welcome him. Hawk was a demonstrative man in private but in public rarely so. Elizabeth was, therefore, surprised when he slipped his arm around her and whispered, "Well, the children won't have to grow up totally ignorant."

"Isn't it exciting?" She turned to him and said, "I know God's in it."

"Yes, I believe He is. The country is getting settled." He thought suddenly of the miles and miles of forest that lay to the west. It was inhabited by Indians who would fight to the death to preserve their ancient hunting grounds, but he refused to consider this now. He squeezed her and said, "God is good to us."

"Yes. He sent us a man to preach His Word!"

A Cabin Raising

Three

The inhabitants of large cities such as Boston or New York, or those who lived in the small towns scattered throughout the eastern seaboard of the country, had almost no concept of what life was like for those who moved into the Misty Mountains across the Appalachians. The first Americans who crossed the Appalachians fought their way through canebrakes unbelievably tall and dense. The bridle paths were sometimes so narrow that the saddlebags of the travelers wore down the cane on each side of the trail. Reaching up to ten and twelve feet and as thick as hemp, it was so high that a man on horseback could barely reach the tops with an umbrella.

The settlers passed through immense forests of trees unknown in the East and witnessed an abundance of wild fauna everywhere. Flocks of turkeys fled fearlessly in the open between roaming herds of deer and buffalo. Bears rolled stones over and ate the grubs and the field mice beneath them. In effect, it was this abundance of wild game and the thickness of the cane that permitted the settlements far beyond the Appalachian Mountains. The cane supported human life until crops and domestic animals were raised and then supported the domestic animals. Without the cane it would have been almost impossible to bring settlements over the mountains and to keep the settlers and their stock from starving in the often harsh winters.

But it was the loneliness of the far-flung settlements that would have baffled and even frightened the more civilized peoples of the eastern seaboard. The migrations trickled on, mostly composed of those who were fleeing civilization for one reason or another. Some, like James Robertson, turned to the West to escape the oppression of a corrupt government that had brought on the Battle of the Alamance between the Regulators and the colonial authorities in North Carolina. Others fled to the wild as an escape from disappointment, seeking new hope, and fleeing the failures that had plagued them. Some came to escape the arm of the law, and some, like Daniel Boone, came because they simply loved the wilds and the life of a hunter, wanting to live where they could not see the smoke of a neighbor's cabin. It became common for the arrest of some to be stamped, "Gone to Kentucky."

And so the tiny trickle of pioneers grew. They came over the Wilderness Road, laid out by Daniel Boone in 1775, which became a monument to the skill and practical engineering ability of the uneducated pioneer. For it did require skill to make a road through more than two hundred miles of wilderness. At first it was a mere trail through the trees and around the mountains, suitable only for horse or foot traveler. As more settlers came, the trail was roughly cleared with axes. But not until the turn of the century would it be improved for wagon travel.

None of those from the East had the vaguest idea of the hardships of the journey west, much less of the life to be eked out once the pioneers arrived. In a short, fragmentary diary kept by Abraham Hanks, the maternal grandfather of Abraham Lincoln, lies a graphic and frightening record of the difficulties of the journey.

Fryday yde 24th March. Come to a turabel mountain that tried us all almost to death to get over it & we lodge this night on the Lawrel fork of holston under a grait mountain & Roast a fine fat turkey for our suppers & Eat it without aney Bread.

Thrusd 30th. March. we set out again & went down to Elk gardin and there Suplied our Selves With Seed Corn & irish tators then we went on alittel way I turned my hors to drive before me and he got Scard Ran wawy threw Down th eSaddel Bags and broke three of our powder goards and ABram's flask Burst open a walet of corn and lost a good Deal and made aturrabel flustration amonst the Reast of Horses Drake's mair ran against a sapling and nockt it down we c acht them all again and went on and lodged at John Duncan's.

Fryday, ye 7th April this morning avery hard snowey morning we still contiue at camp Being in number about 40 men &

some neAgroes, this eaven Comes aletter from Capt. Boon at Caintuck of the inding doing mischief and Some turns back.

Satrd 8th. We all packt up & started corst Cumberland gap. We Met a great maney people turned Back for fear of indians but our Company goes on Still with good courage.

Wedneday 12th. We meet another Companey going Back they tell Such News ABram & Drake is afraid to go aney further

Thursday 13th. ABram & Drake turn Back.

Then began the arduous struggle as squatters dug in and began to wrest a living from the soil. The first settlers were hunters who lived along the rivers where the rocks projected out over the banks, which were called rock houses. Another type of shelter in the early days was the half-faced camp. It was made by setting two forked posts in the ground and placing a traverse pole across the crotches. Then bows of evergreen trees, butts upward, were leaned from the ground against the horizontal pole. Sometimes the skins of animals or even bark of trees were used to cover the shelter. A fire in front of this rude shelter threw its heat upon the occupants.

Some shelters were made of poles and shakes. Even the earliest settlers had an ax or two and some iron wedges. Others owned or could borrow a crosscut saw. The pole house was built from large oaks that had been split into boards by means of wedges. These were called shakes in the north, three or four feet long, and were laid across a roof for protection.

But more permanent houses were soon to be built, and the only alternative was the log house, which became almost an art form with the early settlers. There were no sawmills to rip boards, and the only other way of making a board was by means of a saw pit. It was an arduous, back-breaking task, with one man standing in a pit and pulling one end of a saw. At every draw the dust would fall into his eyes as another man on top pulled the weight of the saw upward. It was the work of two men to make two or three boards a day.

The cabin raising became a symbol of the fellowship and dependency that settlers had to develop out of sheer necessity. It was not only a necessary labor, but one of the few occasions when men, women, and children would come together from far distances. In the thickness of the forest, a cabin raising became the social time everyone looked forward to. And thus the cabin raising of the newlyweds, Andrew and Abigail MacNeal, drew the settlers from far away and became a time of happiness and rejoicing so that no one minded the work.

The new cabin was to be located close to the Spencer cabin, yet far enough away to provide privacy for the newlyweds. The early beams of the red sun beat down on those who had gathered. As the men worked, the women worked beside them doing the lighter tasks. At the same time, some prepared a huge meal on tables made out of cut poles and saplings. Children of all ages were running around playing. The older boys, of course, helped with the task of raising the cabin, but the younger ones were underfoot, and constant cries were heard. "Joshua, get away from that tree. It's going to fall on you!" or "Hannah, come here! Stay close to me! I don't want you to get hurt!"

The bridegroom himself was in charge of making the shakes to cover the cabin roof. Andrew had become quite expert at this, and now he had to caution Joshua again and again to stay back. "I don't want you to get hurt." He grinned at the young fellow. "You sit right there on that log and watch me."

"Whatcha doin', Andy?"

"Well, I'm going to make shakes."

"What's a shake?"

"Little short boards that will go on top to keep the rain from coming in. Just like on your house."

"I help!"

"Well, a little bit, but I have to get started first."

"I help!" Joshua protested.

"All right. I'll tell you when."

Andrew went to work at once along with a son of William Bean and another of John Robertson. The three worked steadily at the painstaking work, but all three did well.

The board-making process began with large sections of oak trunks two to three feet in diameter. They were sawed off into lengths of approximately two to four feet, ready to be made into short boards. The process began when the sections were split into half, then into quarters. Out of this the heart was split, and then carefully, using a wedge, Andrew began to slice the chunks into boards. He went around in a circle, and the oak split well. Each chunk produced around thirty shakes, and then the heart was thrown away.

"I help!" Joshua protested even louder.

"All right. Come here." Holding the boy in front of him, Andrew placed a steel wedge on the next log. He grabbed the sledge in his right hand and said, "Now, you hold on and help me drive it in." He grinned as the boy frowned, and he raised the sledge and let it fall. "That's the way," he said. "We have to hit it hard enough to make this board split." Applying more strength, Andrew heard the noise that meant the split had been made and the wedge disappeared.

"That's a good boy!" he said. "Now you split a log."

"I do more!" Joshua said.

For a time Andrew let the boy help. After chopping a few shakes, it grew tiresome, and he said, "Okay, you go play with your sister now. Watch out for Hannah."

At the same time the pile of shakes was growing, the logs were being lifted into place. The team worked smoothly together with Hawk, the Beans, the Robertsons, and the Fosters performing the same operation over and over again. Each log was notched to fit into the corner. William Bean was, perhaps, the best log notcher in the settlement. His ax flashed in the sun, the chips flew, and in an unbelievably short time, he would call out, "Yo!" At the other end of the log, James Robertson was almost as good as his friend Bean. At first the lift was low enough so men could grab a section of the log and lift it into place. When it got higher, up above their shoulders, the logs were rolled up an incline made of poles.

At noon Elizabeth called out, "Time to eat! Anyone hungry?"

Hawk threw down his ax, wiped the sweat from his face, and said, "I think I could eat a whole buffalo."

"We don't have any buffalo, but we've got everything else. Everyone come on."

All the men gathered around the tables where the hot, steaming food was gathered. Andrew looked toward Reverend Samuel Doak, who had worked as hard as any of the men. "Reverend," he said, "would you make a beginning?" This was the customary way of asking someone to ask the blessing.

Samuel Doak lifted his voice and began to pray. "Oh, God," he intoned in a clear tenor voice, "bless the efforts of our hands for this young couple. Bless their marriage and make it fruitful. Bless this food, and may it strengthen us to finish the task before us. And in all things, Lord, may the name of Your son, the Lord Jesus Christ, be glorified. Amen."

A hearty chorus of "amens" went around the tables, and soon the wooden trenchers were filled with cuts of beef, venison, rabbit, along with fresh bread that had been baked in the fireplaces of various cabins. There were crocks of butter and jars of honey, which the children squealed over when they got their portions.

As they were eating, Leah Foster came over to sit close to Sarah. They were across from Amanda and Abigail. Leah Foster was an attractive girl with pale blond hair and china blue eyes. She had a sweet disposition, a pretty face, although she was not as beautiful as Abigail, but then few young women were.

She began to talk to Sarah under her breath so that the others who were talking about something else could not hear. "I'm sorry about Philip. I haven't had a chance to talk to you since he . . . was taken."

Sarah wished that Leah had said nothing. She had tried to put Philip and her bad dream out of her mind, but now she said quietly, "Thank you, Leah. It's getting a little bit easier."

"I think that it's times like this we really miss Philip," Leah went on, not knowing she was hurting her friend. "He was always so much fun, laughing and playing his fiddle, and he always was so good at the games."

As Leah went on speaking of Philip Baxter, Sarah lost the gaiety that had been in her. She could not help but feel the grief and the sorrow edging back into her.

Across the table, Abigail picked up enough of the conversation to know what was going on and wished that Leah had a little more judgment. *It doesn't do any good to talk about things like this,* she thought. Turning to Amanda, she asked, "How are things going with you and Jacob?"

"Why, fine."

"Well, if you're not going to talk any more than that, I'd better go to Jacob for information," Abigail said.

Amanda looked alarmed. She did have a tremendous affection

for Jacob Spencer, but she tried to keep it hidden. "I wish you wouldn't talk about it," she said. "It embarrasses me. Things are going fine."

Sarah suddenly looked across the table and smiled. "It looks like I might have another sister before long."

Knowing what her friend meant, Amanda said, "I'll really miss Jacob when he goes to Williamsburg."

There was a plaintive quality in Amanda's voice, and Sarah suddenly smiled. She reached across and seized Amanda's hand. "Mother told me that she's talked with your mother about your going with us. I hope you will. I really want you to go, Amanda."

Amanda's eyes brightened. "I'd love to go!" She hesitated, then added, "I think Mother could use the time without me, anyway."

Somewhat surprised, Leah Foster asked, "What do you mean by that?"

Amanda pointed over to where Iris was taking Sequatchie a drink of water. "Look at her. She seems so happy," she said quietly. She studied her mother, who was smiling and laughing at something that Sequatchie had said.

Leah Foster started to ask a question, but Sarah nudged her in the ribs and shook her head.

Abigail said quickly, "I almost wish I could go with you. It'll be such fun."

Sarah laughed aloud. "I'll ask Andrew about that. Maybe he'd be glad to let you go. Do you think?"

"Don't you dare!" Abigail said indignantly. "I was only teasing!"

"What's it like to be married?" Leah demanded, turning to face Abigail.

Something about the question troubled Abigail, and she dropped her head for a moment. Finally she looked up and smiled. "It's not something you can really tell anyone about. You have to experience it for yourself."

There was a peace and contentment in her expression, and Sarah, who was watching her, felt envious. *Her life is all settled,* she thought. *But I don't know what I'm going to do.*

––––––

The men and women separated themselves, more or less—the women speaking about children, cooking, and the mundane tasks they faced day by day. The men, however, as they polished off platters of food, fell into a discussion of the Colonies and Great Britain. George Stevens and Andrew MacNeal were very outspoken about independence. Andrew bit off a large mouthful of venison from the chunk he had on his knife and said vigorously, "We've got to be free of Great Britain, and that's all there is to it. What does King George know about our problems out here? Nothing!"

Charles Foster, age forty-six, was a short man, no more than five six with blond hair and blue eyes. He and his family had moved to Watauga in early 1772. He was a wealthy man, compared to most of the settlers, and an outspoken Tory. His face grew red as he said, "That's treasonous talk, Andrew!"

"I agree. You'd better be careful how you talk about the king," said Joseph Foster, son of Charles and Betty Foster. At the age of nineteen he was taller than his father, but still no more than average. He sat back against a log, his dark hair falling over his forehead. He had light green eyes that watched everything carefully. He was a Tory like his parents, and his intense competitiveness and jealousy were barely covered under his roguish manner. He was a handsome young man and from time to time let his eyes go over to where Sarah MacNeal was sitting with the other young women.

Andrew stared at Joseph Foster, saying, "I don't care if King George hears what I say! I wish I were in England. I'd march right up to whatever palace he lives in and tell him so!"

The argument got somewhat fierce, and Charles Foster suddenly turned and said, "Hawk, what do you think about all this? Are you a loyal king's man or not?"

Hawk had finished eating. He had pulled out his sheath knife and was whittling long slivers from a fragment of cedar. They curled up almost like the curl in a woman's hair and made a fragrant scent that he liked very much. Now looking up, he studied the Fosters for a moment before he spoke. *They're hotheads, both of them,* he thought, *and I don't want there to be trouble.* Finally he said quietly, "I believe men should be free, Charles."

"Englishmen are free."

"Not really. As long as the laws are made in England, we have nothing to say about them."

"Why, that's foolish talk!" Charles said. "We've had the House of Burgesses, and now we've got the Continental Congress. All we have to do is agree to get along with the king and to swear allegiance to him."

"I'm afraid it's not that simple," Hawk said. "A government exists for one reason, to serve the people. And I have to tell you, Charles, and you, too, Joseph, I don't think England has been doing that. They're serving themselves."

Others began to speak, and soon an acrimonious spirit arose among those gathered around. Words were sharp and men's eyes were flashing. Paul Anderson tried to calm the waters by saying, "Well, all the fighting now is over the mountains. There's not any here. Maybe there never will be."

"I wish the Redcoats would come over here up in these mountains!" Andrew exclaimed.

Jacob stared at his brother thoughtfully. "What would you do if they did, Andrew?"

"We'd show 'em what fighting men could do. They wouldn't have a chance in these hills and in these woods!"

Jacob now exchanged glances with his father. The two were thinking the same thing, that it was unlike Andrew to be so aggressive.

Hawk said, "Well, I hope they don't come here, but I'm afraid the fighting will."

"What do you mean, Pa?" Jacob asked.

Shoving the knife back into its sheath, Hawk said quietly, "The British have already turned the Indians loose on the settlers in this country more than once, and they probably will do it again." Seeing no reason to continue the discussion, he stood and said, "Well, let's get back to work."

While the men had been eating, Jacob had been walking around the cabin studying it carefully, thinking, *One day I may want to build one of these for myself.*

As he rounded the corner he met Amanda, who stopped dead still, excitement on her face. "Jacob," she said, "did you know that Sarah's asked me to go with you to Williamsburg?"

"Well, Ma said something about it. What have you decided?"

"I'd love to go. I'd love to meet your family and friends." A roguish smile came to her lips then, and she made a rare joke, "And to keep you away from all your old girlfriends."

Jacob smiled, then laughed. "You wouldn't have much trouble.

I didn't have all that many of them. Only one, really."

As soon as he said this, Jacob's mind went back to old memories of Annabelle Denton. It was almost as if he could remember the softness of her lips as he kissed her. He remembered the fragrance of lilac that was always with her. It seemed so real that it frightened him. He was not a young man given to visions or impressions like this, but for a few moments he stood there completely caught up in those sweet memories of the past. He had blocked her out of his mind for a long time, but now the thought came to him, *I'll see her again. I wonder if she's changed.*

"What in the world are you thinking about? You're a thousand miles away!"

Jacob shook his shoulders and laughed half ruefully. "I don't know. Just thinking."

"About some girl, I'll bet."

Uncomfortably, Jacob shuffled his feet. He put his hands behind his back and tensed his muscles and could think of nothing to say. In truth, he had bad memories of Annabelle, for she had proved herself unfaithful to him in a most painful way.

"I won't go if you don't want me to," Amanda said quietly. She stood before him looking up into his face. She managed to cloak her real feelings for him, but there was pain in her heart now. She recognized that no matter what he said, he was thinking about some young woman he had known back in Williamsburg. She had known for a long time that there was something in his past that he never spoke of, and she had suspected it had something to do with a woman. Now, however, she stood before him and waited for him to speak.

"Don't pay any attention to me, Amanda. I was just thinking how long it's been since I've seen my grandparents." Jacob consoled himself that this was at least partly true. He did have a warm affection for the Spencers, James and Esther, who had raised him while his father had been off in the wilderness. Now he smiled and forced himself to say heartily, "Why, it'll be great, Amanda! You've never been in a place like Williamsburg, and Sarah needs you to go. She'll need one of her girlfriends with her. Why, we will have a wonderful time!"

"Are you sure I ought to go?"

"Yes! Of course I'm sure."

"Do . . . do *you* want me to go?"

Realizing that somehow his reluctance had hurt this girl who had had such a difficult time, Jacob Spencer suddenly reached out and took her hand. He squeezed it and said, "I think it would be wonderful. Can't think of anything better, so it's all settled then. Now I've got to go get something to eat."

Amanda stood quietly and watched Jacob as he disappeared around the corner of the half-built cabin. She remembered how he had kissed her and asked her to wait for him to return from Williamsburg only last week at the wedding. She told herself that she was worrying needlessly. *I think he really does want me to go,* she thought, *but there's some girl there that's hurt him. I wonder if I'll meet her.*

The work went on quickly with the sound of axes splitting logs and men shouting at one another. The poles for the rafters went up, and then the shakes went on very quickly. Andrew had to hold little Joshua up and let him fasten the shake that he had helped to split, and then he sat there looking around holding the boy in his lap. He saw Abigail standing with the women. She looked at him, and as their eyes met, they smiled and waved at each other.

Finally the sun was going down when Paul Anderson said, "All right, that's all we can do for today. It's a little rough, but you're ready to move in."

Andrew and Hawk had been making furniture, and the settlers had all brought something for the newlyweds. They were sparse enough, a table and two chairs placed in the center of the room, a plain worktable with a shelf hung on the wall, tin cups, plates, and a few pots and pans suspended on pegs. The bed's two sides were placed at an angle of the cabin, with the one leg holding up the free edge. The chimney building crew had finished the chimney, but Al Larkin said, "Don't build a fire in it until tomorrow, Andrew. It needs to cure out a little bit."

Other neighbors had brought noggins, piggins, and keelers to hold water. There were cups shaped from wood and shaped baskets from hickory splits. Abigail's mother presented them with the greatest treasure of all, a feather bed made from feathers begged from all the neighbors for months, ever since the engagement.

The bed itself had threaded rawhide thongs stretched tight across the frame to hold the mattress. When the feather bed was laid on it, a giggle went around all who were crowded inside, bringing color to the faces of the bride and the bridegroom.

They all moved outside then, and Paul Anderson said, "Reverend Doak will be holding services on Sunday. I hope to see everyone there."

"Will you be there, Paul?" Hawk asked.

"I don't think so. I'm going to go back to our work with the Cherokee."

"What about Rhoda and your daughter?"

"They're going to stay with Iris while I'm gone with Sequatchie." Paul then said, "Now we're going to ask God to bless this new home." He did not call on someone else, but he himself prayed a fervent prayer. He had a deep love for Hawk Spencer and for his family, and it showed in his heartfelt prayers. His voice was insistent and almost broke once as he thanked God for this new family that was beginning.

"And God bless this man and this woman with children, and may they always love You even more than they love each other. For in this way, Lord, their love for each other will be strengthened. I ask it in Jesus' name. Amen and amen!"

Like an Eagle

Four

$\mathcal{A}$bigail came out of a deep sleep slowly. Somewhere far off she heard a bird beginning to sing. It was a sweet, melodious sound, and she lay quietly in that twilight area, not quite asleep, not quite awake.

Finally, she heard a scratching sound on the roof overhead and opened her eyes almost unwillingly. *Probably a squirrel,* she thought. She listened as the scrabbling sound continued, and then she turned her head slightly to look at Andrew. He was lying on his back and sleeping soundly. Reaching over timidly, she laid her hand gently on his strongly muscled shoulder with a possessiveness she had not known was in her. Color came to her cheeks, for she had not yet come to accept completely his right to be beside her. Pride came then as she thought, *I'm a wife now.*

The quietness in the cabin was almost palpable; then outside faint sounds began to come to her—the champing of the horse in the small corral, the clucking of the four chickens Elizabeth had given her for the beginning of a flock, the barking of a dog far off, thin and insistent.

Suddenly Andrew opened his eyes and, seeing her watching him, grinned broadly. With a quick movement he put his arms around her and pulled her close, squeezing her so hard she gasped.

"You don't have to hold me. I'm not going to run away!" she whispered. She ran her hand down the smoothness of his arm and then touched his thick blond hair. "You need a haircut," she said.

"Not right now," Andrew smiled. "I've got more important things on my mind."

Abigail flushed and then laughed. "You always have more important things on your mind. I'm cutting that hair of yours today. I should have done it for the wedding."

Andrew did not answer. He lay there holding her, marveling at the smoothness of her skin and the strong muscles in her back.

She ran her fingers down his chin, saying, "You know what I like about being married?"

"What?"

"I like this—having you with me here in the mornings so we can talk when it's quiet. You're all mine. As soon as we get out of bed, you'll be gone all day working or hunting, but at night you're all mine."

"I'm glad you like me. It would be difficult if you didn't," Andrew teased her, then he kissed her soundly.

She pushed him away, saying, "I want to talk. What do you think about this war? Do you think it will ever come out here, Andrew?"

"I don't know. Pa thinks it will, and so do some of the other leaders."

"If it does, you'll have to fight, won't you?"

"Yes, I will."

"I hope it never comes this far."

They lay there talking for some time, and finally she kissed him firmly and then got out of bed. "Build me a fire in the fireplace and then you can shave. You're getting stickers on your face."

Quickly Andrew reached for her, but she shoved him away and laughed. He dressed quickly and built a fire expertly and then began to shave. Abigail put a skillet on the grate in the fire, and soon the smell of fresh meat cooking filled the small cabin. She came to stand behind him as he raked the whiskers off, saying, "I'm glad women don't have to shave."

"I don't have to. I could raise a long beard down to my belt."

"No, I'd hate that! Don't you do it!"

"You'd love it. It would tickle."

"I don't want to be tickled. I like you the way you are, all nice and smooth." Abruptly she changed the subject. "What do you think about Amanda going with Jacob and Sarah to Williamsburg?"

"I think it's a good idea. That poor girl needs something good in her life. She hasn't had much of it so far."

"That's true enough. She's such a good friend, too, and so in love with Jacob."

"Is that right?"

Abigail reached out and pulled his hair. "You mean you haven't noticed?"

"I've been busy with other things. A newly married bridegroom has to think about his wife. He doesn't have time to look at other women or think about anything else."

Abigail laughed. "I love it when you talk like that! You just keep on for the next fifty years!" She moved away and set the food on wooden trenchers and quickly made coffee. "Our first meal in our new house," she said, setting it on the table. "Come and eat."

Andrew sat down quickly, asked the blessing, and then plunged into the battered eggs and freshly cooked bacon. There were biscuits left over and butter, and he smeared them with honey to finish off the meal. He washed it all down with several cups of strong black coffee.

"Nothing wrong with your appetite. Marriage is good for you."

Andrew grinned, saying, "Yes, it is."

Looking around the simple cabin, Abigail said with wonder, "I can't believe that we're in our very own home." A thought came to her and she turned to face him suddenly. "I know what we can do. Let's entertain."

"But we just moved in!"

"I know, but wouldn't it be nice if after the service today we could bring some people home? Maybe we could make it a going-away party for Jacob and the girls."

"Well, if you want to go to all the trouble of cooking."

"I do, and maybe we'll have Joseph and Leah Foster over, too."

"I don't know. Joseph's pretty hotheaded. He and I might get into it arguing about this war."

"I'll see that you don't. Let's do it. All right, husband?"

"All right, wife."

Abigail started to discuss the things they would need, but Andrew got up, came over, and pulled her to her feet. Lovingly, he said, "I'm happy to have you as a wife." He kissed her and she clung to him.

When he lifted his lips, she said, "I feel the same way, Andrew, but right now we've got to go to church."

The weather was beautiful, though a little warm, for the service that was held outside in the Watauga community. The Spencers, the Stevens, the MacNeals, the Andersons, the Fosters, and the Taylors were all there to hear the new minister. Some settlers had come from as far away as ten miles, and the space was filled as Samuel Doak stood up. He was wearing a simple black suit and looked rather out of place, for most of the men wore hunting shirts. The women were a little more formal, some having put on their best dresses.

Samuel Doak looked out over the congregation and began by saying, "This is my first meeting with you, dear friends, but it will not be the last. I rejoice that God has sent me to serve as your minister. I might as well tell you now that I see the role of a minister as being that of a servant, and I hereby put myself at your disposal. God has given you to me, and as an undershepherd, I will do my best to serve you as long as He permits me to stay. Now we will have some singing."

It was a simple service—parishioners in large churches back East might have been appalled—but the Spirit of the Lord was strong as people lifted their voices in song. Usually in frontier settlements the hymns had to be *lined* out. The minister would quote two lines of a hymn, and then the congregation would sing them; then the minister would repeat two more lines, and again the congregation would sing.

This was not necessary, for Paul Anderson had schooled his people well. They knew all the words, and even those who could not read from the few hymnbooks that existed lifted their voices and sang enthusiastically. Finally the song service was completed, and Reverend Doak was very pleased and said so.

"It is a good thing to give praise unto God. I have the feeling that He loves to hear His people sing, and I commend you and Brother Anderson. You have all done well."

Doak opened up his Bible, a worn, thick black book, and said clearly, lifting his voice almost like a trumpet, "My text this morning comes from the book of Deuteronomy. Chapter thirty-two, verses eleven and twelve. This says, 'As an eagle stirreth up her nest, fluttereth over her young, spreadeth abroad her wings, taketh them, beareth them on her wings: So the Lord alone did lead him, and there was no strange god with him.' Our text this morning speaks of the nation of Israel, which the passage refers to as Jacob because he was the father of that nation. You are aware that Jacob was not the best of men by nature. His very name means *deceiver*, but he was God's man, chosen by God, ordained by God, led by God, empowered by God. So, too, his descendants were not perfect people, yet God led them and cared for them.

"Despite all of their struggles, the Scripture says that God was leading the nation of Israel as He had led Jacob. He was watching them. You have all seen eagles soaring high in the sky above looking down. The Scripture uses this as a figure. God has not given us actual wings, but *like* an eagle, He looks down on all of us. He is the God of everywhere. As one in the Old Testament prayed, 'Thou, God, seeth me.' Are you aware," Reverend Doak said, "that though you may hide from your husband, or wife, or your parents, or the law, or the minister, God sees you. Every move you make He records; every word you speak is known to Him; every thought and intent of your heart is known to the God who knows all things."

He paused then and for some time spoke about this. Then he said, "If you can, imagine how an eagle would take care of her young eaglets. She would carefully search out food and bring them something to eat so that they would not starve. When something would come to harm them, this mother eagle would fight away anything that would harm her young with a wild scream of anger. If you can imagine that, you have a very small and incomplete idea of how God watches over us.

"Every bite that you have ever eaten was a gift from God. Every drink of water, every breath of air, every escape from danger came from the hand of the almighty and merciful God above."

For some time the minister spoke of the goodness of God, but finally his tone turned somewhat more stern. "God," he said firmly, "can only act in that special way to those who allow Him to. He will lead whoever allows Him to, but as our Scripture says, one cannot have another god. He must have God alone. The almighty God of Abraham, Isaac, and Jacob must be the only God in our lives."

As he preached, Reverend Doak's eyes went over the congregation. He was a man wise in the Scripture, and he understood how easily the human heart gives its loyalty to another. He simply had the gift of discernment. His eyes fell on a young woman who was under some sort of terrible conviction. He did not know her name, but he prayed as he spoke that this young girl, and others, would find Jesus as their Savior.

Finally he completed his sermon. "Anything that comes before God is another god. It must go before one can have a right relationship with Him. I'm going to ask our sister, Mrs. Anderson, to sing 'O God of Bethel.' As she sings, if God has spoken to your heart this morning, I'm going to ask you to come and let me pray with you. Others will be praying. If you feel fear, that is a good thing. God sends it to bring you to himself. He is reaching out this morning, and He is saying, 'Let me be like an eagle. My eye is on you. I want to lead you and guide you.' Through the blood of Jesus Christ you may know that God. By turning to Him and crying out, repenting of sins, and looking to Jesus, you may be saved. Now, sister, will you sing?"

Rhoda Anderson did not move. She simply stood where she was and began to sing:

O God of Bethel, by whose hand
Thy people still are fed,
Who through this earthly pilgrimage
Hast all our fathers led.

Through each perplexing path of life
Our wand'ring footsteps guide;
Give us each day our daily bread,
And raiment fit provide.

O spread thy cov'ring wings around,
Till all our wand'rings cease,
And at our Father's loved abode,
Our souls arrive in peace.

Almost from the first word that Rhoda sang people began going forward. Leah Foster was among them, and she found Abigail and Amanda at her side as she moved forward. They knelt to pray with her, and soon, as the minister came and prayed also, she accepted Christ.

Sarah MacNeal did not go to pray with Leah or anyone else. She had been touched by the sermon, but somehow the thought came to her, *God wasn't watching over me when He let my father die. He let Philip die, too. I don't know why He let this happen to me.*

It was a time of rejoicing for many, but Jacob, who was standing beside his father, caught a glimpse of Sarah's face. *She's not happy,* he thought with a slight shock. *As a matter of fact, she looks miserable. Something's wrong with her. I hope I'm doing the right thing taking her to Williamsburg.*

The service ended with a prayer led by the preacher. Hawk went to him at once and shook his hand firmly. He had tears in his eyes as he said, "I'm not much of a man to cry, but when you talk about Jesus as you did today, I just can't help it."

Reverend Doak reached out and put his arm around the broad shoulders of the muscular man in front of him. "Better men than you or I have cried. David wept often, so we will rejoice, and we will weep together, my dear brother!"

Farewells

Five

$\mathcal{A}$bigail's plan to have her first guests in her new home proved to be quite successful. When they all arrived, the main room of the cabin seemed rather crowded. The guests included the young women, Sarah, Amanda, and Leah, and Jacob and Joseph to balance this trio. They had come home following the service, and Abigail had said, "We're going to eat leftovers, but afterward we're going to make candy."

Jacob immediately brightened up. "Let's just skip the leftovers and make the candy."

"Speak for yourself, Jacob," Sarah said. "I'm hungry."

Abigail had made preparations for the late meal and laid out cold venison, biscuits which she heated in front of the fireplace on a board, honey, and a large pot of beans, also heated until it bubbled over.

"I put lots of peppers in these," Abigail smiled. "Andrew likes them. He likes so much pepper in things, I don't see how he tastes anything."

The young people all sat down, at least those who could find a place around the small table. Jacob and Joseph got their trenchers quickly and sat on the floor, leaning back against the raw logs. Once Joseph leaned forward and said, "These logs are still sticky with sap. It's all over my good shirt."

"It's pretty windy, too," Jacob nodded. "You'd better get this cabin chinked before the cold weather comes, Andrew."

"My next job." Andrew was shoveling the beans into his mouth as fast as he could. Finally he spared time to reach over and pull Abigail's hair. "As long as you cook like this you can stay around," he said.

Abigail slapped his hand and turned back to the young women, who were talking about Enoch Carmody.

Jacob had not been listening and finally he said, "What's this about Enoch?"

Leah turned and said, "Didn't you hear? Why, he put a lock on his door!"

"A lock! That's the most foolish thing I ever heard of! Where'd he get that idea?"

"I don't know, but it wasn't a good one. Nobody around here has a lock on their door," Joseph said with displeasure. He was right about that, for every home the young people knew about had a bar on the inside. It was lifted by a leather thong, but the thong passed through a hole and hung on the outside. The door, therefore, could be opened by anybody who chose to do so.

"Everybody's mad at Enoch," Sarah said. "They say he doesn't trust his neighbors."

"I don't trust them, either, not all of them," Andrew said, "but I wouldn't go so far as to put a lock on the door. It's not neighborly."

For some time the conversation went around in a lively fashion, but soon the meal was over and the girls immediately began to make the candy. Sarah had brought syrup drawn from maple trees she had tapped, and soon it was merrily bubbling in a pot over a fire in the new fireplace. While it was cooking, Amanda said, "I know what we can do while the candy's getting ready to pull! Let's ask riddles."

Joseph scowled. "I never could get those things."

"Oh, you can try," Amanda said. "Come on. I'll give the first one. Here it is: 'Round as a ball, and sharp as an awl; lives all summer, and dies in the fall.' There, what do you think that is?"

Nobody spoke for a moment, and finally Sarah said, "Oh, I know! That's a chestnut. That's just like a chestnut, isn't it? All round but has a sharp point on it, and it does live in the summer and dies in the fall."

Amanda was pleased. "That's right. Now it's your turn, Sarah."

"I've got one." She smiled and looked very pretty as she sat there, the golden light of the single lantern playing over her face. She had a smooth, even complexion, and her eyes glowed as she said, "Here's mine: 'It goes all over the field and through the creek; it has a long tongue but never drinks.' "

Silence reigned for a moment, the only sound being the pleasant bubbling of the syrup in the pot.

"I don't know what that is," Abigail said. "It has a long tongue but never drinks. It couldn't be any kind of an animal, because all animals drink."

"Maybe it's a snake," Joseph said hopefully. "It goes all over the field and creek. And I don't know as I ever saw a snake drinking, and it does have kind of a long, forked tongue."

"No, that's not it," Sarah said. The guessing went on for some time and became quite ridiculous.

Andrew said, "I know what! I can get it!"

"No you can't!" Abigail smiled. "If I can't get it, you can't, either!"

"Sure I can. It's old Mrs. Simpkins. She goes all over the country, and everybody knows she's the awfulest gossip in the settlement. Why, I heard Pa say she had a tongue long enough to sit in the bedroom and lick the skillet in the kitchen."

A roar of laughter went up, for old Mrs. Simpkins' gossiping was legendary. Then Amanda said, "But she does drink."

"You all give up?" Sarah said. When no one had any more ideas, she smiled delightedly. "It's a wagon!"

"Why, sure!" Andrew nodded. "A wagon's got a tongue that never drinks. I guess it's your turn, Abigail. You're the smart one in the family. Give us a good one now."

Using her hands, Abigail said, "Here's mine: 'Big at the bottom, little at the top; little thing inside goes flippity flop.' "

Instantly both Leah and Amanda said, "A churn! That's what it is."

"That's right. Okay, Leah, your turn," Abigail said.

Leah said, "Here's one I bet you can't get." She paused solemnly till she had their attention and then said, " 'Black up and black down, black and brown, three legs up and four legs down.' "

Jacob threw up his hands. "That's the silliest thing I ever heard of! You're just trying to fool us, Leah."

"That's right," Joseph said, looking at his sister with a scowl. "She's always making up things that don't mean anything."

"Well, I made it up, but it's a good riddle! You're just not smart enough to think of it," Leah said. She was a mild-mannered girl, rather quiet, but very intelligent. For a time all of the young people tried guessing everything they could think of, but then finally they all had to give up.

"Well, what is it?" Abigail smiled.

Leah preened herself. "I would think anybody could guess that! It's a person carrying a milk stool upside down riding on a donkey."

A howl of protest went up, but Leah was pleased. "Now," she said, "we know who's the best at riddles."

The syrup was still not thick enough, so they decided to play "Going to Jerusalem." This was a simple game in which the first person said, "My grandfather went to Jerusalem and he carried a churn." The next person would repeat all of that and add an item. "My grandfather went to Jerusalem and he carried a churn and a musket." Each person would add a new item, and the game went on until someone missed. It became obvious very soon that Sarah was by far the best. Seemingly she could not forget. Joseph was very poor at the game. He could never remember over four or five items and would break up the rhythm. Finally he scowled and shook his head. "This is a silly game! Let's make the candy."

"I guess the syrup is about right." Abigail had gotten up and gone over to examine the contents of the pot. "I put some soda in it. I think that makes it whiter." She moved quickly to the shelf and pulled down four pewter plates that were her treasures. Going to the pot, she spooned out a liberal dollop on each plate until they were full, then passed them out. "Two of you take these plates and you pull it out."

At once Amanda moved over to stand next to Jacob and smiled, saying, "Let's you and me pull the candy, all right?"

"Sure," Jacob smiled. "I'm not much of a candy puller. I'm more of an eater."

Joseph went to Sarah, saying, "I ought to be good at this. I'm pretty sweet myself."

Sarah laughed at him. "That's what you say!"

Leah paired off with Abigail, and Andrew said, "I'll just stay out of this. All I want to do is eat the candy."

Abigail said quickly, "Butter the dish as it cools off and put some of it on your hands, then you begin to work this around in a ball."

The candy pulling proved to be a tremendous success. One person would get on one end, and another would take the other side and they'd pull backward. The syrup evidently had been cooked just right, for Abigail cried with delight, "Look how long a string we're making!"

Across the room Amanda and Jacob had taken part of the mass and had backed off, both laughing. It stretched to almost both sides of the cabin, and then they brought it back, balled it up, and pulled it again. Soon the cabin was filled with laughter, and Andrew, leaning back against the wall, was pleased. *I guess Abigail was right,* he thought. *This is a good way to break in a cabin.*

Finally they pulled the pieces out as it started to cool and laid it on the plates. It took a little while for it to harden, but finally Jacob said, "I'm not waiting any longer." Taking out his knife, he tapped at one of the long pieces and it broke sharply. Picking it up, he bit off a chunk and chewed it thoughtfully, "This is the best candy I ever made in my life."

"*You* made!" Abigail laughed. "You couldn't boil water, Jacob Spencer!"

Finally Jacob pulled out his watch. It was a gold watch, the most precious thing he owned, for it had been given to him by his grandfather. On one side was a picture of his great-grandfather, the father of James Spencer. Now he said with surprise as he looked at the face, "You know what time it is? Nigh on to nine o'clock. I doubt if we can get home. The painters will probably get us." By painters he meant the wild panthers that roamed the woods.

Quickly the party broke up, and as they all said good-bye, the young people wished Abigail and Andrew a happy marriage, thanking them for the good time they all had.

Jacob pulled ahead of the others, and Amanda stayed by his side. Once there was a sound she did not recognize, and she drew closer to him. "You think that's a painter, Jacob?"

"Just an owl, I think. You're not afraid, are you?"

"No, not while you're here." They walked on quietly, and finally Amanda said, "Is anything wrong, Jacob?"

"Wrong?" He turned to look at her. The silver moonlight illuminated her face, and her dark brown hair seemed almost black in the night.

"You seem to be troubled."

"Didn't know I seemed that way," Jacob said quietly. "No, nothing's wrong. I guess I've just been thinking about our trip to Williamsburg."

"You're really looking forward to it, aren't you?"

"I miss my grandparents. They were really like parents to me, you know. The best people in the world, James and Esther Spencer. You're going to love them, Amanda." He hesitated, then said, "And they'll love you, too."

Quickly Amanda turned again to study his face. She had always thought him the most handsome young man she had ever seen. He looked so much like his father, and now as she traced the strong features of his face, she noted that he seemed older. He was only twenty-one, but he had filled out, and now the planes of his face had gained strength so that he looked more like his father than ever.

"Do you really think they'll like me?"

"Why wouldn't they?"

"Well, not everybody does."

"Name one!"

"Well, Alice Wilson doesn't like me."

"She's jealous of you," Jacob answered. He turned and grinned and tapped her arm lightly with his fist. "Because you're prettier than she is."

His words pleased Amanda. "She always liked you, Jacob. Ever since you came, she set her cap to you. You could marry her if you wanted to."

"Don't want to." Jacob said nothing for a while, then said, "I'd hate to have Mrs. Wilson for a mother-in-law. She's mean as a snake, and Alice will be just like her when she gets to be her age."

The two walked down the path until they reached Sequatchie's cabin. The lights flickered through the window, and Jacob said, "Your mother is still up. She'll be worried about you."

"Not when I'm with you. Besides, she had supper with Rhoda and Rachel tonight since Paul and Sequatchie are gone."

"You think there's anything between your mother and Sequatchie? It'd be something if they married, wouldn't it?"

"They've never said anything. Ma hasn't, anyway."

"Would you mind if she got married?"

"No, not a bit. I know she gets lonesome."

"What about being married to an Indian?"

Amanda shook her head. "Sequatchie's such a good man. That wouldn't bother me."

"It might bother some people, though. Not everybody likes Indians."

They stood outside for a moment and he turned to her. From far off came the call of some sort of night bird, and Jacob said, "That sound always makes me lonely." He looked down and added, "I'm glad you're going, Amanda."

"Are you, Jacob?"

Something about the way she asked the question moved Jacob Spencer. He had always felt a pity for Amanda, for she had had a hard life. Now, however, she looked so defenseless and vulnerable that something came to him. He reached forward, pulled her into his embrace, and kissed her. It was a light kiss and he released her at once. He smiled then and said, "Good night. It was a good party."

As he disappeared into the darkness, Amanda headed toward the cabin. She stood by the door for a long time, thinking about how much his kiss had moved her. Then she turned and went inside. Finding her mother sitting alone, Amanda smiled and said at once, "It was a good party, Mother."

Joseph Foster had spoken little on the way as he escorted Sarah back to the door. Sarah had spoken lightly of the party, but when they came to the door, she turned to say good night and thank him for walking her home. Before she could speak he said quickly, "Sarah, I want to tell you something."

Apprehension came to Sarah MacNeal, and she said quickly, "Maybe it had better wait until tomorrow."

"No, it's now." Joseph shifted his feet uncomfortably, then tightened his jaw. He was a very competitive young man, and coming from a rather well-to-do family, he was somewhat accustomed to having his own way. Reaching out, he took her hand, and when she looked at him with surprise, he said, "I hope, when you get back from Williamsburg, Sarah, you'll consider letting me call on you."

"Why, Joseph—"

"I know you've been hurtin' because of Philip's death, and maybe it's too soon to speak, but I just wanted you to know. I didn't want to wait until you left, because I want you to think about it. I don't want you to meet someone else."

Sarah was somewhat taken aback. She had known that Joseph

liked her, but his manner was almost demanding. "I don't know what to say, Joseph. I'm not looking for anyone in that way right now."

"Sure, I understand that, but I just want you to know where I stand. I'll be waiting until you get back."

"Why, that's nice of you, Joseph."

At that moment Jacob walked up and said with some surprise, "You still here, Joseph? Getting late. You've got a long ride."

"I guess so. Sarah, think about what I said, will you?"

"Of course I will, Joseph. Good night."

Joseph walked to his wagon, where Leah waited. He climbed aboard and drove toward home. As they disappeared into the night, Jacob asked Sarah, "What was that all about?"

"Joseph asked me to let him call on me."

"Why, you're going to be in Williamsburg. He can't call there."

"No, when I get back," Sarah said quickly.

"And what did you tell him?"

"Nothing, really."

"It might be best." They stood there for a moment, and Jacob said, "I'm not very much at this older brother business." He hesitated for a moment, then reached out and touched her shoulder gently. "I don't think you're really suited for Joseph."

Surprised, Sarah looked up. "Why do you say that?"

"Just a feeling I have, but think about it."

"You don't have to worry." Sarah reached out and took his hands in both of hers. She smiled gently and said, "It's nice to have another brother. I've always had Andrew, and now I've got you to look after me."

Finally Sarah gave a half-rueful laugh. "It's not anything you have to worry about. We're leaving. He'll probably marry someone while I'm gone, or start courting someone anyway."

"Or you might find someone to marry in Williamsburg. Have you thought of that?"

Startled, Sarah shook her head. "I'm not thinking of anything like that, Jacob."

"Just as well. Both of us are pretty young, and with this war going on, it's not a good time to be thinking of getting married."

Sarah shook her head. "That wouldn't bother me if I found someone I cared for. Wars have been coming and going for hundreds of years, and right in the middle of them people fall in love and get married."

Jacob rubbed his chin thoughtfully. He studied her face carefully. There was a depth to this stepsister of his that he had often recognized, and now he said, "You're right about that. People fall in love, they marry, they have children, they get old, they die; then it happens all over again."

"That's the way life is," Sarah said. "Good night, Jacob."

The two went inside. Sarah went to her room and Jacob to his. It seemed lonely there without Andrew to share it with him. As he undressed and got in bed, he could not shake a feeling of dread. His thoughts of Sarah and Joseph and Amanda—and finally Annabelle Denton—intruded on his mind. For a long time he tossed on the shuck mattress, and finally he dozed off into a troubled sleep.

PART II

As Swift as the Eagle Flys

July 1777–August 1777

"The Lord shall bring a nation against thee from far, from the end of the earth, as swift as the eagle flieth."

Deuteronomy 28:49

Seth

Six

*W*earily, Seth Donovan limped down the narrow street, his eyes moving from side to side. He had never been in Williamsburg before and was not surprised that he received several suspicious stares at his Highland attire. Since the battle at Moore's Creek Bridge, he had spent over a year fighting with a few loyalists who had banded together in North Carolina. He had not been involved in any major battles, only small skirmishes, almost like Indian raids. They were to attack, do whatever damage they could, and then run.

As Seth paused beneath a sign with a poorly drawn stag, bitter and harsh memories came back. He had never forgiven the rebels for killing his brother, and every morning he awoke determined to avenge Isaac's death. He had become a silent, morose man, refusing to join himself in spirit to the Highlanders as they fought. He knew he was becoming sour, but the loss of Isaac had been almost as bad as a bullet in his brain. At night he would have dreams of the smiling, cheerful face of the younger brother who had meant everything to him. Then the nightmare would come of the bullet striking Isaac, the blood blossoming on his chest, and his last gasp as he died.

Shaking his shoulders with a gesture of impatience, Seth turned and walked inside the tavern. The place was dark and gloomy, and the ceiling was so low he had to duck to keep from banging his head against one of the greasy timbers that supported the second story. A glance revealed half a dozen roughhewn pine tables and a motley assembly of chairs and stools. The room was dimly illuminated by two small windows that allowed only meager rays of light to filter in from the outer street. Four tin lanterns with intricate punch patterns cast a pale yellowish gleam over the interior. The smell of cooked meat came to him, mingled with grease, sweat, and alcohol—a pungent aroma that reminded him he had not eaten for nearly twenty-four hours. He glanced to the left where a door probably led to the kitchen, and a flight of stairs that gave access to the upper part of the tavern.

Moving over to the counter that served as a bar, Seth said to the man who kept his eyes fixed on him, "I'll have a tankard of ale."

"Right." The man drew the ale into a pewter tankard and said as he set it down, "I'm Hartog. They call me Dutch."

"Glad to know you," Seth nodded but did not give his name.

The burly bartender waited then and a crooked smile twisted his lips. "Everybody's mysterious these days," he muttered. "I guess that's your privilege."

"I'm looking for the home of Edward Denton. Can you tell me where it is?"

Hartog's eyes half closed and he studied the man before him. "You're on the wrong side of town." A wayward thought crossed the bartender's mind, and his lips twisted even more broadly. "I'm sure a gentleman like Mr. Denton would be happy to see a fellow like you."

Seth drank down the ale thirstily. He knew his appearance was not good, for his clothes were tattered from long use. He had a raw scar on the side of his neck that had not healed well, and he had not shaved for three days. "Maybe I'm his rich uncle come to tell him he's inherited a fortune," he said. He smiled slightly, the corners of his broad mouth turning up, but it did not reach his eyes. "Can you name his house to me?" He listened as Hartog gave directions, placed a coin down for the ale, then turned and walked out.

As Seth moved down the street, weariness washing over him, he thought, *I ought to get a shave and clean up a bit before I go to meet Denton. He may think I'm a panhandler come asking for a handout.*

He took the opportunity to stop at a barber, where he received a shave, but the only other clothing he had was filthy and stained. "I'll just have to wear the tartan," he said to himself as he paid the barber. As he left the shop and went on down the street, he thought of Edward Denton—a man he had never met. Seth had gotten his name from his commander in North Carolina, a taciturn man named Burns. Denton, it seemed, was a powerful leader of a loyalist faction and needed someone for a special mission.

"Go see him, Seth," Burns had advised. "You're just the kind of man he might use. You might do more for the king serving Denton than in these raids we've been messing about with."

The sun was dropping toward the hills in the west. There was still plenty of daylight as Seth walked down the neatly paved streets until he reached the Denton house. It was a two-story affair with an opulent look about it. He hesitated a moment, then lifted the brass knocker and rapped sharply.

He had to knock again, but then a servant opened it and stared at him. "Back door for peddlers," she said sharply. She was a short, chubby woman in her late twenties, and she dismissed him with a curl of her lip. "Tradesmen in the back."

"I'm not a tradesman. I've come to see Mr. Edward Denton."

The maid hesitated. She loved to turn away people, but the last time she had turned away the wrong person, Mr. Denton had practically boiled her in oil. "I'll see if Mr. Denton is home."

The door closed firmly, and Seth stood there shifting his weight from one foot to another. Anger coursed through him, for he had not liked the maid's attitude. Still, what else could she think? He thought, *I do look pretty tattered.* Involuntarily, he thought again of Isaac, and the face of his dead brother floated before his eyes like a vision. It did no good to shut his eyes, for it was even clearer then. He bit his lip and slapped his hands against his sides. "Got to stop thinking about it," he muttered. "It doesn't do any good. He's gone, and there's no way to bring him back."

He resolutely put his mind on imagining what Edward Denton might have for him to do, when the door opened and a man stepped outside.

"I'm Edward Denton. What's your business?"

Denton was a tall man with brown hair and intense pale blue eyes. There was an impatience about him, as there often is with men of wealth and influence.

"I'm Seth Donovan. Captain James Burns told me you might have work for me to do—for the cause."

Apprehension washed across the aristocratic face of Denton. He glanced around nervously, then lowered his voice. "Not here. You should not have come to my house! Do you know the town?"

"No, not well. I know where The Brown Stag is."

"I'll meet you there. Take a room."

"I don't have the money."

Fumbling in his waistcoat pocket, Denton took out a coin. "There's a sovereign," he muttered. "Now, get out of here. I'll meet you later."

"When?"

"When I can get there!" Denton snapped. "Now, off with you!" Without another word he stepped inside and shut the door firmly.

"Who was that, Father?"

Edward Denton looked up to see his son, Thomas, who had emerged from the hall and stood there with a question written on his face.

"Oh, just someone looking for a handout. I sent him away."

Thomas Denton was twenty-two. He was a tall young man with reddish blond hair, slightly curly, and blue-green eyes. He smiled sardonically and said, "Well, there'll be lots more of those coming if the colonists continue to rebel against the Crown."

"I expect you're right," Edward nodded. "Well, I must see how your mother is." He turned and went up the stairs. His face was fixed, but he forced himself to smile as he entered the bedroom, putting the matter of Seth Donovan out of his mind.

Thomas moved toward the library, where he found his sister, Annabelle, sitting at the desk writing with a quill.

"Who are you writing to?" he asked.

Annabelle Denton looked up and studied her brother for a moment. She had the same reddish blond hair as Thomas, but her large blue eyes were clear as glass. There was the air about her that a beautiful young girl falls into after having been admired by every man she meets.

"Who was that at the door?"

"Father said it was just a fellow looking for a handout."

"I hope he told him to stay away from here. We don't need any more of those."

"I suppose you're right." Thomas looked over Annabelle's shoulder, then grinned. "You still trying to get Charles Hillyard to chase after you? He'll never do it."

"Get away, Tom! Stop reading over my shoulder!" Annabelle glared at him and said, "I'm not trying to get Charles Hillyard to chase after me!"

"Oh, I thought you were. What actually *are* you trying to do to him?"

Ignoring her brother, Annabelle continued to write. Finally Thomas moved away and began to study the backs of the expensively bound leather books that lined the library wall. He whistled under his breath and finally turned to throw himself into a chair opposite his sister. "I saw James Spencer this morning. He said that Jacob could be arriving any time now for his visit."

Instantly Annabelle looked up. Her lips were beautifully shaped, rich and full with a bow in the middle, and she had added a little artificial color to them. Now the lips pulled together, as they always did when she was thinking hard.

"How long will he be staying?"

"Don't know. Mr. Spencer didn't say." Thomas had not missed the sudden attention he had gotten out of his sister. Now he grinned lazily. "You're always glad to see old friends, aren't you, Annabelle?"

"Of course." Annabelle turned her head away, swinging around in the chair and staring out the window. She did not speak for a moment, but her mind was working rapidly. She had the ability to recall the past in graphic colors almost as if it were a painting. She remembered now as she stared out the window, aware that her brother was watching her, how she had been almost prepared to marry Jacob Spencer at one time. She had, however, felt the same way about Arthur Horton, and now as her mind went back she realized she had played her hand poorly. She had allowed Jacob to overhear her speaking to Arthur exactly as she had spoken to him. Jacob had become bitter and had left for the wilderness almost immediately.

"What's in that pretty little head of yours, sister?"

Annabelle turned and a smile softened her features. She reached up and tucked a stray curl inside the small cap that she wore and said casually, "I suppose we'll have to have Jacob over to welcome him back."

"Oh! So that's what is on your mind."

"Yes, it is," Annabelle said, "and don't smirk! It doesn't become you."

"I thought you might like to see Jacob again. You always were sweet on him, weren't you?"

"He's a nice young man. He's your best friend, so naturally I liked him."

"He was my best friend, and I'd like to have him be that way again. But I hate to think you've got a bead on him."

"You are vulgar, Thomas Denton!" Annabelle said. She rose up, came over, and suddenly reached down and kissed him on the cheek. "Don't worry, we'll just be good friends."

"Annabelle, that's impossible for you. You can't be 'just good friends' with any man."

"Of course I can! What are you talking about?"

Thomas Denton wanted to tell his sister that she was an impossible flirt, and for her, everything between herself and a man sooner or later came to more than a friendship. He dared not say it, however.

"Well," he said finally, "at least you won't have to worry about Arthur now that he's married Ada Watkins. Arthur had something to do with Jacob's leaving the country, didn't he?"

"I think you're being foolish. Anyway, Arthur wasn't suited for me."

Thomas studied her and then rose from his chair. "And Jacob Spencer is?"

Annabelle Denton loved to tease, even with her own brother. She reached out and touched his chin playfully, then smiled thoughtfully. "Who knows?" she murmured. "Time will tell."

The Mission

Seven

$\mathcal{A}$lthough Edward Denton owned a magnificent plantation house surrounded by enormous fields, he was compelled to stay in Williamsburg most of the time. His wife, Phoebe, loved the social life of the city and loathed the lonesomeness, as she called it, of the country. Her one goal in life was to rise in society. Now as she sat at the end of the table for dinner, her dress reflected it. Instead of a simple dress, she wore an open-robe gown made of the finest cream-colored silk. The underskirt was full, and lace and ribbons over-lapped. She wore a large diamond ring on one hand and an emerald on the other; somehow the cost of the stones summed up Phoebe Denton's life.

Annabelle, sitting at her right hand, also had dressed for dinner in a rather ornate fashion. She wore a light blue dress of embroi-dered silk with a square neckline and a bodice tight with tucks in the front. It was accented with dark blue ribbons, white lace, and the funnel-shaped sleeves were done with three layers of lace.

Thomas Denton was dressed casually. His attire consisted of a brown-and-white checked cotton shirt, a pair of fine brown linen trousers, and a pair of high-cut half boots. His curly reddish blond hair fell over his forehead, and he brushed it back from time to time absentmindedly. Engaged in cutting the roast beef, he lifted his eyes to study his father, who was holding forth, as usual, on the political situation in the Colonies.

But Thomas had heard it all before and knew they were ap-proximately in the middle of his father's tirade on how everyone who didn't follow the exact dictates of King George of England was a ruddy traitor. As he suspected, Edward Denton now quoted Dr.

Samuel Johnson, giving his famous opinions of Americans. "The Americans are nothing but a criminal class and should be grateful for anything we give them short of hanging." Thomas actually moved his lips along with his father's words. He glanced over and saw his sister smile and giggle a little.

"What are you laughing at, Annabelle? I'm not aware that I've said anything funny!" Edward Denton was a man jealous of his dignity and now was affronted at his daughter's behavior.

"Oh, nothing, Father!" Annabelle said quickly. "I just thought of something amusing that happened this morning."

"It might do you well to listen to what I have to say. I'm aware that women aren't educated, but it wouldn't hurt you to be conscious of what's happening in this country." Denton frowned and straightened his back as he looked around at his family, awaiting their full attention. When he felt he had received it, he continued his lecture on the evils of Thomas Jefferson, George Washington, Benjamin Franklin, and the rest of them who were not loyal to the king.

Finally Thomas found an opportunity to interrupt his father's comments. "Father, did I tell you that Jacob Spencer is returning from the West?"

"How do you know that, Tom?"

"I talked to his grandfather this morning, Mr. Spencer. He told me."

Phoebe Denton sniffed and held her nose in the air. "And there's no telling what awful habits he's picked up. You know how they are in that place."

"No, I don't, Mother," Thomas said innocently. "What are they like?"

"You know very well what they're like! They're nothing but barbarians!"

"Well, I don't think he's going to offer to come and live with us," Thomas grinned. "He's just returning for a visit, I understand." He took a sip of tea from the fine china cup and shrugged, saying, "I understand he's bringing back his stepsister."

"His stepsister? Who is that?" Phoebe asked with interest.

"She's the daughter of the woman his father married, so I understand. Her name is Sarah. She's had quite a hard time. A close friend of hers was killed by Indians."

"Thomas!" Phoebe said loudly and gave him a freezing glance. "That is certainly not an appropriate topic for dinner conversation!"

"I'm sorry, Mother," Thomas said, trying to look contrite. "I was just relaying information."

Suddenly Edward Denton gave his daughter a quick, searching look. "Do you suppose you'll be seeing Jacob again? You two were quite close at one time." He hesitated and then touched his lips with the snow-white napkin. "As a matter of fact, I've often wondered if young Spencer didn't leave because you broke his heart."

Thomas could not restrain the smile that came to his lips. "It almost seemed that way, didn't it, Father?"

Annabelle spoke up instantly. "Stop being silly, both of you! It'll be very good to see Jacob again."

"Well, who knows what will happen?" Edward said. He was very partial to this daughter of his and had spoiled her completely.

Annabelle had learned as a child that she could get anything she wanted out of her father if she could only talk sweetly enough. As a child she had sat on his lap and pulled at his whiskers, telling him how handsome he was. Now she was a little more sophisticated and had learned other means to flatter her father to get what she wanted.

Phoebe gave her husband a discontented glance. "I don't think a backwoodsman is a good choice for a husband for our daughter."

"Annabelle will have to decide that," Edward smiled. "And I guess you'll have to decide quickly, as you're not getting any younger."

"She's only twenty!" Phoebe said indignantly. "That's not old!"

"I don't know," Thomas said. He leaned back in his chair and looked innocently toward Annabelle. "Almost all of your friends are already married, aren't they, sister? Jane Simmons got married last year. She's the last of your old group and she was nineteen."

Annabelle ignored her brother's comment and looked at her father. "I'll not marry until I find someone like you, Father."

Edward Denton beamed and Thomas was vastly amused. He was completely different from the rest of his family. He had no social aspirations whatsoever and thought his mother's social climbing was absolutely ridiculous. Thomas had some more respect for his father but was well aware that there was a blind spot insofar as Annabelle was concerned. Thomas recognized his father could see no fault or wrong in anything Annabelle ever did. As for Thomas himself, he had been amused by Annabelle's manipulation of young men—until she had used her wiles on his friend Jacob Spencer. Since that time he had been wary of Annabelle, and now he gave her a critical look, thinking, *I hope you don't try any of your tricks on Jacob again. He doesn't need a dose of what you've already given him.* His hopes were dashed at Annabelle's next words.

"Father, don't you think it would be good if we had a reception here for Jacob and his relative? After all, you do have great respect for his grandparents," she said sweetly.

"I certainly don't think that would be in order!" Phoebe said quickly.

"Why, I think that would be a tremendous idea!" Edward beamed. "I do think a great deal of the Spencers, and it would be an opportunity to show it."

"Certainly. It will be a wonderful dinner party," Annabelle said demurely. "And, Mother, you can help me make out the menu, and I'll just have to have a new dress."

Any party, no matter how small, pleased Phoebe Denton. She instantly plunged into a discussion of the new dress, which continued until Edward got up and said, "You take care of the details. I've got to go out on some business this evening."

As he left the room Thomas's eyes followed him. He got up himself shortly after, bored by his mother and sister's talk about the party. Going out into the garden, he leaned back against the house and watched the skies for a time. Memories of his old days of friendship with Jacob Spencer came to him. They had been good friends. He had had none better, then or since. Finally a sense of humor came to his rescue.

"Well, if Jacob has learned to handle wild Indians out on the frontier, I suppose he can take care of one silly girl." He took one last look at the stars, turned, and went back into the house.

Entering The Brown Stag, Edward Denton looked furtively around and spotted Seth Donovan sitting with his back to the wall over in a gloomy area of the room. At once he moved toward him and sat down. When Dutch Hartog approached them, he said, "A glass of ale, please." He waited until the burly tavern owner had brought the drink and then leaned forward. "All right, tell me about yourself. You say your name is Seth Donovan, but I have to have more evidence than your own say-so."

Seth brought out the letter he had brought from Captain Burns, who was a friend of Edward Denton. He handed it over and said, "Maybe this will help."

Quickly, by the light of a flickering candle set in a sconce on the wall, Denton scanned the hastily scribbled lines. He bit his lip and nodded. "All right, I'll have to trust you. I'll trust Burns' word. If he says you're all right, I'll believe him."

"He's a fine officer. I've served under him for the past year."

"Why do you want to leave the army?"

Seth leaned forward in his chair and placed his hands on the table, fidgeting with his fingers. He had large, capable hands burned by the sun with traces of calluses still on his palms from his early years of hard labor on a farm in Scotland. "It doesn't seem to be doing any good. If I'm going to risk my life for the king, I want it to be meaningful."

He looked up suddenly, and his blond hair that reached down to his shoulders, Denton noticed, was clubbed in the back. It was very thick, almost like a lion's mane. The blue-green eyes seemed to bore into him, and the very size and strength of him was almost intimidating for Edward Denton, who was not a man easily impressed.

"Well, you look strong enough for serving the king, but this is a matter of brains, you understand."

Seth shrugged. "Tell me what it is you want done, Mr. Denton. I'll see if I think I'm capable."

"All right, here it is," Denton said. He leaned forward, even though the room was quite noisy and it was not likely that anyone could hear. He narrowed his eyes, and his lips scarcely moved as he muttered, "There is a businessman in Boston who is shipping large amounts of weapons to supply the rebels who are scattered out over the country. Somewhere he apparently has an enormous supply of them received from England. Our agents haven't been able to find out where it is, and we lost one agent in the effort."

"Lost him how?"

"We believe he was captured. These rebels mean business, and it'll be worth your life, Donovan, if you go into this."

"That's what I've been doing for the past year. What's the rest of it? What do you want me to do?"

"I want you to find the storehouse of weapons, and then we can get a force together and capture them. You might be helpful for that too."

"How am I supposed to find out where these weapons are stored?" Seth asked. "I'm not a spy."

"I want you to go to Boston. We know the man who is shipping the arms in. Somehow I want you to get close to him. Find out where the weapons are and when the next shipment is leaving. If possible, get close enough to the man so you can go along with the shipment and find out where all the rest of the arms are stored."

"It does sound a mite dangerous," Seth shrugged, "but I wouldn't know how to go about it."

"Then you're no use to me," Denton said. He took a sip of the ale and shook his head. "All right, that's all there is to it."

"Wait a minute!" Seth said quickly. "Don't be so hasty, Mr. Denton. I'll give the job a try. I'm just warning you that I haven't had any experience along these lines."

"I hadn't supposed you had," Denton nodded. "If you get a job with this man and win his confidence, you might do it. Tell him how much you love the rebels, George Washington, Jefferson, and all that bunch." A scowl crossed Denton's face. "Become a rebel yourself for all practical purposes. If you win him over, it's likely he'll ask you to join in. And if that happens, our mission will be successful." He drank again of the ale and then reached into his pocket. "Here's some cash." He handed Seth a small leather bag that jingled slightly. "There'll be more for you if you succeed, a lot more."

Seth took the money and hefted it in his hands. He studied it for a while, then murmured, "I'm not doing this for money, Mr. Denton. I lost my brother and I'm doing it to avenge him."

Denton stared at the large young man across from him. He looked more and more lionized with his golden hair and strange eyes and lean face. "I see. Well, that makes me think more of you." He smiled then and said, "Welcome to your new occupation."

Seth Donovan slipped the bag of coins into his inner pocket. "What's the name of the man I'm to contact? The one who knows about the weapons?"

Edward Denton drained the rest of his ale and got to his feet. He looked down for a moment at the face of the other and then leaned forward and whispered, "His name is William Martin. . . ."

Martin and Son

Eight

$\mathcal{M}$artha Edwards did not look her sixty-eight years. She was straight as an arrow, and the lines of age had not yet marked her face. Her eyes were clear, and the only sign of approaching age was the liver spots on her hands. As she moved around the dining room arranging the silverware, she thought how strange it was that she should have a home such as this.

Indeed, William Martin and his wife, Anne, owned one of the finest homes in Williamsburg, and Martha had been their servant for a great part of her life. It had never once occurred to her that she should be more than a servant, but when young William Martin, Jr. had fallen in love with her granddaughter, Rebekah, and married, the older Martins had seemed to forget that she was ever a servant and had taken her in as a member of the family.

Old habits die hard, however, and as Martha moved around the room, she still ran her eyes over the service, the table, and the furniture as if she were being paid to do so. It was a large formal dining room lit by silver candelabras. Green-and-gold mica wallpaper and many mirrors caught the light and gave the room a warm glow. The aroma of turtle soup, potted fish, and beef filled the air, and now as the family came in and sat down at the large mahogany dining table, Martha reminded herself that she was no longer a servant and took her seat. The maid, a diminutive young woman named Irene, began bringing in the dishes, aided by a tall black man who was more or less a majordomo. From the large mahogany sideboard were brought silver platters filled with artichokes with toasted cheese, assortments of cheeses, and a truffle for dessert.

Finally William, Sr. bowed his head and asked a blessing, and

Martha began to assist in the feeding of the two youngest Martins, her great-grandchildren, Eve, age four, and David, age three. She paid little attention to the conversation, for her great-grandchildren were her life. Eve had black hair and brown eyes and showed promise of being a beauty. She was very shy, however, unlike her brother, David. At the age of three he had sandy-colored hair, pale blue eyes, and was a very adventurous tyke. He showed no fear of anything, and his grandmother sometimes admonished him, "David, there are some things you ought to be afraid of."

"Like what?" David had piped up.

"Well, like snakes."

"I'll stomp 'em to death," David had said, grinning at her broadly.

It was a warm, friendly room, one in which the expenditure of a large amount of money could be seen in its decor. William Martin, who now sat at the head of the table, looked around it with approval. "I always liked this room, didn't you, Anne?" He was sixty-nine now and somewhat stooped, not as large and robust as he had once been. His blond hair had thinned, and his eyes were not as strong as they once were. He reached across and put his hand on his wife's, saying, "I remember the first meal we ever ate in here. Do you?"

Anne Hardwick Martin was eight years younger than her husband. Her youthful beauty had faded, and now there were lines drawn around her mouth and eyes, and her dark brown hair had turned mostly gray. Still, her brown eyes were piercing, and her complexion was good. At one time in her life she had been harsh, but since the marriage of her son to Rebekah Edwards, she seemed to have mellowed. "Of course I remember," she said. "Do you think I'm getting so old I can't remember anything?" She squeezed his hand and her voice grew more gentle. "I remember it as if it were yesterday. You wore that blue suit that I like so much. I think I fell in love with you because of that blue suit."

William Martin smiled and his face lit up. "Whatever happened to that suit?" he murmured. "I wish I still had it. Maybe I could charm you again."

"You two are acting like a couple of honeymooners." William Martin, Jr., known to everyone simply as Will, found the scene pleasant. He was somewhat under six feet tall with dark brown hair and brown eyes like his mother. He was only thirty-one, nine years younger than his sister Elizabeth, but he still resembled his only sister strongly.

"You be quiet, Will," Rebekah said. The only granddaughter of Martha Edwards, she had been a servant of the house herself. If anything had been needed to convince her that miracles happen, it was the fact that she was now married to the man who had once been her master. She had long black hair, very thick and lustrous, and large emerald green eyes. Her complexion was beautiful, and she had grown more and more pretty as the years of marriage had gone by. "I think it's sweet. I hope you'll talk that way to me when we've been married as long as your parents."

"Well, I'd better start taking lessons, Father." Will grinned up toward the head of the table. "Maybe you could help me write some love poems."

"I certainly could," William replied heartily. "I used to write them all the time. As a matter of fact, it hasn't been so long, has it, Anne?"

"My last birthday," Anne said quietly. "A beautiful poem."

"Oh, it wasn't much, really. I must admit I had to study up a little bit, but I meant every word of it."

The conversation went on for some time, and at the foot of the table, Martha felt a glow of happiness. "What a wonderful family to be in," she said, "and now to be with my great-grandchildren. It's more than I ever dreamed." She paused then and listened as William had begun to speak of business, something he rarely did at the dinner table.

"If it wasn't for the shipping of arms," William was saying, "I think I'd close the business down."

"For a fact, we're not able to do much. Not with the blockade the British have thrown around us," Will agreed. He wanted to say more, but he remembered that he and his father had agreed that the women should not know about the shipment of arms to be used by General Washington. He turned the conversation to other things, but he could not help noticing how his parents had changed. His mother had been strict and harsh during his childhood. Now she had softened and looked even younger than she had seven years ago. He noticed, also, with a pang how much his father had aged. *Even in the past year*, he thought, *he's gotten more feeble. I know Mother is worried about him, and Rebekah is, too.*

William glanced over toward his wife, and as always, he breathed a little prayer. "Thank you, God, for such a good wife." It was a prayer that came from the bottom of his heart, for he had found in Rebekah the perfect companion. His eyes went from there to the children, and once again a sense of well-being and pleasure came to him.

After the dinner was over and the table was being cleared, Anne came closer and said, "Will, I need to talk to you."

"Why, all right, Mother." He moved with her to the library, glancing into the parlor where William was playing with the children while Rebekah sat knitting and watching with a smile on her face. When they were inside, he closed the door and said, "What is it, Mother?"

"I'm worried about your father."

"I know. He doesn't look well, does he? But he's made it a long time. We're praying that he'll last many more years."

"I know, but I think he's getting worse. He doesn't say anything, but I know he's in a lot of pain."

Biting his lip, Will nodded slowly. "I know. The war's taken a lot out of him. It was a hard time when the British first came. It cost him a lot to be faithful to the patriot cause."

"Yes, and after the British left. He's very proud of that, but now that the British are gone, the shipping's almost nonexistent, isn't it?"

Once again Will almost told his mother about the arms, for that occupied most of his attention. There had been little enough to do at the office and at the docks, so he had become very active with the committees of safety and the Sons of Liberty. He had met once with General Washington himself and had been able to encourage him in the matter of shipping muskets.

"Well, we'll just have to pray harder. Suppose we just pray right now."

"Good, son." They both bowed their heads and the two prayed quickly for the man they loved so much. When his mother looked up, she smiled and touched his cheek. "You're a good son, Will, the best a mother ever had."

Will stood watching as she left, and a pang pierced his heart. He knew that time was passing, and no matter what happened with the war, he would not have his father with him much longer.

Will and Rebekah led the children upstairs and to their rooms, tucking them in for the night. After a bedtime story for Eve and a trip back downstairs for a glass of water for David, they were finally alone in their own bedroom. As Will began undressing, Rebekah looked at him curiously. "Is everything all right, Will?"

"Why . . . yes." He stripped off his shirt, hung it carefully on a peg, and then slipped out of his knee britches. As he pulled the stockings off, he asked, "Why do you ask?"

"I know your mother looked worried tonight. What did she say to you?"

"Oh, she's worried about Father, of course."

"I'm worried too," Rebekah said. She began to undress, and as she slipped out of her dress, she promised, "I'll help watch out more for him now."

"That would be good, sweetheart. He loves you very much. You're like another daughter to him."

As Rebekah removed the last of her clothing and put on her shift, she got into bed, then watched as Will slipped into a nightshirt and came to lie down beside her. As he turned to her, she thought, *How much he's changed since I married him. For a time he was so uncertain of himself, and now he's strong physically and spiritually as well.*

"You know, Rebekah," Will said as he took her in his arms and held her for a time, "Elizabeth may have had the right idea by leaving Boston for the frontier."

Surprise washed over Rebekah and she was silent for a moment. "Are you thinking of doing that, Will?"

"Well, of course we couldn't leave with Father so ill, but sometimes I wonder what it would be like to leave all of this business behind. It drives me crazy sometimes."

The two lay there for a long time holding each other. They were still tremendously in love, and even more now than when they had first been married. Finally he drew her closer with his arms around her and kissed her neck. "I'd like to go over the Misty Mountains and just get away from all these affairs that burden me down."

Rebekah ran her hand over his strong neck. "If that's what you want, Will, we'll pray about it, and someday we'll go."

"Way over the Misty Mountains!"

Sickness

Nine

*B*oston Harbor was jammed with ships of every description. The British blockade had been so effective that merchants had almost given up sending any of their ships out, for the British were prone to capture them and declare them as pirate ships, or simply to take them and say nothing.

As Seth Donovan stepped off of the *Marybelle*, he glanced at the forest of masts and spars that seemed thicker than corn in a field.

"Well," he muttered under his breath with satisfaction, "at least the blockade is working. These rebels can't last forever. They'll starve to death."

He joined the other men who disembarked, looking no different in their typical colonial dress, for he had carefully stowed his Highland costume. He could not afford to come into Boston in that, so he had used some of the money Denton had given him to buy a rough-looking suit—used, of course, and a little the worse for wear. This was deliberate, for he wanted to look down at the heels so that it might influence William Martin to give him a job.

The sun was high in the sky, and for a moment a wave of dizziness came to Seth. He stood still, for it seemed as if the earth were moving a little. *Probably just getting off that ship*, he thought. *It was a rough trip.* The waves had been high, and they had encountered a minor storm. Now the solidness of the earth disturbed him even as the rocking of the ship had at first. Taking a handkerchief out of his pocket, he wiped his brow. It did not seem hot enough for him to be sweating. As he looked across to the buildings that lined the harbor, they suddenly seemed to swim before his eyes.

"You all right, mate?"

Turning, Seth saw one of the sailors, a rough-looking, tub-shaped man named Hammond.

"Yes, I'm okay. I haven't got my land legs back."

Hammond grinned at him. "Come on, we'll get us some food and settle our nerves."

"I'd like to, but I'm in a hurry, Hammond. Thanks just the same."

Moving on down toward the low-lying buildings that were set back away from the wharf, Seth saw a man sitting on a cane-bottomed chair tilting back. He was an older man smoking a pipe, and he put his gray eyes on Seth as he approached.

"Can you tell me where to find Martin and Son Shipping?"

"Why do you ask?" the old man snapped. He took the pipe out, punched it in the air, and said, "Or is it you can't read? Martin and Son! See that sign?"

Looking down the row of buildings, Seth made out the sign indicated and tried to smile. "Thanks a lot," he said.

The old man did not answer but jammed the pipe back in his mouth and sent a cloud of purple smoke furiously into the air. Moving on along, Seth reached the two-story building, a wide affair devoid of any social charm. Taking a deep breath he shifted the bag on his shoulder, which had suddenly become very heavy, and stepped inside. The building was a warehouse and was full of goods, but there was no one stirring. Moving to the back, he found a flight of stairs and called up, "Anybody there?" He thought he heard a voice and climbed up the stairs, where he saw a door with *William Martin* on it. Stepping inside, he was greeted by a tall, thin man with a pair of eyes set too closely together.

"What do you want?"

"I'm looking for Mr. Martin."

"What's your business with him? I'm Hosea Simms, his manager."

"Well, Mr. Simms, I'm looking for work."

Simms shook his head. "There's no work around here. Can't you see we're not moving any goods?" He glanced angrily out the window and said, "It's that blockade. We can't get a ship out of the harbor without having it snapped up by the British gunboats."

"Well, I'm pretty down, Mr. Simms," Seth said quickly. He would have said more, but a door to his right opened up and a young man stepped out. "What's this, Simms?"

"Man wants work. I've told him there's not any."

"I'd work just for my keep. Surely there must be something I could do," Seth said quickly.

"What's your name?" the man asked, then said belatedly, "I'm Will Martin."

"I'm Seth Donovan, Mr. Martin. I'd appreciate any help at all."

Seth had his eyes fixed on Will Martin, and he saw the man's lips moving, but suddenly there seemed to be a roaring in his ears. He could not hear and wondered if he was going deaf. He opened his own lips to ask the man to speak up, but then the features of Martin's face seemed to run together. He had never had such a feeling in his life. As he took a step forward the room seemed to tilt upside down, and his legs turned to rubber. Making a croaking sound, he tried to catch himself with his hands, but he felt his forehead strike the rough boards of the floor. He knew that his forehead was bleeding, and he tried to reach up to staunch it, but he could not. All the strength had gone out of him. He suddenly felt the room disappear, and he plunged into a warm darkness, silent as the grave. . . .

———

From time to time Seth was vaguely aware of voices. One was especially soft, and another was more harsh. He wanted to answer them, to call out for help, but he had not lungs nor tongue with which to speak.

Sometimes he was conscious of hands touching him. He felt a coolness, but he could not reach out to touch those who were there. He did not know who they were. Fear came in waves, as he could not remember nor understand what had gone before, nor where he was, nor whether he was going.

And then out of all this came a ray of light. It was different from the light he had known, blinding flashes of it when he was still semi-conscious. This was real light. It touched his eyelids, and immediately he opened them not knowing what he would see.

A woman was standing at his bedside looking at him. He had never seen her before, nor had he ever been in this room. It was all strange to him. Then the woman smiled.

"You're finally awake. It's about time," she said in a firm voice.

Seth's lips were so dried he could not speak and his throat was tight. "Water," he croaked, and at once the woman moved beside him. She picked up a pitcher and poured a tumbler full of water. When she lifted his head and put the glass to his lips, he swallowed frantically. As the water touched his dry throat, the tightness loosened.

"Not so much. You can have all you want but a little at a time. How do you feel?"

Seth looked longingly at the glass and watched as she refilled it. "I don't know," he murmured. "Where is this place?"

"Don't you remember how you got here?"

"No."

"Here, take a little more water. I understand your name's Seth Donovan."

"Yes. How did you know that?"

"My grandson-in-law told me. Will Martin. Do you remember him?"

Memory began to trickle back then, and Seth suddenly nodded. He lifted his head and murmured, "Yes, I was in his office and something happened. I thought maybe it was an earthquake."

Martha Edwards brought the glass to his lips again. She noted how strong he was. His neck was smooth, thick with muscle, and well joined to his powerful shoulders. He was wearing only a nightshirt. She and Will had to struggle to put it on him. He was well over six two or three and heavily muscled; yet at the same time there was something of agility and speed in his frame. "You fell out in my grandson-in-law's office. You were asking for a job."

"I remember, but how did I get here?"

"Will got some help and brought you here."

"Why did he do that? I'm no kin to him."

"He's like that." Martha set the glass down, then pulled the chair and sat down beside him. She put her hand on his forehead. "Your fever is gone. I never saw such a high fever in my life. We had to wrap you in wet sheets to keep you from dying."

"What was it? What was wrong with me?"

"Dr. Steerforth doesn't know. Just something that brought on a fever." Martha studied the smooth features of the man before her, now somewhat haggard with the sickness. "You've been here for three days." She studied him carefully and then nodded. "You had some bad dreams. You must have been a soldier."

"I was once," Seth said quickly. "Did I say anything about myself?"

"Just about shooting and someone named Isaac."

"That was my brother. He was killed."

"I'm sorry," Martha said quickly. "Well, you're better now. Do you think you could eat a little bit?"

Suddenly Seth realized he was enormously hungry. "Yes, ma'am. I didn't get your name."

"I'm Mrs. Edwards. I live here with my grandson-in-law and his family. I'll go get some broth."

"I'd be vurry grateful, Mrs. Edwards."

After the woman left the room, Seth lay quietly. He moved the sheet aside and tried to sit up. The room spun alarmingly, and he was grasping the sides for support when the door opened again.

"What's this? You don't need to be out of bed!"

Looking up, Seth recognized Will Martin. "I thought I'd try to sit up, but I'm as weak as a kitten."

"Lie down there. Mrs. Edwards will bring you some soup in a minute. You haven't had anything to eat for three days. Just what water we could get down your throat." Will pushed the man back and lifted his legs, noting as had Mrs. Edwards how strongly built he was. "You keeled over like you had been shot in the head." Will sat down in the chair and smiled faintly. "I thought you were going to die. Do you remember anything?"

"No, not a thing, sir. I must have got some kind of fever on the ship maybe."

"Where's your home, Seth?"

"Scotland, but I came to America looking for work a few years ago. Haven't been able to do vurry well, though. Thought I might find work here."

"You've come at a bad time." Will shrugged. "With this war and all, most everything's closed down." He saw the lines form on the sick man's face and said quickly, "Don't worry, we'll work out something. Will anyone be looking for you? I can send a letter."

"No, there's no one."

"No family?"

"No, not now." Remembering his dream, he knew it would be safe to add, "I had a brother, Isaac, but he died. No relatives at all now."

"What about friends?"

"None of those either."

"Are you that alone in the world?" Will asked, a trace of regret on his face. "Well, you have a strange way of applying for a job. You'll stay here until you get better. At least we can arrange room and board. Maybe something will break."

The two sat there for a few moments until Martha Edwards came in bearing a bowl of soup on a tray.

"You go along, Will. He's going to eat this and then rest awhile."

"I thank you, Mr. Martin, for your hospitality. It's vurry rare in this world to find such kindness."

Will had gotten to the door. He turned around and smiled. "Well, I try to remember what the Scripture says. I don't always make it, but I try. Get your rest now. We'll talk later."

Seth was able to sit up and eat the soup. He spilled some of it on the front of his nightshirt, but Mrs. Edwards laughed. "I'll get you another bowl," she said. "Don't worry about that shirt. It's washable."

After the woman had left, Seth thought, *It's going to be all right. I can find out what Denton needs to know without any trouble, I think.* But then a thought came to him. *These people have taken me in and I'm going to betray them.* The thought troubled him greatly, but then he remembered Isaac and his jaw grew tense. *He's one of them that killed my brother! He deserves what he gets! He may be a good man, but he's on the wrong side.*

Betrayal

Ten

*W*ell, these are as clean as I could get them. See if you can put them on yourself."

Seth Donovan turned from the window where he had been standing. It had been three days since he had first awakened. The first day he was so weak he could hardly get out of bed, but now he felt much stronger. Taking the clothes she handed him, he grinned wryly. "I'll be glad to get out of this nightshirt. I thank you, Mrs. Edwards."

"Well, the doctor said you could get up for today. Get yourself dressed and you can come down and have breakfast with the family."

"Yes, ma'am, I'll do that." After Mrs. Edwards left, Seth carefully dressed. The clothes were cleaned and pressed, and as he slipped on his shoes and stood up, he felt much better. "Enough of the sickbed," he muttered. "I never could stand that."

Leaving the room, he went out into a hallway and followed it to where curving stairs moved downward. It was a fine home, he saw, full of fine paintings and expensive furniture. Movement caught his eyes, and he turned to see Mrs. Edwards waiting for him. "This way to the dining room. The family's already inside. Come along, now."

Following her, he stepped inside a dining room that was ornate and in which he felt completely out of place. He stood still for a moment not knowing what to say, but Will Martin, who was at the other end of the room, said, "Well, you're down. This is my wife, Rebekah, my mother and father, Mr. and Mrs. Martin, and these are my children, David and Eve. This is Seth Donovan."

"I would like to say how vurry grateful I am for your kindness," Seth said in his Scottish burr.

"He talks funny," David piped up. "Why do you talk so funny?"

"David, don't be impolite!" Rebekah said sharply. "You'll excuse him, Mr. Donovan."

"It's all right, ma'am. I talk funny, young man, because I'm from Scotland. If you were to come and see me, folks there might say you talk funny."

David stared at him. "I don't talk funny! I talk like everybody else. You're the one who talks funny."

"David, hush up!" Will said. He could not restrain a smile and shrugged his shoulders. "Sit down at that place, Mr. Donovan."

Seth took his place carefully and looked at the food that was spread out. There were bowls of thick porridge with cream, sugar, and fruits stirred in, fried ham with gravy, breakfast puffs smothered with fresh butter and honey, and hot coffee. "I've never seen a meal like this," he said. He started to pick up a fork, but at that moment William Martin, at the end, said, "We're glad to have you as our guest," then bowed his head and asked a quick prayer.

Seth realized he had almost made a mistake. He bowed his head quickly and felt strange when the old man offered a prayer for the stranger who had suffered affliction. When the amen was said, he looked up quickly at William Martin and said, "I thank you for that prayer, sir. I well need it."

Seth kept as quiet as possible but enjoyed the breakfast tremendously. At one point he did say, "I am anxious to get to work, Mr. Martin. Quick as I can."

Will shook his head. "Get your strength up, Seth. As soon as you're able, we'll find something for you to do."

A strange feeling came to Seth Donovan at that moment. He looked around at the smiling faces and knew that never in his life had he been shown such love and generosity. Most, if not a great many, of the people he had known had proved to be selfish and uncaring, but this family was so different that he felt some emotion close to loneliness. He had never known what it was like to have an intimate family like this, and now as he sat there he could not bear to look at their faces. The thought came to him involuntarily, *Now I know what Judas felt like. How can I deceive these people after they've taken me in?*

"Well, I thought you'd be staying home today, Father." Will looked up from his desk with surprise as his father entered through the outer office door.

"I just wanted to make sure everything was ready for the arms to go out."

Will got up and moved over to stand beside his father. There was a grayness to the older man's complexion that troubled him, and he said, "Here, sit down. You look tired."

"I am a little tired now that you mention it." William moved over and settled into the leather chair that was positioned directly in front of the desk.

Will stood beside him for a moment, then sat back on the top of the desk and studied his father. "I really think you shouldn't have come in. You need some rest."

"Oh nonsense! You and that doctor are just alike. Always pampering me, and Anne's no different."

"We all want to see you get well."

Suddenly William looked up and studied his son's face. "I don't have much hope of that," he said quietly.

Stunned by the older man's frankness, Will Martin could not answer for a moment. It was a thought that had lurked in his mind many times of late, and now he looked at his father with concern. "You mustn't talk like that," he said gently. "All these things are in the hand of the Lord."

"Yes, I know that, son. 'No man knoweth the day nor the hour of his death,' as the Bible says. But lately I've been thinking more of heaven and about going home. Somehow heaven has gotten richer to me in these last days." William Martin leaned back and closed his eyes. "I suppose that's the way it is when people grow older. It's like when you leave on a journey. The destination's far off and you don't think about it much. But then when you come almost to the end of it, suddenly everything is different." He opened his eyes and smiled gently. "I'm not complaining, you understand. I've had a good life, a good family. I've been especially proud of you in these last few years, Will."

Will's face flushed and he bit his lip. "Thank you, Father. It's good to hear you say that."

"Well now, about these weapons that we have to get out to the fighting men. Will they be ready to go next week?"

"Yes, they will. We're right on schedule."

The two men continued to talk. They did not lower their voices because there seemed to be no need to. What both of them overlooked was that when William had come in, he had failed to close the door. Hosea Simms had moved over to do just that when suddenly he stopped and listened to the two voices. His eyes narrowed, and he did not shut the door but took in all that was being said. His lips grew tight and a tense expression crossed his face. He stood there straining to hear every word, and finally, when he heard William say, "I think I'll go home now, son," he quickly moved back, sat down, and was shuffling papers as William Martin, his employer, moved past.

"Good day, sir. Good to see you."

"Good day to you, Hosea."

———

It was not the part of town that Hosea Simms was most in favor of. He kept away from such places as much as possible, but now he had no choice. Overhead the sky was turning dark, for he had closed the office late, and a fog was rolling in from the waterfront. It was a thick, dense fog, one that would have been called a "London particular" in the city where Hosea had grown up. Now as he made his way down the narrow street, then turned down one that was even narrower, he thought of London, and a sudden wave of nostalgia took him. "I should never have left England," he said. "If I had stayed there, I would have had a good business of my own. There's a curse on me, and I haven't had a happy day since I left there."

He passed mostly sailors as he quickened his pace, until he finally stopped before a tavern with a blue lion on the sign. He glanced at it, then moved inside. He stood just inside the door, aware that he was completely out of place. This was a haunt of the roughest part of Boston's most disreputable population. Narrowing his eyes and peering through the smoky atmosphere, he saw that almost everyone had turned to look at him. There was not a man in there with a suit on, but all wore the garb of sailors or of derelicts of one sort or another. The air was thick with the smell of smoke, alcohol, and unwashed bodies along with the musty smell that age brings to such buildings.

"Well, look who's come to visit. We're honored. Make way for a gentleman."

Hosea whirled quickly and saw the object of his quest sitting at a table. Greasy cards lay scattered on the scarred top, and three rough-looking sailors turned to stare at him.

Simeon Fulton leaned back. He was a handsome man in his own way, for those who admired rough good looks. He had coal black hair and eyes so dark that the pupils were almost invisible. Heavy black eyebrows shadowed them, and when he grinned, his teeth were white against his coppery skin. He was a well-built man of some six feet, strong looking, and dressed better than his companions in a snuff brown suit with a white ruffled shirt. "Make way for the gentleman, lads," he said. "Be off with you! We have business."

Nervously Simms walked across the room and took one of the seats abandoned by the men. He pulled himself up tightly and could not meet the bold eyes of the man who sat grinning across from him.

"Well, I'm glad you've come, Simms. I'm running a bit short of coin. Let's have the cash."

"I . . . that's what I came to talk to you about, Simeon." Nervously Simms cleared his throat and was aware that the smile had disappeared from Fulton's lips. "I'll have it soon, but in the meanwhile I have a proposition for you."

Fulton grunted, "It's not propositions I need. It's money! You're overdue!"

"I know, but—"

"When you lose at gambling, you pay up, or else you pay in another way!"

The threat in Fulton's voice brought a sudden start of fear to Hosea Simms. He was a gambler and a bad one, and now he was head over heels in debt to Simeon Fulton. He had been warned that Fulton was a bad man to owe. He had heard stories of how men had had their legs broken and had been beaten into insensibility when they failed to pay up on time. He said quickly, "There's money in this thing, Simeon. Quite a bit of money, and it'll be easy."

"It won't be as easy as your handing me the cash and putting it right here in my hand."

"I just don't have it," Simms said quickly, his voice threaded with nervous apprehension. "But you can have at least twice, maybe three or four times, what I owe you if you'll listen to what I have to say."

Simeon Fulton took a pull out of the pewter mug and then breathed heavily out as the hard liquor bit at his throat. "All right," he said grudgingly. "What's your proposition?"

Pulling his chair closer, Simms leaned forward on the table. "I'm in a position to get some information from time to time, and I have some now." Simms' eyes narrowed as he began to speak of the arms that were going to be shipped. He was desperately aware that he needed to keep Fulton content and finally said, "It will be easy to steal this shipment and sell it to the British for a great deal more money than what I owe you."

Fulton's eyes narrowed. He was a man with no morals whatsoever and had no objection at all to stealing. As always, however, he weighed the possibilities of something going wrong, and now he said, "Why should I do this? Why don't I just take it out of your hide, Simms?"

"Because," Simms said quickly, "beating me up wouldn't put any money in your pocket, but this could be a lot more lucrative than you think. I don't know how many arms there are, but I know they're worth money."

Leaning back, Fulton studied the thin man in front of him with the close-set eyes. He had nothing but contempt for gamblers who lost and couldn't pay, but he knew that Simms was right. It would give him some pleasure to beat Simms to a pulp, but it would not put cash in his purse. "All right," he said, "where are these arms?"

"That's what I'll find out, and I'll let you know as soon as I do. They're going to be delivered next week, so it won't be past then. I'll have all the information, the time, and the place where the arms will be delivered to the ship so you can take them all—and then we'll be even."

Well aware that he could lure Simms into falling into debt again, Simeon Fulton nodded. "All right, it's a bargain. If I get the arms, all your debts are forgiven."

"All right. I'll be in touch as soon as I find out. Good-bye."

Fulton watched as Simms left and then laughed harshly. "Come on back, boys. Bring some more of that liquor, innkeeper. I just made a deal with a gentleman who's going to make me rich!"

Trouble at the Docks

Eleven

*S*eth Donovan had never been around small children, and to his surprise he found himself a favorite with Eve and David Martin. He discovered he had a natural gift for entertaining them, which manifested itself in his storytelling ability. The two would sit for hours on his lap or at his feet as he spun wildly exaggerated tales. It delighted him to discover that neither of the children found the fantastic stories he concocted unusual or strange. He also discovered they liked fantasy much better than reality, and this shocked him somewhat. He himself had always felt the same way, and one of his most pleasant memories was sitting in the home of an old seafaring man too crippled to work but still able to tell stories of his travels around the globe. Seth had suspected even as a boy that most of the stories were not true, but that had not decreased his delight in them in the least. Now he found the same joy in making up stories and keeping the children entertained.

Several times Rebekah came in to find the large man on the floor with both children on his back playing horsy. She warned him, "You shouldn't do that, Seth. You're not over your fever yet."

"Let him alone, Mommy! He's our horsy," Eve cried.

"It's all right, ma'am," Seth said. "They're no weight at all." He looked up at her and said with a strange expression on his face, "I've never been around the little ones before. I see that I've missed something."

Entertaining the children had not been the only pleasure that Seth had found during his period of recuperation. He had been treated like one of the family. They all addressed him by his first name now and encouraged him to do the same. He had said, "But it won't be right when I go to work for me to call you by your given name."

"We'll worry about that when we come to it," Will grinned. "We're just enjoying having you with us. You've been a real help with the children. I am afraid I'm a little bit jealous of you."

"No need to be that, sir," Seth said quickly. "They both adore you. They can't wait until you get home from work."

"I'm going to spend more time with them, but it's hard working at the office so many hours. I've thought often of taking an easier way, but I don't know what else I'd be suited for."

"I expect, Mr. Martin, you could do anything you put your mind to," Seth replied.

But despite the pleasure in his surroundings, Seth's conscience was giving him grave problems. It cut at him like a razor when he considered how he was being sheltered and loved and accepted, when all the time he was planning to betray the Martin family.

Soon he was able to go outside for short walks and then longer ones. Oftentimes he took the children with him for the shorter trips, but even amidst their happy cries and while occupied with telling them stories and playing simple games with them, he could not forget what the plan was for the future.

For long periods he would walk the streets of Boston taking in the shops and businesses. He was pleased with the neatness of the town and thought he had never seen a finer one. But even while all this was going on in his mind, he was being pulled in two directions. He could not forget Isaac's death. It gnawed at him, and he constantly had to fight away the black grief that crept into his spirit. It was a struggle as powerful as any he had ever known in his warfare as a soldier, and he found it wearied him emotionally.

At night sometimes he would have vivid dreams of his boyhood, and always Isaac was there. He felt himself running through the Scottish heather with his brother by his side, laughing and tossing his hair aside in that peculiar mannerism that had been Isaac's. Faint memories of their young boyhood came in fleeting visions at that time, and then he would think of the time when Isaac had grown up to be a man and how proud he had been of him.

Several days passed, and although his physical strength had come back to its fullness, he felt drained emotionally. More than once he half decided to leave the house and disappear and find another way to serve the Crown, but he always put it off till the next day.

One of those nights when he could not sleep, he got up to read by the light of the lamp on his bedside table and heard faint voices. Glancing at the clock on the mantel, he saw that it was nearly midnight. "Who could that be?" he muttered. Carefully he closed his book and moved as quietly as possible to the door. Turning the knob slowly so that it would not creak, he opened it and then stepped outside. Moving along the hall, he descended the stairs and stopped just outside the library. He had already identified the speakers as William and his son, Will. He stiffened suddenly as he heard the words "arms and weapons" mentioned.

". . . They'll be delivered tomorrow at the dock," Will was saying. "A ship named the *Amazon* is bringing them ashore."

"What will happen then, Will?"

"We'll have them unloaded at the dock, and I've arranged for the *Mary Jane* to deliver them to Williamsburg."

William's voice was fainter than his son's. "I think she can outsail any of the British gunships."

"That she can, Father. I'll be glad to get this done. I don't know as we'll do it again. It's just too dangerous."

"We have to do what we can for the cause, Will," William said firmly.

"I suppose so, but I don't want Mother or Rebekah to know about this."

"No, it would be best if they didn't know. Well, tell me all the details. I'll need to know them."

Outside the door, Seth listened as Will outlined the plan for receiving the arms and for loading them and shipping them. When he heard Will say, "Now it's time for you to go to bed, Father," he turned quickly and tiptoed across the floor and up the stairs. Stepping inside, he closed the door and then leaned back against it. His mind was racing with thoughts, and he knew that it was time to do what he had been sent to do. Heavily he moved across the room and lay back down on the bed. He did not turn out the lantern, and for a long time he lay there, his eyes wide open. He studied the patterns in the wallpaper, but his mind was on the problem before him. Wearily he muttered, "I'll have to do it. I owe it to Isaac," he said.

———————

The air was still, and a quarter of a moon grinned down from above, bright and glittering. It looked like a smile somehow to Seth as he moved quietly along the streets headed for the wharf. He had watched William and Will leave after dinner and had gone to his room early, explaining that he was tired. Then, when the others had gone to bed, he had slipped out and now made his way along the silent streets.

He had no pleasure in what he was doing and had slept hardly at all. "I wish there was some other way," he muttered under his breath. "But I don't see any."

He arrived at the dock and moved along stealthily until he saw movement ahead of him on the wharf. When he got closer he could hear the voices of the men who were unloading cargo. He could not see the name on the ship, but he suspected it would be the *Amazon.* *Who else would be unloading in the middle of the night except something like this?* he thought.

His guess was confirmed sometime later when he heard Will say, "All right, here's the cash."

Straining his eyes through the fog, Seth could see only dim figures by the lantern that hung from a post close to the wharf. He could make out Will's figure, and farther off he thought he saw his father, William, in the background. He waited until the man had counted the money, then gone back on board the ship. He was surprised to see the *Amazon* begin to move almost at once.

"I guess they want to get away from here in case they get caught. Delivering ammunition and arms would get them hanged," Seth murmured. For some time he waited and managed to move in the shadows of the buildings close enough to where he could actually hear the voices of William and his son. They spoke rarely, but once Will said, "The men to move the goods to the *Mary Jane* ought to be here soon."

Seth had all the information he needed for Edward Denton. Still he did not go but lingered. Some time passed, and then the sound of someone approaching caught his attention. It had attracted the notice of Will also, for he said, "Here comes someone. I expect it's the crew to load."

Flattening himself against the wall of one of the offices on the wharf, Seth listened and watched. Suddenly the leader of the three who appeared pulled a pistol from his belt. "You gents hold it right where you are and there'll be no trouble," he said.

"What do you want?" Will demanded.

"I reckon I want what you got in them boxes. You two stand right still, and we got a crew comin' to move 'em."

Seth moved closer. The leader, he could see, was a big man, and the other two behind him were bulky figures in the night. *Something's gone wrong!* Seth thought with alarm. *This isn't the crew they sent for.*

Will Martin also was shocked. "Get away from here! You can't hold us up!"

"Can't I? We'll see about that!" The speaker was Simeon Fulton. He wore a dark overcoat and a hat pulled down over his face. He swelled with satisfaction as he realized this was going to be an easy matter. He waved the pistol, saying, "All right, boys, go get the wagon and we'll have ourselves a time."

One of the men turned to go, but at that moment Will threw himself forward. Seth almost uttered a cry, for it seemed a suicidal move with a pistol in the big man's hand. He saw Will suddenly go down and then struggle to get to his feet.

At that moment Seth ceased to think logically. He did not reason it out, but here was a man in danger who had been his friend. Will Martin had taken him in when he was sick and helpless, and had admitted him to the center of his family. Now he was being harmed by a villain.

Seth shoved himself away from the wall and lunged through the darkness. His feet made a thudding sound that caught the attention of the big man who held the pistol, for he turned and said, "What—" But he had no chance to say more, for Seth struck him a mighty blow in the chest with his fist, the full power of his two hundred pounds of compact muscle driving the man backward. The pistol flew up and hit the stones of the dock with a clattering sound.

Seth was aware that Will was trying to get up, but there was no time to think. He knew the big man would not stay down long, and the two who had accompanied him were rushing forward. One of them had a club in his hand, and his eyes glittered as he lifted it. He struck with all of his might, but it caught Seth a glancing blow on his left shoulder that numbed it. Pivoting, Seth drove his fist full into the face and felt bone and cartilage break. The man cried out and then fell backward full length. Snatching up the club, Seth saw that the other man had drawn a pistol from his belt. He struck out, and the club caught the man on the forearm. He heard the bone snap, and the man uttered a piercing cry. Grabbing his arm, the injured man turned and ran away. At that moment Seth heard William Martin cry out, "Watch out, man, he's going to shoot!"

Seth knew the leader must have recaptured his pistol. He stooped down, and the moonlight glinted on the muzzle of the pistol dropped by the second thug. Snatching it up, he whirled in time to hear an explosion. Something hummed by his ear, and then he aimed and fired without pause.

The bullet struck Simeon Fulton in the mouth and angled up through his cheek. Fulton felt warm blood, and after the numbness, a searing pain ripped through his wound. With a cry of rage, he turned and fled into the night.

Seth took three steps to pursue him and then turned and saw that Will was going to his father. He ran to them and said, "Are you all right, both of you?"

"Seth, what are you doing here?"

"I got worried about you. I knew something was up the way you talked," he said. "So I just followed to be sure it was all right, but look at your father!"

Will turned to see that William had slumped back against the wall and was holding his chest.

"Father, what's wrong?"

"Don't know—pain in my chest!" William gasped.

"We've got to get him home and get a doctor! Help me get him in the carriage, Seth."

"I'll do it. You drive."

Seth Donovan reached down and with his strong hands scooped up the older man as if he were a child. He carried him to the buggy and put him in the seat and then stood beside him, his arm around him. "You'd better drive quick, Will," he said tersely. "He doesn't look good at all."

Going Home

Twelve

For Dr. Phineas Steerforth, the most difficult part of being a doctor was telling a family there was no hope for a loved one. Dr. Steerforth faced such an unpleasant moment as he looked across at Anne Martin. He had been the family physician for the Martins for many years, and he felt a sense of frustration in knowing there was absolutely nothing more he could do. Something close to anger touched him, as it often did, for he had a fighting spirit and would fight death down to the last breath of one of his patients. But now he stood there silently, defeat in his eyes, and he could only say quickly, "I'm sorry, Anne, but there's nothing to be done."

A sob caught at Anne Martin's throat and she choked it back. Tears ran down her face and she turned to lean against William. He put his arms around her, and she pressed her face against the fabric of his shirt, unable to control the grief that overwhelmed her.

Rebekah choked back her own sobs, and she felt her mother's arm come around her. The two women turned and embraced each other, for both of them had a great love for William Martin. He had been a friend to Martha, something few men would have been able to accomplish, seeing she had been his servant for many years. And for Rebekah he had been as much a real father as she had ever known. Now the two women could say not one word but clung to each other as they shared their grief.

"You can all go in," Dr. Steerforth said.

Seth waited outside, his heart heavy. Will had tried to thank him for what he had done, but he had shrugged it off, angry at himself, for he alone knew the villainy of his own heart. He had always been a straightforward man and had fought his battles eye to eye with his enemy. And now he felt like a sneaking coward for what he was about to do. The grief that came to him over the passing of William Martin was the strongest grief he had felt since the loss of his own brother.

For nearly fifteen minutes Seth stood there, and then Will came out. "He wants to see you, Seth."

"Me? He wants to see me?"

"Yes, hurry!"

Bewildered and troubled, Seth Donovan moved inside the room. The lamps threw a cold yellow light over the face of the dying man. Seth moved forward and saw that William's eyes were open.

"I wanted . . . to thank you, Seth." William held up his hand and Seth took it and held it gently. There was no strength in William Martin's hand, for he had said good-bye to the world. Now he smiled slightly and said, "Thank you for saving my boy and doing your best for me."

"It was nothing, Mr. Martin. Nothing at all."

"I couldn't go home without speaking . . . my gratitude. You are a good man, Seth. Learn to love God."

Seth heard the words, and they seemed to inscribe themselves on his mind. He knew he would never forget the man's dying words, and now as he stepped back and put his back to the wall, he felt a strange thing. He had not shed a tear since he had been a child, except at the passing of Isaac, but now his eyes grew misty and his throat grew thick. *I love this old man*, he thought, *and there's nothing I can do for him.*

One by one the family passed and William gave his blessing to each one. He finally looked around and whispered, "Tell Elizabeth I loved her greatly." Then he looked at Anne and put up his hand. She came to him, bent over, and kissed him, her tears falling on his cheeks. "Find strength in God—my dear. You have been . . . God's gift to me."

Unable to speak, Anne put her face against his and held him. She felt his body tense, and then he seemed to sigh—and then he relaxed.

"He's gone," Anne whispered.

At those words, Seth turned and left the room. He had never felt anything like the combination of grief and guilt that weighed him down so heavily, and he fled the house unable to face it.

———————

As soon as Will stepped inside the door, he found Seth Donovan waiting for him. "Hello, Seth," he said. He looked at the man's face and saw something he could not define. "Is something wrong?"

"No, sir. I just need to talk to you." After the death of William, Seth had begun to fear that Will might have some suspicion about him.

As the two men moved into the study, however, Will said, "I hope nothing's wrong."

"I've just been worrying about what I'm going to do. I'm able to work now, and if you can't use me, I'll have to go somewhere else."

Will shook his head. His face was tense and weary, for he had not ceased to think of the loss of his father. Now he said, "Bad news comes again. You've met Hosea Simms?"

"Why, yes, sir. I met him the first day I came to town."

"Well, he's been found dead."

"Do you tell me that!" Seth exclaimed. "He was not an old man. Was it his heart?"

"No, it looks like he was killed."

"You mean murdered?"

"I think that's a possibility." Will had thought hard ever since he had been told of the murder of the manager. Now his mind was not quite clear. There were many things pressing upon him. His mother was not taking his father's death well, and the business, of course, was in poor shape to begin with. Most important of all was the shipment of arms. He had managed to have the arms loaded upon the *Mary Jane* but had no time to make other arrangements.

"Seth, I need help," he said suddenly, deciding instantly to put his trust in the tall, powerful man who had come into his life.

"Why . . . yes, sir. Just name it."

"The shipment on the dock that was being unloaded. It was arms for the Continental Army."

Seth made himself show surprise. "Indeed, sir, do you tell me that!"

"I suppose you know that my family and I are very much in favor of independence. My father risked a great deal and paid a great price for his belief. When the British took over here in Boston, he suffered great persecution and loss, as did all of us, but he had to bear the brunt of it."

"I honor him for it, Will."

"He was a fine man. Not a dishonest thing did I ever know him to do, and not once did I know of him breaking his word."

"There's not many men like that," Seth said solemnly. He waited, wondering what Will would ask of him.

"The arms have been shipped, but I'm thinking I need to move my family from Boston. Someone knew about that shipment. I can't help but think that Hosea had something to do with it, although I'd hate to believe so. He worked for my father for many years, but I do know one thing—he was a bad gambler. He took plunges. I often warned him that if he fell into debt, it might lead to other things."

"You think he might have sold out to some of the king's agents?"

"That's entirely possible. How else would those men have been there at the dock? No one knew we were unloading except my own men, and they're fully trustworthy."

Seth badly wanted to ask where the arms were bound for, but he knew it would not be prudent. "Where were you thinking of going, sir?"

"I've been thinking that we would go see my sister out on the frontier. Several times my father said he wished he could go out and see that new land, and the business isn't doing well, so we won't be leaving anything important behind."

"Anything I can do, I will. You've been so kind to me, I can do no other."

"I just wanted to be sure you wanted to help. It's going to be a chore to get the family all out there, and I'm going to need help."

"Well, you can depend on me, Will. I'd like to see that country myself."

Will put out his hand and found it swallowed by Seth's large hand. He felt the innate strength there and said, "It'll be good to have a strong man to help us. It's a long, hard way, and we'll need all the help we can get. So I'm grateful to you. Now I'll go tell the family what we're going to do, and we can start making our preparations."

———

Several weeks passed after this conversation with Will Martin, and Seth found himself totally caught up with the business of helping Will make the move. Will was busy night and day. He had found a buyer for his business and had gotten a fair price for it, but then the house had to be readied to be vacant for a time.

Anne Martin had been at the center of Will's concern. He had thought she would not care to leave after living her whole life in the city. He was surprised, however, as they all were, to find that she wanted to leave. She had always missed her daughter, Elizabeth, and longed to see her grandchildren who lived so far away.

With the business sold and out of the way, the household was in a swirl making final preparations. All of them worked from morning to night as the final days before their departure passed quickly.

Once Anne said to Will, "I wouldn't have been ready for this trip as long as William was alive. He was too weak for it, of course, but now that he's in his real home with the Lord Jesus, I don't think I could stay here without him. I'm ready for a change, for a while at least."

Will had put his arm around her. "We'll be all right, Mother. We'll be all right."

———

The short, barrel-shaped deckhand of the *Lullabelle* was sitting on the dock fishing. He had been fairly drunk the night before, and his head still ached, so he was in a surly mood.

"Can you tell me, mate, where that ship is headed?"

Turning, the sailor glared at the man who had come to stand beside him. "What's wrong with your face?" he demanded. He stared into the face of the bulky man who was wearing a coat turned up around his chin, but he did not hide the hideous scar. His mouth was twisted and some teeth were missing. Something had torn the flesh from the side of his face so that his right eye was twisted down in a sinister fashion. "Looks like you got your face half tore off. Was you in a fight?"

"Never mind that!" Simeon Fulton snarled, for every reminder of the ruin of his handsome looks brought fury to him. The bullet fired by Seth Donovan had wrecked the right side of his face and turned it into a twisted gargoyle expression. Fulton had been proud of his good looks, and now a burning passion had grown up in him to ruin those who had ruined him.

"What's that ship and where is she bound?"

"Headed for Virginia. Why, was you supposed to be on her?"

"I had some old friends," Fulton said, forcing himself to speak calmly. "Didn't get a chance to see them before they left. I was thinkin' about takin' a trip south. I'd like to see them if I could."

"Well, only one family on it I know of. A friend of mine, the bosun on that vessel, said they were going to Williamsburg in Virginia."

"Much obliged, mate."

Simeon Fulton turned and walked away. "Williamsburg," he muttered. Hatred boiled over in him, and he reached up and touched his scarred face. "Williamsburg, is it? Well, we'll just see Mr. Will Martin and his man, Seth Donovan, in Williamsburg. Then we'll see what befalls them."

PART III

Renewed Like the Eagle

August 1777–November 1777

"Who satisfieth thy mouth with good things; so that thy youth is renewed like the eagle's. The Lord executeth righteousness and judgment for all that are oppressed."

Psalm 103:5–6

Return to Williamsburg

Thirteen

*J*ames Spencer slumped loosely in the horsehide-covered chair that had adapted itself to his shape over the years. The only sound in the room was the ticking of the inlaid mahogany tall case clock and the turning of a page from time to time.

Looking up abruptly, James said, "You know, I think this fellow Thomas Paine is right on target about what he says."

"Is that right, dear?" Esther Spencer looked up from the needlework in her hands, put it down, then flexed her fingers. "What exactly does he say?"

"Pretty much that Americans ought to be Americans and not Englishmen. That we're past the stage when we can be the lackeys of a foreign power thousands of miles across the sea."

"I tried to read a little of one of those books once, that one, I think. What's the name of it?"

"*Common Sense.*"

"Yes, that's the one. I didn't find it very interesting."

A smile creased the lips of James, and he thought, but did not say, *You do not find anything political very interesting, my dear.* Aloud, he said, "I think he's a little bit radical, but the way is clear before us. This country will unite, and one day it will go from sea to sea. You mark my words!"

"Oh dear, I hope this war will be over soon! I can't help worrying over the poor men who have suffered so much. There're so many women we know who are widows."

"Always that way in a war." James read a few more lines of the book, then put it down again and rubbed his eyes. "I'm tired tonight. When a man gets old he loses a lot. I can't see the way I could when I was twenty."

"You can't expect that," Esther said. She had gone back to her needlework but now looked up and smiled at him. The two sat there for a while speaking softly from time to time, the clock beating time metrically with a solemn syncopation. It was an ordinary evening for the Spencers, and finally Esther put her sewing down and said, "I think I'll go to bed. I'm a little bit tired."

"About my bedtime, too," James said as they both stood to their feet.

Esther turned to him and remarked, "I'll be glad when Jacob and his friends come. It seems such a long time. Been a month since they began their journey, according to the last mail we received. I wish they could travel as quickly as the mail."

"Well," James said as he stretched his back, rubbing the small of it with both hands, "one man can travel faster than a party. But they'll be—" He broke off abruptly as a knock sounded on the front door.

"Who in the world could that be at this time of the night?" Esther said.

"I don't know. I'll go see."

She followed him, however, out of the large parlor and down the hall to the door. Reaching out, James opened it, and then Esther let out a small gasp of astonishment. "Jacob, you're here!"

"I'm here all right, Grandmother." Jacob stepped inside, and his grandmother came to his arms at once. He picked her up off the floor and held her for a moment, noting how she seemed to have lost weight and showed some sign of aging even during the relatively brief time he had been gone.

"About time you got here," James Spencer grinned. He waited until Jacob kissed Esther, then he turned to his grandson. Putting out his hand, James said, "You're brown as a berry, and I declare you look strong enough to pick up an ox!"

"You're looking well, too, sir," Jacob said. Indeed, James Spencer did look well. His hair had gotten a little whiter, but he was still strong and firm with an upright posture.

Esther then turned to the young woman who was standing somewhat awkwardly behind her. "Sarah," she said, "come here and give your grandmother a hug."

At once Sarah felt relief. She came and embraced her step-grandmother, holding her tightly. Any doubts she had had about how the

Spencers would receive her vanished from her mind.

"Well, look at you! I was expecting someone I could put on my knee, from what Josh wrote about you, but I don't suppose I can do that!"

James Spencer was grinning broadly. He came over to claim the kiss on his cheek and then shook his head. "It is wonderful having a beautiful young woman like you for a granddaughter."

Sarah glowed warmly as Esther said, "I've always wanted a girl in the family, and now I have one."

"Thank you both so much. You are as wonderful as Jacob told me you were," Sarah said.

Jacob then spoke up. "I'd like for you to meet Amanda Taylor, a very good friend of mine indeed, and of Sarah's. My grandfather and my grandmother."

Esther glanced quickly at her grandson and saw that there was a warmth in his eyes for this young woman. She greeted Amanda warmly and then said, "Well, come into the parlor. We can't stand out here in the foyer the whole time." Moving back into the sitting room, they all sat down, and Esther bombarded Jacob with questions. "Tell me all about Jehoshaphat."

"Jehoshaphat!" Jacob laughed. "Nobody ever calls my father that. He's always called Hawk."

"Well, I can't call him an outlandish name like that. I'm going to call him Josh no matter what he calls himself. Tell me all about him. What about Elizabeth? And tell me about the children."

For a while James listened as his wife peppered Jacob with questions. Seeing that the young man could hardly keep up with them, he finally interrupted, saying, "Esther, you're going to talk him to death. They've had a long journey. They're tired and they need to rest. We can all catch up in the morning."

"Oh, I'm sorry," Esther said, "but I'm so anxious to hear everything. Come along." She turned to see Ellen, the housekeeper, who had poked her head inside the door curiously. "Ellen and I will show you to your rooms."

Jacob followed his grandmother, who led him to his old room. He looked around and said, "It seems like a hundred years since I was here." His eyes went over the familiar things—the books, the comfortable bed, the collection of toys from his childhood. "I spent a lot of time in this room," he murmured.

"I left it just as it was. I like to come in here once in a while and think about the days when you were growing up."

She came and stood looking up at him. She was a small woman really, and tentatively she put her hands on his chest. "You look so much like your father," she whispered. "You look exactly as he did when he was your age. That's a compliment, because I always thought he was the finest-looking man I ever saw."

"Except for Grandfather, of course."

Esther's eyes laughed at the tall young man before her. "Of course except for him." She left him for a moment, went over and turned the bed down, then stood and faced him again. "You look happier than you did when you left here, Jacob. More content. I can tell."

"I am, Grandmother," Jacob said rather slowly. He chewed on his lower lip for a moment and then smiled broadly. "Ever since I found the Lord and got reconciled with Father, things have been different. Like I've been born again in more ways than one."

Tears came to Esther Spencer's eyes. She stood for a moment thinking back over all the long years of prayer for Jacob and Josh to be reunited. Then in a soft voice she whispered, "Sometimes it seems God moves very slowly when He answers prayer. You think nothing's going to happen, and then one day you look at it and it's done."

Jacob came over and put his arm around his grandmother and hugged her tightly. "I know why. It's because you and Grandfather prayed for me every day. Sometimes I'd pass by your room at night, or the sitting room, and I'd hear you praying for me. I never said anything to you, but I thought of it. And finally it just got to me."

"Your grandfather and I have done nothing but walk the floor and praise God ever since we heard about your conversion. We're so happy for you, Jacob." She hesitated for one moment, then said, "Tell me more about Sarah. She doesn't look well."

A strange expression crossed Jacob's face. "It's hard to say, Grandmother. Did you know about Philip Baxter?"

"That was the young man she was attached to?"

"Yes, very attached."

"I heard that he died."

"Yes, he was killed in an Indian attack, and it just about destroyed Sarah. She seems to be better now, but I know she still has nightmares. Mother told me. She won't talk about him very much."

"Well, we'll have to do all we can to help her have a good time while she's here. The Lord is able to heal memories like that. He's healed some for me."

"And for me, too."

Reaching up, Esther pulled his head down and kissed him on his cheek. "Good night, Jacob. You've made two old people very happy. We're so proud of you."

"Well, I'm glad if that's true. If it hadn't been for you and Grandfather, I would never have made it."

Esther turned and left the room, unable to speak anymore. Jacob wandered around touching various objects for a time, and finally he undressed and got into bed. He lay there with his hands locked behind his head, thinking about the years he had lived in this very room. It had been an unhappy time for the most part, for he had felt abandoned by his father. But somehow, as his grandmother had said, God had healed those memories, and now a warm glow of happiness came to him, and he murmured, "Lord God, thank You so much for saving me. Only Your mercy could have reached down and pulled me out of the hatred and bitterness that filled me. Thank You for restoring me to my father. You are a good God and I love You, and I ask in the name of Jesus that You be with Sarah and help her to find peace." He dropped off into a sleep almost instantly and knew nothing until the next morning.

"Have some more of these battered eggs, Sarah," Esther said. "You haven't eaten enough to keep a bird alive."

"If she doesn't want them, I do," Jacob grinned. He reached for the platter and raked off an enormous mound of the golden yellow eggs and then winked at Amanda. "Don't be bashful, Amanda. If you don't eat till you're swollen up like a poisoned pup, Grandmother thinks you don't like her cooking."

"Jacob, what awful talk!" Esther Spencer scolded. "Is that the kind of manners we taught you?"

"No, I think I left my manners at home. Out on the frontier, when we get something to eat, we gulp it down. Glad to get it."

"Is it really that hard, Jacob?" James Spencer asked. He was cutting a piece of ham into small pieces and chewing them thoroughly.

"I suppose you miss a lot of things that you can't get away from the city."

"Well, at first I did," Jacob nodded, "but after a time they don't seem too important."

"What about you, Amanda?" Esther asked. She sipped the tea from a polished china cup and smiled at the young woman who had said very little. "Do you like it out there?"

"I've lived out there for many years now, Mrs. Spencer. Yes, I do like it. It's so different from here." Shyly she looked at the older couple and said, "There's so many people here. I think I've seen more people since we arrived in Williamsburg than I did all of last year out at Watauga."

James Spencer was studying the young woman carefully. He was not as astute as his wife, but she had told him that Jacob seemed to have a special eye for the young woman. She was wearing a simple dress, not at all new. It was an attractive shade of blue, and the lace collar around her neck matched the small lace cap she wore on top of her dark brown hair. There was a shyness in her brown eyes, but he found her quietly attractive. He did not know her age but guessed it to be about eighteen. "What about your family?" he asked.

"There's only my mother. My father died last year."

"Oh, I'm sorry," James said. "I didn't mean to pry."

Jacob thought of how Amanda's father had abused her up until the very last of his life. He changed the subject quickly by saying, "You and Grandmother ought to come for a visit and see what your family is doing out on the frontier."

"Oh no, we're past that," Esther said. "You'll have to do the visiting."

The meal continued pleasantly enough, and finally Esther said, "Oh, Jacob, Thomas Denton has been asking about you ever since James told him that you were coming for a visit."

"Who's Thomas Denton?" Sarah asked.

"Why, he was Jacob's best friend. The two of them used to get into all kinds of mischief when they were young."

Sarah winked at Amanda and said, "Please tell us some of them!"

"I don't think that's necessary," Jacob said quickly, clearing his throat. "It's all ancient history."

James Spencer suddenly laughed aloud. "I remember the time

you and Thomas Denton shaved that fancy dog Mrs. Stratton was so proud of."

"Shaved a dog!" Amanda exclaimed. "Why would you do that?"

"Oh, it was just foolishness!" Jacob said, his face growing red.

"I'll tell it," James said. "Mrs. Stratton said something rude about your grandmother. So Thomas and Jacob got one of my straight razors and captured that dog. He was a little woolly ankle-biting sort of thing, rather hateful, I thought. They shaved every hair off of him." He laughed loudly, and even his wife laughed with him. "He looked like a rat, didn't he, Esther?"

"It was an awful thing to do. Mrs. Stratton thought of that dog as one of her children."

"Well, he was a naked sort of child. Funniest thing I ever saw."

"It wasn't very funny when you whipped me over it," Jacob said, unable to keep back the grin. "You made quite an impression on me."

"It's good for a young man to get a whipping every now and then just to remind him what life is like."

James Spencer then added, "And, of course, you'll be seeing Annabelle, too."

"Who's Annabelle?" Sarah asked. "One of your old flames, Jacob?"

"Certainly is," James grinned. "I guess they had quite a thing going at one time."

"Oh, that was nothing, Grandfather."

"You fooled me, then."

"Isn't she married yet?" Jacob asked.

There was a quality in his voice that drew Amanda's gaze. She kept her eyes fixed on him as his grandfather answered.

"Nope, she still lives at home."

"Oh, I thought she might have been married by now."

Sarah was taking all this in carefully. She had grown to know Jacob very well during their time together, and she could tell he was embarrassed and feeling awkward. *This Annabelle, whoever she is,* Sarah thought rather grimly, *has got some kind of hold on Jacob. I'll have to look into this more carefully.*

"Do tell us more, Jacob," Sarah said. "Just who is Annabelle?"

Jacob flushed and tried to dismiss the question with a wave of his hand. "Oh, she's just my friend Tom's sister." Then turning to his grandfather, he said abruptly, "What about the war?" It was obvious to all at the table that he wanted to change the subject.

James was also aware that Jacob was flustered, so he began to talk about the war. "It doesn't reach us quite as much here. I hope it will end soon, but I do pray that God grants freedom to the Colonies."

After a time James asked, "What are you going to do today?"

Jacob looked around the table, his eyes resting on Amanda for a moment. "I thought I might go see Tom."

"Oh, that will be nice," Esther said.

After Jacob had left and Sarah and Amanda had gone upstairs, Esther said to her husband, "I hope he doesn't take up with that girl again. She wasn't good for him."

"No, she wasn't. Why, that young Taylor girl is a modest, attractive young woman, and you say there's something there?"

"There is on her part," Esther said quickly. "Did you notice how she scarcely took her eyes off Jacob?"

"Well, that was the way I was with you." James grinned and hugged her quickly. "Maybe he'll get smitten with Amanda like I was with you the first time I saw you."

"Don't be foolish! We're too old for that."

"A man's never too old for a little romance," James said, then kissed her on the cheek. "Come on, let's go to town."

Annabelle

Fourteen

As Jacob stepped up to the door of the Denton home, he was suddenly amazed to find that his hand was a little unsteady as he raised it to the solid brass knocker. He thought he had prepared himself for this visit, but somehow, now that the moment had come, he was unsure and could not collect his thoughts. As he waited for the door to open, the ridiculous impulse to turn and run away came to him. "Don't be ridiculous," he told himself firmly. "If you can stand up to wild Indians, you can stand up to seeing a young woman."

The door opened, and a black man dressed in livery nodded and smiled. "Yes, sir?"

"I'd like to see Mr. Thomas Denton, please."

"Yes, sir. Mr. Denton, he's in the library. If you'll come in, I'll tell him you're here."

Stepping inside, Jacob glanced around the foyer. He had forgotten how opulent it was, for Edward Denton was a man who believed in not only making money but in spending it in a way that could be seen. This room had two floor-length windows on each side of the front door covered with dark crimson curtains hanging to the white marble floors. A red velvet-covered bench took its place along one wall just inside the door with a mahogany card table beside it. The walls were papered a brilliant white with gold stripes running through it, and the ceiling was high and coffered, painted white with gold along the edges. Mirrors of all shapes and sizes, all framed in polished brass, decorated the walls along with brass sconces, and along one wall was an elegant set of stairs covered with red carpet runners leading to the second story.

"Well, Jake, here you are!" Thomas Denton emerged, his face beaming, and he came at once to take his hand, then he slapped him hard on the shoulder. "Jake, you old dog, you!"

"Hello, Tom," Jacob grinned. He found himself forgetting Annabelle for the moment as fond memories of the past with this young fellow came back to him. "It's good to see you," he said. "You wouldn't believe how much I've missed you."

"Come on into the library," Thomas said, towing Jacob down the hall and calling over his shoulder, "Matthew, bring us some coffee. That all right with you, Jake?"

"Sure, sounds good." Jacob enjoyed the next half hour tremendously. Thomas, as usual, talked nonstop, reminiscing about some of their escapades. As he did his face was alive with excitement. He was curious about the frontier, as was everyone in the East, it seemed, and Jacob did the best he could to fill him in.

Jacob was in the middle of a story of a wild bear hunt when Annabelle walked into the room. He rose at once and turned to face her. Swallowing hard, he found it difficult to say, "Hello, Annabelle. You look as lovely as ever."

"I thought I heard your voice." Annabelle walked straight up to him with a smile on her lips. She was wearing a formfitting dress of pale green with a square neck and pleats down the front of her bodice, and white lacy funnel sleeves. She did indeed look beautiful. The truth was that she had heard Jacob's voice and had quickly gone to her bedroom and changed and fixed her hair. Now she said, "You look wonderful! So tanned and strong looking! Tom, you've monopolized Jacob long enough. It's my turn."

"All right," Thomas grinned, "but don't get away. We've got plans to make."

"Sure, Tom, I've got plenty of time."

Annabelle took Jacob's arm and led him over to a fine sofa. She pulled him down and sat so close to him that he felt a little uncomfortable at her nearness. "I'm so glad to see you," she said demurely. She reached out and took his hand and held it for a moment, saying, "You can't imagine how much I've missed you, Jacob."

Jacob managed to reply, "It's been lonely out in Watauga on the frontier. I've thought about you many times." He sat there looking at her, and it was as if he had been taken back in time. He had always been somewhat intimidated by her beauty and wondered what she saw in him. Now he felt himself to be the youthful, callow boy he had been years earlier. She still had the same scent of lilac that he remembered so well, and as he watched her lips move, he remembered the times he had kissed her.

Annabelle drew Jacob out, and after he had related some of the hardships in Watauga, she gave a slight shudder. "I wouldn't like it with all those wild animals and savages."

"Not all the Indians are savages. Some of them are very well educated. Sequatchie is a strong Christian and a close friend of the family."

"Oh, but most of them are wild, aren't they?"

"I guess everybody's a little bit wilder on the frontier. It's not Williamsburg or Boston, after all. But I haven't told you the good news," he said eagerly. "My father and I are reconciled now."

"Oh, that's fine! I'm glad to hear it."

Thinking of all that had happened, Jacob said, "I've changed a lot since I've left here. More than you might think."

"Changed how, Jacob?"

"Well, I've become a Christian."

"Why, you were always religious. Your grandparents took you to church every Sunday, if I remember rightly."

"Oh, I suppose I had a little religion, but now I know God in a deep way. It's different somehow, Annabelle."

Annabelle gave him a careful glance. She saw this was a very meaningful thing to him, and so she murmured, "I'm glad." Then suddenly she changed the subject. "We're going to have an October ball for my birthday." Her eyes sparkled and she took his hand again. "You will still be here, won't you?"

"Oh yes. We'll be in Williamsburg all winter, I think."

"Good. Now, we're not going to wait until then for you to come to the house. I know you'll be doing things with Tom, but you mustn't forget me."

"How could I do that?" He suddenly remembered Sarah and Amanda and quickly said, "My stepsister, Sarah, came back with me, and a friend of hers, Amanda Taylor."

"Who is she? Amanda Taylor, that is."

"She's a good friend of ours. I've known her since I moved out there. Her father died and she's had a difficult time." He related how Sarah had lost Philip Baxter, too, and ended by saying, "We thought it would be good for Sarah and Amanda to be together on this trip." He had the impulse to tell her that it was more than that really, but somehow, sitting with Annabelle, he could not bring himself to tell her that he had been practically courting Amanda.

But Annabelle Denton was a very astute young woman, at least where young men were concerned. Somehow she knew from the way Jacob spoke of Amanda Taylor that there was more to it than he was admitting.

She rose finally, and he rose with her as she said, "We'll invite them both to the ball, of course, but that won't be for a time. In the meanwhile, I want you all to myself."

She stood before him and her lips made a small change at the corners. She made a little gesture with her shoulders, and the fragrance of her came powerfully to him. The tone of her personality could charm a man—or chill him to the bone. He stood before her and could not take his eyes from her lips. They were rich with promise, and now, despite his resolutions, he found himself leaning forward. He started to put his arms around her—and at that moment Thomas walked in.

"Oh, sorry!" Thomas said, stopping abruptly.

Annabelle glared at her brother and said, "We were just talking about the ball we'll be having for my birthday."

"Well, that's not for a little while. In the meantime, you and I are going out to visit some of our old haunts."

"That'll be good, Tom."

For some reason Jacob was anxious to get away. "I'll be calling again soon." He turned to Annabelle and she gave him her hand. He took it and said, "I'll see you again soon."

After Jacob left, Thomas lifted his eyebrows and crossed his arms. Staring at Annabelle, he murmured, "Up to your old tricks, sister?"

Annabelle did not answer him. She was thinking, *If Thomas hadn't come in, he'd have kissed me and I'd have had him then!*

More Arrivals

Fifteen

Silas Anderson looked up from the counter where he was slicing rounded cheese into small pieces, and for a moment the knife was perfectly still. He ducked his head to peer over the gold-rimmed glasses on his nose and then exclaimed, "Well, Jacob Spencer, as I do declare!"

"Hello, Mr. Anderson. It's good to see you again." Jacob advanced and put out his hand. When the elderly shopkeeper forgot the knife and extended it, he laughed and shook his head. "I don't believe I'd better shake hands with that. You always kept your knives pretty sharp."

Anderson looked down at the knife and said, "Oh, sorry, I forgot! But I'm gettin' nigh onto seventy now. A man's got a right to forget a few things when he's that age." Tossing the knife down, he once again extended his hand. It was swallowed up by Jacob's, and Anderson shook his head. "My, look at you! You're brown as those Indians you've been out there fellowshippin' with. When did you get in?"

"Just two days ago," Jacob said. "I've got a packet of letters for you from Paul." He reached into his inner pocket, pulled out a small bundle of letters and papers, and handed them to the storekeeper.

"My, all the way from the Far West. Martha will be glad to get all these. She worries about that boy of ours out there." Silas and Martha Anderson were the parents of Paul Anderson, the young minister who had left Williamsburg with a wagon train led by Hawk Spencer. The two had been close friends as boys growing up in Williamsburg. Silas opened one of the letters and ran his eyes across it. "Hard to see with these new spectacles. I'll have to wait and let Martha read them to me."

"How is Mrs. Anderson?" Jacob asked.

"Fine as ever," Anderson beamed. He began to ply Jacob with questions about Paul and his wife, Rhoda, and about their new daughter, Rachel. For a time, Jacob stood there answering as well as he could. Abruptly, then Silas noticed the two young ladies with Jacob. "Well, you didn't up and get married on us, did you, Jacob?"

Jacob grinned. "No, this is Sarah MacNeal. She's my stepsister. Her mother married my father, Hawk."

"Do you tell me that! You've come on a visit, then?"

"Yes, but I've been in your store before, Mr. Anderson." Sarah had been looking about, and now she turned to smile at the old man. "I remember being in this store just before we left to go to Watauga. I first met Jacob's father here. I don't suppose you'd remember me."

"Well, if it happened before last Tuesday, I don't expect I could." Anderson shook his head regretfully. "I'm losin' my memory along with everything else. I do remember when Josh went out . . . and Paul, of course. I've worried about those boys, but I believe the Lord's taken care of them."

"This is my friend, Amanda Taylor. She's come for a visit along with me."

Anderson greeted Amanda pleasantly and said, "I want you two young ladies, and you too, Jacob, to come to our house for supper. We'll pump you dry about all that that boy of ours has been doing."

"He's been doing a great work. I can tell you that," Jacob said. "There's not a better preacher or missionary in the whole territory." He laughed then and said, "Well, to be truthful, there's not but about one or two more. Paul's doing a fine work among the Cherokee. I know you're very proud of him."

As Anderson continued to ask Jacob questions about his son and his family, Sarah was aware that some customers had entered, a man and a woman. Behind them was a tall blond man, much younger, holding two children by the hand. Suddenly her eyes widened, and without thought, she ran toward the man and cried out, "Uncle Will!"

Will Martin was taken completely aback when a lovely young woman suddenly threw herself into his arms. He caught her and then had to catch his balance as he glanced at his wife with astonishment. "Uncle Will?" he said.

"You don't remember me!" Sarah said. "It's me, Sarah MacNeal, your niece! I'm Elizabeth's daughter."

"Well, of all things!" Will Martin was absolutely astonished. He stood there for a moment and then shook his head slowly. "I never dreamed to see you here, Sarah. What in the world are you doing in Williamsburg?"

"I've come for a visit, me and my friend, Amanda. Jacob brought us. Jacob Spencer."

Jacob and Amanda had stood back while this was going on. Sarah asked, "What in the world are you doing in Williamsburg? I was going to try to come to Boston to see you."

With some hesitancy, Will said, "We've just come down for a visit. You remember Rebekah, and these are our children, your cousins, Eve and David."

Sarah greeted them all and then turned with expectation to the large man who did not seem to be part of this group. Her first opinion was that he was one of the strongest-looking men she had ever seen, and he had the oddest color eyes, blue-green, like the sea at certain times.

"This is Mr. Seth Donovan, a very dear friend of ours. He's been of great help to my family. Seth, this is my niece, Sarah MacNeal."

Seth nodded, saying, "I'm glad to meet you, Miss MacNeal."

"And I am glad to meet you, sir."

"Where are you staying?" Sarah asked.

"Well, to be truthful, we just got in. I came in here to get a few things for the children and to ask for a recommendation." He looked over toward the older shopkeeper and said, "Perhaps you can recommend an inn where we might put up."

"Oh, there's no need of that, Uncle Will," Sarah said. "I'm sure Jacob's grandparents would be glad to have them, don't you think so, Jacob?"

"I know they would. They've heard a lot about you," Jacob said.

"Oh no, we wouldn't want to impose!" Rebekah said quickly. Like most women she did not want to be thrust into a strange environment so abruptly and would have much preferred the inn.

"It's a big old house," Jacob said, "and nobody's there except my grandparents, and us, of course. There's plenty of room."

For some moments the discussion went on. The Martins attempted to refuse the kind invitation, but Jacob and Sarah were both adamant that they come and stay with them. Finally Will Martin shrugged. "All right, we'll try it, but your grandparents might not see it like you do."

"That's right," Rebekah said. "My grandmother's with us, too. She's still in the carriage outside, with your grandmother, Sarah."

"Grandmother's here, too! Where is Grandfather?"

"I'm sorry to have to tell you this, Sarah, but he died just a few weeks ago." Will then held his niece as she shed a few silent tears for the man who had been a special part of her childhood.

Jacob waited a time, then quietly added that everyone would be welcome at his grandparents' home.

"But older people don't take kindly to having small children," Rebekah added. "It may be too much for them."

"If they put up with me, I'm sure they can put up with these two. Come along," Jacob said.

Seth had been listening to all this, and now he said quickly, "I'll just find a room at the inn."

"Not a bit of it," Jacob said. "You're welcome to come, too."

Seth shook his head, but Jacob merely laughed. "You can share my room. Be glad to have you."

As soon as Will had made a few purchases from the store, they all left together. After they had disappeared, Silas Anderson picked up the letters and peered at them, then said, "By granny, I've got to get home and let Martha read these letters to me. Find out what that boy of ours has been up to preachin' to the wild Indians out there in the middle of nowhere!"

Esther Spencer had been somewhat overwhelmed at first when Jacob had come rushing in, saying, "Grandmother, I hope you don't get shocked, but I've done something that you may not like."

"It wouldn't be the first time. What is it?"

"We were in the store," Jacob said, "and Will Martin came in. That's Sarah's uncle from Boston."

"Oh yes, I know about them! What's he doing here in Williamsburg?"

"Just on a visit. But, Grandmother, I'm afraid Sarah and I went overboard. We've asked them all to stay with us for a few days."

"Well, that's fine. Is his wife with him?"

Jacob cleared his throat. "Yes, his wife, his mother, and his wife's grandmother."

"Is that all?"

"Well, there's a man named Seth Donovan."

"Any more?" Esther asked, her eyebrows raised.

"Well, only two children about three or four. They won't be any trouble."

Esther could not help but laugh. "Won't be any trouble? A bunch like that, and you think they won't be trouble?"

"I'm sorry, Grandmother. I guess we got carried away."

"It's quite all right. It's been lonely around here. They'll put some life and noise back into this old house."

Jacob was relieved. He squeezed his grandmother and hurried away to tell Sarah the good news. "All is well," he said. "I was a little bit worried, but Grandmother took it like a soldier."

"I knew she would," Sarah said quickly. "I could tell she and your grandfather are some of the most hospitable people I've ever known."

Thus the Martins, Martha Edwards, and Seth Donovan took up their residence with the Spencers. There was a great deal of activity as they were all assigned rooms. Esther Spencer insisted on their lying down to rest after their journey. Then she immediately enlisted the aid of Amanda and Sarah to cook a large meal.

The three women, aided by two servant women, did a magnificent job. Jacob was sent to the shops and came back loaded down with food of all kinds. The women worked furiously, and finally that night they had a fine meal.

As the Martins came into the dining room, Rebekah cried out, "Oh, it's beautiful! I just love fine old houses like this."

The dining room was a large, dimly lit room. It had green carpet covering the hardwood floors, and the walls were papered with a bold green-and-gold mica diamond-shaped wallpaper. There were no windows in this room, but French doors, covered with white lace curtains, dominated the far end of the room. A large oak oval-shaped table was placed in the middle of the room, and it was surrounded by large side chairs with horsehair sets covered with slipcovers in cool yellow chintz. The table was covered with the finest china, decanters of cut glass, crystal, and silver. The large verde and marble chimney piece gave off a warm glow as the logs on the fire began to burn slowly.

"I don't know about the room," Will grinned, "but the food sure looks very impressive. I don't see how you ladies got all this done."

The table was loaded down with platters of beef, potted fish, and venison. The venison had a dish of sugared and spiced wine sauce to be put on top, and bowls of baked pumpkin pudding, potato pie, and green beans with a cream and onion sauce added to the delicious aromas filling the air. There were baskets of freshly baked bread and bowls of whipped butter placed down the center of the table, and smaller plates of cheeses and lemon biscuits for after the main course. For dessert a plate of almond tarts and bowls of boiled custard finished off the meal.

Soon they all sat down, and James Spencer said, "Brother Martin, would you ask the blessing?"

Will bowed his head and gave a fervent prayer of gratitude for the food and for the hospitality. Amanda and Sarah positioned themselves on either side of the two children and saw to it that they were plentifully supplied as the meal went on.

Martha Edwards had insisted on helping fix the meal, and now she sat there saying to Esther Spencer, "I don't know of many women who would take in a crowd like this on a moment's notice. We're very grateful to you."

"Nonsense," Esther said. "James and I get lonely in this big old house sometimes. It will be wonderful having you. And you are family, after all."

James looked up from his plate and said, "What brings you to Williamsburg, Mr. Martin?"

For one brief moment Will hesitated. He had learned a little bit about the Spencers and how they were faithful patriots and supportive of the Revolution. "Well," he said, "it's a rather unpleasant story." He plunged into the details of how he had been importing arms in Boston and then distributing them to the militias and to Washington's army. "But it got a little bit dangerous at the last. If it hadn't been for Mr. Donovan there, I don't think we would have escaped. A man named Simeon Fulton was the head of a group of thieves. I'm very grateful to Seth for pulling me out of that one."

Sarah turned suddenly to look at the young man eating silently at her left. He felt her gaze and turned to meet her eyes. "It wasn't all that much," he said, the Scottish burr very thick.

"I'll bet it was," Sarah said.

"It certainly was," Rebekah Martin said quickly. "He saved Will's life."

All of this bothered Seth, who would have much rather been left out of the conversation. He was glad when the talk turned to other things, and finally the children took their attention by demanding more stories about the Indians from Jacob.

As Jacob obliged, Sarah was studying her grandmother, but a memory came back suddenly. Having now suffered three deaths—her father, Philip Baxter, and her grandfather—she was very conscious of the fragility of life. Looking at her grandmother and noticing how much age had begun to mark her, a coldness crept up on her and she said little more.

Seth had kept his attention on Will, hoping he might reveal the location of the arms that had been shipped in, but he had time to notice Sarah, who had become very quiet and thoughtful. She was a pretty girl, and her features were quick to express her thought. It seemed to him that laughter and the love of life was a part of her, but something had caused them to be diminished. There was fire in her that made her lovely, and yet somehow he knew her beauty would never be for him.

His thoughts were interrupted when Jacob suddenly turned and asked, "This is not your home, I take it, Seth?"

"Weel, no. You can tell that by the way I talk. As the young one there says, I talk funny. I'm from Scotland, of course, but I've been wandering around the Colonies for a couple of years now."

"Well, it's a good thing for us that he did," Will smiled.

Sarah looked at Seth and studied him carefully. There was a strength in him, and she was a woman who admired that in a man, as most women do. She, more than others, looked for it, because it took strength to survive in this world. She took time later in the meal to say, "I'm glad you were able to help my family. Thank you very much."

Seth felt warmed by her praise but said only, "I was glad to be able to do it."

———

Later that night when Jacob and Seth were getting ready for bed, a knock sounded on the door. Moving across the room, Jacob opened it and found his grandmother there. "Hello, Grandmother. What are you doing up so late?"

"I just came to see if you two had everything you needed."

"I guess so. We've got a bed, and that's what we need right now."

Esther looked over at Seth, who had risen when she had come into the room. "This room will be all right for you, will it?"

"Yes indeed, Mrs. Spencer. It's better than anything I've had. I thank you again for your hospitality."

"Oh, by the way, Grandmother," Jacob said, "Sarah, Amanda, and I won't be home for dinner tomorrow."

"Why's that?"

"We've been invited to eat at Edward Denton's house."

A sudden shock seemed to run along Seth's nerves. *Edward Denton—it couldn't be the same!* he thought wildly. *But how many Edward Dentons were there in Williamsburg?* He listened carefully, his mind racing with this new bit of information.

"It would be nice if you could take Mr. Donovan along with you," Esther offered.

"Oh no, I wouldn't care to do that, being a stranger and all!"

"Nonsense, you need to meet some people. I want you to meet my best friend, Tom Denton, and Annabelle, his sister."

For some time Seth protested, but he grew fearful that his refusal might create suspicion.

"All right," he said, "if you insist."

Later, after Jacob had gone to sleep, Seth lay there listening to his heavy, regular breathing. He thought, *Edward Denton. I don't know what all this means. If it's the Edward Denton I know, it could be problems. He won't expect me to be coming into his house as a guest.* Finally he put the matter out of his mind. The last thing he thought of before he went to sleep was the face of Sarah MacNeal.

The Dinner Party

Sixteen

*A*manda turned around and studied herself in the mirror and felt a moment of depression. It was not that her dress was unattractive, but it was not stylish. On the frontier, dresses were made for practical use, not for prettiness. She had only brought three dresses with her, and this was the best one—the one she had thought to wear to church. It was a simply cut dress that buttoned up high in the front with white bone buttons. The color had once been a brilliant blue but now had faded until it was rather dull. She had made it herself, and since it had been one of her first efforts, she was not entirely pleased with the results.

Sarah entered the room and said quickly, "Oh, you look nice, Amanda. I always like that dress."

"Do you really think so? It's a little bit old, and I know it's not very stylish."

"It'll do fine." She herself was wearing a dress she had bought the day before. Hawk had slipped the money into her hand before she had left and winked at her, saying, "Buy a pretty dress that'll knock the eyes out of those young bucks in Williamsburg." It was a light blue dress of embroidered silk. It had a square neckline and dark blue ribbons outlining the full skirt. "If you're ready," she said, "let's go on down."

The two left the bedroom and found Seth and Jacob waiting. Jacob was wearing a black velvet suit with the coat buttoned to the neck. It had a pleated back and fell just below his knees, and consisted of a matching waistcoat and britches that ended below his knees with white silk stockings and shiny black leather shoes.

"Oh, you look nice, Jacob!" Sarah smiled. "Doesn't he, Amanda?"

"Yes he does." Amanda, as a matter of fact, felt rather dowdy standing beside the two. She looked over at Seth and her eyes opened wide, for he was wearing a kilt and full Highland regalia. "Oh, Seth," she said, "I've never seen anything like that."

"It's quite a sight to see an army march into battle wearing the Highland colors," Seth nodded. He thought again of the battle back at Moore's Creek Bridge, and his face darkened as visions of his dying brother intruded into the recesses of his mind.

"Well, I guess we're ready to go," Jacob said. "I've got a coach big enough for all of us."

They stepped outside and saw a large black coach waiting to take them to the party. The coachman had tied the horses and stood now with a smile on his face watching them. He wore a watch coat over a single-breasted suit, a brightly striped vest, leather britches, and heavy jack boots. He yanked his cocked hat off his head to reveal a mass of black, tangled, curly hair and said, "Get in, ladies and gentlemen. We'll be on our way."

The trip to the Dentons' was exciting to Amanda. She was sitting next to Seth facing Jacob and Sarah, and she turned to say to the tall man, "I've never ridden in a coach like this before. Have you?"

"Not very often," Seth answered. "It beats walking, doesn't it?"

Jacob put his glance on Amanda and said, "You'll have to watch out for my friend Tom. He's a little bit too free with his affections. I'm always afraid he's going to be shot by some angry father."

"Is that right?" Amanda said.

"No, it's not *right*, but that's the way he is."

"I understand he says the same thing about you," Sarah said archly. She laughed at the expression on Jacob's face. "Your grandmother's been telling me a lot about your antics with Thomas when you were younger. I hope you've improved some since then."

The coach drew up in front of the Denton house shortly afterward, and the coachman at once jumped down. He handed the ladies out, and Jacob said, "I'll ask you to wait for us. I'll make it worth your while."

"Yes, sir, I'll be right here. You have a fine evening. Don't worry about getting home."

Moving up to the Denton mansion, Amanda felt as out of place as she had ever in her life. She glanced up at Seth Donovan and said, "What a fine house. I've never seen anything so big."

"It would hold a right smart group of people," Seth said. He was tense, for he knew that his meeting with Denton would not be particularly pleasant. As a matter of fact, he had tried to think of some way to get out of coming to the dinner party at all, but Jacob had insisted he join them. Jacob saw that Amanda was afraid and said in a kindly fashion, "Don't worry about it. They're just people. Rich people are just people with money, after all."

Sarah, hearing this, turned her face toward her friend. "That's right, Amanda. They do things the same way we do mostly."

"I don't know about that," Seth said as he watched Jacob knock on the door. "Many a fellow I've known would have been quite a dull chap if he hadn't had twenty thousand pounds a year."

Sarah found Seth's comment amusing and smiled; then the door opened. The tall black butler admitted them, and they were greeted by Annabelle, who came sweeping down the stairs in a beautiful dress. It was made of exquisite pale yellow silk with a green bow decorating the front of it. A dark green brocade trimmed the edges of the neckline onto the full skirt, and the underskirt was layered with yellow pleated panels edged with the same green brocade.

She swept down the stairs so magnificently that Sarah said to herself, *I believe she must have been waiting up there so she could make her entrance.* She took an instant dislike to Annabelle before the young woman came and held both hands out to Jacob, who took them rather awkwardly.

"Jacob, I'm so glad you're here. You look marvelous!" She turned then and her smile was brilliant. "Introduce me to your friends."

Thomas appeared at that moment, and after formal introductions went around, he said, "Let's go into the dining room. We can eat now and talk later."

Annabelle immediately took Jacob's arm and half led him down the hall. Thomas stepped up and said, "If I might, Miss Amanda." She took his arm, imitating the first pair.

"I suppose you'll be forced to escort me. I'm all that's left," Sarah said and smiled at Seth.

"A painless duty, I assure you," Seth said. He put his arm out, and when she tucked her hand inside it, he said, "Your friend, Amanda, is overwhelmed by all of this. You'd better stick close beside her."

"You noticed that?"

"Why, of course."

"Most men wouldn't." Sarah did not know what possessed her, but she looked up suddenly and said, "You must spend a lot of time studying young women to notice a thing like that."

"No man would ever answer a statement like that. He'd be incriminating himself," Seth laughed.

By that time the two were in the dining room, and soon they were seated around the table. Phoebe Denton, Annabelle's mother, sat at one end of the table. She had greeted the guests with perfect courtesy, saying only, "My husband will be a little bit late. You'll forgive him."

Amanda sat at Mrs. Denton's left hand with Sarah beside her, and Seth Donovan took his seat next to Sarah. Across from them Annabelle, Jacob, and Thomas were seated. When the meal began, Sarah noticed that there was no blessing, or even any mention of one, so she assumed that was not part of the Dentons' habits.

The meal was excellent, of course, featuring five courses—fish, beef, mutton, soup, and cutlets. A butler and a maid constantly brought bread and rolls and kept the goblets filled.

Throughout the entire meal, Annabelle dominated the conversation. The tenor of her talk was mostly about the barbaric frontier. She went on so long about the deplorable conditions people had to live under that finally Sarah turned to her and said, "Well, really, Miss Denton, it's not quite as barbaric as you might think. Conditions are hard, of course, and we don't have the conveniences that you do here in Williamsburg, but some of the finest people in the world live there."

"Oh, I'm certain of that, Sarah!" Annabelle smiled quickly. "It's just that it would be so difficult to do without the common conveniences of life, much less the few little luxuries that one becomes accustomed to."

Annabelle then proceeded to continue with her views. She was in her element, and finally Thomas interrupted by saying, "What are your opinions of Williamsburg, Miss Amanda? Miss Sarah?"

Amanda waited for Sarah to answer, and when she felt Sarah nudge her, she said, "Oh, I like it very much, Mr. Denton."

"Mr. Denton is my father. Just call me Thomas or even Tom." Thomas began to question Amanda more carefully, and once

Amanda looked over at Jacob, and he winked at her and shook his head slightly.

He's warning me about his friend, but he's really very nice, Amanda thought. She managed a smile and felt a little more comfortable.

The talk went on for some time. Finally, without knowing why he had done it except that he was strangely irritated with Thomas for showing so much attention to Amanda, Jacob blurted, "Thomas, I don't think I told you, but Amanda and I are quite good friends. We've been seeing each other for some time."

A silence came over the table. Sarah's eyes flew open and she cast a quick look at Amanda, who was staring at Jacob with shock. *He shouldn't have said that!* Sarah thought. *He hasn't been seeing Amanda. They've been friends, but he's implying that they're engaged or something like that.*

Annabelle had been shocked into silence for once. She turned to Amanda and, smiling sweetly, said, "I would never have thought that Jacob would have fallen for a frontier girl." The tone of her voice was clearly derogatory, and then she turned immediately to Jacob and said, "You should have told me about your friend, Jacob."

"Well, it just never came up." Jacob knew he had made a horrible blunder. He kept his eyes down for a moment, but finally he lifted them and saw that Amanda was regarding him with a most peculiar vulnerable expression. Her lips were soft and her eyes were almost pleading, and he knew that once again he had spoken when he should have been quiet.

Sarah said quickly, "Well, I suppose we assumed that you knew that, but there's no reason why you should."

"I've always thought that Jacob would come back after his little playing in the wilderness," Annabelle said, and she gave a little laugh. "I thought he'd come back and marry some wealthy city girl and live in Williamsburg."

Sarah turned to face the young woman and said evenly, "I suppose you were wrong, then, Miss Annabelle."

Amanda had just lowered her face, and Jacob knew she was terribly hurt. *How am I going to get out of this?* he thought.

At that moment Edward Denton stepped into the room. There was a sudden quiet, and then Thomas rose and said, "Let me introduce you to our guests, Father." Thomas went around the room, and when he called the name of Seth Donovan, a change went across his father's face.

"How do you do, Mr. Donovan?" he said simply.

Seth felt the man's gaze burning into him. They all sat down then, and Seth was well aware that no matter what Edward Denton said, his whole attention was on this unexpected guest. As dread rose in him, he had not the faintest idea of how he would talk himself out of this problem that had suddenly arisen.

───────────

"Amanda, don't go up yet. I want to talk to you."

Amanda turned and saw Jacob waiting at the foot of the stairs, where he had come to intercept her. Seth and Sarah had already retired immediately after they came home from the dinner party, and now Amanda paused. "What is it, Jacob?" she asked quietly.

"We can't talk here. Let's go into the library. Nobody's there at this time of the night. They're all in bed."

"All right, if you like."

Amanda followed Jacob inside the library. He turned the lamp up and then turned to face her. "I suppose that you didn't have a very good time tonight."

"I was surprised about some things. Why don't you tell me about Annabelle?"

"Why, she's my best friend's sister."

Amanda stood quietly. She wasn't smiling, and with her head still and straight, she examined him carefully. "There's more to it than that, isn't there, Jacob?"

"Well, at one time there might have been," Jacob said with considerable hesitation. "I saw her a few times. I suppose you could say I courted her." Then he added hastily, "But almost every young man in town did, and it never came to anything."

"Why not?"

Jacob fervently wished he had never been put into this position, and now he said, "It's all ancient history, Amanda. It was never much to begin with. Mostly in my own mind, I suppose. She comes from a very wealthy family and had many suitors."

"She put herself out to be nice to you, Jacob. I think she still cares for you."

Surprise washed across Jacob Spencer's face, but he shook his head stubbornly. "You're wrong about that, Amanda." He desperately wanted to change the subject. "I warned you about Thomas. Did you see what I meant?"

"No, I didn't see anything of the kind. He's very nice and has lovely manners, very elegant."

"You seemed to enjoy his attention enough."

"Why, of course I did. He made me feel very welcome."

The two stood there, both of them awkward and ill at ease. Finally Jacob said, "Well, it's getting late." He suddenly reached out and took her hand and held it. "I wouldn't ever want to do anything to hurt you, Amanda. You've been hurt enough already."

Amanda was silent for a moment. She was surprised and stood there looking up at him. His hand was large and strong and warm. Then she said, "That's nice of you, Jacob. You've always been so kind to me. I can't imagine anyone being any more kind and thoughtful."

Jacob studied her face. She was smiling now, a slight smile that turned the corners of her mouth upward. She had always had a repose about her that he admired. Now he saw in her the will and the pride that drew him to her. She did not move and her composed lips seemed to hold back some hidden knowledge. Her complexion was fair and smooth, rose colored, and a summer darkness lay over her skin. The dress fell away from her throat, showing the smooth ivory, and he was suddenly aware that she was a very attractive young woman. He was still holding her hand, and then suddenly he did something he had never done in his life. He raised it to his lips, kissed it, and whispered, "You're a fine young woman, Amanda." He dropped her hand then and turned and walked away without so much as a good night.

Amanda stared at him, surprised and shocked by the gesture. She moved along the hall and entered the room she was sharing with Sarah. Sarah watched her carefully, speaking of things that had happened at the dinner party.

Finally Sarah said, "I was a little surprised at Annabelle Denton. She's got a way about her that's almost forward. Certainly too much for a woman."

"She's very pretty."

"I suppose so, but so are you."

"Not like she is," Amanda said. She had taken off her dress and slipped into her nightgown, and as she moved to the bed, she said,

"I know Jacob cared for her at one time. I don't know how he feels now."

The two girls got into bed and Sarah blew out the light. "Well, I think men are pretty thickheaded where women are concerned. I can see how Jacob would be taken by her, but I think it's all over now." She waited for a reply but got none, so with a sigh she rolled over and composed herself for sleep.

Seth's Dilemma

Seventeen

As Seth came downstairs rubbing his eyes, he stumbled slightly on the carpet that padded the treads. He had slept much later than usual, for he had lain awake until almost dawn thinking about Edward Denton. Entering the kitchen, he found Martha Edwards and mumbled, "Good morning, Mrs. Edwards."

"Morning, is it?" Martha turned and smiled at him. "A late morning, I must say."

"I overslept. I thought Jacob would wake me up when he left, but he didn't."

"You must be a sound sleeper. He makes enough noise to wake a hibernatin' bear."

"I suppose I am a pretty heavy sleeper."

"Well, sit down and I'll fix you some breakfast."

Seth sat down at the table, and quickly Martha scrambled some eggs, fried some bacon, and put it out along with some rolls. "There's fresh butter and honey to go with the rolls, if you like it."

"I do. It's all very good, Mrs. Edwards." He sat there eating while she worked around cleaning up the kitchen. Finally he asked, "Where is everyone?"

Looking up from the pan she was greasing, Martha said, "Why, they're all gone, except James and Will. They're in the library. They've been holed up there all morning talking about something. Esther, Anne, and Rebekah went to do some shopping, and Jacob took Amanda out for a morning walk."

"What about Miss Sarah?"

"She's out in the garden watching Eve and David. She's very good with children, do you know?"

"No, I didn't know that." Seth layered his roll with golden butter, then poured dark brown honey over it. "This is good honey," he said. "Back in Scotland we had honey almost like this. It wasn't always the same, though."

"I think it depends on what the bees eat. Back home we always thought that clover honey was the best of all, but a friend of mine says alfalfa honey is good, too." She watched him eat, admiring the strength of his hands and the breadth of his shoulders. She wanted to ask more about him, for he was an attractive man, though more silent than most men.

When he was finished, Seth rose and said, "I thank you vurry much. It was a vurry good breakfast."

"You're welcome. Why don't you go out and see Sarah? As I said, she's out in the garden."

Seth hesitated, then nodded, "I think I will just see how she is and those children. I've had a lot of pleasure out of them."

"You have a lot of brothers and sisters?"

After a certain hesitation, Seth said quietly, "I had one brother, but he died last year."

"Oh, I'm so sorry to hear that!"

"Nothing to be done for it," Seth said heavily. He turned and moved out of the house. The garden was on the west side of the house itself and was filled with yellow, red, and purple flowers of all kinds. Roses bloomed along a low-lying brick wall, and over in an open space a fountain bubbled merrily. Eve and David Martin were dabbling in the water, and Sarah sat on the curbstone. She had been watching them, but she turned her face as Seth approached. "Good morning," she said. "You finally got up, did you?"

"Afraid I sleep late every chance I get." He sat down on the well stone, and Eve came at once and said, "Look, fish, Seth!"

"That's right. They're big ones, too," Seth said, looking down at the goldfish. They were very large and he marveled at the size of them. "I didn't know goldfish got that big."

"They must be very old," Sarah nodded. "I think some people call them carp."

"Goldfish sounds better, don't you think?"

"I suppose so." Sarah smiled at him. His tawny yellow hair was ruffled, and he had not shaved, so the bristle of his beard was almost a golden red. "If you didn't shave, I think you'd have a red beard."

"It is red," he admitted. He smiled at her, and his teeth showed white against his tan. "My mother was redheaded, as red as you ever saw. It all got in my beard. None in my hair, though."

Sarah asked idly, "When did you raise a beard?"

"When I was in the army, but they made me shave it off. The major didn't like it."

"I bet you didn't like that, did you?"

"Didn't like what?"

"Being told what to do."

Looking up swiftly, he caught an amused glimpse in the young woman's eyes. "Why have I got that reputation, I wonder? I thought I was a pretty agreeable fellow."

"Oh, I'm sure you are. If not, you've got Uncle Will fooled. He thinks you're quite a fellow."

A streak of guilt ran through Seth as it always did whenever Will Martin's approval of him was spoken. "He's a fine man, Mr. Martin. Got a good family."

The two sat there for some time, and soon David came to say, "Help me catch a fish, Seth."

"No, we can't catch these fish. Maybe there's a stream around here, and I could take you fishing later."

"Will you really?"

"If I can."

"I think there is a creek just outside of town. Grandfather Spencer was telling me about it. I always liked to fish when I was a little girl."

"Maybe we could all go," Seth said.

Immediately the children set up a clamor begging to go fishing. Seth had nothing particular to do, and soon the four of them were on their way out of town. Seth carried both children, Eve on his shoulders, and David on his back. The creek was not actually very far, nor was it very big, but soon they had their corks out, and within minutes Eve's cork disappeared with a firm *plunk*!

"You've got him! Bring him in, sweetheart!" Seth said. He and Sarah laughed as the girl struggled and finally landed a plump red-eared perch. Skillfully Seth took it off and placed it on a stringer, then said, "Another fifteen or twenty and we'll have enough for all of us to eat."

"I'm going to catch one, too. You wait and see!" David said.

For Seth Donovan it was a pleasure such as he had rarely known. The rigors of war that had followed the years of hard labor in the fields had left little time for moments such as this. Now the sun shone down brightly on the fiery red hair of Sarah MacNeal, and he said once, "Your hair's the same color as my mother's. It takes me back, Miss Sarah, to think about it."

Sarah ran her hand over her hair. "I hated it when I was little. The kids made fun of me and called me carrot top."

"I suppose every redhead has to put up with that, but it's beautiful now."

Sarah flushed and looked down at the running waters of the brook. She reached her hand down, and the water made a small fountain as it bubbled over the knuckles. After a moment she straightened up and said, "What about the rest of your family?"

"I don't have any. I had a brother, my only kin, but he was killed last year."

Sarah turned still as a statue. She had been looking down at Eve, who was watching her cork avidly, but now she turned to face the big man beside her. "I know something about that. I've lost people, too."

"Have you, now? I'm sorry to hear it."

Sarah found herself telling the story of how her father had been killed in an Indian raid, and then how Philip Baxter was another victim of Indian violence. She also spoke of her Grandfather Martin. Seth nodded, remembering his death, but said nothing, as he was afraid Sarah would stop talking. She spoke slowly at first, for she had buried it for a long time in her heart, but now she somehow found herself speaking more freely. There was kindness and gentleness in the eyes of the big man who sat beside her, and although she was a young woman who opened herself up easily to anyone, somehow the fact that he had lost his only brother made her more willing to speak. She sat there speaking softly, saying things that she had kept bottled up for a long time concerning the death of her father. The raw wound that the death of Philip Baxter had left was also evident to young Donovan.

"Do you still have the pain in you, Sarah?"

"Yes, you can't help that. I was looking at Grandmother the other day, and I realized that I'll lose her someday, too—maybe not too far off."

"That's the way life is," Seth said. "We don't have forever on this earth."

"No, but it's so hard when someone you love is suddenly snatched away, taken without a moment's notice."

"The young man, his name was Philip?"

"Yes. Philip Baxter."

"You loved him, did you?"

The answer did not come quickly. Sarah watched the water as it pearled over a branch that had dropped from the opposite side. She saw a group of silvery minnows schooling in the clear waters, all darting instantly at the same time. Finally she looked up and said, "You know, Seth, I'm not sure. I liked him greatly. We were such good friends. Out on the frontier there aren't many people, and those you get close to become very . . . very precious, I suppose you would say."

Sarah ceased speaking, and Seth sat there watching the children. Finally, he said, "I hope your grandmother lives a long time."

"Thank you, Seth. That's kind of you." She turned to him and smiled tremulously at first, then she said without thinking, "You don't have a family. Are you married?"

"No, not that."

"But you must have a sweetheart somewhere."

"No. I never found one that would put up with me."

"Well, I can see how that would be very difficult."

He blinked with surprise and then saw that she was smiling at him, teasing him a little bit. "That's right," he said. "I wouldn't ask any woman to put up with me."

The afternoon wore on, but finally Sarah said, "The children are getting tired."

"Well, we have enough fish for them to eat. I'll clean them, and maybe Mrs. Edwards will cook them for their supper. Would you like that, kids? To get to eat these fish?"

"They're slimy," Eve said. She shuddered and said, "No, I don't want to eat those nasty things!"

"I'll eat them!" David announced proudly. "I'll eat all of them."

"Good boy," Seth laughed. He picked the children up again and said, "Sarah, if you will carry those fish home, we'll have a supper fit for a king. And I'll bet you'll eat some, too, Eve, when you smell how good they are."

———

For two days Seth could make no decision, but finally he knew it must come. At eleven o'clock, after spending some time working with the gardener out of a lack of something to do, he had straightened up and his jaw was set with determination. *I've got to go see Denton,* he thought in his mind. *No way out of it.*

An hour later he was walking up to the steps of Edward Denton's home. When the housekeeper came and he announced his wish to see Denton, she said, "I'll tell the master you're here. You can wait here."

Stepping inside, Seth waited, his muscles tense. A moment later Edward Denton stepped out of a door down the hall followed by the maid. He came forward at once and said, "Step outside, Donovan."

"Yes, sir."

The two went outside and Edward Denton led the way around to the side of the house. There was a grape arbor there that sheltered them as they moved to the north side of it. "No one can hear us here. Now tell me why I haven't heard from you. I nearly had a heart attack when I saw you in my house the other night. Why didn't you report?"

Seth immediately related the difficulties in Boston. "There wasn't much else I could do, but one good thing about it, Mr. Denton—I'm in very close to the Martin family now. Shouldn't be any trouble to find out what we need to know."

"You must find those weapons!" Denton insisted.

"I'm working on it, but I can't make the man tell me, can I?"

"All right, all right. Get close to the family, but not too close, you understand?"

"What do you mean by that, Mr. Denton?"

"I mean your first job is to find out where those guns are. There's money in it for you, and besides, you owe it to the Crown."

"I'll do the best I can."

"You'd better! If you don't, we'll both be in trouble. Now get out of here! Leave word at The Brown Stag if you want to get word to me. It's too dangerous to have you coming here."

From a window upstairs Annabelle Denton was watching. She had seen Seth coming and was somewhat surprised. When her father had led him outside the house and they had taken up a position behind the grape arbor, she watched intently. "I wish I could hear them," she murmured. "There's something going on." Finally she saw Donovan move away and her father head toward the house. He was looking around carefully to see if he had been noticed. "He looks guilty," Annabelle said. "I'll have to find out what's going on with those two."

Under the Apple Trees

Eighteen

*B*y the end of the first week of October, fall weather had begun to envelop Williamsburg. The trees had turned to a riot of orange, red, and gold. Some of them had already begun to lose their leaves, which floated to the earth and settled down in a colorful carpet. There they would slowly disintegrate and form new earth. The old cycles repeated themselves always, and Amanda thought of her home in Watauga and knew that there, too, the seasons were changing.

Ever since Jacob had spoken to her after their visit to the Dentons, Amanda had been confused. She had seen something in Jacob's expression she had never noticed before. Somehow she knew there was something in his heart he had not expressed that night, and since that time he had been oddly withdrawn. She sensed something was going on in his heart that was causing him to struggle.

None of this did Amanda reveal to Sarah, but as the days passed, she would see Jacob looking at her from time to time when he thought she was not aware of his scrutiny. Often when this happened, he would hold her gaze for a while, as if trying to determine what was going on inside her heart. Amanda was puzzled by all of this and yet encouraged to think that he was more interested than his words implied, so she continued to keep her own silence.

On the eleventh day of the month she left the house one afternoon. It was her birthday, and they were celebrating both hers and that of Anne Martin in the evening, even though Anne's was not until the following day. She moved through the streets of Williamsburg and delighted in all the activity that went on. She passed a broom seller with a wicker basket stacked high with brooms. He was calling out, "Brooms! Brooms!" at the top of his lungs, and when he asked Amanda, "You want to buy a broom, lady?" she shook her head and he moved on disappointed. Farther on down the street, she passed by a farmer wearing his homespun jacket, and his wife wearing a man's felt hat, an apron, and a skirt.

Stopping to peer in at the blacksmith's shop, she watched the sparks that rose as the powerful smith beat an iron bar that was white hot. He wore a woolen cap, a checkered linen shirt, and a leather apron. Looking up, he grinned at her, exposing gaps between his teeth.

"Howdy, missy," he said. "Something for you?"

"No, I just like to watch people work."

The smith grinned even more broadly. "I'd rather watch 'em as do it myself. Come back anytime."

For nearly two hours Amanda wandered the streets encountering wagoners and purveyors of various items. At one corner she saw a chimney sweep with his long, sectioned broom slung over his shoulder. A boy, evidently his son, was with him, and both were covered from head to foot with so much black soot. The boy winked at her impudently. He was no more than fifteen but had a cheerful, impish expression.

Amanda laughed and nodded, then moved on down to the shop that sold vegetables. There she picked up a few things for the supper and then turned homeward. As she came out of the store, she was greeted by a most unusual person. A young man wearing an outfit that she had never seen the likes of.

"Well, what have we here? How are you today, my pretty lady?"

Amanda was not taken at all by the young man. He wore a bound, cocked hat with silver cords, a cambric neck cloth, and a fine, ruffled linen shirt. His vest was bound with silver lace, and he wore two watches with tasseled fobs descending below the skirts of the vest. His silk stockings had embroidered clocks or patterns from ankle to calf. But all of this finery was not the crowning glory of his strange attire. That honor belonged to his coat that was spotted like a leopard. It was a light color, and the spots were irregular, which gave him an odd look indeed. He swept his cocked hat off his head with his free hand, for he carried a cane in his other, and powder flew from his wig. His eyes were close together and his smile rather foolish. "Perhaps I might help you carry your parcels, miss?"

"No, thank you. I'm not going far," Amanda said.

"Oh, but I insist!"

The young man reached out and took hold of Amanda's parcel. She held on to it as tightly as she could, for she was frightened of the young man. He wore a sword on his left side, and the handle was gold and encrusted with jewels.

"Come now, don't be troublesome!" he said and smiled at her. He was so close she could smell the liquor on his breath and was troubled how to behave.

"Please, I don't need your help. Thank you very much," she said quickly and tugged at the package. But the young man refused to let it go. He stood there grinning and hanging on to the package.

"You are a pretty one! Come along, we'll go celebrate today with some drinks down at the finest inn in town."

Amanda was in a quandary. She did not want to make a scene, but people had stopped to glance sideways at her and the leopard-coated young man. She could not let the package go, and yet she could not free it from his grasp. Just at that moment a voice behind her said, "I think you may let the lady's parcel go, fellow."

Amanda turned quickly to see Jacob standing there. He was frowning at the fop, who still held on to her package. Taking a step closer, he said, "I must trouble you, sir, to take your hand off the package. Or do you need help to do that?"

The young man began to curse. His face grew red and he dropped his hold on Amanda's package, reaching for the hilt of his sword.

Quickly Jacob stepped forward, and in a movement so swift that Amanda was shocked by it, Jacob delivered a powerful right-hand blow right between the eyes of the young man. It drove him backward into the mud and filth of the street, and he lay there, his arms and legs thrashing feebly. He was practically unconscious and several people laughed at the scene.

"Come along, Amanda, unless you'd care to stay and watch me give him a proper thrashing."

"Oh no, Jacob," Amanda said quickly. "Let's leave before he gets up. He has a sword, you know."

"I know. I was thinking about ramming it down his throat, but I took pity on him."

Jacob offered his arm and Amanda quickly took it. "Let me carry your parcel," he said, and reaching over, he took it from her. They moved down the street and once Jacob looked back and laughed. "He's still floundering around like a fish out of water. I never saw such a silly-looking fellow."

"I'm glad you came along, Jacob," Amanda said with gratitude. "I don't know what I would have done if you hadn't."

"He wouldn't last long on the frontier, would he? The first Indian that came along would have him for that coat. Wasn't he a sight, though?" He laughed and Amanda joined in. "Yes, sir, I'd like to put him in the middle of a Cherokee war party and see what they'd make of him. They'd fry him on a spit, I think. They'd think he was some kind of strange monster with that spotted hide."

The two walked on down the street, and Jacob fell silent. When they approached the lane that led to the Spencer house, he slowed his pace. As they turned into the yard, he said, "Amanda, I need to talk to you."

"Why, of course, Jacob! What is it?"

"Not here. Privately." Jacob looked at the house, then shook his head. "Too many people in there. Come along, let's walk a bit more."

"All right, Jacob."

Amanda could not imagine what he would have to say, and yet her heart, for some reason, had begun beating faster. He walked on down the street, and somehow a silence fell upon him. From time to time she stole a glance at his face, which was far more serious than was his habit. Finally he turned down a street that had not been built up but was covered with fruit trees.

"This is where I played when I was a boy," he said. "I used to come and eat the apples. There's a bench over here. You can't see it." He led her through the maze of apple trees and finally reached up and pulled one off. "Not quite ripe yet, but they will be soon. I'm an expert, you know. I've eaten enough of Mr. Simpson's apples to know the good ones. It seems like a long time ago, though."

They reached the wooden bench, old and silvered with age, but he did not sit down. Instead, he glanced around and saw that they were secluded. Taking a deep breath, he turned to her and reached out and took her hands. "Amanda, I've been thinking ever since I talked to you the night of the Dentons' party."

"Yes, Jacob," Amanda whispered, as he seemed at a loss for words. "What is it?"

"Well, I've been thinking of the times we've had. How I first met you . . . and what's gone on since then."

"I think about that a lot, too, Jacob. If it hadn't been for you and your father and your family, I don't know what would have become of us. My mother and I needed help terribly." She did not put a fault to her father, for she was grateful that he had found the Lord before his death.

Jacob suddenly reached out and pulled Amanda close. For some time, he had been aware of the attraction this young woman had for him, and now as she lay soft in his arms, her nearness stirred the feelings he had had for a long time. Her hand came up and rested on his shoulder, and he pulled her closer. As he bent his head slowly, giving her time to reject him, he thought, *I love this girl. I wonder how long I've loved her.* She did not resist but came to him shyly with reserve. The kiss was sweet and pure as she herself was, and he released her and said quietly, "Amanda, I've thought about you constantly these last few days. You're the woman I'd like to spend my life with. Would you consider marrying me?"

Amanda stood stock-still. It was a question she had often dreamed of Jacob asking, but never really believed he ever would. Now, as she stood there in the circle of his arms, she felt a glow of happiness fill her heart. Overhead the skies were gray, but there was a joy in her such as she had never known. She nodded and a sweet smile touched her lips. "Yes, Jacob, I will."

He kissed her again, and then they stood there in each other's embrace. "It'll be quite a surprise for everyone," Jacob said.

"It was a surprise for me," Amanda said somewhat shyly. "I've loved you a long time, Jacob, but I didn't think you would ever care for me."

"I guess men are slower than women in that way." He laughed suddenly, saying, "Well, when we go back to Watauga, I'll have to ask your mother."

"Maybe I'll have to ask your father," Amanda said impishly. "He might not want me for a daughter-in-law."

The two walked blindly around the orchard, unaware of the late birds that sang in the trees, or of the white clouds that came scudding across the gray sky. The winds blew pleasantly, but they heard only the sounds of their own voices. Jacob found that he had not the words to say all that he felt, but it was a time neither would ever forget. Finally Jacob said, "Come along, we've got to break the news to the family."

"All right, Jacob. I wish Mother were here. I'll have to write her and tell her."

"Yes, and I'll have to write Pa, too. They'll both be glad, though."

"You won't want to live here in Williamsburg, will you?"

"No. Once a fellow has a taste of the openness of the Misty Mountains, he can never get over it, I suppose. Come on, let's go tell everyone."

A few days later was Annabelle Denton's birthday, and her party was an elaborate affair. Edward Denton and his wife, Phoebe, had spared no expense for decorating the house. The largest room in the house was the ballroom, second to none in private homes in Williamsburg. It was a large rectangular room with many gilded, mirror-backed sconces for light. The floor was an alabaster-colored marble, and the tables along the edge held cut-crystal punch bowls and cups and delectable-looking food.

As for the food itself, silver tureens of soup, and platters of cold lobster, beef, and cooked goose filled the room with their aroma. There were large bowls of oyster sauce, chestnut stuffing, spinach, and peach flummery filling other tables along with a selection of cheeses. Candied fruits, puffed pastries, jams and wafers of all sorts covered a dessert frame in the center of the dessert table.

The musicians had arrived early and had tuned up, and now the sound of fiddles, flutes, and a harpsichord filled the room as the Martins and the Spencers arrived. James and Esther Spencer led the way, followed by Will and Rebekah. Jacob and Amanda, Seth, and Sarah were also at the party.

As the small group entered the room, they were met by Thomas Denton. "Well, it's good to see you all!" He went around shaking hands. "Make yourself at home. Annabelle isn't down yet, but she will be soon, I'm certain." He moved over to Amanda and bowed, but when he straightened up, there was a pixyish look in his eye. "I understand my friend Jacob has beaten me out. Congratulations on your engagement."

"Thank you, Thomas," Amanda said. A slight color rose to her cheeks. She could not yet speak of her engagement without a warm feeling rising in her.

"Well, I'm put out with you, Jacob! Here I set myself to courting this beautiful young woman, and you defeat me by proposing marriage!" He punched at Jacob's arm with a closed fist, striking him lightly. "You old dog, you're going to do it, aren't you? Soon you'll be an old married man, and a few years from now, you'll have half a dozen little children hanging on to you."

"I hope so, Thomas," Jacob smiled. "That's what a man gets married for." He reached out and took Amanda's arm. "Beauty in a woman and lots of children. That's what a man needs. You'll find that out one day for yourself."

"Well, I'm claiming the first dance with your bride-to-be. Come along, Amanda."

Jacob surrendered Amanda, pleased that his best friend approved of his choice. He himself moved over to the side of the room and stood talking to some of the guests he had known for a long time. All of his old friends were here. They came by from time to time to congratulate him. One of them, Roger Macklin, winked and said, "I'm glad you're out of the way, Jacob."

"What do you mean by that, Roger?"

"Well, I've always thought that Annabelle was in love with you. She's turned me down a number of times, and other fellows, as well. Now that you're off the market, so to speak, I think some of the rest of us might have a chance."

"There's nothing to that, Roger, and I wish you well."

Even as Jacob was speaking, he heard one of the young women standing close say, "Here comes Annabelle."

Looking quickly toward the stairway, Jacob saw Annabelle descending. As he had expected, she had a new dress for the occasion. It was a light rose-colored dress made of silk. The sleeves hung loose and ended with lace ruffles, and a snug bodice with small white ribbons accented her figure. The overskirt was worn over large hoops edged with lace, and the petticoat was made of white silk with small roses embroidered on it. Her hair was done up in the latest fashion, and she was indeed beautiful, Jacob thought as she came into the room. She was stopped half a dozen times, but soon she came to stand before him.

"Are you going to ask me for my first dance, Jacob? I see your fiancée is already occupied." She nodded toward Amanda, who was standing beside Roger Macklin.

"Of course."

The musicians were already filling the ballroom with the music of a minuet as the two moved out on the floor. As they took hands to begin the dance, Annabelle said almost at once, "I was surprised when Thomas told me you were engaged to Amanda."

Jacob felt uncomfortable and could only say, "Yes, I'm very happy."

"You should have told me yourself," she smiled.

"I suppose so, but really it happened quite suddenly."

"Well, it's a very important matter for a young man when he chooses a bride. I hope you're certain. Quick decisions aren't usually good in cases like this."

Jacob stared at her, not knowing what to make of her words. He was somewhat startled when she suddenly stopped and raised her voice. "Stop the music! Stop the music!"

The musicians broke off their playing, and everyone turned to look at Annabelle. She was smiling now, but there was an odd look in her eyes, Jacob saw. *What's she going to do now?* he thought. Annabelle Denton was known for outlandish behavior, and apprehension grew in him as she caught everyone's attention.

"I have an announcement to make! May I have your attention!"

The room grew still, and Annabelle said, "Amanda, come over here, please!"

Amanda wanted to shrink away. She hated to be noticed in public like this. Furthermore, she was apprehensive of what Annabelle would say. There was no escape, however, so she slowly and reluctantly moved across the floor, coming at last to stand beside Jacob, her eyes riveted on Annabelle Denton.

"I want to say to all of you that I am very happy for this young couple. But I am also forced to say, in all honesty, that I can't believe I have let Jacob Spencer slip through my hands."

There was a shock that ran across the room at these words, for a young woman did not say such things in public. But this was Annabelle Denton, and she would say and do exactly what she wished.

Annabelle was aware that every eye was upon her, and she well understood that Amanda made a poor showing next to her. Amanda's dress was the same faded blue one she had worn before, and in contrast to Annabelle's finery, she looked rather dowdy.

Annabelle was gloating at being the center of attention, and even enjoyed seeing how uncomfortable Amanda was. She had planned all this out, and now she said, "I am sure that Amanda won't mind my getting a birthday kiss from my former fiancé. After all, we were engaged at one time."

Amanda stood there in total shock. Jacob had never told her about being engaged! She watched numbly, expecting Annabelle to kiss Jacob on the cheek. Instead she reached up, pulled his head down, and kissed him firmly on the lips, holding him there for what seemed like an eternity.

Practically everyone in the room was shocked by what was taking place. Annabelle's parents stared at her. "What is that girl doing?" Edward mumbled. "She's making a spectacle of herself."

Others were even less kind. Roger Macklin said, "Well, she's going to do everything she can to see that he doesn't get away."

Amanda did not even wait for Annabelle to release Jacob. She turned and walked blindly away. She was followed at once by Will and Rebekah, and Sarah said, "Come on, Seth, let's get out of this place!"

As for Jacob himself, he suddenly realized he had been caught in a trap he had not even imagined. He knew that Annabelle was capable of outrageous things, but this surpassed everything. He finally put his hands on her shoulders and pulled his head away. "Annabelle, what are you doing?" he whispered, but everyone close could hear.

"Why, I'm just getting a kiss from my former fiancé. Nothing wrong with that, is there, Jacob?"

Disgusted and humiliated by the scene, Jacob looked around. He saw impudent grins on some faces, frowns of disapproval on others, and then his eyes came back to Annabelle's. He did not speak, but he saw she had accomplished her purpose. She had humiliated Amanda. Without another word he turned and left the room, aware of the babble of voices that had arisen as he left.

Thomas went at once to Annabelle, took her by the arm, and practically dragged her off the floor.

"You're hurting me, Thomas!" she said. "Let me go!"

"What do you think you're doing?" he demanded as soon as they were out of the hearing of the rest of the guests.

"Well, what have I done? I just told the truth."

"You were never engaged to Jacob."

"Why, of course I was. He asked me, and I told him I'd never marry any man but him."

Thomas laughed harshly. "And how many others have you told that to?"

"But I really meant it with Jacob. The others I just entertained myself with."

"You made him look foolish in front of the young woman he loves, and you branded yourself as a silly girl with no judgment whatsoever!"

"I assumed that Jacob had told Amanda about us."

"You didn't assume anything of the sort! You're just a spoiled brat, and you've taken this way to hurt a fine man and a fine girl!"

Annabelle watched Thomas whirl and leave her standing there. She was not overly concerned, for although she knew she had behaved badly, she had always found a way to reconcile with her parents and brother. There would be a bad scene with her parents, she knew, but a smile touched her lips. "I'm going to get Jacob no matter what I have to do. If I've broken them up this time, that will give me a chance at him."

She stood there already planning what she would do when she next met Jacob. She would be filled with remorse. She would cry and weep and throw herself into his arms, begging for his forgiveness. "He'll believe me. He'll soon forget that dowdy little frump from the wilderness."

———————

By the time Jacob got outside, the family had gone. He was totally shaken by what had taken place at the birthday party. "I've got to talk to Amanda," he said, "but not with everybody around. I'll wait until everybody goes to bed. I know she's hurt, but I can explain it to her."

For hours he walked the streets, and when he arrived back at the house, he went at once to the room Amanda shared with Sarah. He knocked lightly and called her name. The door opened and Amanda stood there. "What do you want, Jacob?" she asked, her voice unsteady.

"Come downstairs. I've got to talk to you, Amanda."

"It's late. We'll talk in the morning."

"No. Now!" He insisted so strongly that Amanda finally agreed. "You go on down. I'll get dressed and come down."

"All right, I'll wait for you." He left the top floor and went down the stairs and lit a candle in the study. He paced the floor until finally he heard the sound of soft footsteps and turned and went at once to Amanda. "Amanda," he said, "I'm so sorry. I wouldn't have had that happen for anything."

Amanda had wept when she had finally gotten alone. Sarah had tried to comfort her, but still her face was drawn. "Why didn't you tell me that you had been engaged to Annabelle?"

"I wasn't engaged to her, not really."

"What is that supposed to mean?"

"Well, I did ask her to marry me once, and she said, 'I'll marry no man but you.'"

"That's an engagement," Amanda said quietly. Her heart was breaking, but with great effort she kept her face still.

"I thought so, too," Jacob nodded, "until I found out she had said the same thing to another man. As a matter of fact, I heard her say it to him. We had quite a brawl about that. That's when I left Williamsburg and came to live with my father in Watauga."

"Do you still care for her, Jacob?"

"Care for her? Why, Amanda, how can you ask such a thing?"

"You wanted to marry her once. You must have loved her then."

Jacob was totally miserable. He put his hands behind his back, clenched them, and shook his head. "I am not very old now, Amanda, but I was much younger then. She was beautiful and everyone admired her. All the young men were chasing after her. I just joined the crew. I didn't know anything about women." His face suddenly drew up into a scowl, and he said, "I still don't know much about women! I should have told you all this. I see that now. I'm sorry."

"I can't quite believe you, Jacob. The first time I heard her name mentioned was at home, and I saw something come into your face then. Every time she's mentioned you have an odd look."

"There's nothing to that," he said, shaking his head.

Amanda stood very still. She had been brought down from a happiness she had never known to a misery she could not define. It filled her whole heart now, and she forced herself to say, "I can't be engaged to you now."

"Why not?"

"You've got to figure out whom you love, Jacob. You don't know right now. It's obvious that you've been thinking of Annabelle ever since you left Watauga. You weren't honest enough to tell yourself, and you certainly didn't tell me."

"Amanda—"

"I won't talk about it anymore, Jacob. Good night."

"Amanda, don't leave," Jacob pleaded, but she turned and was gone. As soon as she was out of the room, Jacob struck out with his fist as if he were in a physical fight. But this was not physical. He knew somehow that he had hurt the purest, sweetest young woman he had ever known, and a shroud of dark despair settled on him. "I've got to do something to show her I don't care for Annabelle," he muttered, and then her words came back to him: *"You always have an odd expression when her name is mentioned."* He was troubled by the thought. *Do I really care for Annabelle? Is there anything left of that first love?*

In all honesty Jacob Spencer could not say. He was confused, and he knew that upstairs Amanda was crushed and bitter over what he had exposed her to in front of all those people. He went to his room and found Seth Donovan sitting at the table reading a book. Seth looked and opened his mouth to ask a question, but when he saw the look on Jacob's face, he closed it again.

Jacob was grateful for the big man's tact. Others might have plunged into a long conversation, and the last thing Jacob Spencer wanted to do was to talk about the awful evening that he had just endured.

Plots and Plans

Nineteen

Anne Martin and her daughter-in-law, Rebekah, had been joined by Sarah MacNeal in the oversized kitchen that dominated the first floor of the Spencer home. The three women had asked permission from Esther to come and do the cooking for the day, since the hired cook was off due to a death in her family. Now the three gathered and were busy discussing what to make for the day. A fire had been built up in the enormous chimney, and Anne said, "I'm hungry for some pease porridge. I think I'll make some of that."

"All right. I'll make a pilgrim cake," Rebekah said.

Sarah quickly added, "And I want to make some hasty pudding. It'll be good for breakfast."

The three of them soon were engaged in their activities. Sarah filled a pewter pot with water, added some salt to it, and then brought it to a boil over the fire. She slowly poured in some yellow cornmeal and stirred it all the while. When the mix was thick enough so a spoon could stand up in it, she ladled it out into three bowls. She dropped some butter into each portion, then sprinkled on ground nutmeg and some molasses.

"Here, let's eat it while it's hot. I do love hasty pudding," Sarah said. The three women sat down and all three began eating.

Rebekah tasted the concoction and then exclaimed, "This is wonderful, Sarah!"

"Anybody can make hasty pudding."

Rebekah took another bite after blowing on it and then said, "How do you think Amanda's doing after that awful night at Annabelle's party?"

"She doesn't say much," Sarah replied, "but I can tell she's hurt.

It's been two weeks, but she's trying to do her best."

"I think Jacob's troubled, also," Rebekah nodded and took a sip of tea.

"Well, he ought to be!" Sarah exclaimed. "I can't believe what he did to Amanda and how much he's hurt her! I love my stepbrother, but I would like to give him a thrashing sometimes."

Anne Martin said quietly, "You must be patient, Sarah, and pray that God will work it out."

"That's right. Sometimes God wants to chastise His children," Rebekah said.

Sarah, however, was not to be mollified. "Maybe He wants me to do the thrashing! I'd be glad to take the job on if God would give me His permission."

Anne laughed aloud at that. "I don't think you had better start chastising God's children until you are certain of that." She got up and said, "Now I'm going to make some pease porridge. You young women better pay attention. I got this recipe from my grandmother."

The three continued talking while Anne fixed the pease porridge. She took a quart of green peas and put them in a quart of water. She added a little bundle of dried mint, a little fat, and then began boiling it. Soon it began bubbling, and after a time, she put in some beaten pepper and a piece of butter rolled in flour.

"I'm going to let this boil for a while, then I'll add two quarts of milk. Take out the mint, and it will be ready to serve."

"Will loves pease porridge, but he loves pilgrim cake, too. Let's make that while we're waiting."

Pilgrim cake was relatively simple to make. Rebekah rubbed two spoonfuls of butter into a quart of flour and wet the dough with cold water. When it was done, she raked open a place in the hottest part of the hearth, then rolled out the dough into a cake an inch thick. She floured it well on both sides and then placed it on the hot ashes. Then she covered it with more hot ashes and then with coals. "Now when it's done, we'll wipe off that flour and it'll be the best pilgrim cake you ever had!"

"Did I hear somebody mention pilgrim cake?" Will Martin entered the room and sniffed the air. "It smells good," he said.

"Well, sit down and have some hasty pudding. I've got a little left."

Right willingly Will sat down, and after noticing the pensive look on his face, Anne said, "Sarah, why don't you take Amanda to town and cheer her up. She needs to get out of the house more."

"All right. I think that's a good idea. I'll help with the cooking when I get back. Maybe Amanda will help, too."

"Go on and have a good time."

As soon as Sarah was out of the room, Rebekah turned to Will. "Something's wrong with you, Will. You didn't say a word last night."

"That's right, son. You don't cover your feelings very well." Anne Martin smiled, reached over, and put her hand on Will's. "What's the matter?"

Will stared down at his plate for a moment, then looked up, a troubled expression on his face. "I've heard from Peter Jennings in Boston, my friend there. They've asked me to see if I could help them."

"What sort of help?" Rebekah inquired.

"They're ready to ship more arms here to Williamsburg. They came in on a large ship from England, all under cover, of course."

"Don't they have someone here that can do that?" Anne asked.

"They did have, but he was apprehended by the British."

"What happened to him?" Rebekah asked quickly.

"Well, he was hanged as a spy." Will shook his head. "I know it's dangerous, but somehow I think we've got to help. I feel like we have to go on with the thing that Father started."

"I think you're right, son," Anne said.

Rebekah thought for a moment, and then she said, "Why don't you ask Seth to help you? He was such a big help last time, and I'm sure he'd be willing."

"All right, I think I will. I'll go talk to him as soon as I finish breakfast."

Thirty minutes later Will found Seth out in the garden. He seemed to be doing nothing, and Will asked, "Are you thinking of doing a little gardening, Seth?"

"I used to do some when I was a boy growing up at home. My mother loved gardening. I can still see her there, red hair shining like fire in the sunshine, pulling peas, grubbing potatoes. She just loved to be out in it. So do I."

"Never was much of a gardener myself. I like what comes out of it, though." Will hesitated and the two men spoke generally for a while, and then suddenly Will said, "Seth, I need some help."

Instantly Seth Donovan turned to look at him. "It must be something about the arms."

"That's right." Will related how he had been asked to distribute some muskets and other arms. Finally he said ruefully, "I hate to ask you for help again. It's dangerous."

"That doesn't matter. I'd be glad to help."

Relief washed across Will Martin's face. "Well, that's good to hear." Leaning forward, he said, "What we'll do is oversee the transfer of the arms to an abandoned farm. It's a couple of miles out of town. Shouldn't be too difficult."

"You can count on me."

"Thanks, Seth. I knew you wouldn't let me down."

He turned and left immediately, and Seth moved slowly along the garden rows. *Here I go again,* he thought. *This family's been so good to me, and now I'm going to betray them.* He thought again of Isaac, as he often did, but somehow the pain was not as sharp, and the urgency for revenge seemed to have waned. "I wish I was out of this," he said aloud. A mockingbird lit on a branch above his head and flashed the white part of his feathers. "I wish I didn't have any more troubles," Seth murmured. "But I'll get out of this somehow or other. Then I'll never betray a friend again."

———

There was no moon, and the stars were almost all hidden except for a few that beamed feebly over The Brown Stag. Seth paused outside and wondered if Edward Denton would be there. He had sent word through the servant whom he had been instructed to use and hoped that Denton had gotten the message. He moved inside and took a seat in the corner. When the innkeeper came, he refused food but allowed the bulky man to bring him a cup of tea. He sipped it slowly and was only half finished when Edward Denton came inside. He spotted Seth and came at once and sat down. Without preamble, he demanded, "What's so urgent? Do you have news?"

"Yes. There's going to be a shipment of arms to a house somewhere out in the country. I don't know where," he said. "Will Martin hasn't told me yet."

The two spoke in normal voices, for the inn was almost empty.

Only two or three other customers were there. Over to their left, a man wearing a cloak pulled across his shoulders and a floppy black hat pulled down over his face seemed to be dozing. Probably drunk, they both decided.

Finally Denton nodded with satisfaction. "That's what I've been waiting for. Come along, I want you to meet some of my men who will be in on the action."

As soon as the two men left, the man with the floppy hat sat up straight. A scar twisted his face, for it was none other than Simeon Fulton. He had come to The Brown Stag several times while plotting his revenge against Will Martin. Now his dark eyes gleamed, and he muttered, "Well, that's good fortune. I'll not only put the quietus on the man that gave me this scar, but I'll take those guns I should have had the last time." He stood to his feet and moved over toward Dutch Hartog, the innkeeper. "Another tankard of ale. Mighty good ale you serve, innkeeper."

Gratified, Hartog filled the tankard. "On the house," he said. "Glad you like it."

Fulton drained half of the pale yellow ale, and then said, "Who was that fellow there? I thought I knew him, the one who just left." Actually Fulton recognized Seth instantly, but he didn't know the other man.

"I don't know the big fellow, but the other man's Edward Denton. Prominent man in town."

"Is he, now? He looks familiar to me."

"Pretty well-known fellow. Lots of money."

"Where does he live?"

Hartog thought it was strange, but he told the man with the terrible scar how to find Denton's house.

"I'm obliged to you." Fulton drained the rest of the ale, put some money on the counter, and then left. When he was outside he walked slowly back toward his room. "Now I know as much as I need to know. A few good men, one little action, and I'll put Mr. Will Martin and Seth Donovan where they belong, pushing up flowers!"

A Man-to-Man Talk

Twenty

*E*sther Spencer leaned back in her walnut rocking chair and looked across the room to where her husband was half dozing. He was sitting in his favorite chair with a book open in his lap, but he had not moved for several minutes. She smiled as she saw him nodding. *He's about as tired as I am,* she thought. *We're not used to all this company. It's a little bit hard on old folks.*

As if he had heard her thoughts, James Spencer's head snapped up, and he gazed at her with confusion in his mild blue eyes. "Must have dropped off to sleep," he admitted. He rubbed his eyes and stretched luxuriously in the chair, then looked around the sitting room. "What's that I hear?"

"I don't hear anything."

James grinned at her. "I think that's what I hear—nothing. Hard to take silence. We've had so much racket around here in the past few weeks." He closed the book and got up and replaced it on the shelf, then turned and came to stand beside her. Looking down, he said, "I'm afraid all this excitement may have been a bit much for you, Esther."

"Nonsense!" Reaching up, she took his hand and held it. It was thin now, and she suddenly remembered when it had been as strong and muscular as that of his grandson, Jacob. She said nothing of this, however, for she knew that age had touched her as well. "I've enjoyed every minute of it."

"Have you? Well, that's all right, then." He squeezed her hand and walked over to the window and stared out. "Don't those children ever get tired? Look at them out there playing and screaming like young Indians."

"They're healthy, aren't they?"

"I can't keep up with them. They're too much for me." He remained where he was watching them, and finally, without turning to look at her, he remarked in what he considered an innocent tone, "I suppose Jacob hasn't said anything to you."

"You mean about Amanda?"

"Yes, or about Annabelle." He considered her for a moment, then said, "I can't make him out. What do you think of it?"

Several weeks had passed since Annabelle's birthday party, and during that time there had been an armed truce, it seemed, between Jacob and Amanda. No one had talked with Jacob about it, although Esther suspected that Sarah had gotten something out of Amanda. She picked up her embroidery hoop and peered down at the intricate design. As she pushed the needle through, she shook her head. "I'm concerned about Jacob, but at least I know he hasn't gone to see Annabelle."

"No, and I think that's a good thing. That girl's too flighty. She won't do."

"Men are never put off by flighty girls." A smile touched Esther Spencer's lips, and she said mildly, "I remember you and that McCartney girl."

"Amy McCartney?" A shocked look seemed to creep across James' face. "Why, I haven't thought about her in forty years!"

"You thought about her a lot once. As a matter of fact, I think you were about ready to go crazy out when she turned you down."

"I think your memory is overactive. I don't remember anything like that."

"You've always had a selective memory, James, or a selective forgettery, I might say. But you were just as foolish over Amy McCartney when you were Jacob's age as he is over this Denton girl."

Snorting impatiently, James shook his head. "How is it you can always remember things that never happened?" Anxious to change the subject, he said, "I've been thinking about selling that thirty acres over on the—"

"Don't change the subject, James! We're talking about our grandson. I don't want to talk about buying or selling land."

"Well, what about him, then? It's a little bit out of our hands, isn't it, Esther? I mean we can't tell the boy not to see her."

"No, I don't think we could do that, but something has occurred to me." Pulling the scarlet thread through the material, Esther looked up and said, "Jacob's birthday is next week."

"Is it? Seems like there's been a lot of birthday parties, but that's right, isn't it?"

"Yes. And I've been thinking that maybe we could give Jacob a big party."

"I think it's a great idea. How about if I go down and talk to Jacob about it? He was in the library the last time I looked."

"You go do that and be nice."

"I'm always nice." He walked over, leaned down, and kissed her on the cheek. "You're a smart woman, Esther Spencer, and the smartest thing I ever did was to marry you."

Leaving the room, James went at once to the library, where he found Jacob tilted back in a chair, his feet up on a table.

"Get your feet off that table, Jacob! Do you know what that cost?"

"Sorry, Grandfather. It's just that I can seem to read better with my feet up."

"You're trying to tell me your brains are all in your feet?" James grinned. He sat down across from Jacob and asked, "What are you reading?"

"A book called *Gulliver's Travels* by a fellow named Jonathan Swift."

"Oh yes, I've heard about that. Kind of a fantasy, isn't it?"

"Yes. He was a pretty bitter man, this fellow. Didn't believe in government, or family, or anything else apparently. And the writer was a minister of the Anglican church."

"I wouldn't waste my time on that sort of thing."

"I think you're right. It's interesting but pretty depressing. He sees the worst of everything and everybody."

"I've been talking to your grandmother. She thinks we ought to have a big party to celebrate your birthday."

"Oh, that's too much trouble. I'm too old for birthday parties."

"You are? Well, I'm not. I'd like to have one every year. Cake, good cooking. You know your grandmother's plum cakes, what they taste like."

"I know, but I'm not really in the mood for it."

"Oh, I think you'll have to do it. Esther's mind is made up. Anyway, it'll be something for you young folks to do. You don't need to lock yourself up in this library. You haven't gone out this week, have you?"

"Not much. Just catching up on my reading."

Something evasive in his grandson's tone caught at James Spencer. He leaned back in his chair and said nothing for a moment. Finally he let his eyes run around the leather covers of the books on the shelves, and a thought came to him. "We've had quite a few talks in this room, haven't we?"

"Yes, we have. We'd have a talk," Jacob grinned, "and then we'd go outside and you'd whip me. I often wondered why you didn't do the whipping here."

"Didn't want to pollute the library. No sense having a lot of screaming going on in a nice room like this."

"I never screamed when you whipped me!" Jacob protested.

"That's right, you never did. Maybe I didn't whip you hard enough."

"You did very well, Grandfather," Jacob said. "I think I still have a few scars from some of those whippings."

"Well, I hope you remember more about our enjoyable times together than getting punished."

"Of course. I was just teasing." Jacob closed the book, put it on the table, leaned forward, and locked his fingers together. Then he, too, let his eyes gaze around the room and said finally, "It seems like a hundred years ago, but I remember our talks very well. Not all of them were when I was in trouble. Sometimes it was just talk about other things. I enjoyed those talks, I think, more than anything else."

"So did I, and I'm glad to hear that you did. You were a good boy growing up, Jacob. I don't think there were as many whippings as you remember. But there were lots of talks. I remember in the winter we'd build a fire over there and put chestnuts on the hearth. As they roasted we would crack them and eat them and talk our heads off. One night I remember we got so excited we stayed up till nearly two o'clock. Your grandmother came down and scolded us both. I felt like the one who had gotten a whipping that night."

Jacob laughed softly. "I remember that. You were in hot water all right, but I don't expect you got more than a little lecture. Grandmother's not capable of whipping anybody."

"I'm surprised you'd say that. You don't remember about her tulips?"

Jacob's eyes flew open. "I do remember that!" he exclaimed. "It's the only time she ever laid her hand on me."

"I think she shocked herself. I know she shocked me. She was always the one who stood between me and you when there was trouble."

Jacob's mind went back to that day. "I deserved it," he said. "I made myself a new slingshot, and the best targets I could find were Grandmother's tulips. By the time she caught me I'd shot most of them to ribbons." He laughed and said, "I remember thinking when she came up, *It's a good thing Grandfather didn't catch me doing this. He would have whipped me, but Grandmother never will!*"

"What'd she do, boy?"

"Marched me out to the peach tree and made me peel off a big switch. I tried her on a little one and she just scoffed. Finally I got one big enough to suit her and trimmed it with my pocket knife. I still didn't think she'd do it, though."

"I'd like to have seen that!"

"Well, she grabbed me by one arm and took that switch in the other, then I heard a whooshing sound, and then it felt like my legs were on fire. She began flailing me, and I began screaming and hollering, but none of it did any good."

Jacob suddenly stopped smiling. His face grew serious, and he said, "You know, Grandfather, I learned something from that. It didn't always stay with me, or at least I didn't always live with it."

"What was that, Jacob?"

"I was trying to get away from Grandmother and I couldn't. She had all the room in the world to swing that big switch. She could get a good swing at it, and it would whistle through the air and whack me on the legs. Well, I was trying to get away, and in my confusion I turned toward her and ran into her. I grabbed her around the legs and held on to her and pressed my face against her. I began crying, 'I love you, Grandmother! I love you, Grandmother!' And that was when I made my big discovery."

"What was that?" James asked, fascinated with this part of the old tale.

"I discovered that the closer I got to Grandmother, the less room she had to swing that switch. All she could do was kind of pat me with it, so I kept telling her I loved her, and she kept tapping me, and finally she gave up. Finally she threw it down. She was crying and she held me. I remember she had tears running down her cheeks, and she said, 'I love you, too, Jacob, more than I love life.' "

James Spencer was silent. "That's a good story, son."

"Well, I got something out of it. I came to see it later during a sermon I heard when the preacher said, 'Kiss the Son lest he be angry.' And I learned that if you disobey God and displease Him, you shouldn't run away from Him. You should run *to* Him, and throw your arms around Him, and tell Him you love Him. And then He doesn't have to chastise you."

James Spencer was thunderstruck. He had never heard such profound words from his grandson before, and he studied him carefully. "That's good, Jacob. I wish all of us were able to put that into practice."

"Well, I didn't always put it into practice, but I know it's true. So now I guess the thing for me to do is to go to God and tell Him I'm sorry."

"You're talking now about this business with Amanda?"

"Yes, I think I've wronged her greatly. It was just carelessness, stupidity, really, on my part, but she's very hurt."

"Well, I think she is. But it's not too late."

"Grandfather, I just can't seem to sort out my feelings. I love Amanda, but . . . I feel *something* for Annabelle."

"What is it that you like about Amanda, Jacob?"

"Why, I enjoy being with her. I like talking things over with her, doing things with her. I always have, but lately I've noticed I've enjoyed it even more."

"What about Annabelle?"

Jacob bit his lip. "Well, she's always been a lot of fun, and she's the most beautiful girl I've ever seen. She'd make any man proud."

"I'm not talking about any man, I'm talking about you. Now, Jacob, who loves you the most?"

Jacob did not hesitate. "Amanda. She cares more about what happens to me than what happens to her. She's always been that way."

"Well, I think you'd be better off with someone like that than someone who's just fun. Fun only lasts for a while and then life sets in. The most important thing, Jacob, is to choose someone who will stay by your side through the rough times as well as the good times. And choose someone who you can share your faith with. Do you talk much about the Lord with Annabelle?"

"Not at all."

James shrugged his shoulders. "The most important thing in life is God, and if two people can't talk about God, they don't have much of a foundation. Someday the fun will be all gone. You can't live on a dance floor, or going to parties, or having a good time. There's poverty, hard times, the difficulty of having children, sometimes a war comes along. All kinds of difficult things happen, and when those things happen, you want a woman by your side who will never leave you."

Jacob was absolutely still for a moment, and then he looked up with shock and surprise written across his face. "I've been so stupid, Grandfather! How could I even think of choosing Annabelle over Amanda? I ought to be tarred and feathered."

"Well, not quite that bad, but I have to agree you've been stupid. Or unthoughtful at least."

"Well, what do I have to do?"

"I think you have to give Amanda some time, and I think you have to pray about how you can act with her and win her back if it's God's will."

Jacob nodded slowly. "That's where I went wrong in the first place, not praying about what to do."

"Well, God's always ready to listen. It's us weak folks who don't seek Him with all of our heart that get into trouble." He rose to his feet and said, "Pray about it, boy, and know that your grandmother and I are praying with you. And when two or three are gathered together, it'll be done."

As soon as his grandfather left the room, Jacob sat down. Somehow he felt that he had been given a new insight, a new way of thinking, and he knew that his grandfather had brought him a word from the Lord. He knelt down beside the library table, pressed his face against his forearm, and began to pray, "Oh, God, give me wisdom. . . ."

———

"There's a man to see you, Mr. Denton."

"What sort of a man? Who'd be calling at this hour?" Edward Denton looked up from his desk with surprise at the butler.

"I don't know his name, but he looks mighty bad."

"What do you mean 'looks bad'?"

"Well, he's got his hat pulled down over his face, but he's all scarred up, and the side of his face is twisted. You want me to tell him to go on his way, Mr. Denton?"

"Yes, I don't know anyone like that."

Plato, the butler, turned to leave. "All he said was to tell you something about Seth and how the guns gonna get delivered to Williamsburg."

"Wait a minute! He said what?" Denton listened as Plato repeated the words, then a shock ran through him. "Wait a minute. Show him in. I will see him."

"Yes, sir. I'll do that, but he don't look good to me."

"Never mind what he looks like to you. Show him in."

Edward Denton threw his quill down and stood beside his desk. He heard the sound of footfalls, then the door opened. The man had removed his floppy hat, revealing a face that was handsome enough on the left side but terribly twisted on the right. It was obviously a recent thing, for the scars had not fully healed. The right side of his mouth was twisted up, and somehow the scar on his cheek had pulled his eye down so that he seemed to be leering in a sinister fashion.

"My name is Simeon Fulton. You're Mr. Denton, I assume."

"Yes, what's your business, Mr. Fulton?"

"The same as yours, I would think," Simeon said coolly. He took off his cloak and tossed it on a chair and then tossed his hat on top of it. "We have an interest in arms, and I have some information to give you."

"I don't know what you're talking about."

"Oh, I think you do. Don't worry, I'm not an agent for the rebels. My interest is with King George and England, the same as yours, sir."

"Do you have any identification? Who sent you to me?"

"My identification is this. I know that there's a shipment of guns arriving to be taken to a house just outside of town. I also know that Seth Donovan is your agent, and you are trusting him to be sure to give you all the information."

Denton paused. "That's right," he said. If the man knew this much, then certainly he would have turned him into the authorities already. "What's your interest in this?"

"I have no loyalties to anyone but those who pay me the most. If these guns can be taken, it will achieve two things. First, they will not be in the hands of Washington's soldiers. Secondly, the British would be most happy to buy them back. I understand they're first-class weapons."

Edward Denton hesitated. "You've made a mistake, sir. You can't prove I'm involved in any of this."

"I can prove to you that your agent is not reliable."

"Donovan? Impossible!"

"Did you know, Mr. Denton, that when the arms were delivered to the dock at Boston, my men and I were there to take them for the Crown, and it was Seth Donovan who broke up our raid?"

"You must be mistaken."

Anger flashed in the dark eyes of Simeon Fulton. He reached up and touched the twisted scar on his face. "That's not likely, since it was Donovan who gave me this scar. I was a nice-looking fellow before this happened. What woman would look at me now?"

Edward Denton hesitated. "Sit down, Fulton. I want to hear more about this."

For over thirty minutes the two sat there talking, and finally Denton knew the man spoke the truth. He made a quick decision and said firmly, "I'll hire you, Fulton, as a safeguard."

"And when we get the armaments back?"

"The profit will be yours. I'm not doing this for money. I'm doing it for my country, but I need your help."

"I think you do. Seth Donovan and Will Martin deserve what they get, and I must warn you, I've got no good feelings for either of them."

"Don't be an idiot. I'm interested in just the arms. If you shoot them and are taken, you will hang for it."

Fulton thought, *Why, the man's foolish! Doesn't he know I'll hang if they catch me with just the guns?* But he said smoothly, "Perhaps you're right. We'll take the guns and let them go their own way."

Fulton got to his feet, put on his cloak, and pulled his hat down over his face. "We're agreed, then? As soon as Donovan tells you where the guns are, you pass the information along to me. I'll be staying at The Brown Stag."

"Very well, Fulton. I don't think it will be long. Donovan said it would be this week probably. In the meantime, I think you might follow Donovan. He might give something away. He may know where the guns are already. In that case, we could go get them now."

"I'll follow him. I'll be a shadow to him. You may be sure of that."

For a long time Edward Denton stood watching the door that closed behind Fulton, then went and sat down heavily. He was confused by this change of events, but he knew he had to do what he could to keep the rebels from getting the armaments. He couldn't shake the feeling, however, that he had just made a deal with the devil.

Jacob's Choice

Twenty-One

Amanda, are you awake?"

As a matter of fact, Amanda had been awake for some time. She had awakened when the first soft birdcalls began drifting through the window. It was cold and she had snuggled down into the feather bed under the heavy comforters. She had lain there remembering how at times she had shivered on a shuck mattress with a thin blanket over her growing up as a girl. Blankets, comforters, and feather beds had been luxuries beyond her wildest dreams. Now, however, she pulled the comforter down and turned to look at Sarah, who was blinking at her owlishly.

"Yes, I'm awake." She hesitated for a moment, then said, "I suppose we ought to get up and help prepare for the party."

Snuggling down into the warm comforter, Sarah said lazily, "No, Jacob ought to do it himself."

"Now, Sarah," Amanda pleaded, "we ought to all pitch in and help him celebrate. You're not still mad at him for what happened at Annabelle's party, are you?"

"Mad at him? I'd like to pinch his head off!"

"You don't mean that, Sarah."

"Don't I? Just give me a chance!" Sarah pulled the cover back and sat straight up in bed. "I'm surprised you're taking it like you are!"

"Well, don't be mad at him for my sake. You know the Bible says not to take up the offenses of another."

"I never read that."

"Well, I can't remember the verse, but I'll look it up and give it to you. Anyway, he's your brother."

"My stepbrother!" Sarah said peevishly. She ran her fingers through her hair and exclaimed, "I'll never get these tangles out! I think I'll cut it all off!"

The idea of that made Amanda laugh. "Don't be silly! You'd look ridiculous."

"I might look ridiculous, but I wouldn't have to spend half my life washing and fixing my hair. Yours is nice and straight. You don't have to worry about it."

Now Amanda sat up and threw the covers back. She stepped out onto the mat that covered the pine floor and quickly reached for the woolen robe Esther Spencer had given her. Slipping into it, she said, "I've always wanted curly hair. I guess we always want to be something we're not."

"Seth told me he likes my hair," Sarah said. She could not bring herself to get out on the floor. "Don't you think he's a gorgeous man?"

"He's handsome all right. Do you like him?"

Sarah shrugged. "He's all right for a foreigner."

"He's not a foreigner; he's Scottish!"

"Well, that's foreign."

"No, it's not. Most of us came from England or Scotland or Ireland, or somewhere in that part of the world. He just got here a little later than the rest of us."

"He is nice looking. I never saw such hair! He looks like a lion, and he's so big! It makes me feel almost like a little girl."

"You've been spending a lot of time with him. What does he talk about?"

"Oh, we talk about lots of things," Sarah said. She jumped up and began struggling into her clothes and went over and washed her face, blowing and sputtering over the cold water. "I wish we had hot water, but it's too much trouble to heat it in the fireplace and bring it up here. I'm going to take a bath before the party."

"I'd like to do that, too."

"Good. It'll take all morning. Let Jacob carry the hot water up."

"Oh, we couldn't ask him to do that. I wouldn't want him to. It wouldn't seem decent somehow."

"What do you mean decent?"

"I mean his carrying our bath water."

Sarah burst out laughing. "You are too modest, Amanda! What

difference does it make who carries the water?"

"Oh, I don't know. I'm just being silly, I guess."

The two girls talked and giggled together as they washed their faces, combed their hair, and dressed. Amanda said, "You'll be the prettiest girl at the party. It's such a beautiful dress your pa gave you the money for."

"Oh, it's all right, I suppose. But your dress is nice, too."

"That old thing? I've worn it every time I've been out, but I'm not complaining. I'm just glad I got to come."

Finally the two girls were dressed, and as they were preparing to go downstairs, a knock came at the door. When Amanda went over and opened it, she found Esther standing there, and Anne Martin was right behind her. They were trying to hide something, and Esther Spencer said, "Close your eyes, Amanda, we have a surprise for you."

"A surprise for me? What is it?"

"Never mind," Anne said. "Close your eyes."

Obediently Amanda closed her eyes, and Esther propelled her backward into the room. When they were inside, she heard the door close, and she also heard Sarah stifling a giggle. "What is it?" she demanded.

"All right, you can open your eyes and look."

Opening her eyes, Amanda stood stock-still for one moment and then gasped. "Is that for me?" she whispered, staring at the beautiful dress that Anne was holding up.

"Well, it's not for Sarah, and it's not for either one of us, so it must be for you," Esther Spencer said. "Do you like it?"

Amanda went closer and timidly reached out and touched the dress. "I've never seen anything so beautiful!" she whispered. "It can't be for me!"

The dress was indeed a beautiful creation. It was a bright yellow sacque gown decorated with tiny flowers and green foliage. Red shirring bordered the front opening, the sleeves, and the turban that Anne held in her hand. Amanda could do nothing but stand and admire it.

"Well, put it on!" Sarah laughed. "If it doesn't fit you, I'll wear it!"

"No, you won't! It'll fit me," Amanda cried. "You wait and see!"

Slipping out of her clothes except for her shift, all the ladies helped her put on her new dress and fit the turban.

She turned around, and since there was only a small mirror, she could only see portions of herself.

"Come down to my room," Esther said, "and you can see the whole effect."

The four of them went giggling down the hall, and they passed by James, who said, "It sounds like a bunch of gabbling geese. What are you doing?"

"Go away, James! Why don't you help somebody do something," Esther said. "Men!" she added as they entered the bedroom. "He didn't even notice your new dress. He wouldn't notice it even if I wore it."

In front of the mirror, Amanda turned around again and again. "It doesn't seem like me," she said, her voice filled with awe.

"You'll be the belle of the ball," Sarah said. "I'm so glad you got it."

"How can I thank you all?" Amanda said. Tears came to her eyes, and she brushed them away and smiled tremulously. "Nobody was ever so kind to me before. I don't deserve it."

"Well, none of us deserve much of anything," Anne said, "but sometimes we get to treat ourselves a little. Now go take that dress off. We want it to be nice and fresh when you make your entrance tonight."

"That's right. I want you to make a grand entrance!" Sarah exclaimed. "That'll show Annabelle Denton who she's dealing with."

"Oh, I couldn't do that!"

"Yes, you can. If it takes all three of us, you're going to come out looking like a queen."

———

Jacob stood beside Seth at the door greeting the guests. It was a rather large party. He had determined to fight back every attempt on the part of his grandmother to invite a large group. Now, however, he was thinking how he had lost. He was wishing he was somewhere else when suddenly the Denton family arrived—all of them: Edward and Phoebe along with Thomas and Annabelle. Esther's hospitality had won out over her anger at Annabelle. She had not wanted Annabelle at the party, but she knew she could not invite Jacob's best friend and not invite his family, too. Jacob greeted them all, and Thomas shook his hand, smiling warmly. "Well, happy birthday, old friend. Many of them."

"Thank you, Tom."

Edward and Phoebe made their greetings, and then Annabelle came and offered her hand. "Happy birthday, Jacob. I'm so happy for you."

Jacob blinked, for this was another Annabelle. She was usually outgoing, but now she seemed rather subdued. She leaned forward and whispered, "I hope you have the happiest life in the world, Jacob. I was sorry to hear about your engagement being broken, but these things happen."

"I guess they do," Jacob muttered. Annabelle squeezed his hand, and then they moved on as he turned to greet other guests.

Seth was standing back against the wall. His eyes met those of Edward Denton, but the older man's expression did not change. *He's like a statue*, Seth thought. *Never can tell what that man is thinking.* It seemed to him that Denton had been cooler in recent days. Perhaps because he had not been able to ascertain the hidden location of the armaments. Now he watched as Denton moved over to speak with James Spencer. *It's strange how those two don't know each other very well. Denton for the Crown and James Spencer for the Revolution.* He hesitated and then the thought came into his mind, *And where are you? Somewhere in the middle.* He felt foolish, as the weak often do. *A man ought to know what he believes in*, he thought. *But I wander around between two opinions, not knowing what I am or who I am.*

The guests had all arrived when Sarah came up to Jacob and said, "I wonder what's keeping Amanda?"

"I don't know. Why didn't she come down with you?"

"She wasn't quite ready yet—oh, here she comes now."

Jacob missed the mischievous grin on his stepsister's face as he turned to look toward the stairs leading up to the second floor. For one moment, he did not recognize the young woman who was coming down. He was so accustomed to Amanda wearing homespuns or linsey-woolsey that the young beauty who gracefully descended the staircase seemed to be another individual entirely.

"Amanda—" he whispered and could not take his eyes off of her.

"She's beautiful, isn't she, Jacob?"

"Yes," Jacob nodded in answer to Sarah's question. "It's as if I never saw her before."

"You never looked, Jacob, not really. She's always been a beautiful girl, but you were fooled by expensive clothes."

Jacob moved toward Amanda, but at that moment Annabelle stood beside him and put her hand on his arm. "Jacob, I need to talk to you."

Also at that moment, Jacob saw Thomas Denton approach Amanda, and she had taken his arm. He watched as his best friend led her toward the refreshment table.

"All right, Annabelle," he said heavily. It was not what he wanted to do, but her hand on his arm was insistent.

As she led him away, Sarah was watching them when a voice behind her startled her.

"They make a good-looking couple, don't they?"

Sarah turned quickly and found Seth Donovan standing beside her. He was wearing a new suit made of a black-and-gray striped material, with a double-breasted coat, worn buttoned to the top and cut away in the front. He also wore a pure white silk shirt with ruffles at the neck and wrists, and a solid gray waistcoat. Tight-fitting white britches ended just below the knee with white silk stockings that were tucked into black leather shoes with silver buckles.

"Yes, they do, Seth."

"You look very nice, Sarah."

"So do you. Is that a new suit?"

Seth flushed. "Yes, it is. Will Martin bought it for me. I think his wife pressured him. They were tired of looking at my ugly hairy legs and my Highland kilt."

Sarah could not help smiling. "Well, I like your Highland outfit. I think it's very manly. That surprises me," she said, "a man wearing skirts but looking manly."

"We Scots take a lot of ribbing about our kilts, but I don't mind." He moved his shoulders restlessly. They were large and heavily muscled and seemed to swell against the fabric. "I feel like I'm about to pop." He looked around the room and watched Jacob and Annabelle. The young woman had pulled him over to a corner and now seemed to be dominating the conversation. "I don't understand about all of this. Maybe you do."

"About Amanda and Jacob? I've known them both a long time.

They've both had lots of problems, Seth."

"What kind of problems?"

"Are you really interested?"

"Of course I am. Why wouldn't I be?"

Sarah looked up at the tall man. "I don't know. I suppose I just didn't think of you as that sort of man."

Seth stared at her. "Am I that cold and unfeeling?" he asked. "I didn't think I was."

"I don't know you very well, Seth. You're mysterious. Everyone is a little bit puzzled by you. You don't have any background or any family. You have no ties in the world."

"That's true enough. That makes a man moody, I suppose. But I wouldn't have you think I'm entirely uncaring about others. I've grown very fond of Jacob. He's been kind to me, but he seems— well, all mixed up."

"You know his history. His father abandoned him when he was a child, just a baby. He didn't come back for him until he was a young man. That embittered him greatly."

"I can see how that would happen. But he seems happy with his relationship now from what he tells me."

"That's true. Amanda has had a much harder life." Sarah went on to tell how Amanda's father had mistreated both her and her mother. She shook her head finally, saying, "I don't see how she's come through it as emotionally unscarred as she has."

"She looks very beautiful, but I don't understand Jacob. First he was telling everyone he was going to marry her, announcing it publicly, and then he wasn't."

"It wasn't all Jacob's fault," Sarah admitted.

As she stood there before him her soft fragrance slid through the armor of his self-sufficiency. He thought, *There's fire in this girl. She's a lovely lass—but a headstrong one behind that cool reserve of hers. Yet I like her spirit.* As Seth stood there, he suddenly realized he was drawn to her as he had never been drawn to a young woman before. He listened carefully as she explained Amanda's terrible background, and finally when she ended, he said, "That makes it look all the worse for Jacob. If she's had that much trouble, he didn't need to give her any more."

Sarah hesitated. "I've been angry at Jacob ever since the night of Annabelle's ball. If I had been a man, I would have given him a whipping for the way he treated poor Amanda!"

"Well, is he in love with Annabelle?"

"Of course not! She's just the candle and he's the moth."

Suddenly Seth laughed. "I've seen moths do that. Flying right into a candle flame and shriveling up. Is that your opinion of men?"

"They can be so thickheaded! Why is he drawn to Annabelle? She's beautiful enough, but what does that mean?"

Seth shrugged. "Well, it means a lot to a man for a woman to be attractive. That's not to be sniffed at."

"But she lives for nothing but pleasure. And the Bible says, 'She that liveth in pleasure is dead while she liveth.' "

"You know your Bible," Seth said, lifting his eyebrows.

"I know that much of it. If you ever read the book of Proverbs, you'll read chapter after chapter warning men against being taken by the snares of women."

"You're pretty hard on your fellow ladies, Sarah."

"Not all of them. Not on Amanda." Then she suddenly tried to smile and failed. Biting her lip, she shook her head. "I know I'm too hard on people. I love Jacob, but he's so wrong."

"Well, I'm hoping he'll pull out of it," Seth said slowly. He looked at the couple across the room, at Annabelle's beautiful face, and then shook his head. "She's not for him."

His discernment pleased Sarah. She said, "Look, they're starting to dance. I know it's not proper for a lady to ask a man to dance, but I'm asking you."

Seth immediately brightened up. "I always like a woman who knows her mind. Come along."

She put her hand on his arm, feeling the muscles swell under it, and once again was impressed with the power that lay in this man. She was puzzled by him, drawn to him, and found him extremely attractive. As they began to dance, it did not occur to her that since she had met Seth Donovan, the dreams and the awful memories of Philip Baxter's death had not appeared. She noticed how graceful he was for such a large man, and at this moment she was content.

As the dance came to a close, Sarah and Seth moved to join Jacob and Annabelle, who were helping themselves to some punch. Thomas and Amanda then joined the group.

Jacob could not take his eyes from Amanda. He had never seen her looking so beautiful. After praying for God to direct him in the matter of Amanda and Annabelle, he realized that the only choice for him was this girl from Watauga who had always been there for him from the first day they had met. It was Amanda who had stuck by him when he had acted so horribly toward everyone on the frontier. It was Amanda who had eventually led him to the Lord. It had always been Amanda, and he now knew that it always would be. Jacob found his voice to say to her, "You look especially beautiful tonight, Amanda. I love your new dress."

Surprised by Jacob's remarks, Amanda lowered her eyes and answered quietly, "Thank you, Jacob."

"Jacob, you haven't noticed *my* new gown," Annabelle interrupted with a pout. Annabelle did not like that Jacob was paying more attention to Amanda than he was to her. She turned to Amanda with a sly smile on her face. "Wherever did you get such a pretty dress, Amanda? It appears too fancy for a frontier girl to own."

Sarah, fuming at Annabelle's treatment of her friend, interjected, "It was a birthday gift from my grandmother to Amanda. It was made by a seamstress in Williamsburg who specializes in copying Paris gowns for rich colonial men to buy their spoiled daughters."

Catching the not-so-subtle insult, Annabelle started to retort when James Spencer called for attention. "I think it is time my grandson, Jacob, the guest of honor, says a few words."

Jacob reddened slightly as he moved to the center of the room. "I want to thank all of you for coming and celebrating this occasion with me. It has been wonderful visiting with my grandparents, but I must confess that I miss my family in Watauga. I plan to return there soon, but I will always have a special place in my heart for all of you. I know that you join me in praying for a future of freedom in this fine land of America!"

Edward Denton seethed inwardly as he listened to what he considered treasonous words from Jacob Spencer. He consoled himself with the thought that he would help bring the rebels to their knees before the might of England.

James Spencer joined his grandson and put his arm around him. "No grandfather could be prouder of his grandson than I am of you, Jacob." After they embraced, James said, "Now, Jacob, it is time you choose a young lady to join you in the special dance of the evening."

Jacob smiled at the group and said, "There is only one choice for me. I want to dance with the prettiest lady here—or anywhere else for that matter—Miss Amanda Taylor."

Shocked by his words, Amanda could only stare at Jacob. He held out his arm to her. Amanda finally took his hand and joined him.

Annabelle's smile of expectancy had turned to a look of venomous hatred. She had thought Jacob would pick her. She had been sure of it when he had talked about choosing the prettiest girl there. Then she thought her ears had deceived her when he had spoken that frontier girl's name. But the evidence was there in front of her as Jacob danced with Amanda Taylor.

Sarah noticed the change in Annabelle's demeanor and leaned toward her as she whispered, "You really shouldn't stand around with your mouth open, Annabelle. It is quite unbecoming of a lady."

Annabelle glared at Sarah and stormed from the room.

Jacob, thrilled to be dancing with Amanda, stared deeply into her eyes. "Amanda, I owe you an apology. I should have told you everything about Annabelle before. I hope you believe me when I tell you that I never meant to hurt you and that I love you with all of my heart. Will you please forgive me?"

Amanda asked, "What about Annabelle?"

"Annabelle is definitely a part of my past, a past before I met you and found Jesus Christ as my Savior. I know now that I never really loved her as I know I love you. My feelings for her were based purely on her appearance, and that is nothing to build a future together on. I want you as a part of my future, a future built on serving God the rest of my days on this earth. Will you, Amanda Taylor, honor me by sharing this future with me as my wife?"

Tears came to Amanda's eyes as she said quietly, but with a surety, "I do forgive you, Jacob Spencer. And yes, I will share your future with you as your wife, as I love you with all of my heart."

The two seemed to meld into one as they continued dancing, oblivious to everything and everyone except themselves and the love they shared for each other and especially for God.

Valley of Decision

Twenty-Two

*T*he hour was growing late and soon the party would be over. Sarah was so happy to see Jacob and Amanda together at last. She also couldn't help being pleased at the looks Annabelle was giving Jacob. Sarah murmured to herself, "I hope I'll be as happy as Jacob and Amanda one day."

"You will be!" Seth had come to stand beside her and heard her wish. Seth noticed Sarah turning pink. Leaning down, he whispered, "Come on, Sarah, you need to get away for a moment." He led her out of the crowded room into the front foyer. "It's a little chilly, but would you go outside with me?"

"Yes, that might be nice. It's a bit warm in there for me."

"Where's your cloak?" Seth asked.

"It's on the rack over there." She moved over and picked up a gray woolen cloak that came down to her ankles and handed it to him. He slipped it over her shoulders and they walked out through the front door. Seth stretched and said, "I like parties but not too much of them."

They walked around the back of the house to the garden. A pale moon cast its silver light on the flagstones beneath their feet, and a crisp autumn breeze refreshed them. They could hear the sounds of the party faintly in the distance and the crunch of dry leaves on the path. Seth said suddenly, "I like this weather, these fall days. There's something in the air that's good. It makes a person feel alive."

Sarah smiled. She stopped and turned to him. "Fall is beautiful in Watauga, too. In October the colors are breathtaking. I think it's probably the prettiest place I've ever seen."

"You miss your home, don't you?"

"More than I thought I would. I miss my family, too."

"I'm sure they all miss you, too," Seth smiled. "Especially all of your suitors. You do have suitors, don't you?"

Sarah feigned a cross look. "As if that is any of your concern!"

Seth held up his hands in surrender, and Sarah smiled at him.

They were quiet then for a moment, and the sound of the fiddle and the fife coming from inside the house sounded far away. "It sounds like fairy music," Sarah said. "Do you believe in fairies, Seth? I know Irish people do."

"We Scots are far more hardheaded. Not much romance in us."

"That's too bad," Sarah said.

She stood before him, and he was, once again, impressed with her beauty. The oval of her face was shining from the silvery light of the moon. She had a beauty that stirred his loneliness, and there was a faint lift to her head that sent her jade earrings into motion. He saw something then in the depth of her eyes.

"What do you think of me, Seth? That I'm just a silly, headstrong woman?"

Seth Donovan stood very still. He did not speak for a moment, but something had been working in him ever since he had seen this woman. And now he said, "A man has reasons for what he thinks about a woman. All he knows is what she does to him, and how she makes him feel." He grew very still and suddenly reached out and put his hands on her arms. When she did not protest, he said in a soft voice, "Sometimes he looks at a woman, and then he seems himself, and he knows what he is."

"What if she's the wrong woman for him?" Sarah whispered, mesmerized by the touch of his big hands on her arms.

"If she's the wrong woman," Seth answered slowly, "then he'll search for the right one."

"What if he never finds the right woman?"

"Why, I suppose he would make it in life, but he would be lonely. When a man finds the right woman, he's complete, he's whole. My father and my mother were like that. They were like one being, really. That's what the marriage vows say—one flesh. They were one spirit, too. All my life I've looked for that kind of thing."

"Do you find it often, Seth?"

"Not vurry often. I see it in James and Esther Spencer, though, don't you?"

"Yes, they love each other dearly," Sarah agreed. "And I've seen it in my mother and stepfather. My mother had one great love with my father, but when he died, she thought she would never find another man, nor want one. But she did."

"I'm glad for them. It's a rare thing indeed. Vurry rare."

Suddenly Sarah knew he was going to kiss her. Instead of turning her head or stepping back, she lifted her face. And when his lips came down on hers, she was stirred as she never had been by a man's kiss. His arms were strong around her and gave her a sense of security, and she yielded herself to his embrace. Her softness was met by the hardness of his muscles and the firmness of his lips. As he continued holding her, she made no attempt to pull away.

When he raised his head, he said, "All men carry in their head the picture of the kind of woman they want to spend the rest of their lives with. Sometimes it's a mixture of many women—a picture they've built up of the good women and the beautiful ones they've seen."

"That's not very fair to a woman, Seth," Sarah whispered, still stirred by his caress.

"When a man finds the right woman, all the things that he's seen in the others will be in her. There'll be sweetness and honesty and self-sacrifice." He hesitated, then added, "And there'll be disagreements, too. That goes with it, I suppose. The sand and the sugar. I'd rather have it," he said suddenly, "than a lifetime of dullness. You're a woman who can touch a man's heart, Sarah, and here's where I tell you that I think I'm falling in love with you."

Sarah suddenly put her hand on his chest, for he was bending his head down to kiss her again, but she was confused. She looked up at him, her lips soft and vulnerable, and the thought came, *I don't know him. He's able to stir a woman, but that may not be good. It may come from long practice.* She turned suddenly and said, "We'd better go back in the house, Seth."

"All right." He took her arm, and as they made their way back, he said quietly, "I've never told a woman I loved her before."

His words startled Sarah. "You mean that, Seth?"

"Yes."

He made no protest and did not argue, and somehow she knew he was telling her the truth. It touched her, and she said without looking at him, "It's a compliment, then, but it's too quick. We don't know each other that well."

"You don't know me," Seth said as they reached the door. "But I know you."

They went inside and the sound of the music filled their ears again. Sarah left him at once, and Seth moved across into a dark corner of the room where he watched the others dancing. He was not seeing them, however, but was thinking of the honesty in Sarah's eyes and remembering the soft embrace they had shared in the moonlit garden.

Will Martin moved across the room to where he saw Seth standing in the corner. He went to him and said in a low tone, "Seth, I've got to talk to you. Come with me."

The two men left the room, and as soon as they were in the library, Will said, "I've just had a messenger. The armaments are in. We've got to go immediately."

"You mean we're going to move them from the ship to the hiding place?"

"That's right, and it has to be done quickly tonight. The ship's leaving early in the morning. We'll have to go right now."

"All right, Will. I'll have to change clothes. I can't go like this."

"So will I."

"Do you have enough men to move the arms?"

Will chewed his lips. "I haven't been able to find anyone. Maybe you and I can do it alone. It'll take longer, but the fewer who are in on it, the better off we'll be. Go change and I'll meet you out at the back of the house."

Will turned and left, and Seth walked back to the party. Some sort of alarm was going off in his mind, a reluctance he could not explain. Of late he had thought less of Isaac's death. The anger and bitterness didn't seem as strong as before. More and more his memories had been of their boyhood, pleasant times, but now he was committed. A man could not change his mind as a weather vane changes. Stiffening his tall body, he moved across the room to where Edward Denton sat in a chair, his back against the wall. Seth motioned for Denton to follow him. When they were in the library, Seth turned to him. "It's time, Mr. Denton. The shipment's going to be moved now. Will Martin just told me."

"All right," Denton said. "As soon as you find out the exact location, we'll need to know it."

"All right, I'll do it." Seth turned and headed to his bedroom to change. Edward Denton followed him out of the library. Unbeknown to either man, Annabelle Denton stepped out of the shadows of the room, smiling without forcing herself to for the first time that evening.

———————

Edward Denton walked out to his carriage. "Harry," he said, "I want you to go to The Brown Stag. Take this note to Fulton. You know him, don't you?"

"Fellow with the scarred face? Yes, sir, I do know him."

"All right, on your way then." He watched as the carriage drove off, then moved back inside.

Annabelle Denton saw her father preparing to leave. She knew that her time was short, and she went to Sarah, whom she disliked intensely. She disguised it, however, by saying, "Sarah, I think I need to warn you about something."

"Warn me about what?" Sarah said abruptly. She had no time for Annabelle Denton and could not imagine what the girl was talking about.

"It's about Seth Donovan."

"What are you talking about, Annabelle?"

"I'm talking about the fact that Seth is working for my father."

Sarah stared at the young woman in front of her. "What do you mean working for your father?"

"I mean he's working as a spy, and he's spying on your family, on the Martins. There's something going on. I don't know all of it, but I do know that Seth is involved with it."

Sarah refused to believe it and said so. "Annabelle, as far as you are concerned, I don't believe a word you say! After the way you've treated Jacob and my friend Amanda, I wouldn't believe you if you took an oath on the Bible!"

"You can believe it or not, but I've seen them. As a matter of fact, Seth is leaving with your uncle now to betray him and turn a shipment of arms over to my father. I am just warning you to stay away from him," she said, then turned and left.

Sarah stared at Annabelle as the girl swept away. She found herself thinking about the possibility that Annabelle might be telling the truth. *I've got to talk to Jacob,* she thought. She walked across the room and touched Jacob on the arm. He was standing with Amanda, and she said, "Come outside. I've got something to tell you. You too, Amanda."

Both of them looked surprised, but they followed her. When they were outside, she turned and quickly repeated what Annabelle had told her. "I don't know if she's telling the truth or not, but I do know that Uncle Will and Seth left abruptly a little while ago."

"Yes, I saw them," Jacob said. "Didn't they say where they were going?"

"No, they didn't tell anyone that I know of. Jacob, I think you'd better go see what's happening. You remember the last time there was trouble, Seth and Uncle Will were involved with some armaments in Boston. I think that could be what they're doing tonight, moving guns for the Continental Army."

"I'll go right now." Jacob turned and left at once. He grabbed his coat and hat and mounted a horse that his grandfather had been keeping for some time. "They're probably at the dock," he said to himself. "I'll have to follow them and see what they're doing."

Will and Seth had had foresight enough to take two wagons that Will had rented to carry the guns. It had been relatively easy to get the wagons loaded, for some of the deckhands had volunteered. There was a surreptitious air about them all, and two armed men had gone out into the darkness to stand guard.

What Will and Seth did not know was that Fulton had gotten the message from Denton. He had made no attempt to interrupt the unloading of the arms, but as the two wagons pulled out, Fulton followed stealthily in the darkness with four armed men.

Finally the wagons rumbled off the wharf, and Seth had taken his seat beside Will in the lead vehicle. The other was driven by one of the crew that had volunteered for the job.

It was a dark night with the moon hidden behind shreds of dark clouds. The stars gave no light, and as the horses moved along steadily, Seth peered ahead in the darkness. "Do you know where you're going, Will? I can't see a thing."

"Yes, we stay on this road for four miles outside of town. We'll have to be careful. I don't want to miss the turnoff."

Seth said no more. His nerves were giving him problems. As the wagon rolled down the road, Will began to talk about the Revolution. He spoke with such warmth about freedom for Americans that Seth suddenly found himself listening with a new ear.

"It's not like the Old Country. I know some men think that Englishmen have more freedom than anyone, and they do have more than most," Will said. "But they've kept their heels on the necks of Irishmen for years."

"And the Scots, too," Seth said.

"I'm surprised to hear you say that. It's the first time I've ever heard you make a remark of that nature," Will said. He peered through the darkness at Seth's face and shook his head. "I suppose you think it's not your fight. I thought the same thing myself, but it's just not right, Seth, for men sitting three or four thousand miles away in a Parliament to make decisions about the lives of men they will never see or never know. All we want as Americans is the right to govern ourselves. That's what Englishmen have, but we don't have that here."

Seth was going over this in his mind, and then finally he said, "There's some justice to that, Will. I wouldn't want to go back to Scotland again, or even to England. This is a good country."

Will nodded in agreement. "It has its faults, but if we can win this war, man can do as he pleases. He'll have a vote, a say in his own destiny, and that's what this Revolution is all about."

There was a long silence then, and finally Will began to talk about his family. "I want my boy and girl to grow up in a place where there's freedom."

"They're fine children, Will. I've never seen finer."

"Yes, they are, but they won't have a chance unless we win this war."

Somehow the thought of Eve and David Martin growing up under any kind of oppression struck at Seth Donovan. He had learned to love the two children greatly. They were the first children he had ever really grown attached to. And as Will continued to talk about them, his conscience smote him a hard blow. Somehow it was all confused in his mind with what he felt for Sarah MacNeal. But now the idea of a free country where men could vote and choose their own way, where small children like David and Eve could grow up not being afraid of what men thousands of miles away would decree for them, appealed to him.

For over an hour Seth wrestled with his conscience. Finally, as clear as day, he heard his own voice saying abruptly, "I can't do this!"

Will turned with surprise, for Seth had spoken loudly. "You can't do what? Help me unload the guns?"

And then Seth Donovan knew that no matter what it cost him, he had to tell the truth. He turned to Will and said simply, "I'm not what you think I am, Will."

"What does that mean?"

"It means that I've sold you out. Edward Denton is a Tory, and he hired me to find out where the guns were."

Will Martin sat stock-still and tried to take in what Seth was saying. He was so shocked at Seth's confession, he could not believe his ears. "You don't know what you're talking about, Seth."

"Don't I know my own heart?" Seth answered. He grew calmer then and said, "My brother, Isaac, was killed by the Revolutionary forces at Moore's Creek Bridge. I was there with him. I saw him die. I swore I'd get revenge for his death, Will, and before I met you, I'd fought for a year with the Tories in North Carolina. But then they told me I could do more good by helping Edward Denton, and that's what I've done."

"You're an agent for the British?"

"I'm afraid that's the size of it."

Will felt a surge of anger. "After what we've done for you? How could you betray us when we took you into our family?"

"No, I can't betray you. That's why I'm telling you, Will. I can't go through with it. All the time I've known it was wrong and indecent, and that's why I had to tell you the truth. I know you won't want me around now, so as soon as we get the guns unloaded, I'll be out of your way."

Will Martin drove in silence. As the wagon bounced along the rutted road he could hear the boxes of muskets banging against the floorboards. He went swiftly over in his mind the events since he had met Seth Donovan. But soon the anger began to fade. After all, hadn't the man told him the truth? He spoke up and said quietly, "I'm glad you told me, Seth."

"I had to. It was tearing me to pieces."

"What are you going to do now?"

"I'm going to try to find my way, Will. I'm like a man without a star. There's nothing to guide me."

"A man needs God for that."

"I'll say aye to that," Seth said, "and maybe I'll find Him now that I've got this awful thing out of the way. Will, can you ever forgive me for what I've done to you and your family?"

Will Martin did not hesitate and said, "Of course I can, and I'll help you, too."

The two men rode on for another five minutes, and then Will said, "There's the turn."

Seth suddenly held up his hand. "Did you hear something, Will?"

Holding his head up, Will said, "No, I don't think so. What was it?"

"I thought I heard horses."

"We'd better get off this road and into the house. I'd hate for anyone to catch us here."

He turned off the side road and drove the horses forward at a gallop. Seth held on. He also held on to the pistol in his belt. He was certain he had heard horses.

When they got to the house, they could scarcely see it in the darkness. "That's it," he said. "Let's get these wagons unloaded."

The three men jumped to the ground and had moved only a few cartons of the muskets when suddenly the sound of a voice startled them.

"Hold it right where you are!"

A man advanced into the light of the lantern that they had lit to see their way, and instantly three other men spread out behind him.

"They've come to steal the shipment of arms," Will whispered. "We can't let them have them. Try to get away, Seth."

"You can't fight them alone. Did you bring a pistol?"

"Two of them."

"So did I. That makes four, and we've got four shots."

"I've got a pistol, too," said the rough-looking sailor who had driven the other wagon.

"Throw those guns down!" Fulton yelled. But at once the sailor lifted his pistol and fired. A man to the right of Fulton fell with a gasp, and the silence of the night was instantly broken with the sounds of gunfire.

Will never really remembered much of the fight. When the loads had been expended, it became hand-to-hand combat. He only knew that he was down and Simeon Fulton was sitting on him holding a knife at his throat. His eye was gleaming, and his twisted face looked diabolic.

"Ruin my face, will you? Well, I'm going to ruin yours now, then I'm going to put this knife in your heart!"

Will felt the knife as it touched the side of his cheek and tensed himself for the pain. Right then a shot rang out. He felt Fulton's body stiffen and heard him cry, "Ahhh!" Fulton's eyes rolled upward and he slumped forward.

Frantically, Will shoved the body aside and then stood up. He saw Seth, who had fought off one of the other men successfully, rising from the limp form, and there in the lamplight Will saw Jacob Spencer holding a smoking pistol in his hand.

"Jacob," Will gasped, "how did you get here?"

"Sarah told me about you two leaving. She asked me to follow you."

"It's a good thing you did," Will said. "This fellow was going to kill me."

Seth came up to Jacob and stood facing him squarely. "You've got to know the truth, Jacob. This was all my fault." He repeated all the details of his confession to Jacob. When he was finished, he said wearily, "I'm no man. No honest man could've done what I've done. But Will's forgiven me, so I'll ask for your forgiveness too, Jacob."

Jacob was shocked, but seeing Will's quick nod, he said, "If a man's been wrong and says so, then no one can hold his wrong against him. God doesn't, so why should I? God's forgiveness is what you really need, but you have mine, for what it's worth."

Seth nodded. "I know that. I guess I'm what you call a seeker."

Will said, "The Bible says, 'He that seeketh findeth.' You'll find God, Seth, I'm sure of it." He hesitated, then said, "We can't leave these guns here. We'll have to find another place to hide them. Fulton's dead, but two of those fellows got away. We'll have to store the weapons somewhere else."

The men quickly loaded the few boxes they had carried into the house and then started for the wagon. Will moved over and looked down into the twisted face of Simeon Fulton. *He was a wicked fellow, but I'm sorry he had to go out like this*, he thought. Then he looked at Jacob and said, "You saved my life, Jacob."

Jacob Spencer nodded. "I'm glad I did, Uncle Will. You would have done the same for me. We're family."

Partings

Twenty-Three

Seth looked awkwardly around at the small group that had gathered and met their gazes one at a time. James and Esther Spencer, Will and Rebekah Martin, Anne Martin, Martha Edwards, then Jacob, Amanda, and Sarah. They had all gathered at the dining table, but Seth had come late. Now he stood there, a tall figure with a strange expression in his bright blue-green eyes. He had rehearsed his speech well the night before and now said, "I suppose Will has told you about me. Well, what can I say? I betrayed a family that showed me more love and hospitality than I had dreamed existed." He hesitated, then shrugged his broad shoulders. "I'm sorry, and I regret that I let my thirst for vengeance take me so far. All I can say is I was wrong and I'm sorry. I've been thinking a lot about this war and about the freedom that Will talked about. I've been wrong. I always felt that the patriots had a just cause, but I was with the High-landers for Britain. I don't know what I'll do now, but I know I can't stay here. So this is my farewell speech to all of you."

Jacob spoke up at once. "I think we've all done things we were mighty ashamed of, Seth. The important thing is to get it out of our hearts and get on with it." He, too, had been thinking, and now he said, "I've got a suggestion for you, Seth."

"For me? What might that be, Jacob?"

"This is a big country. You told me you didn't ever want to go back to Scotland again. What would you think about moving to the frontier?"

A startled look leaped into Seth Donovan's eyes. "Well, actually Will asked me about that when we were in Boston, but I hadn't thought about it anymore . . . after what I had done."

"You ought to consider it," Will said quickly seeing his discomfort. "You're a strong man and a young one. You could pick up the ways of the frontier and make a good life for yourself out there. My wife and I have decided that that's the place for us. Why don't you come with us, Seth? We would truly love to have you with us."

Surprise washed across Seth's face. "Well, it's a thing that will have to be thought on," he said. Actually he had not one other single idea in his mind, and even as he stood there before them, the idea grew on him. His eyes went to Sarah, but she was looking down and not saying a word. Finally, he said, "I think I might like to try it. At least go out and see what it's like. I've heard so much about it. Not that I might stay. A man never knows about that."

"As soon as everyone gets ready, we'll see to our journey," Will said.

Anne then surprised them all. "You won't need to make plans for Martha and me. We're staying right here in Williamsburg."

"In Williamsburg!" Rebekah exclaimed. "What do you mean?"

"I'm getting lonely," Esther said. "James and I have asked Anne to stay with us, and Martha's going to stay, too, so we'll be company for each other."

Will asked, "Are you sure, Mother? We would miss you terribly."

Anne smiled at her son. "Yes, I'm sure. I will miss all of you, too, but you need to start your new lives with your own family." As Will started to protest, Anne added, "Besides, Martha and I are too accustomed to our creature comforts. The frontier would be too rough for us."

Will had a huge lump in his throat as he embraced his mother. He then turned to the others and said, "Let's make some plans."

After they had decided on a spring departure to allow time for Will to travel to Boston to sell the house and settle affairs there, Seth agreed to accompany Will, in order to get away from Edward Denton as soon as possible.

As the planning continued Jacob stood and said, "Well, if you'll excuse me, I've got one piece of business I have to take care of." He glanced at Amanda, who was watching him carefully. They did not speak, but somehow, as Jacob left, an image of her face remained implanted on his mind.

Leaving the house, he went at once to the Denton home. He had made up his mind what he had to do, and now he knocked on the door firmly. Thomas met him instead of the servant, and his face was tense. "I heard what happened last night, Jacob. I have to apologize for my father."

"You didn't know anything about it, Thomas?"

"No. I knew he was an ardent Tory, but I didn't know anything about this shipment of guns. He didn't really mean for it to come to violence. He just wanted to help the Tory cause." Thomas ran his hand through his hair and gave Jacob an anxious look. "Is this going to make any difference in our friendship, Jacob?"

Summoning a smile, Jacob shook his head. "Not between you and me."

"Well, something else might. I'm thinking of joining a Tory regiment."

"That doesn't make any difference either, Thomas. If that's what you feel you have to do, then God be with you. Now I need to see Annabelle."

"I thought you might. That's all over, isn't it? It's better for both of you. I'll get her for you."

Jacob went into the library, which was empty. He stood there as Thomas disappeared, and soon Annabelle came to stand before him. "Annabelle," he said quickly before she could speak, "I've got something to say." He noticed she did not look her usual best. He thought she might have been crying, perhaps over her father's involvement in the arms business. He said quickly, "I'm leaving, Annabelle."

"I knew you would. You're going to marry Amanda, aren't you?"

"Yes, I am. I know I love her."

"She won't make you happy," Annabelle said petulantly.

"I know she will. God's the only one who can make anyone happy, really. And since she loves God more than she loves me, she will make me very happy."

Annabelle turned her face away. She did not want to hear this talk and repeated, "You'll be sorry, Jacob. She's not the woman to make you happy."

"Annabelle, you and I would have been miserable together. We've got different goals, different ideas about how to live. I'm sorry if I've hurt you. I didn't intend to."

Annabelle turned and stiffened her back. She forced a smile and said, "All right. Good-bye, Jacob. And don't worry about me. I'll be just fine!"

"I know you will, Annabelle," Jacob said quietly. He returned her smile, but it did not quite reach his eyes. "Good-bye, Annabelle."

Jacob turned and left the house, knowing he had made the right decision, but feeling sad for Annabelle and the true need in her life that she would not face—her need for Jesus Christ.

From her bedroom window, Annabelle Denton watched Jacob Spencer walk out of her life. "I'm better off without him," she tried to convince herself, but the words held little conviction. As Jacob disappeared from her view, she realized she felt lonelier than she had ever been in her life. A single tear fell down her face as she turned from the window. "Mother," she called, "I think we need to plan a big party. . . ."

Seth was ready to leave to purchase supplies with Will, but he knew he had one more thing to do. Sarah had not said one thing to him, and finally he made up his mind. "I've got to talk to her." He knew she usually was out in the garden in the afternoon, so he walked out and found her trimming the old growth away. It was cold, and she was wearing a dark blue woolen coat with a hood. She straightened up at once as he walked up to her. There was a stillness in her face and a resistance that disheartened Seth. Nevertheless, he spoke up, saying, "I've got to talk to you, Sarah."

"I don't want to talk to you, Seth."

"I just wanted to say I'm sorry."

"You've already said that!" Her voice was cold and her tone was clipped. She stood as straight as a soldier and gazed steadily into his eyes.

"I told you that I loved you."

"I know you told me that. You told us all a lot of things, but most of them were lies, weren't they?"

"That wasn't a lie."

"The rest of them were all lies, but that's the one truth in all you said?"

Seth knew then that it was hopeless. He stood there silently but could think of nothing else to add. "After I help your uncle, I'll be moving to the frontier."

"The frontier's a big place. I won't have to see you, and that's fine with me."

Seth started to say more, but she turned her back abruptly. "I don't want to talk to you anymore, Seth. Good-bye."

Seth stood there for one moment but knew that there was no point. "Good-bye, Sarah, and remember, I do love you, no matter what other wrong things I've done or said. That's the one true thing in my life." He waited for her to move, but she did not. Turning, he walked away.

When he was gone Sarah suddenly lifted her head. There were tears in her eyes and she bit them back. *I don't know what to believe anymore*, she thought. *I've lost so many, and now this. I'm afraid to trust anybody.* She knew this was not normal for her. She had always been an openhearted girl, quick to respond to affection, but Philip's death had hardened her. She knew that this big Highlander who was walking out of her life had touched her as no man ever had. But could she believe him? Deep down she knew she did believe him, but she also realized that she was afraid of losing him. *Maybe I could open my heart to him. . . .*

"No, I'll have nothing to do with him," she said aloud, and then wiped the tears away and continued to trim the dead plants out of the garden.

PART IV

Mount Up With Wings as Eagles

May 1778–November 1780

"But they that wait upon the Lord shall renew their strength;
they shall mount up with wings as eagles;
they shall run, and not be weary;
and they shall walk, and not faint."

Isaiah 40:31

Home Again

Twenty-Four

*S*equatchie moved across the clearing, making no more sound than did the white cloud that drifted across the slate blue sky overhead. It was not a thing he did intentionally, but from his youth he had learned to move through the forest silently. It had been a matter of life and death at times, for the enemies of the Cherokee were fierce and cunning. Now he did it as a matter of course, his feet avoiding twigs, dry leaves—anything that might make a sound.

Sequatchie was forty-six years old and had the typical look of the Cherokee. He was very tall with smooth bronze skin, dark eyes, square jaw, and high cheekbones. He had a long face with a broad forehead and an aquiline nose. His scalp was shaved except for the topknot that was tied and hung down his back. Even at his age, it still showed no sign of gray.

Approaching the cabin, he called out softly, "Iris!" He waited until the door opened and then smiled. "Are you ready for your first bee hunt?"

Iris Taylor, at the age of forty-two, was still an attractive woman. Her hair was dark and she had dark blue eyes to match. The hard life and a merciless first marriage had put a few lines in her face, but since her husband had died, those had seemed to fade. She moved almost as lightly as a young girl. She wore a buckskin dress and a pair of Indian moccasins with leggings. Flushed lightly, she said, "I don't feel quite right dressed like this, Sequatchie."

"You look fine, and when we go to my people, you will be more like one of us."

Iris Taylor came and stood beside the tall Indian. It had come as a shock to her that she had agreed to marry him. A bad first marriage should have soured her, but somehow her first husband, for all his cruelty, had not been able to quench the natural goodness and sweetness that lay in her. She had allowed God to heal her hurt and pain. She reached up and put her hand on his arm and said, "I can't believe that all this is happening."

Sequatchie's dark features broke into a smile. He had good teeth, a brilliant white that made his skin seem even more coppery. "It is hard for me to believe, too. I have not had a wife for so long, I will probably not be a good husband. I've forgotten how, if I ever knew."

Iris laughed and struck his arm lightly. "I'll have to teach you, then."

"Good. Now, we Cherokee love honey, and it's time that you learned how to lay some in store."

"I'm ready."

"Good. Come along. You will get your first lesson in how to get sweetness out of a tree."

The two moved away from the small cabin, glancing briefly at the larger house where the Spencer family lived. It was midafternoon, and the two younger children were out tumbling and playing in front of the cabin while Elizabeth tended to her flowers. She called out and waved to them. "Where are you going?"

"Going to get honey," Iris said.

"Good. Bring me some, Miss Iris," Joshua called out.

"Me too!" Hannah yelled.

"They're growing up so fast," Iris murmured.

She moved quickly, keeping pace with Sequatchie's long legs. As they disappeared quickly into the deep forest that lay to the north of the cabins, she said rather timidly, "I'm a little bit nervous, Sequatchie."

"About what?"

"It's going to come as quite a shock to Amanda, our getting married, I mean."

"Maybe not as much as you think. She has very sharp eyes, that daughter of yours. I think she's seen the great affection I have for you."

"I hope so. I haven't said anything to her, but still, it's a lot for a young woman to take in."

"You think she will object to your marrying an Indian?"

"No, she loves you very much. She's seen the kindness in you that she never saw in—" Iris broke off quickly. She had almost said, "In her father," but she had schooled herself not to say anything about the evil ways of her first husband, especially since he had come to know the Lord before he died. She changed the subject quickly, saying, "Well, how do we catch these bees?"

"I will show you." Sequatchie stopped and looked around. They were in a small clearing, and he studied the terrain carefully. Finding a stump where a tree had been cut to build the Spencer cabin, he reached into the leather sack he bore from a sling and pulled something out. It was wrapped in a piece of old cloth, and Iris moved closer.

"What's that?" she said.

"A corncob soaked in honey." He placed the bait in the center of the stump and added, "Soon, if there are any bees, one will find it."

"What if there are no bees around here?"

"Then we will go someplace else."

They had been there no more than ten minutes when Sequatchie said, "Look! You see him?"

Squinting her eyes, Iris saw a bee that had lit on the cob. He soon rose into the air, and she said, "Do we follow him?"

"No," Sequatchie said, shaking his head. "We could never follow one bee, but he will go tell the others of his hive. We will soon see more of them."

Within a short time, more bees appeared. Iris was amazed and watched as they lit upon the corncob.

Soon Sequatchie rose and said, "Now we have a line to the tree."

"I suppose that's where the saying comes from, 'making a bee-line' for something."

"I have not heard that saying, but watch carefully. We must not lose track of the bees."

Iris moved with Sequatchie. It was great fun trying to keep track of the bees. More than once they had to stop. It seemed that Sequatchie could even hear the bees, for he would put them back on the line again.

Finally Sequatchie grunted, "Good, there is your honey, Iris."

Iris looked ahead and saw a black oak that had a bulge on it. The bulge had a split, and she could see the bees constantly coming and going. "Is the honey in there?" she asked.

"Yes. Now we have to get it out."

The extraction of the honey from the tree was quite exciting. Iris had carried an empty tub for the honey, and Sequatchie warned her, "You are probably going to get stung even if you stand far back, but there's no help for it."

"Go ahead," Iris said. "I guess some good honey is worth a sting or two."

"You sound like a good Cherokee woman. Stay back until I get the tree cut."

Sequatchie, before beginning his cut, built a fire some fifteen feet away from the tree. The bees did not seem to bother him, and soon, using a mixture of dry and green wood, he had a smoky fire built. He moved the fire stick by stick around the base of the tree, informing her, "It seems to make the bees sleepy. If you try to get the honey without smoking them, it's bad medicine."

After waiting for the bees to settle down, Sequatchie took an ax and cut into the tree across the grain two feet above and two feet below the hole. Then he split with the grain and lifted out a slice of trunk four feet long and several inches wide.

"That makes them mad," he said, and indeed a number of bees came boiling out. Sequatchie kept smoking the bees and cutting away. Finally he said, "All right, you want to see what the inside of a beehive looks like?"

Iris moved forward. A few bees buzzed around her head, and Sequatchie leaned over and pulled one out of her hair. "Look, there's the queen right there. You see? If we wanted to start our own hive, we'd have to be sure to take her."

"Could we do that?"

"Not this time," Sequatchie said. "You have to have a bee gum."

"A bee gum, what's that?"

"It's a section of a hollow tree. You put a top on it and put bees in there, and they make their honey there outside your cabin. You don't have to hunt a tree down, but we don't have a bee gum, so today we'll just take the honey. Stand back, now. Let me get it. I don't want you hurt."

Iris moved back and watched as Sequatchie stooped inside. He moved rapidly, and several times he flinched as he was stung around the neck and on his hands. Quickly he filled the bucket up with the dripping, golden cone and then moved away. Slapping the bees off, he said, "Want to taste it?"

The honey was not clear but had dead bees and chips of wood in it. Nevertheless, she stuck her finger in it, then raised it to her lips. "Oh, it's delicious!" she said. "This will make good honey cakes."

"Let's get along. I don't want to get any more stings."

They moved away and stopped at a creek, where Sequatchie washed his hands. He also put some cool mud on the stings on his hands and on his neck.

"Doesn't that hurt dreadfully?" Iris asked.

"Good honey's worth a few stings, as you said. Come along."

The two made their way back toward the cabin, and Iris was happy. She said, "When do you want to get married, Sequatchie?"

"That's up to you. You'll be the bride."

"I'd say very soon, then. As soon as Amanda gets back and can be here for the wedding."

"Good."

"As soon as we're married, I want us to go to your people. I'm anxious to get to know them better."

Sequatchie looked over at Iris with affection. It was a source of amazement to him that he had decided to give up his free roaming life and become a family man again. But he had roamed for years and longed for some sort of peace in his life. "We will get married twice. Once the white man's way and once the Cherokee way."

"All right, Sequatchie. It will be as you say."

They were almost to the cabin when Sequatchie said, "We have visitors."

Iris could hear nothing for a while, but when they had gone a bit farther, she did hear the sound of many voices. "I wonder if Jacob and Amanda and Sarah are back?"

"Yes, that is so." Sequatchie had keen eyes and caught a glimpse of the crowd outside the cabin. "There are more people than that. I do not know some of them."

The two went quickly forward, and soon Iris saw Amanda turn and catch sight of her.

"Mother!" she cried and came flying toward her.

Iris ran forward and the two embraced. "I've missed you so

much, daughter!" Iris said. "And look at that dress! Where did you get it?"

"I brought you one even prettier, Mother," Amanda said. She turned to Sequatchie and went to him at once. "Have you taken good care of my mother?"

"Better than you might think, daughter." A glint of humor flickered in Sequatchie's dark eyes, and his lips turned upward in a smile. "Things have happened since you've been gone."

Amanda stood stock still. Her eyes went quickly to her mother, who was suddenly blushing, and Amanda cried out, "You're going to get married—or maybe you're married already!"

"Not yet. We wouldn't do that without waiting for you."

"And I had to ask your permission," Sequatchie said. "How many horses will you have to have for your mother? At least three or four, I would think. She's a good woman. Worth that many."

The three stood there in a close group, and Amanda's heart filled with the joy of happiness. "Oh, Mother. I'm so happy for you." She gave her a kiss on the cheek, then said, "Come on. I want you to meet some new friends."

As they moved toward the group, Iris's eyes went from one to the other. She saw Elizabeth standing with a tall man she had never seen before and wondered who he was.

———

Elizabeth had gotten no warning at all about the visitors. She had heard the sound of someone coming and said, "Hawk, I think we have company."

"Yes," Hawk said, going to the window, "and quite a bunch of them, from what I can see."

Almost at once Jacob, Amanda, and Sarah entered. Sarah threw her arms around her mother, and then Elizabeth turned and gave Jacob a hug. "I'm so glad you're all back," she said.

"Mother, we've got a surprise for you. Close your eyes."

Elizabeth looked involuntarily, for she knew that some others were outside the door but she could not imagine who. Immediately she closed her eyes and heard the sound of movements and whispering.

"All right, you can open your eyes."

When Elizabeth opened her eyes, she was astonished to see her brother standing directly in front of her grinning broadly. "Will!" she screamed and threw her arms around him.

"Well, sis, we just dropped by for a visit, since we were in the neighborhood."

Elizabeth hugged him hard and tears came to her eyes. "I've missed you so much, Will," she said. She felt his strong arms around her, and for a moment the two stood there shut off from everyone else, caught by old memories. Then Will stepped back and said, "I know this comes as a shock, but after Father died we all started talking about coming west to Watauga."

Rebekah came forward and greeted Elizabeth with a kiss. "We decided to cross the Misty Mountains. You've written so much about it we just had to come and see for ourselves." She turned and said, "Oh, this is Seth Donovan." She gave a quick history of how Seth had helped the family so much, and Elizabeth greeted him warmly.

"My goodness, we've got to start cooking something!" Elizabeth said. "Where are those children of yours?"

Soon the cabin was filled, and Hawk moved over to speak to Seth Donovan. "Glad to meet you, Seth," he said. He liked the looks of the young man and engaged him in conversation. He soon knew there was more to the young man than he was being told, for Seth seemed uncomfortable.

It took quite a while to put together a meal for such a large company, and at one point Amanda went out to get a bucket of water from the well. She was pulling it up when a hand closed over hers, and Jacob's voice said, "Let me do that, Amanda."

Amanda turned and said, "All right, Jacob."

The trip had been good for both of them. When they had started out in the company of a large group of settlers, Jacob had somehow managed to spend time alone with Amanda every day.

Now Jacob said to her, "You are so beautiful, Amanda. I can't believe you love me after all I've put you through."

"That is forever in the past, Jacob. Let's leave it there."

"Then you'll still marry me?"

"Of course I will marry you, Jacob. How many times must I say it?"

Jacob let out a whoop like a wounded mountain lion.

"Jacob, you'll have everybody out here!"

"I don't care!" Jacob yelled. "I think it's time we let everyone know. Come out here, everybody! We've got an announcement!"

At once the door of the cabin flew open and everyone came out and stood before Jacob Spencer.

"What is it, Jake? Is it Indians?" Hawk asked his son, but there was a smile on his face, for he knew there were none.

"No, no Indians, but Amanda and I are going to make grandparents out of you! After we're married, of course," Jacob said. He let out another whoop, and then David and Eve, along with Hannah and Joshua, all thinking it was a game, began to whoop and do a little war dance.

Iris came over and pulled Jacob's head down and kissed him. "You be good to her or I'll cut a switch to you, Jacob Spencer."

"I will, Ma. Don't you worry about it." He looked at Sequatchie and said, "I guess the two of us will have to learn how to be good husbands to these Taylor women."

Elizabeth came into Sarah's room and found her getting ready for bed. She was wearing a shift and combing out her hair. She went over to Sarah and hugged her again, saying, "I can't believe you're back. It's been almost a year."

"I know. It has been a long time, hasn't it?"

"Now tell me all about it. I want to hear everything."

"No, you don't, Mother," Sarah said, smiling. "You just want to hear the exciting things. There were lots of dull times in Williamsburg."

"You've forgotten how lonely it gets out here, and we don't know anything. Tell me everything. Tell me about your grandmother and Martha. I wish I could see them, but I think they made the right decision in staying with the Spencers. What are the women wearing for hats these days? Tell me more about Hawk's parents. What about the dances? Did you meet any young men you liked?"

As soon as she said that, Elizabeth saw that Sarah's face seemed to be swept by an odd expression. "You did meet a young man! I knew it!"

"Not really."

Quickly Elizabeth said, "That young man, Seth Donovan, is it him?"

"No!" Sarah said. "He's nothing to me."

The answer came so quickly and sharply that Elizabeth was silent for a moment. Then she said, "Will told me a little of his history. It sounds like he had a bad beginning but a good ending."

"I suppose so," Sarah said.

A sudden moment of insight came to Elizabeth. She said quietly, "You haven't gotten over the death of your father after all these years, and you're still thinking about Philip, aren't you?"

"I haven't learned how to forget things like that, Mother. I don't think you ever do."

"I think about your father quite often, but it's a good memory for me. It was his time to go, and God has made wonderful provisions. It's not that I love your father any less, but these things happen. I don't think God wants us to sit around and be sad, but to take the new day He gives us."

"I don't know how to do that," Sarah said, her lips compressed tightly. She ran the brush over her hair, then turned to face her mother. "I don't know if I'll ever be able to let myself love anyone completely, because there's always the chance of losing them."

"Sarah, you've got to open your heart. Even if you risk loss, it's better to have love even if you lose it."

"I don't believe that."

"Then you'll be a bitter woman the rest of your life."

Suddenly tears came to Sarah's eyes. "I know it, Mother," she whispered. "I just can't help myself. To tell the truth I . . . I did find myself becoming interested in Seth."

"He seems like a fine man. He's so big and handsome, and according to Will, he's very brave. He'll make some woman a good husband."

"I suppose so, but I've got to forget some things first."

"We'll pray, and God will give you peace about all of this, Sarah." Elizabeth went over and hugged her daughter and then said fondly, "Good night. I'm glad you're home."

"I'm glad I'm home, too, Mother."

Wedding Day

Twenty-Five

$\mathscr{I}$t's the first time I've ever seen you nervous, Sequatchie." Hawk grinned broadly at the tall Indian, who gave him a stoic glance back. "I've seen you face a big war party when you weren't as jumpy as you are now."

Sequatchie knew his friend was prodding him with the rough frontier humor that he was accustomed to.

"A man has a right to be nervous when he puts his life in the hands of a woman."

"Why, I expect you know that Iris is going to take good care of you. No sense being jumpy."

"I've been alone a long time," Sequatchie said. "I don't know if I can properly handle all the ropes that tie a man down once he's married. The Cherokee way I know, but the white people have many strange customs."

"You're right about that," Hawk nodded. He sobered and said, "You and Jacob are both taking a big step. Jake's never been married, and you haven't for a long time."

Jacob, who was standing stiffly with his back against the cabin wall, licked his lips. "I didn't think I'd feel like this, Pa. Right now I'd rather go up against a grizzly bear with nothing but a switch than to go through with this!"

"Every man feels like that, son," Hawk nodded encouragingly. "I think it took two or three good men to hold me down when I was about to marry your mother. There's just something about it that frightens a man."

Not a hundred feet away in the Spencer cabin, Iris and Amanda were having somewhat the same conversation with Elizabeth.

After a time Elizabeth finally said, "Well, I'm glad that we're going to be close together." It had been arranged that Jacob and Amanda would live on the Taylor family homestead. Iris had given it to them as a wedding present. Iris was going with Sequatchie, in any case, to the Cherokee, and afterward they would come back and Sequatchie would build her another house near Jacob and Amanda.

Now Elizabeth looked at the two and started to speak, but suddenly Joshua came running, saying, "The preacher's here! The preacher's here!"

"I suppose it's time. There're a lot of people out there," Elizabeth said.

"I wish none of them were here," Amanda said. She was wearing a light pink dress that had a square neckline with delicate rows of white lace decorating the tight-fitting bodice. The sleeves were made up of three layers of white lace and pink ribbon bows along the edges. The overskirt had light blue ribbon along the edging, and the underskirt had embroidered roses decorating it. Amanda looked very nervous as she finished getting ready.

Iris also had on the first new dress she had owned in years. She wore a jade green dress with a high neck and full elbow-length sleeves. It had black ribbon decorating the bodice and along the edges of the overskirt, and the underskirt had small black bows along the bottom.

At that moment Will stuck his head in the door and said, "The minister's here. Are you brides ready?"

Taking a deep breath, Amanda went over and put her arm around her mother. "Let's go," she said. She smiled then and said, "I'm happy for you, Mother."

"And I'm happy for you, too, Amanda. You're getting a good man."

"We both are."

They moved outside and found the yard filled with people who had come to share this special day. Paul Anderson was standing there smiling at them, and beside him stood Jacob and Sequatchie. The two women moved forward and Paul arranged them facing him, saying, "Take your brides by the hand, gentlemen."

The ceremony was long as such things go. Paul Anderson spoke the words of the binding part of the ceremony, and after this gave a rather lengthy discourse, much like a sermon, speaking of the responsibilities of husbands and wives to one another. Afterward he prayed a prayer with a great voice, calling out a blessing on their union, and asking God to watch over both husbands and wives.

Amanda's hand lay on Jacob's arm firmly while the words rolled over them. From time to time she would look up and pull his eyes toward her. There was a love in his expression that gave her great courage, and finally Paul Anderson's voice became gentle as he spoke of the holiness of the marriage tie, the goodness of God, and the mercies of the Lord Jesus.

As Paul continued to pray, Sequatchie, who was holding Iris's hands, felt suddenly that he had done exactly what God had commanded him to do. He could feel Iris's eyes on him and turned to smile at her as Anderson spoke of the blessings of health and love and neighborly kindness, the joys of sins forgiven, and the comfort of the Spirit.

Finally Paul Anderson said, "I now pronounce you man and wife, Amanda and Jacob. And I pronounce you man and wife, Sequatchie and Iris. May the Lord watch over you and keep you faithful to himself and to each other as long as you both shall live."

———————

After the ceremony was over, Seth Donovan, who had kept at the back of the crowd, watched as Sarah congratulated both of the brides and then stepped back. He went to her at once and said, "It was a nice wedding."

"Yes, it was, Seth."

"No slight meant to the brides, but I think you're the most beautiful lady here."

Sarah flushed and stammered, "You shouldn't say that. This is their day."

"I know it, Sarah. I seem to have a genius for saying the wrong things to you."

At that moment Joseph Foster, who had been standing close enough to hear Seth's remarks, stepped up. He said, "Sarah, perhaps you need some help serving all these people."

"Why, thank you, Joseph, that's nice of you." She hesitated, then said, "I don't believe you've met this gentleman. This is Seth Donovan. Seth, this is Joseph Foster."

"Glad to know you," Foster said, but he did not offer his hand,

and the smile on his lips did not go to his eyes.

"Thank you," Seth said. He ascertained at once that this man disliked him, and from Foster's possessive touch on Sarah's arm, it was not difficult to figure out why.

"Well, I guess I'll go congratulate the new grooms."

As soon as Seth moved away, Foster said, "Who is that fellow?"

"He's from Scotland."

"I can tell that from his talk. What's he doing here?"

"Oh, I don't know, Joseph. He's good friends with Will Martin, my uncle."

Joseph cast a hard look at Seth's departing back, then turned to say quickly, "I missed you, Sarah."

"Well, I missed you and everyone else."

Foster could not get his mind off Seth Donovan. "He came all the way back with you from Williamsburg?"

"Yes. As I say, he's good friends with my uncle and his family."

Joseph nodded but something was in his mind. He was a possessive man, and having set his head to winning Sarah, he would brook no opposition. "I wonder if he's a Tory."

"Not at all!" Sarah almost related what had happened between Seth and the Martins and how he had changed, but she felt it would be wrong. "He's not loyal to the Crown. I'm sure of that."

"Maybe so. In any case, come along. You can wait on me. Get me the best of the food."

For hours people stayed and visited. There were games, tests of strength for the young men, and the women of the outer settlements could not get enough talk. It was lonely out in their cabins, and they made the day last as long as it could.

Hawk finally moved over to Sequatchie after people began leaving and said, "I hear that the Indians are attacking some of the areas to the south."

"I heard this, too. I think it's the followers of Dragging Canoe."

"Dragging Canoe! I had hoped we'd heard the last of him!" Hawk said.

"Well, he was beaten at the last battle, but he escaped to the Chickamauga area."

"I think someone's stirring the Indians up to this."

"I agree."

Hawk sighed heavily and looked at the happiness on his son's face and murmured, "It looks like this Revolution has caught up with us, and I hate to see it. . . !"

Anniversary

Twenty-Six

*A*manda was bent over the fireplace stirring a delicious-smelling stew. She was concentrating so thoroughly on this that she did not hear Jacob as he approached her. His eyes were gleaming with humor, and he suddenly reached out and grabbed her around the waist. He snatched her up in the air and swung her around in a wild, careening arch, ignoring her squeals.

Finally he put her down, and when she turned around and opened her mouth to scold him, he enfolded her in his arms and stopped her protests with a firm kiss.

"Jacob, you ought to be ashamed of yourself!"

"I am ashamed!" Jacob's eyes gleamed and he pulled her even closer, ignoring her attempts to escape. "I'm ashamed that I don't pay more attention to you. I've got to stop working so hard. It's not right for a woman to be ignored like you've been."

Amanda could not hide the smile that leaped to her lips. "Ignore me! Why, I can't turn around but what you're there. I didn't know you were going to be such a pest, Jacob Spencer!"

"Well, I read in the Bible that in the old days when a young Jewish man married he didn't do any work for a year. He stayed home and paid attention to his wife, let her wait on him, and things like that."

"You made that up!"

"No, I didn't! It's in the Old Testament somewhere. I'll ask Sequatchie about it. I'll bet he doesn't intend to do any work, either."

The two newlyweds had only enjoyed the bliss of marriage for two weeks, but it had opened a new world to both of them. Neither Jacob nor Amanda had known a happy childhood, Jacob being abandoned by his father and living a lonely life, and Amanda enduring the hardships of an abusive father. Now, however, Amanda was rejoicing every day in the new happiness that had filled her life. She stopped still, a thoughtful look coming into her clear eyes. "I'm happier than I've ever been, Jacob," she said evenly. "I didn't know what real contentment was. You make me feel so—well, so wanted and so secure. I never felt that before."

"I'm glad, and you make me feel the same way, Amanda. I like being married."

The two stood there for a moment, then Amanda's shoulders lifted. "Well, I've got to get this food cooked. If we're going to have this celebration for Andrew and Abigail's first anniversary, we've got to have food to eat."

"Hardly seems possible that they've been married a year, does it?"

"No, and I think they're almost as happy as we are."

Jacob went about his chores while Amanda finished the cooking; then an hour later Andrew and Abigail came in. It had been Amanda's idea to have them in for a meal to celebrate their anniversary, and they had also invited Sarah MacNeal, Seth Donovan, and Joseph and Leah Foster. It was late afternoon when they all had arrived, and the cabin was soon filled with the sounds of laughter. It was Jacob who suggested playing One-oh-Cat. They all went outside to an open space where a stake had been driven into the ground about three feet high. Jacob found a stick about a foot long and placed it on top of the stake, then when the others spread out, he said, "All right, here it goes!" Using an upward swing, he struck the second stick with a bat whittled out of white oak and sent it spinning into the air. It drove directly at Andrew, who adroitly picked it out and said, "Easy! Now it's my turn." The object was to hit the stick so that no one would catch it. If it was caught, the player would be declared out, otherwise he ran to a base. If the stick was not caught but hit the ground, one of the players picked it up and threw it at the batter. If it hit him before he reached base, he was out. If not, he stayed on base.

The game went on for some time with a lot of chiding of the young women by the young men. Seth Donovan found himself the master of the game. It was not only that he was larger and stronger than anyone there, but he seemed to have tremendously good hand-to-eye coordination. He could strike the stick and drive it into the air so that it would fall between two players. Or, from time to time, he would hit it a hard blow and make it fly over the heads of all of them.

Joseph Foster, although he was strong and agile, seemed to have no skill at the game. He spent most of the time scowling and muttering, "This is for children!"

Sarah had laughed at him and said, "Come on, Joseph, loosen up! Have a little fun. It beats working, doesn't it?"

Joseph managed to smile, but it was a feeble effort.

Finally, when Seth knocked the stick so that it fell almost in Joseph's hands, Joseph wheeled and drove the stick directly at Donovan's head. It struck him in the cheek, and since he was only a few feet away, it was obviously unnecessary.

"Seth, are you all right?" Sarah asked. She ran to him and reached up, saying, "Oh, you've got a cut there! Come along, I'll put something on it."

"No need of that," Seth protested, but Sarah had come up and studied the wound. "I think that's enough of this game. It's a little bit too violent."

"Sorry about that, Donovan. I didn't mean to hit you so hard. I guess I got carried away." Joseph Foster made his apology stiffly and stood there defiantly.

Seth shrugged. "Doesn't matter. It's not a bad cut."

Nevertheless, that ended the game. When they went inside the cabin, Sarah said, "Let me look at that a little bit more closely. Do you have any liniment, Amanda?"

"I think so. I believe it's in the barn."

"I'll get it," Jacob said, then left at once.

Meanwhile, Sarah said, "Let me at least get the blood off. Do you have a piece of cloth, Amanda?"

When Amanda came back with a small piece of cloth, Sarah said, "Sit down here, Seth." He protested, but she shoved him firmly down. "Now you sit and be still." Taking the cloth and dipping it into a pan of cool water, she wiped the blood off, then studied it carefully. "I'm glad that stick wasn't higher. It might have hit you in the eye."

"Never worry about things that might have happened," Seth said, smiling, very conscious of her hands on his face. When Jacob returned with the liniment and she applied it, Seth did not flinch. "That's enough of this," he said. "I've gotten worse scratches in a briar patch."

It was time then to eat, and Sarah, Amanda, Abigail, and Leah put the food out. It consisted mostly of wild game, including raccoon and venison. As they were eating, Andrew asked, "Seth, how do you like the frontier?"

Seth was chewing on a piece of venison. After he swallowed, he said, "I like it right well. Vurry well," he said, "except some of the things take a little getting used to." He looked at Jacob, saying, "Your father's done a lot to teach me how to live out here and how to do things, but I've got a long way to go."

"You'll learn," Jacob said. "I didn't know anything about this country when I came, but Pa and Sequatchie helped me. You've got a good eye, a good shot, and we need more defenders in the settlement here."

"That's right," Joseph said quickly. "The more men with arms we have, the more we'll be able to fight off these attacks by the Cherokee."

Quickly Sarah looked at Joseph. "You don't know that there'll be any more attacks by the Indians."

"Why, of course there will!" Joseph said, somewhat surprised at her words. "They'll be coming back. The British are constantly trying to stir them up. I thought everyone knew that."

"I expect Joseph's right," Andrew said. "I heard Pa talking with Mr. Sevier. They said it's just a matter of time before Dragging Canoe launches another attack on the settlements."

"Well, they're not really prepared to attack. They don't have the guns or the ammunition or the powder," Jacob said.

Suddenly Joseph slid his eyes over to Seth. He smiled and said, "They'll have to have somebody to give it to them, and since you used to fight for the British, maybe it'll be you, Seth." Then he laughed and said, "That's just a joke, of course."

The joke fell flat, however, and no one even smiled. Jacob shook his head and said, "That's not funny, Joseph."

"I'm sorry. I was just having a little fun. You don't mind, do you, Seth?"

"No, not at all."

Joseph then added, "Of course, people around here are suspicious of anybody who's fought in the British army. You'll have to get used to that."

"That's all over for you, isn't it, Seth?" Sarah said quickly.

"Yes, it is. I'll never fight for the king again."

Joseph Foster's attempt at a joke had taken some of the fun out of the celebration. Leah, his sister, quickly began to tell a story that amused them all and the moment was passed over.

————

"I'll see you home, Sarah."

"You don't really need to, Joseph."

"Don't be so silly. I want to."

The two thanked Jacob and Amanda for the party and wished Andrew and Abigail a happy anniversary, then left. Andrew and Abigail volunteered to take Leah home, and soon Joseph was taking Sarah to her cabin. She said little enough, and finally Joseph broke the silence by saying, "I hope you're not mad at what I said about Seth."

"No, of course not."

"Well, he's new, of course, and he did serve in the British army. There're not many Tories around here, and people are pretty suspicious of them."

"Seth certainly isn't one of them."

"But he did fight on the British side."

"Joseph, I don't want to talk about it anymore."

Joseph kept silent for a while, and then finally they reached her home. Joseph walked Sarah to the door. He reached out and caught her arm. He had been preparing a speech, and now he said, "Sarah, what would you think about it if I called on you as a suitor?"

Instantly Sarah knew what he meant, but she hesitated. He had said something like this before she had gone to Williamsburg. She had filed it away in her mind, but now, after looking into his eyes, she saw that he was serious. "I'm . . . just not ready for anything like that."

Joseph reached out and put his arms around her and kissed her. He did it so quickly she could not protest, but she stepped back quickly. She had not returned the kiss and half angrily said, "You shouldn't have done that, Joseph!"

"I probably shouldn't, but I'll probably do it again."

Abruptly, Sarah said, "Good night!" and went into the house.

Turning away, Joseph shook his head. "She's playing hard to get," he murmured as he strolled along in the darkness, "and I can tell she's stuck on Donovan." Anger came to him then. He was a jealous young man determined to have his own way, and now his jaw tightened as he said, "I'll fix that! See if I don't!"

Two Birthdays Celebrated

Twenty-Seven

*F*or the settlers over the Misty Mountains in Watauga, the war still seemed very far away. Their greatest fear was not that the troops of King George would come to give battle, but that the British would incite the fierce Indian tribes to sweep down upon them. After Washington and his tattered Continentals had endured a terrible winter at Valley Forge in 1777, the nature of the Revolution had gradually begun to change. Despite the harsh conditions that winter, the troops had emerged from the experience in better shape than ever before. Baron von Steuben had taught them close-order drills and how to march, and for the first time they had come forth able to meet the trained troops of King George.

Washington still suffered defeats at Monmouth and Morristown, but by November of 1778, he had twelve thousand troops fit for duty, as large an army as he had ever commanded. Now they were waiting for the spring of 1779 with more hope than they had experienced at the beginning of the war.

The struggle for independence, however, passed over the heads of those who were cut off by the mountains to the west. As Christmas of 1778 approached, they managed to put away their fears of Indian raids and the war coming any closer and looked forward to the holiday season with joy and anticipation.

On Christmas Eve all of Hawk's and Elizabeth's families were gathered together to celebrate. Will Martin and his family were at the Spencers' cabin along with Jacob and Amanda, Andrew and Abigail. Seth Donovan also had arrived, feeling a little bit uncomfortable and like a stranger.

The children were all engaged in threading popcorn on a string to decorate the tree that took up a large part of the corner of the cabin.

"I've got to have a bigger cabin," Hawk said ruefully. "This one's as crowded as an anthill."

Elizabeth smiled at him. She was happy and her face glowed. "Be glad we're all here. It's good to have a big family for a Christmas celebration."

"Yes, it is," Hawk agreed. He looked around fondly and picked up Hannah as she came begging him to help her with the popcorn. His big hands struggled with the needle.

Elizabeth smiled to see the tiny girl sitting in her husband's lap. "She looks like you sometimes, Jehoshaphat."

"Jehoshaphat!" Hawk looked up with surprise. "You only call me that when you're mad at me."

"No, I don't."

"You call me other things, too." He winked broadly at her. "A lot sweeter than any of those."

Elizabeth flushed and looked around to see if anyone heard, then said, "You hush! It's not nice to talk like that!"

Across the room Seth was sitting with Eve and David Martin. He had sat down on the floor beside the children and now was helping Eve Martin with her popcorn the same as Hawk with Hannah. He listened idly to the chatter of the child, answering her from time to time, and finally saw that Sarah was watching him with a strange expression in her eyes. When he finished one string, he said, "Eve, you try this one for yourself. You're old enough to string your own popcorn." Ignoring her protests, he moved across and stood beside Sarah, who was cutting up venison into small chunks. The fireplace made a pleasant roaring sound as the logs crackled, and outside the wind blew, trying to force itself down the chimney.

"Pretty cold outside today," Seth said. He found it difficult to talk to Sarah. Ever since he had come to Watauga, he had spent most of his time in the woods hunting with Jacob or Andrew. Will Martin had done a great deal of this, too. Both of them were anxious to learn the ways of the woodsmen, and the long days out under the open skies had tanned Seth's skin to a coppery tone. His hair hung down clubbed in the back, and he wore a soft deerskin hunting shirt, fringed and molded to the muscles of his upper body. His neck was thick and strong, and his hands had toughened and looked very powerful.

"I haven't been seeing much of you lately, Sarah."

Sarah continued cubing the meat with a sharp knife and dropping bits into a large black pan. "No," she said, "I've been busy."

"Can't tell you how much I appreciate your father's help. He's taught me a lot this fall."

"He's good at teaching people," Sarah said slowly. She finished up the meat and then looked directly into his eyes. "Have you had any more trouble about being in the British army?"

"A little, but it's not too bad."

As a matter of fact, Seth had suffered some insults from some of the more fiery patriots of the settlement. A few of them had been forthright about it, accusing him of being a traitor to the patriot cause. Seth had endured it patiently, explaining that like many others, he had come over from Scotland or England with little idea of what was going on in the Colonies. He had merely said, "I was loyal to my king, but I no longer agree. So I can't serve him any longer."

This had calmed many nerves, but the rumors persisted. Seth was fairly certain that it was Joseph Foster who kept the rumors from being laid to rest, but he made no comment and said nothing to Joseph about it. Now he looked over at Sarah and wanted somehow to express himself, but this young woman had built a wall around herself. She met his glance, and he saw the shadow and shape of odd things come and vanish in her eyes. She was a complex and unfathomable woman, he thought, and now he noticed she was breathing quicker, and color ran freshly across her cheeks. He saw the hint of her will and her pride in the corners of her eyes and lips and marveled again at her eyes that were colored by a tint that seemed to have no bottom.

Not knowing what else to say, he rose and went back to sit between Eve and David again.

———

The big meal had been consumed, and presents had been exchanged. At the end of the evening, Hawk Spencer said, "Before you all leave, I want to do one more thing." The cabin grew quiet. It was packed almost, and the children were tired and quiet for the first time that day. "I want to read the Christmas story. After all, this day is meant to celebrate the coming of One who delivered us all from our sins."

Moving across the room, Hawk picked up a black leather Bible from the mantel and turned. The firelight flickered on his strong cheeks as he opened the Bible and began to read the old story from the Gospel of Luke.

As the account was being read, Seth found himself feeling more strange than he could ever remember. He had heard this story read from the Scripture many times, for his family, his mother and father, had been God-fearing Christian people. Somehow, though, as the words filled the cabin, Seth realized suddenly, *Why, this story's being read all over the world. Even as far away as the jungles, or even in the north country of ice.* Somehow the enormity and the miracle of the Christmas story sank into his heart. The words began to create vivid mental images. It was almost as if he could see the manger with the animals, their breath steaming in the night as the baby's first cry came. And then as the story continued in the second chapter of Matthew, he seemed to see the men from the East as they came bearing gifts, acknowledging the coming to the world of the One who would save it from its sins.

Sarah, across the room, kept her eyes fixed on Seth's face. It was a strong face, the firelight making the planes of his cheeks almost cavernous, and his eyes were sunk back under a heavy bone structure. She was somewhat shocked to see that he was moved by this story. She knew he was a man who kept his emotions under tight control, and as the story came to the end, his eyes suddenly seemed to glisten. She realized with a distinct shock that these were tears. It was a side of Seth Donovan she had never seen before, and as she watched him wipe his eyes furtively with the sleeve of his hunting jacket, she thought, *Why, I don't know him at all, not at all!*

Finally Hawk closed the Bible and said, "I think it would be well if we have a prayer. Maybe you'd lead us, Will."

Will Martin prayed fervently for all the family and for those in the settlements. He was not an eloquent man, but somehow the prayer stirred the hearts of those gathered.

As soon as he was finished, everyone decided to turn in for the night. The Martins left for their nearby cabin. Abigail and Amanda were staying with Sarah. Jacob and Andrew were staying with Seth in the small cabin that had once belonged to Sequatchie. Seth had been staying there since coming to the frontier.

Elizabeth turned to Hawk after everyone was gone or in bed. She put her arm around him and said, "It was good, wasn't it?"

"Yes, wife, it was very good."

———

As Jacob, Andrew, and Seth were undressing for bed, Jacob turned to Seth and asked him, "How did you like the evening?"

"It was different, and it was good, Jacob."

"I always love hearing the Christmas story, especially now that I'm a Christian."

Seth seemed somewhat uncomfortable at Jacob's mention of faith. "It's a wonderful story," he murmured. He had been staring out the window at the clear stars sparkling in the sky, and now he looked over at Jacob and said, "I envy everybody who's got God in their hearts."

"Why, Seth," Andrew said with surprise, "you don't need to do that! God doesn't have any favorites."

Seth did not answer for a time. He was studying the configuration of sparkling points made up by the stars. They always fascinated him, and now he murmured, "Those stars didn't all make themselves. I know that God made them."

"Of course He did. Just like He made you and me and everything else."

"Tell me how you both became Christians."

Andrew answered quietly, "My father led me to the Lord as we were traveling to Watauga when I was just a boy. He was always so close to God. He lived it before me every day of his life. It was the last true conversation we had." As tears came to his eyes, he added, "God is as close and wonderful to me today as He was then."

Jacob then said, "I had a tougher time coming to the Lord. I allowed bitterness at being abandoned by my father to keep me from my heavenly Father. He never stopped loving me, however. He kept putting people in my life to witness to me—my grandparents, my father, Sequatchie, my stepmother, even Andrew." He smiled at his stepbrother. "Finally, I was at the end of my rope, and Amanda spoke to me in a very straightforward manner, basically telling me to get saved. I learned then to listen to her, and it was a good thing I did, since I wound up marrying her!"

After they all shared a laugh, Jacob asked, "What about you, Seth? Have you come to know God in a personal way through His Son, Jesus Christ?"

"I've been so angry at God since the death of my brother, Isaac, I doubt if He will ever listen to me again."

"Don't be foolish, Seth," Jacob said quickly. "We all offend God. You know He says in His book that He loves us even when we offend Him. Think of that prodigal son, how badly he had offended his father. But when he came back, the father ran to greet him."

For a long time the three men sat there talking, and finally more and more Seth Donovan felt a loneliness and an emptiness in his heart. He had heard someone say that there were enormous distances between those stars overhead, but they were nothing to the emptiness that he felt deep inside!

As for Andrew, he knew his sister had some sort of special feeling for the big Scotsman, and as he talked he prayed silently, *Oh, God, let Seth find You. He's lonely and lost, and has no life!*

Finally, after a long time, Jacob said quietly, "It's not difficult to be saved, Seth. God is on our trail. All we have to do is repent of our sins and have faith in Jesus' sacrifice on the cross. When we have that, all we have to do is call, and He'll answer."

Seth did not answer, but Jacob saw his hands were trembling and that he could not lift his head. Quickly Jacob pressed his advantage. "We're going to pray for you, Seth, and I want you to pray for yourself. It doesn't have to be an eloquent prayer. You're praying to a God who loves you, who sent His only begotten Son, Jesus, to die on the cross for you. Now let's just pray that that same Christ who was born in a stable in Bethlehem will be born in your heart right now."

As Seth prayed a simple prayer, he felt a loosening in his spirit. He began to weep silently, for he knew something was happening. All of the guilt and all of the anger that had built up in him throughout the years of his life seemed to be dissipating like a mist—and then it was gone! Looking up, Seth said, "Jacob, Andrew, something . . . has happened to me."

"I think so. God has touched your heart," Jacob replied.

Seth could not speak for a long time. Andrew began to quote Scripture to him, and finally Jacob threw his arms around the big man and said, "Seth, you know that baby in the manger in a new way. From now on, you can celebrate your spiritual birthday on the same day we celebrate Jesus coming into the world."

The whole family was gathered around the table for breakfast, but before they could begin, Seth cleared his throat and said, "I've got something to tell you." When everyone looked at him with surprise, he swallowed hard and said, "Jacob and Andrew talked with me a long time last night, and then they prayed for me. I prayed for myself, and . . . I don't know how to say this, but something happened to me."

Hawk Spencer rose at once and came over and put his arm around Seth's shoulder. The two big men seemed to dominate the cabin, and Hawk's voice was husky as he said, "I know what it's like, what happened to you, Seth. It's like you've been lost out in the cold and the dark, and then suddenly you come into a room where there's warmth and fire and people who love you."

Shocked by the recognition that came at Hawk Spencer's words, Seth Donovan nodded, paused, and then replied in a voice filled with emotion, "Yes, that's what it's like."

And then the whole family came to welcome the tall Scotsman into the family of God. Sarah came too, but there was a reserve in her. Although she was happy about Seth's newfound faith, somehow she felt an odd reticence about entering into this man's joy as she knew she should. It troubled her, and later on that day when she encountered him out beside the well, she said, "Maybe I didn't express myself very well when you told us you had found the Lord, Seth." She was a proud girl and an honest one, and now she turned to face him. "I'm very happy for you. Very happy, indeed." She put her hand out and he took it.

He squeezed it and said briefly, "That's like you, Sarah. You have a strong will, but I know deep down you're one of the kindest people I've ever met."

Sarah was somehow touched by his words. "I do have a strong will," she admitted, "but I thank you for reminding me of it. In any case, Merry Christmas, Seth Donovan, and welcome to the family of God!"

Mount Up With Wings

Twenty-Eight

*H*awk Spencer always awoke, even out of the deepest sleep, with an almost shocking abruptness. One moment he would be unconscious in that twilight world, and the next his eyes would fly open and he would be totally aware of his surroundings. Others he knew, such as Elizabeth, awakened slowly, but he himself leaped from sleep to the world of reality about him in one instant.

A cock was crowing far off, his clarion call clear and sharp and insistent. The chuffing of the bay mare that was about to bear a foal came to him from the pasture as his eyes flew open. For a time he lay there savoring the sounds of early morning. Moving his head slightly, he saw that the eastern horizon was already turning a silvery buttermilk color. Ordinarily he would have leaped out of bed, but instead he lay there for a time, and as was his custom, he took the time to thank God for the blessings that had come into his life. His praying was as plain and simple as the clothes he wore. He disliked ornate prayers almost as much as he disliked a full dress suit. His mind moved quickly over his family and all his blessings. When he had named all of his family and friends, he ended by praying, *Well, Lord, these are all in Your hands. I don't need to tell You how to take care of them. I'm just asking You to do it, and I especially pray for these young ones who are marrying and starting families. Be with them, for the way is hard and rocky sometimes. But with Your help they will make it. So I am thanking You in advance for the work You are going to do.*

Now he was aware that the light was growing a long line of crimson along the eastern hills, and he turned over abruptly in the bed, propped his head up on his hand, and smiled as he looked at Elizabeth. She was sleeping soundly, as usual, and for a long period, he simply let his gaze wander over her features. He had done this often, and now a special sense of happiness came to him, a joy he often wished he could express to Elizabeth but lacked the words. Now he reached out and laid his hand on her cheek, and lowering his head, he kissed her on the other, whispering, "Wake up, wife. Time to start a new day." He smiled as she squirmed and tried to turn her head away. She dearly loved to sleep late, and ordinarily he might have let her, but there was much to do on this Sabbath day.

"Wake up. We've got to get ready to go to meeting," he whispered again. This time he put his hand on her hair and stroked its soft glossiness. "You're the prettiest wife in all creation," he said, "but you sure do sleep sound. Now, wake up before I pour cold water all over you."

Elizabeth shut her eyes tight and murmured, "Go away. Leave me alone."

Hawk reached over, threw the coverlets off, and Elizabeth grabbed at them futilely. It was March and the air was still cool, and being pulled out of the warmth she loved so much brought a protest from her. "Leave me alone, Hawk!"

"What do you want me to do, go fix breakfast? That's your job, woman!" Hawk simply reached over and rolled her to him and pressed her to his chest.

"All right, I'm awake!" she said. "Let me go!"

"After a while. I haven't got my money's worth out of you yet."

Accustomed to his mild teasing, Elizabeth lay there, coming fully awake slowly. She enjoyed more than she had ever expressed to anyone the little attentions her husband paid to her. Attentions like this when he simply held her, stroked her back as she came out of a sound sleep. He had not always been a demonstrative man, but he had somehow come to not only speaking his love for her, but showing it with little gestures and caresses. Reaching up, she pulled his head down, kissed him, and smiled as he showed surprise. "Now, that's a reward for being such a good husband."

"Well, I think I've been a better husband than that," Hawk said, kissing her again. The two lay there for a few moments talking, and sometimes Elizabeth would giggle at the wild and rather ridiculous things he said. "No one would ever know how foolish you are! You're so stately and dignified sometimes before other people. They don't know how you carry on when the two of us are alone."

"I can't help it," Hawk said solemnly. "Your beauty drives me mad!"

"What!"

"I read that in a book once. It was a book of poetry, I think. This fellow said that about a woman. Your beauty drives me mad. I've been saving up to tell you something like that for a long time. Now you know the truth. I'm plum crazy, and you can't expect any sensible behavior out of me."

Elizabeth laughed and shoved him aside. He grabbed for her, but she escaped and came to stand on the floor. Quickly she moved over to the washstand and began washing her face. She talked as he lay watching her, and finally she said, "Come on and shave those whiskers. They nearly rubbed my skin off last night."

Hawk grinned broadly. "You didn't complain, I noticed." He got out of the bed, came over, and began preparations to shave. As he lathered up, Elizabeth went over and removed her shift and began to dress. She put on a clean white chemise, a pair of drawers, and then a petticoat made out of heavy cambric material. She then slipped into a plum-colored outer petticoat of linsey-woolsey and a white blouse with tucks down the front, long sleeves, and a high neck.

Hawk lathered his face up, tested his straight razor, then began drawing it down across his skin. "It's been nice having Reverend Doak and his family here permanently, hasn't it, Elizabeth?"

"Yes, it has," Elizabeth said, drawing the brush down over her hair that fell almost to her waist. "I love Paul, but I know he's got to follow his call to preach to the Cherokee. It's been good to have preaching on a more consistent basis."

"Sure has." Hawk removed the lather from the shining blade on a towel, then carefully drew it down the other cheek. "A lot of churches are being established around here these days. The Buffalo Ridge Baptist Church just started up. I expect Doak will pick a place to start a Presbyterian church soon."

"Some have complained because there are so many denominations coming in, but I don't think that's right. I hope they all come. The more churches, the better the moral atmosphere this country will have."

"We're gettin' civilized." Hawk wiped the lather off his face and then pulled on his pair of gray trousers. He slipped on a single white shirt, and as he buttoned it up, he said, "You know, now that we've got a county seat here, the country's going to grow faster. And James Robertson is still gone to pick out an area farther out west to start another settlement."

"I think that's good. It'll be a long time before we have anything like the cities back East, but I feel safer with more people living in the area."

"Well, I like the churches moving in," Hawk murmured as he brushed his hair, "but that means taking more land from the Cherokee."

Elizabeth glanced at him abruptly. "And that means more fighting, I suppose."

"Probably does."

"Well, we'll have to pray even harder for the Cherokee and for our people, too. Now, let me fix your hair. It looks like you slept upside down for a week. . . ."

———

A small graveyard had been started next to the church in a little clearing near the main part of the settlement. To one side, a few tombstones were clustered in the tall grass. Most of them were simple wooden boards with a name and date of death carved in them. Two or three were made out of rock hauled in from the river and had the names more permanently carved in the soft stone.

As the sun rose higher, families began arriving at the church. Preaching appointments were generally happy occasions, for the people lived far apart, and services were held only as often as the minister was able to make it into the area. When the preacher arrived he would find the fenced-in yard around the small building crowded with men, women, and children. Numerous guns would be leaning against the log cabin meetinghouse while every man took his place on a bench, wearing his shot pouch, tomahawk, and scalping knife. There was always a great deal of handshaking before the meeting.

As Hawk and Elizabeth arrived, Hawk noticed that many of the congregation had already abandoned their shoes, especially the children. He also noticed that some of the women carried their shoes in their hand until they reached the meetinghouse, whereon they slipped them on. Shoes were too valuable to be used up when bare feet would do just as well!

"It looks like we've got more dogs for the service than people," Elizabeth said to Sarah, who was walking closely beside her.

"Some of them are better behaved, too," Sarah smiled mischievously. She made a quick count and said, "If every family in this area has five dogs, which I believe they do, that means we must have over a hundred dogs here for services this morning."

"That's about right," Jacob said. He was right behind his parents and Elizabeth, holding on to Amanda's arm. "Forty-five babies and seventy-five dogs, with about sixty adults to take care of all the dogs and children."

Amanda laughed. "What a thing to say."

Seth was walking beside Sarah. Since he had been converted, he had not missed a service and had become an avid reader of the Bible. Sequatchie and Iris had given him one for a "birthday present," as they called it. He treasured it greatly, and it was quickly discovered that he had a prodigious memory. If he ever once read something out of the Scriptures, it never seemed to leave his mind, and he could remember the chapter and verse, as well. Hawk had laughed at him, calling him a walking Bible, but Seth had merely smiled and said, "I guess that's a good thing for a man to have in his head, the Bible. I've had a lot worse."

The church itself was a rough log structure that had been built by the combined efforts of the men and had little in the way of decoration. The pews were made of split logs with pegs driven in for legs. There were no backs to them, of course, and often splinters found their way into the worshipers. There were three windows along each side that let in not only light but also mosquitoes and bugs of all sorts, and even birds from time to time.

Seth leaned toward Sarah after they had sat down and said, "It's not like this back in Scotland. In the churches I went to, everyone was very quiet. If a young one got out of hand, he was taken outside and thoroughly thrashed."

"What were the sermons like?"

"I guess I wasn't listening," Seth admitted. "Some of it must have stuck with me. I know some of the Scriptures did, but then my parents read the Bible to me a lot."

"Everybody's amazed at how well you've done studying your Bible," Sarah said.

"I've never read anything as exciting as the Bible. It's like a history book, an adventure story, and a book of poetry all rolled into one. It's as though God wrote it just for me. I keep seeing myself in it."

Sarah had not yet allowed the wall she had put between herself and Seth Donovan to be breached. She still kept him formally at arm's length. Now she realized this was the most intimate conversation they had had since his conversion. She was grateful that he had experienced a change of heart. Still, she was having difficulty in her own heart learning to let go and allow herself to get close to someone because of the losses she had suffered.

As the two sat there, Seth looked around and noticed that the Spencers, the Andersons, Sequatchie and Iris, the Stevenses, and the Fosters were all there. *I've gotten to know these people pretty quick,* he said to himself. *I never had friends like this before. I never stayed in one place long enough after I left home, I suppose.* His thoughts were interrupted when Reverend Samuel Doak walked in through the front door and was greeted on every hand. Doak came by and shook hands with every individual. Seth had not met him before, and when he stood up to greet the preacher and was introduced by Hawk, Doak looked at him with a pair of level dark eyes. "I'm glad to finally meet you, dear brother. Do you know the Lord?"

"Yes, Pastor, I was converted on Christmas Eve. Jacob Spencer and Andrew MacNeal led me to know the Lord."

A pleased smile lit up Doak's features. "I thank God for your salvation. And are you walking in the light?"

"I'm doing the best I can, Preacher, with a lot of help from Brother Spencer here and his family."

"I can't think of a better family to nourish a newborn child of God. Welcome into the kingdom of God, my dear brother."

Doak left and took his place at the front of the room, leaving a warm glow in Seth's heart. He sat there content, unaware that several in the congregation, including Joseph Foster, did not share Doak's fondness for him. Hawk and Elizabeth noted it, however, and Elizabeth whispered, "I wish people wouldn't hold Seth's past against him."

"So do I, but that's the way some people are, I guess."

The song service lasted for nearly forty minutes, and then Samuel Doak stood to his feet. He opened his Bible and said, "My text is taken today from Isaiah, chapter forty, verses twenty-eight through thirty-one. It says, 'Hast thou not known? Hast thou not heard, that the everlasting God, the Lord, the Creator of the ends of the earth, fainteth not, neither is weary? There is no searching of his understanding.

" 'He giveth power to the faint; and to them that have no might he increaseth strength. Even the youths shall faint and be weary, and the young men shall utterly fall;

" 'But they that wait upon the Lord shall renew their strength; they shall mount up with wings as eagles; they shall run, and not be weary; and they shall walk, and not faint.'

"I take it that this text is applicable not only to the children of Israel, but to every living human being," Doak said, his voice a clarion call, reaching even those who were outside the building. "Not a man or a woman who ever lived has escaped this experience. Weariness comes to all of us. Some of you have labored harder, hacking and hewing a home out of this wilderness in a way that people who live in the cities of this continent will never know. Early and late you have labored, and sometimes you have been so tired you could barely crawl into your beds."

For some time Doak stressed that weariness was part of human life, and as his keen eyes went over his congregation, he saw that his words struck home. The women indeed knew what it was to labor, even as the men, who worked from sunup to long after sundown, knew what it was to be weary. Doak's words came to pierce their very hearts.

"But there is another kind of weariness," Doak said, "that is even more trying, and that is the weariness that comes to the spirit, to the soul, to the heart of all of us. It is worse, because when we are physically tired, we can lie down and sleep and be refreshed, but the weariness of the heart—who can give rest from that? Our text tells us that it is the Lord God, the Creator of the ends of the earth who can give us rest. He himself does not faint and is not weary, and it is His delight to give to every one of his children rest from the trials and troubles that weigh down our hearts."

Seth listened quietly, taking in the words. He had discovered that he loved hearing the preaching as much as he enjoyed reading the

Bible for himself. It was a relief and a rest to hear the Word of God proclaimed.

Doak preached for some time, and finally he said, "All who are not living for the Lord must be weary. One of the key factors in finding rest is found in our text, the thirty-first verse. 'They that *wait* upon the Lord.' Waiting is something that we do not do easily. We are willing to work but not to wait. God says there comes a time when we must simply wait upon Him. To believe that He knows what is best for us, and that He will be with us through everything. I will ask you, my dear brothers and my dear sisters, have you learned to wait upon the almighty God?"

As Reverend Doak spoke these words, Sarah felt a pang in her heart. She bowed her head and stared down at her hands, for she realized she had been living under an intolerable burden. As the preacher continued, she began to confess to God that she had not let Him help her. And finally she began to plead with Him. *Oh, God, I have not waited upon You. I have borne the burdens that the minister speaks of, and right now I open my heart. I open it to You.*

As she prayed she knew something was happening. A freedom began to manifest itself. She took a deep breath and was suddenly aware of a presence, and she knew it was the power of the Spirit of God.

He's taken away the load! It was as if a terrible, heavy burden had been lifted, and joy began to bubble up in her.

Seth was aware that Sarah had been touched and moved by the sermon as well. He had seen her clench her hands together tightly and had noticed that they trembled. He leaned forward and said, "What is it, Sarah?"

When Sarah turned to face Seth, her eyes were filled with tears. "It's just . . . God has taken away a heavy load from my heart."

"I'm glad," he said simply. He did not touch her or reach out, but there was a warmth and something in his clear eyes that encouraged her, and she held his gaze for a moment before turning back to listen as Reverend Doak concluded his sermon.

Sarah had been so happy over what God had done for her in setting her free, she did not notice as she made her way back home that Joseph Foster had cut across the path until he stood beside her.

"Sarah, I've got to talk to you."

"Can't it wait, Joseph?"

"No, it can't." He took her arm and turned her around.

The others of the family looked, and Hawk Spencer frowned but shook his head and they moved on. Seth gave the pair a keen glance, but he, too, shrugged and moved away, heading back toward the homestead.

"Sarah, I think I've been patient with you," Joseph said, "but I need an answer. You know that I care for you."

Somehow his insistence grated on Sarah. "Joseph," she said, "I don't want to talk about this now. As a matter of fact, I'm just not ready to even think about such things." She tried to tell him about what had happened in the church, but he shook his head.

"I'm glad you had a good service, but you've led me to believe that you like me."

"I've always liked you and Leah. We've been friends for a long time."

"I want more than that, Sarah. I want you to marry me, and I want your promise now."

"I can't give it to you, Joseph. I'm sorry, and please don't talk about this to me again. Not for a long time."

"For someone who doesn't want anybody courting them, you're getting awfully close to that big Scotsman."

"He's just a good friend of the family."

"I don't believe that!"

"Well, I'm sorry, Joseph, but you'll have to accept it. Now I've got to catch up with my family. Please let's not have a scene like this again. Let's just be good friends."

Joseph Foster stared at her as she left. Anger burned deeply in him, and he put his gaze on the broad back of Seth Donovan, and the jealousy and envy that had been in him for some time seemed to boil over.

"He won't get her!" he muttered between clenched teeth. "I'll see that he doesn't get her!"

Accusations

Twenty-Nine

$\mathcal{S}$equatchie glanced over at Hawk Spencer with curiosity in his dark eyes. He and Iris had spent much time with the Cherokee, where they had helped Paul and Rhoda Anderson minister. They had come back now for a rest. Balancing the maul in his hands that he was using to split locust rails, Sequatchie asked, "How are things going with the newlyweds?"

"Why, I reckon they're as happy as two pigs in the sunshine."

Sequatchie laughed aloud. "I was not aware that pigs had such happiness."

Hawk set the steel wedge in the crack of a locust tree, tapped it in with his maul, then swung it easily. The tree made a loud ripping sound as it fell apart into two sections. "I wish everything in life was as easy as splitting locust rails," he commented, then picked up the maul and held it in his hands for a moment before turning his dark blue eyes on his companion. "I'm glad for Jacob and Amanda. They're happy with each other."

"That was what Iris said. She was concerned about Amanda. She was afraid she would not make a good wife."

"Why would she think a thing like that?"

"She told me that because her father mistreated her, she might be afraid of men. But they've had a lot of secret talks since we've been back, and she tells me that all is well."

"It's good for a man to get married when he's young."

"I suppose that's a jab at me for waiting so long to remarry," Sequatchie said. He tapped his own wedge into the crevice of a locust, swung the maul, and the log fell apart easily. "But you yourself waited many years before you married again."

"That's right," Hawk said. The two men worked steadily for a time, and finally Hawk said, "I've been a little concerned about our girl Sarah."

"I know."

"You know? How do you know? I haven't said anything about it!"

"Do you think I'm blind?" Sequatchie shrugged. "Iris and I have been watching Sarah for a long time. We feel like she's our own really. We know she's had a hard time getting over the death of her father."

"It all happened so long ago. I can't believe she's still troubled with that."

"I think it's as much losing Philip Baxter as anything else."

"That's what her mother says, but life is hard out here in this place. Everybody has to learn to give up a loved one. I don't know a single family who hasn't lost someone in the fighting, or to the wild beasts, or just to the elements. It's a hard country, Sequatchie."

"It's just as hard in white man's big cities." The Cherokee shrugged and a thoughtful expression came to his eyes. "The Scripture says that we're nothing but a breath, a vapor, that will disappear in a moment."

"That's right. Or like a flower that blooms and then is gone the next day. But God gives us some good times, doesn't He?"

"That He does, but what about Sarah?"

Heaving a sigh, Hawk laid the maul down and moved over beside the cabin. A bucket of water was there and he lifted it and drank out of it, then held it to Sequatchie. "Have some of this. It's still pretty cool."

Sequatchie took his drink and then waited for Hawk to speak. He knew that, like himself, Hawk Spencer was a man who knew how to keep his own counsel. Others might speak quickly what was on their hearts, but something about being a longhunter, spending months or even years alone in the wilderness, created a silence within men that was not easily broken. Now the dark face of the Cherokee was patient as he waited for Hawk to speak his mind.

"It's obvious is she taken with Seth, and that worries us a little bit."

"You do not think he's a good man?"

"I think he is now. Like all of us, he's got things in his background he's not proud of," Hawk shrugged. "But since he's given his heart to God, I can't fault him."

"There's a lot of talk about his being a British soldier. People don't like that, and they can't seem to forget it," Sequatchie commented. "It's not right, but there it is."

"It's not even that that worries me. It's the fact that Sarah's built a wall about herself. If she loves the man, Elizabeth and I could accept him as a son-in-law easily."

"He learns fast," Sequatchie agreed. "He's become a good hunter in a brief time. Another few years and he will be as good as you." He smiled slightly and said, "Perhaps even as good as me."

Hawk glanced abruptly at the Cherokee and caught the sly humor that came out of Sequatchie from time to time. He smiled in return. "I guess you're right about that, but I had a better teacher than he does."

"Where are they now?"

"In the barn looking at the new calf. At least that's what they said they were going to do."

"They're more likely looking at each other. That's far more interesting to young people than looking at new calves."

"I suppose so. Anyway, I know you're praying for them, and so are Elizabeth and I. Seth Donovan is a good man. He'll make a good husband, but Sarah will have to give up some things that've been in her heart."

"You know, I think she's already begun. I was watching her in the service when Reverend Doak preached at the last meeting. God was doing some kind of work in her heart, and after it was over, I could tell that she was relieved."

"I noticed that, too," Hawk said, "but on the way home Joseph Foster spoke to her. He's been after her for a long time now, but Sarah doesn't care for him. At least not in that way."

The two men spoke openly and freely, for they were closer than most brothers. Finally Hawk said, "Well, it's in God's hands now. We'll just pray that those two young people will do the right thing."

————

Inside the barn Seth Donovan was seated on a keg watching Sarah as she stroked the silky back of the young calf that was feeding from its mother. He thought, *Never seen a prettier sight than that.*

Young calves are pretty anyway, and as for Sarah, I don't know how to say what I feel about her.

"Isn't she precious," Sarah crooned. "Her hide's just like silk. Now you go on and have your lunch, Sweetie Pie."

"Sweetie Pie! Is that the name of that critter?"

"Yes, it is. I named her myself. Sweetie Pie."

"I named her before you did."

Surprised, Sarah turned around to stare at the big Scotsman. She was wearing a simple gray dress with a white apron over it, and she made a fetching picture. "Who told you you could name my calf?"

"Nobody told me," Seth said. "I just did it."

"I'll bet it's an awful name!"

"Delilah."

"What?" Sarah stared at him and her eyes flew open. "Delilah? Why would you name a beautiful calf like this an awful name like Delilah?"

"I think it's a pretty name."

"Haven't you ever read about Delilah?"

"Of course I have. She was a barber," Seth said innocently. "I understand she gave very nice haircuts."

Suddenly Sarah saw that his lips were tightly held together as if he were withholding a laugh. She had noticed before that there was a comical side to this big man that slipped out from time to time. She burst out laughing and shook her head. "You're awful, Seth Donovan! Just awful! And you know what a terrible woman Delilah was!"

"Must have been pretty, though. Samson thought so."

"He was a foolish man for giving his heart to a woman like that!"

"Man can't always choose. When love comes it just comes."

Suspiciously Sarah turned away from the calf. She came over and sat down on a keg beside him and gathered her skirts around her ankles. "What kind of talk is that? When love comes it just comes. Have you been reading some kind of romances?"

"I've read a few. Haven't you?"

Sarah shook her head and turned away. "I think they're low!"

"I like them," Seth grinned. "That's the way love happens. A young fellow is just walking along, sees a young woman, and something just turns over inside of him. From that moment on, just one look and he's a gone coon."

"A gone coon? I'll bet it didn't say that in that romance you read."

"I don't remember what it said. But anyhow, this young fellow took one look at this girl, and then for the next five hundred pages, he chased around after her." He glanced over at the calf. "He was mooning like Delilah here does for her mama when she's hungry."

"Don't you call my calf Delilah! Her name is Sweetie Pie!"

"You call her what you want to, and I'll call her what I want to."

Sarah reached over and grabbed Seth's hair. It was caught up in a club in the back. She loved the looks of his hair. It was thick like a lion's mane and a golden blond, or tawny color, she had never seen before. It had a little red in it, too, for sometimes the sunlight caught it. She pulled at it and said, "I'll pull your scalp off if you don't stop it!"

His neck and shoulders were so strong, Seth scarcely felt her pulling with all of her might. He endured it for a moment, however, then turned around and caught her wrist.

"If I'm going to be scalped, I want it to be by a wild Indian, not by you, Sarah MacNeal!"

Sarah tried to get to her feet, and he rose with her, still holding her hands pinioned in his large grasp. He looked down at her and, holding her hands together, shook his head as if in wonder. "You know, it's a strange thing," he said quietly. "Here I can hold you, both of your hands in mine, and you can't move a muscle. Physically I can make you do anything I want to, but there's the other side of it."

Sarah was very conscious of being held. The Scots burr was evident in his tone. That was something else Sarah liked about him, he didn't talk like anybody else. His strength was tremendous, and she felt like a little girl, almost, in his grasp. He was so tall she had to look up to him. She was less than five feet six inches, while he towered over her a full six feet two. He had measured beside Hawk and discovered to be two inches taller. He was also so broad and his muscles so rounded that he gave the impression of tremendous strength. Now she stood there and, looking up, whispered, "What do you mean by that?"

"I mean that I am stronger than you are in one way, but you have the power to draw a man, Sarah. Did you know that?"

"Any woman can do that."

"No, they can't. At least not like you draw me. Sometimes when I'm out in the woods all alone, not a soul around, I think about you. And I stop, and I turn, and I face back toward this homestead, but it's not a cabin I'm turning to, it's you. I saw a little magnet once that would draw metal to it. I'm like that metal, and you're like that magnet. You could draw me if I were halfway around the world. I'd come back if I thought you wanted me."

A silence then fell in the barn, only the sound of the calf nuzzling her mother, and outside the pleasant hum of the two men talking, from time to time the splitting of a locust log, but Sarah was not conscious of any of this. What she was conscious of was the strength of the man before her. Ever since the load had lifted from her heart, she had looked on Seth differently. Perhaps it had something to do with Joseph Foster's insistence upon some sort of decision from her. Now she quietly whispered, "Let me go, Seth."

"Sure." Seth loosed his grip at once but did not step back. Rays of sunlight filtered through the cracks in the barn and touched Sarah's hair. It was a fiery red, and she had told him that her father had had hair exactly like that. Her hair hung in long ringlets that cascaded down her back, and as she looked up at him, her eyes, an unusual bluish green, were fastened on him. She would be strong, Seth knew, as a woman had to be in this part of the world. She would be a woman to stand beside a man, working, and bearing children, and enduring the hardship down through the years.

"I don't know how to say this, Sarah," Seth said quietly. He reached out and ran his hand over her hair. Just the action caused a slight shiver to run through Sarah, but he did not notice it. His voice was quiet and intent, and his eyes were filled with her image. "I've never cared for a woman like I care for you. The rest of them are all like ghosts. I can't even remember them, but I'll remember you if I'm an old man who lives to be ninety. I'll still remember this moment. I remember everything about you from the first time we met. I don't know why it is," he murmured, his voice soft as the breeze outside the barn, "but everything you do stays with me. At night when I'm lying in my bed, I go over it again and again. The time you pulled the fish out of the creek and nearly fell in and I caught you."

"I'd forgotten that," Sarah whispered, deeply moved.

"I haven't. You were wearing your checkered dress, and you had a yellow bow in your hair. When you slipped I caught your arm and then pulled you out of the water, and you laughed up at me. That comes to me again and again, that and a thousand other things."

"I didn't know you felt like that, Seth. I didn't know any man did. It's women who remember things."

"Maybe they do, too. I can't say. I just know that no matter where I go from this place, I'll remember you."

"Go?" Sarah was startled. Involuntarily almost, she reached out and laid her hand gently on his chest. "What do you mean go?"

"I'll have to go, Sarah," Seth said quietly.

"Why? Why would you have to go?"

"It's too hard to be here, to be around you and not have you," he said simply.

At that moment Sarah MacNeal knew something had changed in her spirit. For years she had endured a weight and had resisted forming any sort of permanent relationship for fear of loss. But God had taken that from her, and now she saw that she was about to lose the man that she truly loved. It came to her almost like a vision, or a dream, with the suddenness of a bolt of lightning that lit up the skies. *Why, I love him, and I can't lose him! He can't go away!*

With a voice that was not steady, she said, "Seth, please don't go. I . . . I need you."

Hope sprang into Seth Donovan's blue eyes, and he reached forward and put his hand gently on her shoulders. "Does that mean that you care for me a little bit, Sarah? For I love you as no man ever loved a woman."

"I . . . I have learned to care for you, Seth," Sarah said.

At those words, almost spoken in a whisper, Seth suddenly smiled and a wonderful goodness broke across his face. "I think, next to my hope of heaven, my hope of having you is the strongest thing in me. I do love you, Sarah MacNeal." He pulled her forward then and spoke her name. She gave herself to him, and a great, powerful sensation moved in her as he kissed her. She wasn't quite crying when she kissed him, but an emotion, strong and full, flooded through her, and as his arms went around her and pressed her tightly against his chest, she suddenly felt as if she had come home again.

As for Seth, her nearness brought up a constant, never-lessening want, and the pressure of this desire held him there as he pressed her closer. There was suddenly, to him, a bottomless softness, a sweetness, and she was a fire burning against him and a wind rushing through him.

Finally he released her and, looking down, saw a flood of emotions in her eyes. The sunlight fell across her face, and he saw there what he had seen so many times, a beautiful woman with a soft depth, and a strong and fiery spirit. She looked at him silently then, and a woman's silence could mean many things. Seth said quietly, "It means a lot just to be able to say these things to you, Sarah. They've been in my heart a long time."

As for Sarah MacNeal, she was experiencing an emotion she could not define. She remembered how he had kissed her back in Williamsburg and wanted, at that moment, to speak all that was in her heart. Still there was some reticence in her, and she pushed him back and then ran her hand, which was trembling, over her hair. "We'll talk about this later," she said in a voice that was not steady.

Seeing that she was shaken by the experience, Seth nodded, "I'll be here," he said.

———

"I think I hear someone coming," Sequatchie said. He looked up at Hawk, who had heard the same thing.

"I'll see who it is," Hawk said. The family was gathered around for the noon meal, and now as he went outside, he saw Colonel Evan Shelby and a group of eight or ten men, including Joseph and Charles Foster. He stepped down on the ground, aware that the others had filed out to see what the group had come for. "Hello, Colonel Shelby."

"Hello, Spencer," Shelby said. He seemed nervous, and when he stepped down off his horse, he slapped the reins across his palms and stood there as if reluctant to speak. Finally he said, "We've come on some rather unpleasant business, I'm afraid."

Instantly Hawk's eyes narrowed. "Speak your peace, Colonel."

"All right then, here it is. There's been a lot of talk about Seth Donovan. We have reason to believe that he's in with a group that's inciting the Indians to come against us."

"What sort of evidence do you have?" Hawk said, his voice turning hard.

"That will come out at the trial." Shelby's eyes went to Donovan and he said, "You'll have to come with us, Donovan."

Seth moved forward. Somehow he was not greatly surprised that this had happened. The rumors concerning his loyalty to the settlement had been called and questioned, and his eyes went to the Fosters, and one look revealed that they were the source of the accusations.

Colonel Shelby said, "We'd like to search this man's cabin."

"You don't have to permit that, Seth," Hawk said quickly. "Colonel Shelby, you're not the law in these parts."

"The law hasn't caught up with us yet, Hawk," Colonel Shelby said. He was a mild-mannered man except in battle, then he turned fierce. But now he said firmly, "Until the law gets here, we have to be our own. Your were a sheriff in the Watauga Association for a time. You understand that we have to handle these matters ourselves."

Hawk shook his head. "Seth's as loyal as I am, Colonel."

"I trust that he is, but we've got to get these rumors settled. Will you permit a search?"

"They can search. Let them do what they want," Seth said, his eyes locking with Joseph Foster's.

Colonel Shelby said, "I'm sorry we have to do this. Some of you men go do it."

At once Joseph Foster slipped off his horse and said, "You come along, Ransom." The two men went inside the cabin, and Hawk said coldly, "Go ahead, Joseph, but you're wrong!"

"I'm sorry to have to do this. I know you're a friend of Seth's, but if he's not loyal to our cause, we've got to find out." Shelby then went up the stairs, followed by Eli Ransom. They were gone only a few moments, and when they came down Shelby had a sheaf of papers in his hands. "Look at this!" he said.

"Let me see that!" Hawk demanded.

Colonel Shelby took the papers back and studied them for a moment.

"These are from Alexander Campbell!" he exclaimed. "You know what that means, Hawk and Sequatchie. He's the one inciting the Indians to war!" He turned to face Seth Donovan. "How do you explain these?"

"I never saw those papers before."

Shelby hesitated for a moment. "You'll have to come along with us, I'm afraid. You're under arrest. There'll have to be a trial."

Sarah had observed all this with a heightened fear. She watched as Hawk brought a horse out. Before Seth could mount she went over to him. "Seth," she said, "you didn't do this, did you?"

"No, I didn't." He didn't argue or attempt to explain. His lips were set in a thin white line, and as he looked down on her, he said not another word.

He turned away but she caught his arm. "I believe in you, Seth."

Joseph Foster had observed this and he jerked at the lines of Seth's horse, saying, "Come on, fellow, we'll get the truth out of you."

Hawk and Elizabeth watched along with the others as Colonel Shelby led his band out.

"I don't think they got the right man," Sequatchie said so quietly that only Hawk could hear it.

"I agree."

"The person that makes the most noise about something is guilty in most cases."

"I think we'd better look into this ourselves, Sequatchie," Hawk said as he looked at Sarah, who was staring after the self-constituted posse. "This hits Sarah hard," he murmured.

Elizabeth gripped his arm. "We can't let it go on like that."

———

Later in the evening Elizabeth came to Sarah's room. She found her sitting in a chair staring blankly at a wall.

"You mustn't worry too much. I'm sure there's a good explanation."

"I don't know what to think, Mother. I was just getting to trust Seth again, and now this happens."

"If Seth is truly your friend, if you really care for him, now is the time to stand behind him and believe in him."

"But he betrayed us all once, or tried to."

"But he couldn't go through with it, could he?"

Sarah turned to her and could not answer for a moment. "I think I'm learning to care for him as a woman cares for a man."

"Of course. I saw that long ago, but now is the time for you to show your trust in your love."

Sarah stood there for a moment and then her lips grew firm.

"Thank you, Mother. I will. I can't let my fears get the better of me."

"We'll all be praying, and your father will get to the bottom of this. He's very fond of Seth, you know."

"I know," Sarah whispered. She could say no more, and after her mother left, she paced the floor for some time, and finally spoke out loud, "He can't be guilty. I just won't believe it. He's not that kind of man!"

Truth Revealed

Thirty

*T*he clearing around the meetinghouse was well filled with men who had gathered at the insistence of Colonel Shelby. Some of the women drew near to the outskirts so that they could hear the words of Shelby. The children, as usual, had to be forcibly quieted.

Colonel Shelby looked around at the gathering, and his expression was serious as he said, "Men, I have some news that is not good. Some of you remember Dragging Canoe, the son of Little Carpenter."

"I remember him," Hawk spoke up at once. "He's nothing at all like his father. Little Carpenter is an honorable man, but Dragging Canoe wants nothing but blood."

"That's right, Spencer," Shelby nodded, "and Akando has joined with him. I received word that they put together a sizable band, and if my informants are correct, they'll be raiding the settlements at any time."

A murmur of protest and indignation went around the men. One of them, a tall, bearded frontiersman spoke up. "I say we go out and put a stop to them murderin' varmints!"

Sequatchie had said nothing. He was well aware of the danger of raids by Dragging Canoe, for he had known him all of his life. Of all the Cherokee, Dragging Canoe was probably the most vicious and the most adamant against the white man. It was he who had said at a tribal meeting at which the whites had attempted to make peace, "This will be a bloody ground for you whites if you try to take it away from the Cherokee."

Colonel Shelby was an excellent leader of men. He waited until the group had worked itself up into a fighting mood, and then he said, "I'm going to ask you to follow me in a raid against the Chick-amauga Indians. Dragging Canoe has made himself their leader, and if we strike them, I think we may be able to handle the situation. How many of you will be willing to go?"

While the men were volunteering, Sequatchie had stationed himself so that he could watch Joseph Foster carefully. There was a great deal of milling around, and Sequatchie noted rather absently that Andrew and Jacob had both volunteered to join the raid. His eyes, however, were on Foster, and when the young man slipped away, Sequatchie moved over quickly to where Hawk was standing close to the colonel. He said nothing but touched his arm, and when Hawk turned, Sequatchie moved away and Hawk followed.

As soon as they were out of the hearing of the others, Hawk asked curiously, "What's the trouble, Sequatchie?"

"I think we need to follow Foster."

"Joseph Foster? Where has he gone?"

"He was here until a few minutes ago, until the colonel made his announcement. I've got the feeling that he's left to pass this word on to someone who could warn Dragging Canoe."

"Why would he do that?" Hawk asked. "What would he get out of it?"

"I don't know. I don't understand that young man. He seems to have something twisted in his mind. I do know that the English have paid money for information about what we are doing here. That might be it."

Hawk said instantly, "Let's follow him, then."

Following Foster proved not to be difficult. He was not a very good woodsman, and he never got the slightest hint that he was being followed as he made his way from the settlement. Hawk and Sequatchie stayed far behind, out of his sight for the most part. From time to time one would pull over as a flanker and catch a glimpse of him.

"He's turning off the road, on the old trail," Sequatchie murmured.

"He's up to something," Hawk nodded. "He wouldn't leave a meeting like that unless there was something going on."

Moving closer, the two darted behind trees, muted their footsteps, and after half an hour, Sequatchie motioned to Hawk, who stopped instantly. "Someone's ahead. I suspect whoever it is that's meeting him."

The two men watched carefully and soon were rewarded by the sight of a tall Indian of the Chickamauga tribe. Both men recognized him instantly as Running Arrow, one of the leaders that had given the settlers much trouble. He was a follower of Dragging Canoe, and now as the two spoke, Sequatchie and Hawk crept closer to hear their words.

"Pass the word to Dragging Canoe that there will be a raid on the Chickamauga settlements," Foster said.

Both Sequatchie and Hawk heard these words clearly. The Indian began to ask for more details, and Hawk whispered, "We can't let him get away and take that message back. We'll have to take them, Sequatchie."

Sequatchie nodded and the two men suddenly rose up from their hiding places, and Hawk called out, "Stop where you are, Running Arrow!"

But Running Arrow had his musket in his hand and it was primed. He threw it up and got off one shot that went humming by Hawk's ear. Hawk threw his musket up, but a shot rang out and Running Arrow fell back, a bullet in his chest. Hawk looked over to where Sequatchie was lowering his rifle, and then the two advanced.

"You'll have to come back with us, Joseph," Hawk said.

"What for?" Joseph Foster tried to brazen it out, but there was fear in his eyes, for he knew he had been caught. His only hope was that the two had not heard what he was saying. "I was just trying to arrange a meeting with the Indians so we could talk about peace."

"That's not what you said," Hawk replied, his eyes hard. "We heard you making arrangements to let Dragging Canoe know about the raid on the settlement. Come along, you'll have to face up to it, Joseph."

Foster turned and started to flee, but he was no match for the two woodsmen. Hawk was up with him in a moment and struck him in the back of the neck with a forearm. The blow drove Foster to the ground, and Sequatchie yanked him to his feet, pulling out his knife. "If you would rather I scalp you here, that can be arranged!" he said, his eyes glittering.

"No, don't let him do it, Spencer!"

"Come along, then," Hawk said.

As they were trudging along back toward the settlement, Foster spoke not a word. When they reached the group, most of the men had dispersed, but Colonel Shelby was still there. Hawk drew him aside, saying, "I've got some bad news, Colonel."

"What is it, Spencer?"

Hawk related the circumstances of Joseph Foster's treachery, and the colonel said at once, "Let me see him!"

The meeting was short and harsh. Shelby was angry to the bone at what had happened. He got the truth out of Joseph Foster almost immediately, and then said, "I don't know what you did this for, why a man would betray his own! I'm going to take you into custody!"

They took him at once to the jail. After releasing Seth, the colonel threw Joseph Foster inside the single cell. He began at once crying for someone to send for his father. Shelby said, "Shut your mouth! You'll get justice. I'll see to that!"

Turning to Seth, the colonel said, "I'm sorry about all this, Donovan. I think it's pretty likely now that we know how those papers got into your things."

"That's all right, Colonel, I understand." He hesitated, then said, "I'd like to join the raiding party if you'll have me."

"You've had some experience in the army. Fighting's a little bit different here, but we can always use another good shot."

Seth immediately left for the homestead, accompanied by Hawk and Sequatchie. The three men said little on their way, but finally Sequatchie said, "Justice sometimes comes slowly, but it did come. At least this time."

The raiding party had prepared itself so that on April the tenth they were ready to strike out. Abigail and Amanda were at the Spencer cabin saying good-bye to Jacob and Andrew. Each of the young women had decided to stay with her family while the men were away.

Sarah had hung back, and finally she left the room and walked slowly down toward the creek that cut across the northern part of the property. The spring had brought mild weather, and now the warm breezes blew across her cheek. It stirred the waters of the small creek, and she watched as the silvery bodies of the minnows darted here and there. Farther downstream a bass broke the surface, thrashing as he took his prey.

"Sarah?"

Quickly Sarah turned to find Seth standing before her. She stood at once and turned to face him. For days now she had tried to sort out her feelings to understand what was going on inside her heart.

"I haven't had a chance to talk to you, but I wanted to ask you how you felt about Joseph Foster."

"It's hard for me to believe he did a thing like that," Sarah admitted. "I've known him a long time, and he has a good side to him."

"I don't know why he did it either, but he's never liked me. Perhaps because he knows how I feel about you. He's cared for you a long time. What will you do now that he's been disgraced?"

"I went to see him," Sarah said slowly. "He's a broken man, Seth. He admitted he didn't know why he had done such a thing." She dropped her head and was silent for a moment. "He cried while I was there. I couldn't believe it. It was embarrassing for both of us. I feel so sorry for his family, too. They are so humiliated by what Joseph did that they are moving back to Williamsburg. I will really miss Leah."

Overhead a woodpecker began to hammer on the trunk of a dead tree. It made a staccato sound in the silence, and after finding a large grub, it flew off. Seth watched it go and then turned back and said, "I'll miss you, Sarah, and I wanted to ask you to pray for me. Will you do that?"

Sarah felt a lump in her throat. She knew somehow she loved this man, yet she could not speak. "Yes," she whispered, "I'll do that, of course."

Seth could not understand this young woman. He stood looking at her for a moment, then shrugged. *I guess she just doesn't care for me as I thought.* The thought came to him and he turned quietly and walked away.

Later, when Jacob, Andrew, Hawk, and Seth left to join Shelby, Sarah stood out on the porch and watched them leave. Somehow she knew she had failed once again. "I thought I was over all my fears," she murmured, then walked out to where she could watch them go down the path riding their horses at a slow walk. She watched them disappear around the turn, and misery came to her then. She was afraid for all of them, and the fear rose in her throat and seemed to fill her whole body. "God, bring them home safely" was the only prayer she could pray.

———————

Eliazbeth stepped outside her cabin to get some water from the nearby stream. After she filled her bucket, she paused a moment to rest. She had worked furiously for weeks to fill the time up so that she would not miss Hawk so much. She sent one of many prayers heavenward for the safety of her husband, sons, and friends. As she got up to head for the cabin and resume her work, she suddenly spied two men heading toward the cabin. Her heart skipped as she recoginzed her husband! She ran to Hawk and threw herself into his arms.

Hawk took her in his arms and said, "Somebody would think that you missed me!"

"You crazy man, of course I missed you!" Seth was behind Hawk and Elizabeth gave him a hug, too. "It is good to have you back, too, Seth."

"Thank you vurry much. Is Sarah around?"

Elizabeth smiled at the large man. "She's in the house, Seth. Go on in. I know she will be happy to see you."

Seth grinned and walked hurriedly toward the cabin. Hawk and Elizabeth took a more leisurely pace as they walked with their arms entwined. Elizabeth then asked, "Where are Jacob and Andrew? Are they all right?"

"They are fine. They were anxious to see their wives. They will be over to see you a little later, so you had better get a big supper going."

"Was the raid successful?"

Hawk sighed. "Yes, it was. I hate that we had to do it, but we would have not been safe otherwise. We hit them pretty hard. I doubt they will try to bother us again. Dragging Canoe and Akando both escaped, but it will be a while before they can muster the strength to bother us again."

"I'm just glad you're all home safe and sound."

"For now."

"What do you mean for now?" Elizabeth asked.

"I'm afraid this is just the beginning. The war is beginning to reach across the mountains. Soon the British will be after us, too."

Elizabeth replied firmly, "Well, I'm just going to thank God for keeping you safe now and let Him worry about the future."

"That is the best thing to do, wife." Hawk smiled down a Elizabeth and said, "Now I'm ready to see those kids of ours. I hope you haven't ruined them while I was gone!"

"Oh, you! I now wonder what it was I missed when you were gone!"

But one look into his wife's eyes told Hawk all he needed to know as he gently kissed her.

Sarah was startled by someone calling her name. She turned from her chore of dusting to see Seth Donovan filling the doorway of the cabin. She sucked in her breath and almost flung herself into his arms, but she held herself back at the last instant. "It is good to have you back safely, Seth."

Seth was disappointed by Sarah's greeting. "It is good to see *you* again, Sarah. I really missed you. Did you miss me?"

"Of course I did." She then moved to him and gave him a quick hug and a kiss on the cheek.

"I had hoped for a better greeting than that."

"Seth, I need some more time to sort out my feelings. It was hard while you were gone. I was afraid that you might not . . ." She stopped what she was saying and looked at the floor.

"Afraid that I might not come back? Sarah, I thought you had given that over to God."

"I need you to be patient with me. Please, Seth?"

Seth smiled slightly. "As long as I know you still care for me, I can wait as long as you need me to."

"Thank you, Seth. I do care for you, and I am very glad that you are home safely." Sarah watched as Seth quietly made his way to his small cabin. She wanted to run to him and tell him all that was in her heart for him, but then memories of losing Philip and the pain and grief that came to her for so long held her back. Tears came to her eyes as she prayed, "Help me, dear Father. I am so afraid."

Muster at Sycamore Shoals

Thirty-One

The year of 1780 was disastrous for Congress and for the American cause. Later historians label it by the title "The War Moves South." The British strategy involved moving into the southern Colonies, and they were fast overrunning Georgia and both of the Carolinas. General Cornwallis and his trained army moved forward, seemingly invincible. The patriots suffered defeat after defeat; Washington himself had grave doubts, and Congress practically gave up the fight. Because of short-term enlistments and shortage of supplies, the American force had dwindled to fewer than five thousand men. The American currency was worthless—a month's pay would barely purchase one good meal—and Congress had lost its authority and seemingly had no strength to make a move.

General Clinton, having failed in a campaign against the northern states, sent Colonel Campbell with three thousand troops to attack Savannah, Georgia. Campbell proceeded to plunder that city, and with a strong fleet and an army of thirteen thousand, he moved on and laid siege to Charleston. Two months later, on May 12, 1780, the patriots surrendered. The Hessians immediately pillaged the city, the homes of the patriots were taken or burned, and General Clinton, taking advantage of his victory, sent out his dispatchments in all directions. He wanted to subdue the patriots and demonstrate to the people that it was much better to take an oath of allegiance to the king than to fight.

Even worse news came to the American cause when General Horatio Gates was thoroughly trounced at the Battle of Camden in South Carolina. Gates, an incompetent general at best, lost his head and fled. The entire army was either killed, captured, or scattered.

Gates himself ran like a rabbit and did not stop until he had ridden two hundred miles away. This was the low point of the American Revolution, and those who had pursued the war in England were now confident that victory lay not far ahead.

At this point in history, as often happens, a small, almost insignificant event proved to be the hinge on which the larger events turned. The Battle of King's Mountain has never been recognized by most Americans. Nevertheless, it signaled a turning point in the Revolutionary War in the South. This in turn gave Washington in the north time to regroup and rise to fight again. The Battle of King's Mountain, therefore, is a watershed in the American Revolution.

To understand the Battle of King's Mountain, one must understand a British soldier, Colonel Patrick Ferguson. It was Ferguson, able soldier that he was, who led his troops into a losing battle, and therefore succeeded in turning the tide of the Revolution. Ferguson, an aide to Cornwallis, was sent to organize the Tories into a fighting force. He settled at a town called Ninety-Six, his headquarters, and for a time those who favored the king rushed to the British standard in large numbers. Ninety-Six was so named because it was ninety-six miles from the Indian town of Keowe, located just across the river from Fort Prince Charles.

Ferguson and his staff trained the Tory recruits thoroughly so that they learned good discipline. They also began a reign of terror in South Carolina and Georgia, ransacking, burning, and killing innocent civilians. Homes were burned, and mothers and children had to find shelter in the forest, and soon the name of Ferguson began to be spoken with hatred throughout the South. At that point in time, Colonel Ferguson, riding high with his successful campaign, had visions of becoming a general. He hated the overmountain men who had been a thorn in his flesh, causing him to make the most serious mistake of his life. Thinking to frighten the uncouth barbarians from the overmountain country, he wrote a message to Colonel Shelby, which he sent by his aide, a Lieutenant Phillips. It said, in effect, that if these back woodsmen did not stop their opposition of British arms, he would march over the mountains, hang their leaders, lay waste the country, burn every home, and destroy all the livestock.

As soon as Colonel Isaac Shelby received this message, he saddled his horse and rode at once to speak with Colonel John Sevier.

Sevier had recently married Katherine Cheryl, who had been known as Bonnie Kate Cheryl. It had been a romantic match because he had saved her life when she fled from the Indians in a most dramatic fashion. Leaning over the stockade, he had reached down, risking death by the musket balls of the Indians, grabbed her wrists, and hauled her to safety.

At once plans began to fall into place. As a result, September 25, 1780 was declared the date for a muster at Sycamore Shoals. Riders were sent over the country to call in for volunteers. Money for the undertaking was secured from John Adair, who said, "I have no authority to make disposition of the money, but if a country is overrun by the British, our liberty is gone! Let the money go, too!"

And so the word went out, and men all over the area began to move toward Sycamore Shoals.

All of the settlers were agitated over the news of the gathering. Wives bit their tongues, knowing that it would be useless to argue with their men. The spirit of patriotism had swept over the entire area, and events swept forward so rapidly that it was difficult to realize that soon the husbands and brothers and fathers of the settlements would be risking their lives in the war that had finally reached across the mountains and threatened to demolish them.

Elizabeth had kept her own fears to herself. At supper her eyes often rested on Hawk, who seemed cheerful. *He's not afraid of what might happen,* she thought, *but I am. I can't help it!*

After supper she stepped out on the porch and saw Sarah walking slowly along the path that led away from the homestead. Taking off her apron quickly, she followed her and finally called out, "Sarah!" When Sarah turned, she said, "What's wrong? You haven't said a word all day."

"I guess I can tell you, Mother, but I've been so confused I don't know which way to turn."

Elizabeth reached out and brushed a lock of Sarah's hair back from her forehead. "It's Seth, isn't it?"

Immediately the words began to fall. Sarah had been storing them up, afraid to speak, but now in the silence of the evening that was closing around the world, she nodded, "I've been afraid that if

I loved him and if we married, something would happen to him as it did to Father and to Philip."

"Sarah, we've talked about this before. You can't live life without taking chances. Don't you think I feel the same way about Hawk? Don't you think I'm afraid? But what would life be without love?"

"I know, but—"

"Sarah, you can't stop caring about people because you're afraid they will die. It was so hard when I lost your father. Nobody will ever know how I grieved. I had to be strong in front of you and Andrew, but it tore me apart inside." Elizabeth thought back to that time and the grief and the pain that she had gone through, and her lips tightened, but then she smiled slowly, saying, "If I had it to do all over again, even knowing the future, I still would have married your father. We had such good years, and I have you and Andrew, and there'll be grandchildren. And I have my memories of Patrick. He's part of me and will be as long as I draw breath. I'm glad that I married him."

"I wish I could feel like you do, Mother."

"It's the same way with children, Sarah. Think how risky it is to have a child, especially out here on the frontier. With Indians, and wild beasts, sickness, and no doctor, who knows which child will live past the first year? There's no way of telling that, but we have to throw ourselves into living and risk loss."

For a long time the two women stood there. The sky grew darker and the soft summer wind brushed their cheeks. Sarah listened to her mother with her heart open, for she had struggled with this problem until she did not know what to do.

"Love is a gift from God," Elizabeth said. "It's one of the things, perhaps the greatest thing, child, that He gives us to enjoy. Caring for Seth can be a good thing if you keep it all under God."

"I never thought of that."

"Well, it's time you thought. And let me ask you this. Do you wish you'd never known your father, that he had died before you were born?"

"Of course not!"

"Well, then, you should be glad for the time you had with him, and you should be glad with the time you have with your brothers and sisters . . . with your friends. The Bible says, 'God sets the solitary in families.' Those who aren't set in families are lonely people.

We all need each other, so I think it's time for you to think about the selfishness that you developed."

Startled, Sarah looked up. Her mother's face was almost stern. "Selfishness? What do you mean by that, Mother?"

"I mean you're withholding yourself from others. Didn't you know that the Scripture says, 'Who so would be a friend must show himself friendly.' It's almost the same thing to say, 'He who would be loved must love others. He who would have a lover must be a lover.' We have to give in order to receive."

Slowly Sarah nodded. "That's true. I think of old Mr. Ryerson, who's all by himself by choice. He's cut himself off and refuses to have anybody close, and he's like a dried-up stump."

"And that's the penalty of withholding love. That's why the Dead Sea is dead. It takes in fresh water but it doesn't give it out."

"Mother, I've been so miserable and unhappy."

Quickly Elizabeth put her arms around her daughter. She huddled close and nestled her against her as if she were a small child. "God will be with you. You must put Him first. You can't help those fears that come to you, the fear of losing someone, but God is greater than our fears. He has not given us the spirit of fear but of power and of love and a sound mind. You've got to turn to Him and release all these things, Sarah."

"Pray for me, Mother."

Elizabeth closed her eyes and prayed for her daughter. She had prayed for her for years, but now the words poured out of her lips and out of her heart.

Finally Sarah, with tears streaking down her cheeks, said, "Mother, God has spoken to me before about this in church."

"I remember, but you fell back and let your fears put you in prison. You have allowed your fears to keep Seth at arm's length for the past year, too, even though you know he loves you and you love him. Never take counsel of your fears, Sarah. Always take counsel of God."

Sarah straightened up. There was a new strength in her eyes, and now she stood straighter. Taking a deep breath, she said, "All right, Mother, I'll put this fear behind me."

"And about Seth?"

"I love him, Mother. I've just been afraid to let myself say so. I guess I haven't been fair to him by keeping him at bay all this time.

It's just that I was so afraid I would lose him when he went to fight the Cherokee at Chickamauga."

"Do you think he loves you?"

"Yes, I know he does. He's said so."

"He'll be going away with the men to fight. Don't let him go without telling him this time."

———————

The next afternoon Seth was surprised and even a little shocked when Sarah came by where he was chopping wood for the fire and said, "Seth, I'm going out to the river. Would you go with me? I need to talk to you."

"Why . . . of course!"

Seth tossed the ax down and turned at once. The two left the house and went toward the east, where a small river, hardly worthy of the name, wound around through the hills. All the way there, Sarah spoke of nothing but unimportant things. But when they got to the river, she turned to him and said, "I don't know how to say this, Seth, but—" For a moment her courage almost deserted her, but she was a courageous young woman and turned and faced him fully.

Seth saw her lips make a small change at the corners, and her eyes deepened almost to a greenish gray. Her hair was shining in the sun, and as Seth looked at her, he tried to fathom her expression. "What is it, Sarah? You can tell me."

A summer darkness lay over Sarah's skin, and she was shapely in a way that struck any man, and the light was kind to her, revealing the full, soft lines of her body. "I haven't been fair to you, Seth. I know that now. God's been dealing with me for over a year now, ever since that service in church when He spoke to me, and now I want to tell you that I love you."

Instantly Seth felt a rush of joy and happiness such as he had never known. He reached forth and took her hands and almost crushed them. "Sarah, I can't believe you're saying this! I've dreamed of winning you, but it seemed so impossible." And then, because he could do no less, he reached out and pulled her close. She came to him quickly, and when his lips met hers, she gave back the caress that he gave her. There was a roughness in him that she was astonished to find that she liked, and she held him closer, pulling her arms around his neck. For Sarah MacNeal, this was what she had been searching for. When he pulled his head back, she said, "I've been afraid to love because I've been afraid to lose."

"I know that, but there are no guarantees."

"No, except one." She looked at him steadfastly and said, "No matter if we only have a day, or a week, or a month, I'll have that and I'll be grateful for it."

The two turned and walked down beside the river. Neither one knew what to say, for happiness overwhelmed them. Finally he turned to her and said, "When I come back from the war, will you marry me, Sarah?"

"Yes."

He smiled and touched her cheek. "I have nothing, no money, no prospects."

"You have one asset." She laughed suddenly and reached up and grabbed his hunting shirt in her fist. Gathering it up she tried to shake him, but he was so big she made no effect. "You have me," she said.

"Then I'm rich."

He put his arms around her, held her close, and as he did, she prayed, "Oh, God, bring him back safe—bring him back safe!"

The muster at Sycamore Shoals was like nothing that had ever happened in the settlement before. The men who came were frontiersmen, hardened through their life in the new country. They were bold, resolute men who were self-reliant, independent, and individualistic. They depended upon the forest and the streams for life, and they could fight, scalp an Indian, or wrestle a bear.

Seth stood beside Sarah as the two of them watched the crowd swell. "They don't look like any army I've ever seen," Seth murmured. Indeed they did not. Most of them wore the long, fringed hunting shirt made of dressed deerskin. The pants were made of skins or homespun. Some wore leggings and moccasins made of leather and sewed with strips of elk hide to protect their legs and feet. Caps were made of animal skins, beaver hides, or coon, sometimes with the tail hanging down behind.

"Do you think they'll fight as an army, Seth?" Sarah asked. Somehow the sight of the army gathering together awed her. She was not accustomed to seeing such large groups, and there were over a thousand men already gathered. Many of them had brought their wives and some of their children so that Sycamore Shoals was swarming.

"They don't know close-order drill, but then they're all dead shots. That's more than I can say for the British. Of course, some of the British forces will be militia. They'll be as good a shots as we are, but these men are fighting for their homes, and I'd say they're going to do well."

The date was September 25, and every man there, and every woman also, knew they would never forget it. The women had been busy with their looms and needles, making and mending clothes for their menfolk. Some of them had made lead bullets in bullet molds. Others had whipped up all of the bread and provisions the men could possibly carry.

Hawk was standing beside Elizabeth, with Andrew and Abigail at his side. In front of him Jacob and Amanda stood watching the gathering. He looked at his sons, their wives, then looked down at Elizabeth. "You're not afraid, are you?"

"I'm putting my trust in God," Elizabeth said. She refused to answer directly, for if she had she would have said, "Yes, I'm afraid. I'm afraid for you and Andrew and Jacob and Seth and for all the men." Instead, she said, "God will be with us. He'll bring you safely home again."

That night campfires glittered all over Sycamore Shoals like the glittering of many eyes when seen from the distant mountains. There was singing, there were tears, there were all the things that come when men march off to war and leave their women and children behind.

The next morning Colonel Sevier asked the Reverend Samuel Doak to speak to the men.

Samuel Doak stood on a small knoll and looked out over the men for a moment. His heart swelled up within him, and then he said, "My countrymen, you are about to set out on an expedition that is full of hardships and dangers, but one in which the Almighty will attend you! The mother country has her hands upon you, these American Colonies, and take that for which our fathers planted their homes in the wilderness—our liberty! Your brethren across the mountains are crying like Macedonia unto your help. God forbid that you shall refuse to hear and answer their call, but the call of your brethren is not all. The enemy is marching hither to destroy your homes."

At these words a mutter went over the congregation, and men drew their wives closer and their jaws hardened. Jacob looked at Amanda and thought, *I'll fight to the death for you just like all these other men will fight for their wives.* He glanced at Andrew and their eyes met. They had had their difficulties, but now they were united and brothers indeed.

Reverend Doak concluded by saying, "Brave men, you are not unacquainted with battle. Your hands have already been taught to war and your fingers to fight. You have wrested these beautiful valleys of the Holsten and Watauga from the savage hands. Will you tarry now until the other enemy carries fire and sword to your very doors? No, it shall not be! Go forth, then, in the strength of your manhood to the aid of your brethren, the defense of your liberty, and the protection of your homes, and may the God of justice be with you and give you victory!".

A rousing cheer went up, and then Doak raised his hands until silence reigned again. "Let us pray! Almighty and gracious God, Thou hast been the refuge and strength of Thy people in all ages. In times of sorest need, we have learned to come to Thee—our Rock and our Fortress. Thou knowest the dangers and snares that surround us on march and in battle. Thou knowest the dangers that constantly threaten the humble, the well-beloved homes which Thy servants have left behind them. Oh, in Thine infinite mercy, spare us from the cruelties of the savage and the tyrant. Save the unprotected homes while fathers and husbands and sons are far away fighting for freedom and helping the oppressed."

Seth felt Sarah's hand close on his upper arm, and he turned to look down at her. She was smiling at him, but still there was a tremendous soberness in her. "I love you, Seth, and God has promised me that He will be with you. But be careful."

"I will," he said. He put his arm around her and left it there while the Reverend Doak finished his prayer.

"Thou who promised to protect the sparrow in his flight, keep ceaseless watch, by day and by night, over our loved ones. The helpless women and little children we commit to Thy care. Thou wilt not leave them or forsake them in times of loneliness and anxiety and terror. O God of battle, arise in Thy might. Avenge the slaughter of Thy people, confound those who plot for our destruction, crown this mighty effort with victory, and smite those who exalt themselves against liberty, justice, and truth. Help us as good soldiers to wield the sword of the Lord and of Gideon. In the name of Jesus, amen."

A mighty chorus of amens rent the air, and Hawk Spencer, looking around at his family and his brethren, knew that the British would have to face a formidable army.

Battle of King's Mountain

Thirty-Two

*A*s the overmountain men made their way from Sycamore Shoals in pursuit of the enemy that had threatened their homes, the instigator of the battle, Patrick Ferguson, took the threat of their army lightly. Ferguson, as proud and arrogant as his message to Colonel Shelby reveals, was in many respects a brilliant officer.

One of the chief marks of his brilliance was the fact that he had invented the first breech-loading rifle used in the army and had secured a patent on it. The weapon could be fired much more rapidly than a muzzle-loading piece, was highly accurate, and was reliable in wet weather when the flintlock was simply unusable. But the breech-loading gun was never used, for General Howe, who resented the young officer's invention as well as his inclination to independent action, shelved the notion. The guns were used to good effect at Brandywine, but then were put into storage, and the muzzle-loading flintlock musket remained the standard arm of the British infantrymen for decades to come.

One interesting footnote to history must be tied to the name of Patrick Ferguson. At the Battle of Brandywine, Ferguson, who was an excellent shot, was close enough to General George Washington to have easily shot him, but he refused to do so. He did not fire, because in the code of the British Officer-gentleman, it was bad form to kill enemy officers. In Ferguson's own words, "It was not pleasant to fire at the back of an unoffending individual who was acquitting himself very coolly in the light of his duty, so I'll let him alone."

What would have been the result if Ferguson had killed the commander in chief of the patriot forces at Brandywine? It is not impossible that without Washington's firm leadership, the Continental

Army would have fallen apart, and America would have remained colonies under the authority of Great Britain.

One other factor contributed to the Battle of King's Mountain. Patrick Ferguson's successes had all been in open warfare, almost invariably forays where speed and surprise were essential. He had no experience whatsoever with a different defensive operation, and his men likewise were untried for such forms of battle. The one remaining problem was an Englishman leading American Tories. He was the scion of an aristocratic Scottish family who had stayed out of military service initially because of bad health. But in 1768 he had bought a commission as captain in the 70th foot regiment and hence had been sent on duty to America. The Tories, though loyal to the Crown, were sometimes resentful of the officers sent from England to lead them, and this, no doubt, was a factor in the Battle of King's Mountain.

Ferguson left Ninety-Six bound for Charlotte, taking a circuitous route to the west to cover the left flank of General Cornwallis. He also hoped to scatter such rebel militia as he might find and had some hope of enlisting recruits for the king's cause from the scattered inhabitants of the South Carolina Blue Ridge. This proved to be a forlorn hope. The area was composed of "the most violent young rebels" that one of Ferguson's officers had ever seen. Finally, after receiving many reports of an army of three thousand back-woodsmen all armed with rifles, which they used with uncommon skill, Ferguson began sending urgent messages requesting support from Colonel Krueger at Ninety-Six. He also sent couriers to General Cornwallis. One of them read, "I am on my march toward you by a road leading from Cherokee Ford north of King's Mountain. Three or four hundred good soldiers, part dragoons, would finish the business. Something must be done. This is their last push in this quarter." But none of the messages that Ferguson sent ever reached their destination, and finally, on October 6, he took up a defensive position on King's Mountain, a spur of the South Carolina Blue Ridge, where he turned to face his pursuers, hoping to drive them off.

King's Mountain was a strong position in many ways. Ferguson placed his men on the crest of a steep hill littered with thousands of pine needles and immense boulders lying between trees that grew to an imposing height. One of his flanks was protected by an escarpment, which the backwoodsmen, for all their renowned agility, could not possibly climb. Ferguson felt confident that his men, a thousand or so of militia, and a hundred Provincials, all of them American, would have no difficulty in withstanding attacks in the front and his other side by a force even twice as strong as the thousand or so men he believed himself to be facing. Now Ferguson waited for the arrival of the overmountain men, confident in his position and of his soldiers.

But he sent two hundred of his best men out on a foraging expedition, leaving him with nine hundred men, eight hundred militia, and a hundred soldiers from the king's American Rangers, the most famous Tory regiment. And so the die was cast, and Ferguson and his Tories waited for the advance of the overmountain men.

————————

Andrew MacNeal marched alongside his stepbrother, Jacob Spencer. The two of them were worn out, for the march had been long and arduous. Finally Andrew groaned, "Do you think we're ever going to get there?"

"I reckon sooner or later we will." Jacob lifted his musket and shifted it to another position, saying, "Old Sweetlips here is going to kiss some of those Redcoats pretty soon."

"Sweetlips! What a name for a rifle! You take my musket," Andrew said. "I've decided to call it 'Hot Lead.'"

Jacob grinned at his stepbrother but made no answer. He looked back along the line of marching men and thought of the long days they had spent. Most of them had no other equipment than a blanket, a hunting knife, and a bag of parched corn sweetened with molasses or honey. They had already started living off fresh-killed game, and as they trudged along, he looked up to see his father suddenly appear.

"How's it going, boys?" Hawk asked. He was wearing his hunting shirt, as were the rest of them, with leggings and deerskin moccasins. His dark blue eyes were clear and he did not appear tired.

"Not as well as you, Pa," Jacob said. "I've about worn my feet down to my ankles. I don't see how an old man like you can keep up the pace."

Hawk laughed. "You youngsters just don't have it. How are you doing, Andrew?"

"All right, Pa." Andrew looked questioningly over the line of men that stretched out in front of him. "When do you think we'll get there?"

"Scouts came in just a while ago. They say that Ferguson's finally stopped running."

"Well, I'm glad of that. Where did he hole up?"

"On top of a place called King's Mountain," Hawk remarked. "And from what I understand, it's a pretty strong position, but Colonel Shelby thinks we can take it."

"Who's in command of the army, Pa?" Jacob asked. "We got so many units that have come in, and we don't really have a general."

This was true enough, for the various leaders for the four separate bands were commanded by a miller, an innkeeper, a future member of Congress, and a man named Isaac Shelby, who was to be the first governor of the new state of Kentucky. All of them were under the general direction of Colonel William Campbell of the Virginia Militia. He was married to Patrick Henry's sister and was a giant of a man and a fierce fighter.

"Well, there was some argument about that." Hawk shrugged as he trudged along beside the boys. "They couldn't decide on who the leader would be, so what they are doing now is having a staff meeting every morning and one of them is chosen officer of the day. Good a system as any, I reckon. When the fightin' starts, generals aren't much good anyway."

"You don't really believe that, do you, Pa?"

"Well, I'd have to excuse General Washington from that, and maybe Nathaniel Green and a few others, but we're not the kind of army that a general will help. The best thing they can do is say pick a tree and take your best shots."

Andrew looked up and said, "Look, here comes Colonel Shelby!"

Colonel Shelby did indeed ride by. He stopped beside Hawk, who was a particular friend of his by this time, and said, "King's Mountain is no more than five miles ahead. How do you think the men are feeling, Spencer?"

"Well, we got soaked in the rain last night, but all that did was make the men mad. I reckon they'll be like a bunch of bees warning a bear trying to rob their honey."

Shelby laughed. He was in good humor and said, "The scouts say that Ferguson and his men are on top of a mountain."

"That means we've got to climb up to get at him."

"Yes, but that's not all bad," Shelby said. His horse skittered sideways under him and he brought him back sharply, saying, "Stop that, Jackson!" then turned back to Hawk, his face serious. "Here's what I think. There are plenty of trees and rocks. It won't be open ground, so we can make our way up frontier style, Indian fashion. And you know how hard it is to shoot downhill. Those Tories will have to stand up to get a shot, and in most cases they'll overshoot."

"I've missed several bucks shootin' downhill," Hawk Spencer nodded.

"That's right. So it will be that kind of a fight. He's got some well-trained troops up there, but he's trapped himself. There's no way off that mountain, and we're going to throw our men around it like a ring and all start for the top. Hang on to your scalp, Hawk."

"You too, Colonel."

All the soldiers had gathered around, Seth included. And now he said, "A little bit informal, isn't it? I'm used to armies that line up in ranks and obey orders."

"Good way to get killed around here, Seth," Hawk smiled. "I'm not interested in getting killed. All I want is to run these Tories out of the country and the Redcoats all the way back to England."

Seth said nothing, but the thought occurred to him, *I've come all the way around, a full circle. I came over to fight the rebels, and now I'm fighting on their side.* However, as he looked at the faces of Hawk Spencer and his two sons, he suddenly felt good about it. "I'm doing the right thing," he said. "This is going to be my home and I'll fight for it."

The sun came up quickly, rising over the mountains and casting a reddish glow as Seth Donovan ate the cold beef and washed it down with spring water. He glanced over at Jacob and Andrew, and then around at the other members of the company. Hawk was standing alone, looking toward the west as if he could see the mountain where the enemy waited. Straightening up, Seth picked up his rifle, checked the priming, and moved over to stand beside Hawk. "You think it'll be today?" he asked quietly.

"Yes, it'll have to be. King's Mountain is right over there, and the officers have said we'll attack. Should be getting the order soon."

"I haven't been able to put this into words, Hawk, but I love your daughter, Sarah. I want to marry her, and I'm asking your permission."

Hawk suddenly turned and stared at the large, burly Scotsman. "You picked an odd time to ask." A slight smile tugged at his lips. "What would you do if I said no?"

"What would you have done if Elizabeth's father had refused to let you marry her?"

Hawk laughed deep in his throat. "I didn't have to worry about that, since he was too far away, but I guess I'd have married her anyway. But I want you to know that I've become very fond of you, Seth, and Sarah loves you. So her mother and I are glad that you two have found each other."

"I've made a crooked track around the world. I haven't done much with my life."

"You've done as much as I have," Hawk shrugged. "I hid from life for years and almost lost my son doing it. But God is good. He's kept us both."

At that moment a lieutenant came riding by. "Form up! Form up!" he shouted. "Ready to march!"

"I guess this is where we find out if Mr. Patrick Ferguson and his Tories are as tough as we hear," Hawk said. The two men went back, got their sparse belongings, and soon the lines were moving through the undergrowth headed for the battle. Within an hour they broke out of the heavier timber and looked up to the hill that lay ahead.

"That's a pretty strong-looking position, but we can take it," Hawk remarked.

"It's a good thing there're trees there and those rocks," Seth said. "I'd hate to climb up a hill into the face of those guns without any cover."

"That's what the British did at Bunker Hill and got their ears shot off. No, our leaders know that we're able to do it." He looked around at his sons and said quietly, "Look out for my boys as well as you can, Seth."

"I'll do that . . . or they may be looking out for me."

"You know, what I'm most afraid of is the bayonet. We don't have any here, and these rifles are slower to load than muskets."

"They're more accurate, though."

"Yes, but if we're up close and we fire a volley and they rush at us with those bayonets, we'll have to retreat. A man can't stand against a naked bayonet without anything to fight with." Although Hawk did not know it, all of the Tory militia on top of King's Mountain were well trained in the use of the bayonet. Actually they did not have regular bayonets at this point but crude bayonets, actually a long blade jammed down the muzzle of their musket. This meant the musket could not be fired, of course, but a line of naked bayonets rushing toward men who had unloaded guns was a frightening sight.

Seth moved along until Colonel Shelby ordered the men to stop, and soon the different units began to surround the mountain itself. By noon all of the troops had made a complete ring around the foot of the mountain. They now waited for the signal for the attack to begin. As it happened, this honor was given to Colonel Campbell's men, of which Hawk, Jacob, Andrew, and Seth were members. Colonel Campbell, a huge man, bulky and blunt of face, led the way. He yelled, "Come on, boys, remember your liberty! Do it, my brave fellows!"

Seth moved out quickly and kept his eyes on the crest of the hill. Although it was too far for a musket ball to reach, he kept carefully behind trees. From time to time he glanced at Jacob, Andrew, and Hawk, who were also taking cover as they moved upward. Ferguson had obviously put his men in picket lines along this area, which was the most approachable area for an attack.

Soon the air was full of the sounds of muskets exploding. It sounded to Seth like the crackling of thousands of small sticks. Smoke covered the line of picketers, and more than once Seth heard the whiz of a bullet passing close to him. He was grateful for the training he had received from Hawk and Sequatchie, for he moved quickly from tree to rock, never exposing himself for more than a few seconds to the enemy fire. A musket ball struck the hard rock and went off, making eerie sounds like the wailing of a banshee.

He did not attempt to fire his musket until they were halfway up the sides of the steep incline. At that point he heard Hawk yelling, "Now we can get a target! Pick your man and don't waste a shot!"

Seth steadied his rifle and waited until he saw a flash of an enemy uniform. He carefully squeezed the trigger, and the weapon bucked against his shoulder. He saw the uniform disappear and knew that he had hit his man. Quickly he began to reload, pouring the powder down the barrel, then the ball in on top, and finally putting another bit of powder in the pan. He had learned to do this very efficiently, but still it took time.

Ten feet down the way Jacob was firing and loading rapidly, as was Andrew, who was very close. They did not speak to each other, but finally Andrew yelled, "Look out, they're coming with the bayonets!"

Jacob looked up to see the sun flashing on what seemed to be hundreds of bayonets. He knew logically there could not be that many, but his lips went dry. He had just fired a shot, and he knew that the others were not loaded, either. His hands began to tremble as he poured the powder in, but looking up, he saw he would never make it. At that moment a shout came, "Retreat! Back down the mountain!" It was Hawk calling, and at once Jacob scrambled back. He did not need to hunt for cover, for he knew that there would be few shots fired during a bayonet charge.

The battle raged, and three times the troops charged, then went back toward the summit. Bodies were lying still, and the wounded were already beginning to cry out. Seth kept firing and retreating, all the time keeping his eyes on Andrew and Jacob.

Finally Colonel Campbell came to shout, "One more time and we'll have them, boys! Come, shout like devils!" He had lost his horse, but for such a large man he covered ground very rapidly.

As they moved up the hill, Hawk came to shout at Seth, "Watch out for a man on a horse wearing a checkered shirt. That'll be Ferguson. If we can get him, the rest will collapse."

"How do you know that?"

"One of the spies found it out. All the officers are passing the word along. Get Ferguson!"

On top of the mountain Patrick Ferguson was fighting like a maniac. He, indeed, did have on a checkered shirt. He also had a whistle by which he gave orders, and as the enemy drew closer, he seemed to be everywhere. More than once a small group would try to raise a white flag, and Ferguson would cut it down with a swipe of the sword that he carried.

One of his officers said, "Sir, we can't hold this position. We must surrender." But Ferguson screamed at him, and the officers all knew there would be no surrender from this man.

Finally the ring of attackers grew closer to the top. Now they were actually over the crest, and Seth saw there was no way that Ferguson's men could escape. They were being driven farther and farther in toward the center, and now many of them were huddled together behind the wagons and tents. "We've got them!" he yelled.

At that moment, however, a British officer suddenly appeared. He had a pistol in his hand, and he leveled it directly at Jacob.

Seth's musket was empty, but he threw himself forward, putting his body between Jacob and the officer. He heard the crack and felt the ball strike him high in the shoulder, between his shoulder blade and neck. It drove him down, and he rolled over, ignoring the pain, to see Jacob raise his musket and put a ball in the forehead of the officer.

Leaning down, Jacob cried, "Are you all right, Seth?"

"Yes."

Jacob reached up and pulled his hunting shirt back. The ball had passed through the top part of his muscle over the collarbone. "It went right through," he said. "Come on, we've got them now."

The battle ended quickly, for there was little hope. Hawk had kept his group close together, and now someone yelled, "Look, there goes Ferguson!" Every eye, it seemed, turned to the man on the big gray horse wearing the checkered hunting shirt. He was making an attempt to break away, but muskets cracked out and he fell to the ground, riddled by eight balls. Both of his arms were found to be broken, and the battle was over.

Some units that arrived late did not know the Tories were trying to surrender and fired into the masses. But finally Colonel Campbell, plunging into the center of the milling men, got them to hold their fire.

"Well, I guess it's all over," Hawk said slowly. "You boys all right?"

"All except for Seth," Jacob said. He turned to face the big man and said, "Why'd you put yourself in the way of that bullet for me?"

"Well, you did as much for me once," Seth said slowly. The loss of blood had made him somewhat sick, but he managed a grin. "Now we're even until the next time."

———

The Tory survivors—and there were not many—were marched

off to the interior of North Carolina. The defeat was a crushing one, for it destroyed beyond question Lord North's southern strategy. This was based on the conviction that a British expeditionary force could defeat any Continental Army put into the field against it. They thought they could intimidate the patriot militia and encourage the far more numerous loyalists to take control of their own colonies in the name of His Majesty's government. But King's Mountain had destroyed that theory completely. All of the victories that the British had won went up in smoke. At King's Mountain a spontaneous patriot army had risen to wipe out one of the best and most successful units in the entire British military establishment. It was a turning point, and from the moment the news of it swept through the country, General Clinton said, "It was the first link of a chain of evils that followed each other in regular succession until they at last ended in the total loss of America."

And so as the men marched back toward their homes, despite the death of some of their neighbors and friends, the aura of victory was in the air, and it was Hawk who said to Seth, "We've won. If we can do this once, we can do it again. The British can't take these kinds of losses."

Seth was moving slowly because of the wound in his shoulder, but he sensed the exultation in Hawk Spencer, and his thoughts went ahead to the woman who would be waiting for him back in Watauga.

Battle of the Heart

Thirty-Three

*W*ell, there it is. It looks mighty good to me." Hawk looked at the cabin that lay down in the clearing and glanced over at the smaller one over to the west. "I guess you boys will be glad to see those wives of yours, won't you?"

Jacob's face was drawn with fatigue, but he brightened up. Straightening up on his horse, he said, "Sure will, Pa. How about you, Andrew?"

"I guess you know about that. I never thought I could miss a woman so much." He turned and looked down at Seth, who lay with his eyes closed between two horses in a deerskin stretched on poles. "I'm worried about Seth, though. I wish that wound hadn't gotten infected."

Seth had made little of the wound, but by the second day of their journey home, he began to complain of fever. By the third day he was practically unconscious. They had slowed their pace, but all of the men had been discouraged, for they had seen what an infected wound could do. It could kill as surely as a bullet at times.

"Well, let's get him home and into a bed. Elizabeth's good with things like this, and we can maybe get a doctor to take a look at him."

They wound down by the trail, and when they were within calling distance, Hawk raised his voice. "Hello the house! Where are you women?"

Almost at once the door opened and Elizabeth ran out, followed by Abigail and Amanda. Hawk slipped off his horse and grabbed Elizabeth, who threw herself against him. "Well, I'm back," he whispered.

"Thank God!" Elizabeth said. She blinked back the tears and held him as tightly as she could.

Amanda and Abigail had also greeted their husbands, and for a time there was a babble of voices mixed with laughter and a few furtive tears on the part of the women.

"What's wrong with Seth?" Elizabeth asked, moving over to peer down into his face. "He looks terrible! Look how pale he is."

"He took a ball at the battle. We thought he was all right. It went right on through, but it got infected."

Elizabeth lifted the cloth that covered the wound and blinked. "It looks bad," she whispered.

"Where's Sarah?" Andrew asked. "She'll want to see him."

"She's out feeding the hogs. There she comes now."

Sarah had indeed heard the sound of Hawk's shout and had turned and run quickly to the cabin. As she approached the small group, she saw them all looking at her in a strange way—and she saw also that Seth was not among them. A cold fear gripped her, and she could not speak but stopped abruptly.

"It's all right, Sarah," Hawk said, coming to her. "Seth took a musket ball. He's not feeling too good, but he'll be better now that he's home."

Sarah went at once to stand beside the litter and looked down at the face of the wounded man. He was pale and had dark circles under his eyes, and she leaned over and put her hands on his hair. "Seth—oh, Seth!" she whispered. He did not move or open his eyes, and she said, "We've got to get him into the house!"

"We'll put him over in the other cabin where he's been staying," Elizabeth said.

As Andrew and Jacob took over the job of moving the big man, Elizabeth said, "How did it go?"

"Went well, Elizabeth. We wiped them out completely. I think that things are going to change from now on. It's a turning point. Cornwallis was the best general they had with the biggest force, and we robbed him of a big part of that when we took Ferguson and all of his men."

"I'm glad you're back," she said.

"I'm glad to be back." He glanced over to where the boys were lifting Seth out of the litter. "I'm worried about Seth. It didn't seem to be too bad, but it got worse."

"Sarah would be lost if anything happened to him."

"Yes, she would. He asked me just before the battle if he could marry her."

"What did you say, Hawk?"

"I said yes. Was that right?"

"Of course," Elizabeth nodded. "She loves him very much, but we'll have to pray that she doesn't lose him. I don't know what that would do to her."

———

Sarah was exhausted, both physically and emotionally. For two days she had scarcely left Seth's side, often sleeping in a chair beside him. Others came and went, but she could not tear herself away. It was late on Thursday night when she dropped off to sleep and gave a jolt finally when she realized that Elizabeth had come in and was sitting beside her.

"Why don't you go to bed, Sarah? Get some rest."

"No, I want to stay here beside him." She turned to her mother and said, "Why is this happening, Mama?"

Elizabeth, of course, had no answer. There was no answer for these things, but she sat quietly for a time before saying, "Now, you remember you made a commitment to God, Sarah, that you were going to love no matter what. You weren't going to shut any doors on anybody. Well, don't shut a door on God. Seth's alive and many men are dead. God hasn't brought him this far for you to lose him."

"Do you think so, Mama?"

Looking at this daughter of hers that she loved so dearly, Elizabeth suddenly felt one of those moments of insight. "God has really given me great confidence about Seth," she said quietly. "This may be the final test of your faith. You remember when Abraham was told to sacrifice his son?"

"Yes, Mama."

"I've often thought about it. That moment when he lifted the knife and was about to plunge it into his son's heart, what did he feel? How awful it must have been for him." Shaking her head, Elizabeth was quiet for a moment, then said, "That's where you are right now. Abraham is the father of the faithful because he believes that God was able to bring forth his son back from the dead if necessary, but he was going to obey God, and that's what you must do."

The two women began to pray, and Sarah felt the comfort that her mother brought, which lifted her spirits. She began to praise God, and as she did so aloud, Elizabeth knew a moment of quiet but fierce pride. *She's made it through the hard times. Now, God, give her the victory. Spare this man.*

Seth opened his eyes and for a moment could not think clearly. His lips were dry, and he felt as weak as he had ever felt in his life. He was confused, also, for the last memory he had was being jolted over a road in a rough litter.

Suddenly a shadow fell across his face, and he looked up to see Sarah. He whispered her name through cracked lips and saw her eyes were glistening with tears. "Don't cry," he whispered.

"I can't help it. I'm so happy you're awake."

"How long . . . have I been here?"

"Almost a week. We've been feeding you like a baby." Sarah put her hand on his forehead. "Your fever's gone. It went down last night. I knew then that you were going to be all right."

Seth lay there quietly. His head was swimming, and he struggled against the weakness. He waited until she sat down beside him and took her hand in his, then he whispered for a drink. When she brought it, he drank it thirstily. When she sat back down, he said, "Have you changed your mind?"

"About marrying you?"

"Yes."

"I wouldn't be here if I had changed my mind. But I'll never change my mind, Seth. You can't get rid of me. I'm on your hands forever."

Seth looked up and suddenly a great peace came into him. "It seems like a dream," he said. His voice grew stronger, and his grip tightened on her hand. "I know what a hard time you've had. You've lost so much, but you're not going to lose me. Not for another forty years at least."

Sarah leaned over and kissed him on the lips. She laid her head down beside him, putting her cheek against his. "My time with you is a gift from God, and I'm going to savor every moment of it, and you must do the same. Right now we have today," she whispered. "I don't know what's coming tomorrow, but right now I'm happy."

Then Seth Donovan said, "I'm happy, too, as long as I have you."

The small church was full. The date was November 16, 1780. Sarah looked up at the tall man beside her and said, "I do." She felt his hand tighten on hers and their eyes met. The church at Jonesboro was full, and as they repeated the rest of their vows and listened as Paul Anderson pronounced them man and wife, Sarah MacNeal Donovan received her first kiss as a wife from her husband. He was well and strong now but held her as if she were some fragile, gentle thing.

Neither of them ever remembered a great deal of what went on after the ceremony, but finally they got back to the small cabin where they had their first meal as man and wife.

They sat at the table laughing at nothing, and from time to time he would reach over and take her hand in his.

Finally Seth said, "I have something to tell you, wife. I don't know whether you will like it or not."

Somewhat apprehensively Sarah opened her eyes wide. "What is it, Seth?"

Silence came over the big man for a moment, and for a time it seemed he would not answer. Sarah did not interrupt, for she had learned already that there were times like this with this big man of hers. He would say what was on his heart if she waited long enough.

"It may be that the Lord is calling me into the ministry."

Sarah smiled suddenly. She reached over with both of her hands and held his. "I'm not surprised. God has done a great work in you, Seth. You know the Bible, and you love it better than any man I ever saw. And you love to talk about your Savior, and you love people. Any man who has those things, God is going to use."

"It'll be a hard life. We won't have much."

"I'll have you, and I'll have the children that God's going to give us, and I'll have Jesus every day. What more could a woman want?"

Looking across at the strong features of Seth Donovan, Sarah held his hands tightly and was silent for only a moment, and then she said with something like awe in her voice, "I can't believe that I found a husband among the king's soldiers."

"But now I'm going to be a soldier for *the* King." Seth smiled at his wife as the promise of a future serving his Lord awaited.

Epilogue

$\mathscr{I}$t seems that children were everywhere as Hawk and Elizabeth sat in cane-bottomed chairs outside their cabin. It was a mid-November day in 1781, but it was one of those mild days of winter when winter is gone for a time and a cheerful sun sends down warm beams. After the cold spell everyone was glad to be outside.

Hawk watched the children who were playing and shouting at the top of their lungs. Hannah, age eight, was the oldest. She was directing the others and, as always, was thoughtful. "That's a sweet girl I've got there. She takes after me," Hawk nodded with satisfaction.

"I don't think so. Joshua's like you. He's spoiled and wants his own way."

"Well, he's only seven. He'll get sweet like me as he grows older." Hawk reached over and pulled at Elizabeth's hair. "Just be glad you've got a sweet husband and sweet children."

The other children, Rachel Anderson, age seven, was the liveliest one of the group, while Eve Martin, at eight years old, and David, age seven, made up the others.

"Eve is always the shiest of all the children," Hawk remarked.

"Yes, she is. She's a precious child. But that David Martin, I don't know where he gets it from, but he is a daredevil!"

"Like me."

"Yes, like you."

The two had just come from a celebration dinner in honor of Seth and Sarah's first anniversary. They had also made it a celebration of Washington's defeat of Cornwallis at Yorktown. The others were still inside, Jacob, Amanda, Andrew, Abigail, Sequatchie and

Iris, the Martins, the Stevenses, and the Andersons, but Hawk and Elizabeth had stepped outside to watch the children.

"What's it going to feel like being a grandfather?" Both Abigail and Amanda were expecting children, and now Hawk said, "Well, I don't mind being a grandfather." He pouted slightly and said, "But I sure do hate being married to a grandma. Makes me feel old."

"You crazy thing!" Elizabeth reached up, grabbed his hair where it was clubbed at the back, and pulled.

Hawk turned and smiled. "You're the finest-looking grandma I've ever seen. You'll always be young to me."

Elizabeth was content. She said quietly, "It's good to see Sarah so at peace with herself. God's truly worked in her life."

"It was quite a struggle, but she and Seth are happy now. And we have a minister for a son-in-law. It's hard to believe they've been married a year now."

"I'm glad Seth has been called to be a minister. I think we need one. He'll have his hands full keeping track of this family. Don't know if he'll have time for anyone else."

Elizabeth ignored him. "You think the war's really over?"

"Yes, it is. There'll be a few more skirmishes but no major battles." He leaned back in the chair and his eyes grew thoughtful. "There'll be a new country now. It'll be free and independent."

He looked down suddenly at the children, and a thought came to him. "It'll be up to these to decide what direction it takes."

Elizabeth Spencer watched the children as they screamed and played and rolled, and peace came to her. "God has been good to us. We'll have to pray that they'll trust in God to help them through their hard times, for they'll have some."

"Yes, they will, but God's brought you and me, and all of us through hard times. He'll be with these, too."

The two suddenly rose and went back into the house. The children watched them go and then returned to their games. They did not know fear, and now that America was a country of its own, only Hannah had a thought. Looking at the others, she suddenly wondered, *I wonder what it will be like when we grow up like Ma and Pa. . . .*

Notes to Our Readers

We have come to the end of another journey over the Misty Mountains. Gilbert and I hope you enjoyed this one, too. We have certainly enjoyed all of your kind and encouraging letters! Thank you so much for supporting our books! God is truly great!

We especially enjoy weaving spiritual truths into our stories. Sarah MacNeal was like so many people today. We have become afraid of opening our hearts to other people and truly showing them the love of Christ. We must follow the commands of our Savior and love others as He first loved us, no matter the cost we may suffer.

We find the history of this place and time fascinating. It is fun to intersperse these true events into the story. The battle at Moore's Creek that Seth fought in was a battle between the patriots and Scottish Highlanders who had been persuaded by Governor Josiah Martin of North Carolina to fight for the Crown. Flora McDonald, along with her husband, Allen, was a true hero of the Scottish and led them in America, too. Allen and his son, Alexander, were captured during this battle and imprisoned in Halifax. After many months and finally arranging his and his son's exchange, Allen was stationed in Nova Scotia, where he was later joined by his beloved wife. They both finally returned to Scotland. Flora died on March 5, 1790. Her funeral shroud was a sheet that Prince Charles Edward, her "Bonnie Prince Charlie," had slept on when she had helped him to escape his pursuers so many years ago.

Colonel Shelby did lead a raid against the Cherokee, who were under the leadership of Dragging Canoe. It did effectively put a stop to the British using them to raid the American settlers and took the Cherokee out of the American Revolution.

The Battle of King's Mountain was one of the most important battles of the American Revolution. By stopping Ferguson, the overmountain men kept his forces from joining General Cornwallis in Virginia. This allowed General Washington to defeat him at Yorktown approximately one year later and ensure freedom for the American colonies. The battle site is now a national park, located near York, South Carolina, close to the North Carolina border.

Thank you again for joining us on these journeys. There will be future trips beyond the quiet hills. We will look into how Washington County, North Carolina, struggled to first become the state of Franklin, and finally became the state of Tennessee in 1796. We will especially watch the next generation of children, Hannah and Joshua Spencer, Even and David Martin, and Rachel Anderson, grow and deal with their own struggles on the frontier. We hope you join us! God bless you!

Gilbert Morris &
Aaron McCarver

INSP
FROM
MOR

Morris, Gilbert.

Among the king's
soldiers.

Spirit of Appalachia

$9.99   BK 3

DATE			
JA 5 '99	AR 10 2003		
MR 4 '99	MAR 15 2005		
~~MR 27 '99~~	JA 29 '07		
AP 6 '99			
JE 14 '99			
OC 28 '99			
JE 1 '00			
NO 16 '00			
MY 29 '01			